SINFUL LIES

THE SINFUL SERIES

MARIE ANNILLA

CW01619772

Copyright © 2025 MARIE ANNILLA

All rights reserved.

No part of this book may be reproduced, distributed, or transmitted in any form or by any means, including photocopying, recording, or other electronic or mechanical methods, without the prior written permission of the publisher, except in the case of brief quotations embodied in critical reviews and certain other noncommercial uses permitted by copyright law.

Published by:
Marie Annilla
Amazon KDP

ISBN: 978-2-9595228-3-3

Cover Design: Vikki/ Fiverr
Formatting: Shannon / Fiverr

Printed in USA

First Edition

Disclaimer: This is a work of fiction. Names, characters, places, and incidents are either the product of the author's imagination or used fictitiously. Any resemblance to actual events, locales, or persons, living or dead, is entirely coincidental.

For information, contact:
Marie Annilla
marie.b.annilla@gmail.com
Instagram: @authormarieannilla
Tiktok: @authormarieannilla
Threads: @authormarieannilla

THE SINFUL SERIES:

Sinful Promises (2024)

Enter the world of Mikhaïl Volkov—a brutal mafia king whose dangerous allure pulls you into a dark and seductive romance.

Sinful Games (2024)

An arranged marriage with Alexsei Romaniev turns into a game of survival and temptation, where every move raises the stakes and blurs the line between love and hate.

Sinful Lies (2025)

Secrets and lies intertwine as Angelo Lazzio's story unfolds—a tale of betrayal, obsession, and fiery passion that consumes everything in its path.

A Note to the Reader...

Trigger Warning

This book contains themes and content that may be distressing to some readers, including but not limited to: explicit sexual content, strong language, scenes of violence, psychological manipulation, isolation, trauma, murder, death, abuse, and the use of weapons.

Reader discretion is advised.

Please proceed with caution if these themes are triggering for you.

For the queens who lie in whispers, sin in shadows, and conquer hearts without mercy—this one's yours.

To the fearless women in my life who showed me the path to redemption: may our roots intertwine beneath the earth, unseen yet unbreakable, as we rise together—taller, stronger, and forever united.

Let's always be girls together.

PLAYLIST:

BAND PERRY – If I Die Young

LANA DEL REY – Happiness is a Butterfly

ARIANA GRANDE - God Is a Woman

MANESKIN - I Wanna Be Your Slave

KELLY ROWLAND - Motivation

RIHANNA - Love On The Brain

TWO FEET - Love Is a B*tch

BILLIE EILISH - When the Party's Over

EMINEM FT RIHANNA - Love the Way You Lie

Duncan Laurence - Arcade

BEYONCE – All Night

Sinful Lies is split into two parts.

The first part recounts the eight years of Jade's life, from ages 22 to 29, highlighting key moments and pivotal events from each year. These moments build up to a dramatic conclusion, which transitions into the second part, set in the present day as Jade turns 30.

PROLOGUE

"The angel is nothing without the demon."
— **A.D. Aliwat**

Angelo

Four inches.

Four inches to my computer screen, four inches to the picture frame of Georgino with my parents. Perfectly centered —always where I kept my backup burner phone.

That old black case? Worn and cracked, but it had been my lifeline over the years.

I bought it for one reason: to dig into Cyrus's project—a multi-million-dollar scheme to wipe out a ghost town in Boston, a place left to rot since the auto industry fell apart and everyone bailed for bigger cities.

Jonathan Cyrus, a so-called friend of my old man, Carlos Lazzio, had some grand vision.

Bulldozers would come in, and he'd turn that dump into a shining paradise of luxury hotels, exotic zoos—think Babylon with all the bells and whistles, celebrating the seasons in style. Lake Kendrick would wrap around it, flashing lights, fine cigars, and money pouring in like it was a goddamn fountain.

That was his plan, anyway.

Cyrus snatched that project right from under my nose. My father thought I wasn't tough enough to handle it, thought I couldn't carry the weight.

So he gave this project to him.

I was just twenty-seven back then, and I had spent a decade proving myself in this ruthless game. Ten years of blood, sweat, and tears, and it still wasn't fucking enough.

So, I wanted to take matters into my own hands before everything blew away.

That damn burner phone was the key to everything.

But when I reached for it tonight and found it missing from its usual spot, a cold knot twisted in my stomach.

I knew something was wrong. I could feel it in my bones, and I knew who was behind it: a tall, pale demon with long black hair, a pretty face and a wicked glint in her eye.

The very reason I found myself in this room to begin with.

The air in the interrogation room was stifling, thick with the kind of humidity that clings to your skin like a second layer.

I tugged at the cufflinks, the sharp metallic clink echoing in the silence, and shrugged off my blazer. It slid off my shoulders and draped itself over the wooden chair behind me, forgotten.

A bead of sweat meandered lazily down the curve of my neck, tracing heat over already simmering flesh.

My arms folded across my chest as I sat there, unwavering, my gaze fixed on the mirror in front of me.

I didn't need to guess what was behind it—probably a handful of faceless, self-important bastards. Watching. Waiting. Hoping I'd crack or beg for mercy.

The thought almost made me laugh, but I kept the smirk buried deep.

The room was deceptively serene, considering the weight it carried.

This was a place where suffering lingered, soaked into the walls.

How many grown men had screamed for their mama here?

How many women had collapsed, beaten by exhaustion?

How many desperate fuckers had promised to sell out their loved ones for a taste of freedom?

My reflection stared back at me from the mirror—hair disheveled, shadows under my eyes, a restrained wrath simmering just beneath the surface.

I glanced down, twisting the face of my Rolex to clear a smudge.

2:35 a.m.

The door creaked open, pulling my attention.

Detective McLaren stepped in, a file under her arm and two cheap plastic cups of coffee in her hands. She set one down in front of me before sliding into the seat at the far end of the table.

The file landed with a dull thud.

"Murder, kidnapping, embezzlement ..." Her voice was calm, measured as she flipped through the papers.

Finally, her gaze lifted, catching mine. Her eyes widened for just a fraction of a second as her focus lingered on my face, a slight blush creeping onto her cheeks before she snapped her attention back to the file.

Blonde, petite, and sporty.

The kind of woman I'd rather see tangled in my sheets than across an interrogation table.

She cleared her throat, taking a sip of coffee. "Is your lawyer on their way?"

I shook my head.

Her frown deepened. "Mr. Lazzio, these accusations are serious. You need legal representation."

I shook my head again, slower this time, letting a smirk curl at the edge of my lips.

Her eyes flicked down, catching the movement, before darting back to the file.

She reached for a photo and slid it across the table.

"Do you recognize this woman?"

I didn't bother looking. I already knew.

Pauline Dupont. French-American actress. Dead. Closed eyes and a ghost of a scream frozen on her lips.

Her voice faltered just slightly. "Of course you do."

I let the silence stretch before asking, "What's your name, Detective?"

Her posture stiffened. "Why?"

"I'd like to know the name of the beautiful woman accusing me of murder."

Her arms crossed defensively, her lower lip trembling. "That's irrelevant to the investigation, Mr. Lazzio."

I let my tongue glide slowly across my teeth. "I'm sure it's something lovely. Lucie? Gloria?"

"Naomi."

I smiled faintly. "Pretty."

Her hand moved almost unconsciously, tucking a stray strand of hair back into her tightly wound bun. Her voice dipped. "Thank you."

The pulse at her neck betrayed her calm, quickening in

time with the faintest flush creeping up her skin. Her eyes darted to my lips, just for a moment too long.

I glanced down again, adjusting my watch.

2:42.

"Pauline Dupont," she began, her eyes steady on mine. "An actress working at The Sunflower on 42nd Street—your theater. Found dead in her apartment three months ago. A bullet between her eyes, a gun in her hand. Ruled a suicide. And you even gave a statement to the press about her mental health struggles."

"Poor woman did struggle," I said, the corner of my mouth twitching upward in a ghost of a smile.

"But your COO, Miss Jade Whitenhouse, seems to disagree. She claims you're the one who pulled the trigger."

At the mention of her name, something sharp and ugly tore through my chest.

My throat tightened, my fists clenched against the cool metal of the table.

Jade.

Her face flashed before my eyes—too perfect, too intoxicating, and yet somehow marked with the stain of betrayal.

Her sleek black hair that always fell just right, her honey-drenched voice that could cut glass, the scent of her skin mingling with mine, long nails dragging down my back, pretty mouth kissing mine.

"She said that?"

"She did."

A scoff left my lips, humorless and cold.

My thumb brushed along my jaw as the silence stretched between us.

The fire in my chest flared, scorching its way through my lungs.

Betrayal—raw and jagged—settled in my veins, thick and suffocating.

The weight of her whispers still lingered, those soft words that had once felt like salvation now echoing like a curse.

I love you too, Angelo.

Nausea coiled in my stomach, climbing my throat like a slow burn. It tasted like bile.

"Do you believe in love, Naomi?"

"No," she whispered, a hint of doubt in her voice, like she couldn't quite believe what she was hearing. "Do *you*?"

"If love is obsession," I murmured, my voice slipping through the air like smoke, dark and thick, "then I am already drowning in its flames, trapped in the deepest circle of hell."

I stood, slowly pulling my blazer from the back of the chair, letting the fabric fall over my shoulders.

Her gaze never wavered; I knew she was watching me, taking in every detail as if she couldn't tear herself away.

I slid my cufflinks on one by one.

I could almost feel the flicker of admiration in her gaze, the way her lips parted slightly, almost imperceptibly.

"I never would've believed a man like you could ever fall in love," she said, her voice softer now, as if she'd let a piece of herself slip.

I gave her a dark smirk, the kind that didn't reach my eyes.

"Me neither, Naomi. Not until I met the devil herself." I leaned in, as my voice dropped lower, darker. "She stole my soul, and now I'm willingly bound to her mercy ... for all eternity."

Her head tilted slightly to the side, her cheeks now a deep crimson.

I turned, the door opening in front of me.

Without looking back, I stepped into the hallway and left.

PART ONE
THE PAST

CHAPTER
ONE

"All a woman actually wants is to feel special."
— **Matt Dunn**

Jade
22 years old
Eight years ago

"Your nurse, Lana, told me you don't take your medicine anymore. You flush them down the toilet or hide them in the food you don't finish in the canteen. What's going on, Jade?"

I leaned back against the bed frame, its cheap wood digging into my spine. Arms crossed, I stared at the blank white wall ahead, ignoring Doctor Morano's gaze.

Tall, serious, and composed, she was everything you'd expect from someone with a psychology degree from Harvard. The tight bun of silvery-white hair, the spotless white blouse, and those glasses perched high on her nose screamed old money.

A nepo baby through and through.

Yet, she had this annoying tendency to actually care—heart of gold, they said.

Gag-worthy, really.

Her legs were crossed as she sat, one manicured hand resting on the arm of the chair, the other adjusting her glasses. She was waiting for me to crack, but she should've known better.

I was an expert at playing the game. Feigning ignorance, dodging questions, putting on my little "I'm totally fine" act.

"Jade," she said finally. "If you won't take your medicine, I'm afraid we'll have to administer it intravenously."

My head snapped to her, eyes narrowing. "You wouldn't dare."

A flicker of amusement crossed her face—brief, but there. "Oh, I would. If it means my favorite patient finally gets better, I absolutely would."

I exhaled sharply, kicking the covers off as frustration bubbled under my skin. The hospital gown clung uncomfortably to my body as I swung my legs over the edge of the bed, the cold floor biting at my bare feet.

Wordlessly, I padded to the bathroom, pulled open the cabinet beneath the sink, and grabbed the cup where I'd stashed my tiny rebellions.

Returning to the room, I held the cup out in front of me like a peace offering before tossing the pills into my mouth and swallowing them dry.

Back on the bed, the mattress sagged under me as I sank into it, the sour taste of compliance lingering on my tongue.

"You say that to every patient, Doc. You're a liar—I'm not your favorite."

A small, knowing smile crept onto her lips. "Really? Because I've never given this to any other patient before."

She reached into her pocket, her slender fingers digging deep, and retrieved a small velvet box. Without a word, she placed it on the bed beside me.

I frowned hesitantly before picking it up. Turning it over in my hands, I analyzed the box, its soft texture unfamiliar in the stark, clinical setting of the hospital.

Finally, I opened it.

My lungs tightened.

Inside was a dainty gold necklace, its pendant a delicate butterfly—the same one *she* used to wear.

Hands trembling, I gently removed it from the box. A small sob escaped my lips as I brushed my hair to the side, struggling to clasp it around my neck. When the pendant finally settled against my skin, I reached up to hold the butterfly in my palm, tears slipping freely down my cheeks.

"Thank you," I whispered, my voice breaking, barely audible.

Dr. Morano stood, moving from her chair to sit beside me on the bed.

She took my hand in hers, her grip warm, grounding.

"It may sound unprofessional, but you really are like a daughter to me, Jade," she said, her voice soft. "You're so, *so* young, with *so* much ahead of you. I want you to get better. To live your life, to overcome what you've been through. I *want* to help you."

A bitter laugh tried to escape, but all I managed was a shaky breath.

"What if I'm beyond help?"

Her eyes softened, her hand tightening slightly around mine. "No one really is, Jade. We all just need the right people around us—the ones who genuinely believe we're capable of a second chance at life."

I shook my head, tears blurring my vision as fear clawed its way through my chest.

The words slipped out before I could stop them. "I can't, Doc. I can't keep living my life after what happened. I can't live without her."

"To breathe, you have to start by inhaling, Jade. And to heal, you have to open the gates of your pain and let it out. You admitted yourself to this psych ward because, deep down, you knew you needed help. You know you can't do this alone anymore. So, no more avoiding, no more flushing your medicine, no more silence. This time, we talk it all out."

Talk it all out.

My voice wavered. "How did you know about the necklace?"

Her lips curved into a soft, knowing smile, her eyes flicking toward the nightstand beside my bed. I followed her gaze and saw it—the small picture frame I kept there.

It was a photo of us. Me and her. She was smiling, her cheeks flushed, her eyes alive with laughter. The butterfly necklace rested around her neck, shining against her skin.

Of course.

The memory hit like a punch to the gut.

I could still hear her laughter, feel the warmth of her hand in mine. She used to play with that necklace, her fingers brushing over the pendant whenever she felt nervous or excited. She'd called it her symbol of hope—her reminder that change was possible, even when it felt impossible.

My throat tightened as my gaze dropped to the delicate butterfly pendant hanging from the gold chain around my neck.

"She always said it symbolized transformation," I whispered, my fingers brushing over the butterfly. "That no matter how broken or lost we feel, there's something beautiful waiting to emerge."

Dr. Morano didn't speak right away.

She let the silence settle, her hand steady on mine.

"And she believed that, Jade. For herself and for you. Even now, through this necklace, she's asking you to believe it too."

A sob slipped free. I gripped the necklace like it was the only thing keeping me from falling apart completely.

"She was my everything," I said, my voice cracking. "She made me feel safe, like no matter how bad things got, I could survive it. And now ... now she's gone, and I don't know how to keep going."

Dr. Morano leaned forward slightly. "She was your sister, Jade. Blood wasn't the only thing that tied you together—it was deeper than that. A connection like that doesn't just disappear. It's okay to feel like your entire world has shattered."

I bit down on my lip, hard enough to taste blood.

The weight of her words felt crushing, like I was sinking deeper and deeper, with no way out.

I had no way out.

CHAPTER TWO

"Wear your heart on your skin in this life."
— **Sylvia Plath**

Jade

23 years old

Seven years ago

I lined up the powder on the table with the man's business card, smoothing it out until it formed a perfectly straight line. Setting the card down, I leaned forward, pressing one finger against my right nostril. With the other, I inhaled sharply.

The powder burned its way up my nose and hit the back of my throat like fire.

My eyes clenched shut as the familiar wave of relief washed over me, and I let out a long sigh, sinking back against the couch.

The cold tiles beneath me chilled my legs, but I didn't care.

Tiny stars flickered in my vision as the weight in my chest lifted, leaving nothing but a strange, hollow lightness behind.

Six months out of the psych ward.

A whole year spent there trying to *heal*, trying to rebuild myself, to become something better.

I almost laughed at the thought—what a fucking joke. All it had done was nurture a darkness in my chest, one I hadn't even known could exist.

Now I try to smother it in whatever way I can—sex, adrenaline, cocaine.

Sometimes it works. Most times, it doesn't.

And in those moments, when the darkness claws its way to the surface, nothing calls to me louder than the sharp edge of a razor blade.

"Alright, get up." His rough voice cut through the haze. "My wife's comin' home sooner than expected, and the last thing I need is for her to find you here. She'll chew my ear off for days."

I groaned, struggling to push myself upright. My balance was off, and I stumbled slightly.

"You're such a piece of shit, you know that? You don't even deserve her."

He smirked, leaning against the doorframe. "That's not what you said last week, babe. Besides, I'm a catch. She's the lucky one, not me."

I laughed bitterly, grabbing my jacket from where it had landed on the floor. "Right. A middle-aged asshole having a crisis, hanging out with girls half his age, handing out coke and booze so he can pretend he's not an old, washed-up loser. Total dream husband."

His smirk faltered for a second, and I felt a flicker of satisfaction. He recovered quickly, tossing my shoes toward me.

"Whatever you say, babe. Now hurry the fuck up and go."

I shoved my feet into my shoes, not bothering to tie them properly, and yanked my jacket over my shoulders.

I turned to leave, but not before throwing one last glance at him.

"You're pathetic," I said, voice flat, before stepping out the door.

But really, I was the pathetic one hanging with a stranger who sells me highs.

The apartment stairs creaked under my weight as I made my way down to the street. The air was icy cold, cutting through my foggy mind.

I started walking, my destination clear—the tattoo shop.

The streets were busy now, people rushing home from their nine-to-five jobs, returning to their loved ones.

Family.

The word lodged itself in my chest like a shard of glass. I stopped halfway down an alley, leaning against the brick wall to catch my breath. My hands shook as I closed my eyes, trying to push the word away, but it stuck there, stubborn and cruel.

Family.

The ones I loved, but constantly hurt.

The ones I'd lost—not just my sister, whose death had shattered something vital inside me, but the rest of them too. Not because they'd left, but because I'd pushed them away.

Grief consumed me, guilt weighed me down, and shutting them out seemed safer than letting them see the wreckage inside.

Family binds us by blood, weaving an invisible vow to stay together. But when *she* had died, it felt like that cord had snapped, and I'd been cutting the frayed edges ever since.

I swallowed hard and forced my legs to move, ignoring the tightness in my chest.

The tattoo shop wasn't far. Just fifteen more minutes.

Fifteen minutes, and I could forget it all again.

"You're late," Jasmine said flatly, not even glancing up as she poured herself a cup of coffee.

Jasmine Miller.

We'd been inseparable in high school—cheerleading together, devouring greasy burgers and strawberry milkshakes every Wednesday after practice, gossiping about boys and dreaming up the futures we'd both believed we deserved.

But life had kicked us hard.

She'd married her high school boyfriend fresh out of graduation, and he'd turned out to be a monster. The abuse had ended when he was arrested for domestic violence, but not before he left her with a baby to raise on her own—a little girl she named Star.

Now she was the only tattoo artist in Bay Village, turning pain into art for anyone who walked through her door.

I followed her as she gestured toward the back room, her shop smelling faintly of ink and antiseptic. She closed the door behind us while I slipped off my jacket, draping it over a rickety coat rack.

I settled onto the tattoo chair, the leather cold against my skin.

"Yeah, sorry, I got caught up with work," I lied smoothly.

She let out a heavy sigh, turning her honey-brown eyes on me. Her gaze flicked over my face, zeroing in on my pupils.

They must've been blown wide, judging by the way her lips tightened before she spun around to her computer.

Clicking through a few screens, she finally pulled up the design we'd discussed.

The dragon glared at me from the screen—fierce and alive, its bold black lines coiled into vivid swirls of color that would crawl across my back, its tail curling just above the dimples at my spine.

A dragon to mark my transformation.

Not just a rebirth—a reckoning.

The new me, built from fire and pain.

"Still sure you wanna do this, Jade?" Jasmine asked, turning her head just enough to catch my gaze.

"Yes."

She studied me for a beat, then shook her head. "You know it's gonna hurt like hell. It'll take at least six hours, and that's just for the outlines. You'll have to come back in a month for the color, and that'll hurt even worse."

"Perfect," I replied, without missing a beat.

Her eyes narrowed slightly, and for a second, I thought she might call me out. But instead, she sighed again and nodded, pulling on a pair of gloves.

"Alright," she said. "Let's do this."

I slipped off my top and bra, setting them aside before lying face down on the leather chair. The cold surface pressed against my skin, and I felt the antiseptic wipe glide over my back, cool and clinical. She carefully aligned the stencil, smoothing it into place before stepping back to inspect her work.

The buzz of the tattoo machine filled the silence.

I closed my eyes as the needle met my skin, the first sting sharp enough to pull a hiss from my lips. But I stayed still, letting the sensation wash over me.

I welcomed the pain.

Welcomed it like an old friend.

Because for those hours, the darkness in my head went quiet, retreating into the corners of my mind. All I could feel was the sting, the burn, the steady rhythm of the needle carving the dragon into my flesh.

And for a little while, that was enough.

CHAPTER THREE

"The urge to destroy is also a creative urge."
— **Mikhail Bakunin**

Jade
24 years old
Six years ago

"But you don't know anyone in New York, Jadie! I can't let you leave. For what? A fresh start? To escape the ghost of your sister? To run from *me*?"

I didn't answer.

I just kept packing, each item I folded neatly into my bag as if it was the last time I'd ever touch any of it. I knew it deep in my gut—once I walked out that door, I wasn't coming back.

I moved into the bathroom, the cold tile floor beneath my feet as I grabbed my shampoo, my toothbrush, the little things

I needed to survive on my own. I stuffed them into a plastic bag, careful not to let anything spill.

"Jadie, please," my mama's voice broke. I could hear the desperation as she sank onto the bed behind me. "You can't leave me too."

I stopped for a moment, the weight of her words hitting harder than I expected.

But I had to keep going. I had to finish this.

I zipped the bag closed and slowly turned to face her. She was sitting there, her face buried in her hands, shoulders shaking with sobs that sounded like they were tearing her apart.

I sat down beside her, pulling her into my arms without a second thought.

This was the reason I had to go.

I wasn't just running from the past—I was hurting her. Every day, the more I stayed, the more I dragged her down with me. She didn't deserve that. She deserved peace, not to be tied to the mess I had become.

I couldn't keep dragging her into my darkness.

I sighed, leaning back. "Mama, I've been arrested three times in the past month. I can't stay here. This town is tearing me apart, and everything tied to it is dragging me down with it. You know it better than I do."

Just the night before, I'd been released from custody after a bar fight. I had been so far gone, I didn't even remember what happened until the flashes came back—the tequila, the coke, throwing up all over some poor lady's dress in the bathroom. The cops had shown up because she'd called them on me.

When they saw the state I was in—blown pupils, the five-gram bag in my jacket—they didn't hesitate. But Officer Kennedy, my mama's high school sweetheart—who for some reason still had a soft spot for her—let me go, just like that.

I couldn't help but think of my papa. He must have been rolling in his grave, watching me from wherever he was. Disappointed. Ashamed.

And my mama, who was flirting with a man she hated just to get me out of trouble.

She sniffled, her hands trembling as she reached for mine again. "What about Dr. Morano? You told me she was nice. Maybe if you go back, spend some time there ... she could help you again."

My shoulders slumped as I looked around the room, my eyes wandering over the remnants of who I used to be. Posters of boy bands, vinyl records from high school, my old pom-poms, teddy bears, paintings from my art classes—all those pieces of a life that felt so far away now.

I shook my head and forced myself to stand, pulling on my jacket and grabbing my bags. "I need to go. I'm gonna miss my bus."

She sobbed. "Jadie, my baby, why New York? Why not Boston? It's just twenty minutes away. I could come by, spend time with you, and—"

I couldn't look at her anymore.

I turned away, my hands white-knuckling the bag handle. "I'll text you once I'm there."

Without waiting for a response, I left the room, walking through the living room where Aunt Kristine, my mama's sister, sat on the couch. Her sad, knowing eyes followed me before she stood up and pulled me into a tight hug.

"Take care of yourself, birdy. Don't trust anyone. New Yorkers are ... something else."

I nodded, swallowing hard, my throat tight with the weight of everything I couldn't say. "I will."

She reached into her jacket pocket and pulled out a small

envelope. Slowly, she opened one of my bags and slipped it inside.

“Some money for your first two months of rent. Leila’s waiting for you. I had to convince her to take you in. So don’t disappoint me. No drugs. Not in her house.”

I wanted to tell her that last night had been the last time. That I’d never touch any of it again. That I’d be better, that I’d change.

But the words stuck in my throat.

“I promise.”

She gently tucked a strand of hair behind my ear, her touch soft, but the sadness in her eyes was almost unbearable. “Try to find peace, birdy. Try to heal, okay? And don’t forget about us. Please, Jadie. Call us.”

I clung to Aunt Kristine for a moment longer, breathing in the last of her warmth.

I let go, but before I could leave, Mama grabbed my arm. Her grip was desperate and tight, holding me like she was afraid I’d slip away forever. Her tears soaked into my neck, her sobs muffled by my shirt.

Aunt Kristine gently pried her away. “Clara, let her go. She’s made up her mind.”

I couldn’t look back.

I knew if I did, I’d fall apart, and I needed to keep moving forward, no matter how heavy my heart felt. Without a word, I turned and walked out the door, closing it quietly behind me.

The streets of Bay Village stretched out before me, the familiar white brick houses lining the road, their gardens quiet now. The places I’d once played, laughing with friends, felt like they belonged to someone else—a version of me that was already fading away.

The memories of neighborhood barbecues, families gathered in front yards, felt distant, unreachable.

I stopped at the bus station, the same one I'd used to catch the bus to school.

The gray bus rolled up in front of me, the words "New York City" shining in bold letters on the front.

I breathed out, the tightness in my chest finally loosening as I handed over my ticket. I made my way down the aisle and shoved my bags into the overhead compartment before settling into a seat at the back.

As the bus pulled away from Bay Village, I exhaled, feeling the weight of the past slipping away with every mile. I didn't know what really awaited me in New York, but for the first time in what felt like forever, it didn't matter.

I was finally leaving.

"I have a job interview. Wish me luck!" I called out, making my way to the door.

Leila barely spared me a glance, her attention consumed by *The Housewives of Atlanta*.

She waved her hand lazily in my direction, a cigarette perched between her lips, her eyes glued to the chaos unfolding on screen. One of the housewives had just tossed her champagne glass at another, all over some petty accusation.

I shrugged into my coat, the cold air outside already biting at my skin as I let my hair cascade out from under the collar. The harsh New York winter gripped me the moment I stepped out, and no matter how many months I'd spent here, it still felt like a shock to the system.

Living in the Bronx wasn't something I'd ever imagined for

myself, but Leila had made it work. She'd won the lottery years ago and built herself a life from it. She'd bought this small house and put in the work to turn it into something that felt like home. But it was too big for just her now, so she rented it out.

First to her friends, then to people trying to make it here—like me.

I'd asked her once about how she'd met Aunt Kristine, and I could've sworn I saw a flicker of something cross her face. A hesitation. She claimed they'd been *close* in college, but something in her eyes didn't match the story. Aunt Kristine had only lasted a month in college before she ditched it all to open a nail salon.

Maybe Leila wasn't telling the whole truth. Maybe she didn't want to.

She had told me the house had become too big for her alone, though I could tell it was really just the right size for two.

But I guess, deep down, she knew she needed the company.

I slid into the taxi heading for Manhattan and crossed my legs, the black tights clinging to my skin, my high-heeled boots digging into my toes.

I let my eyes wander over the cityscape. The cold air sliced through the towering skyscrapers while the neon lights of the city flickered by in a blur, painting the night in electric colors.

It had been six months.

Six months since I'd touched *anything*. No drugs. No alcohol.

Nothing to dull the pain or silence the voices in my head or the faces that haunted my dreams. I'd been facing my demons alone for all this time. But the only thing that kept me going was work—and *revenge*.

I spent my mornings serving breakfast at a diner, grinding away to keep my head above water. It was the kind of work that kept me distracted, kept me from completely losing myself.

But in the afternoons, I switched gears. I worked at a vintage boutique—one that Leila knew the owner of. The store was small, but it was my escape.

It gave me the time I needed, the time to sit quietly, take in the city, and plan my next move. Between folding clothes and ringing up customers, I would watch. I would think.

But at night? That's when the real work started. That's when I built my plan.

There were many sleepless nights, endlessly scrolling through Google, LinkedIn, even Facebook. I didn't care how long it took, how much I had to dig—I wasn't going to stop until I had what I needed.

And then, I found it.

A name.

The one person who, unknowingly, would be the key to my revenge.

The cab driver's voice snapped me back. "There. Lazzio Exhibits Inc. That'll be fifty bucks."

I couldn't help but roll my eyes. This city was way too expensive.

I pulled out the cash and handed it over.

He snatched it quickly, offering me a half-hearted smile. "Good luck. The Lazzios are known to be evil."

My gaze drifted to the towering glass building of the museum, gleaming under the night's light snow, standing like a fortress in the heart of the city.

A slow smile crept across my face. "They haven't met me yet."

I was the real evil here.

. . .

The secretary's frown deepened, accentuating the lines carved into her forehead.

"You need an appointment to meet Mr. Lazzio," she said, her voice clipped, like I was wasting precious air just by standing there. "And it's Christmas Eve. Shouldn't you be with your family instead of showing up here unannounced?"

I tapped my heel against the marble floor, annoyed.

Grace—the name pinned neatly to her chest in gold—sat stiffly at her desk, her pen clicking against the wood in a maddening rhythm as her eyes bore into me.

Getting this far hadn't been easy.

When I first approached the museum, a wall of muscle in a navy-blue coat and cap had blocked the doors. The security guard looked like he benched SUVs for fun, and he wasn't budging.

"It's after hours," he said, his voice flat. "Museum's closed. Come back another day."

Desperation clawed at me.

Okay, Jade. You can do this!

I gave him my best wide-eyed look and launched into the performance of my life.

"But I have a job interview with the manager for the curator position! If I don't get this job, I'll be homeless! I'll have to ... resort to prostitution, leave the path of God—" My voice cracked, and I let a few fake tears spill. "And it'll all be *your* fault! On Judgment Day, you'll have to answer for this. My failures will be *your sins.*"

He raised an eyebrow, unimpressed.

I wasn't done. "It's Christmas Eve! Don't you believe in miracles? In second chances? Can't you let me have this one tiny win?"

For a moment he had just stared, his face unreadable.

Then he'd sighed, stepping aside with a grudging shake of his head. "Fine. Go. But hurry up before I change my mind."

I'd lit up like a Christmas tree, clapping my hands in exaggerated joy.

"You won't, I promise!" I'd chirped, practically skipping past him.

Now, standing in front of *Miss Judgmental*'s desk, I felt my patience wearing thin.

"Mr. Lazzio doesn't meet with people without appointments," she said, her voice colder than the December air outside. "You should've called ahead."

I leaned in slightly, dropping my tone to something softer. "Grace, it's Christmas Eve. I'm not asking for much, just a chance to talk to him. A few minutes—"

"No," she cut me off, her pen clicking again, louder this time. "This isn't happening."

My smile froze, and I let out a slow breath.

Fine. She wanted to play hardball? I could play too.

"Listen oldie," I said, meeting her eyes, "Christmas is about compassion. About opening doors, not closing them. You might not believe in miracles, but I do. And if I have to sit here all night to make one happen, I fucking will."

She stared at me, unblinking, as if trying to decide if I was bold, foolish, or both.

Then, with a long-suffering sigh, she picked up the phone.

"Wait here," she said, her voice tight.

I smiled sweetly, settling into the chair across from her. "Thank you. I knew you'd see reason."

She shot me a side-eye that could probably kill a man in two seconds, then dialed a number with all the enthusiasm of someone ordering coffee at a drive-thru.

When she got Mr. Lazzio on the line, her voice was stiff as she spoke into the phone, her tone clipped.

"Mr. Lazzio, sorry to disturb you, but there's a twenty-three-year-old woman from Philadelphia here to see you. She's really interested in the vacant curator position."

Yeah. Philadelphia.

Never been there, probably never will.

No way I'd tell them where I'm really from—some secrets are better left buried.

No one can know my real motive.

She paused, listening to whatever he was saying, her whole face lit up with a devilish smile.

"Yes, sir, I understand." She hung up and turned to face me. "He said no."

I blinked, momentarily speechless. "No?"

This was a joke, right?

Christmas miracle? More like Christmas fucking nightmare.

Was the universe actually working against me?

She shrugged, arms crossed, clearly enjoying this way too much. "He said you're too young, not enough experience, and that you're not what he's looking for."

"How would he know if he's never fucking met me?"

She didn't even flinch at my crazy outburst, just stood up and gestured for me to follow. "Come on, Miss Whitenhouse, I'll walk you out."

I wanted to scream.

The nerve.

But instead, I clenched my jaw, stood up. Smoothing down my skirt as my coat fluttered open, I grabbed my bag and followed her. My heels clicked sharply on the floor, each step making me feel like I was walking to my doom.

When we reached the elevator, she pressed the button.

As the doors opened, she turned back to me with her insincere smile. “It was a pleasure to meet you, Miss—”

“I’m *so* sorry for what I’m about to do.”

Her eyes narrowed in confusion.

I didn’t waste a second.

I shoved her into the elevator with a force I didn’t even know I had in me, hearing a startled gasp escape her lips as she stumbled back.

Without another thought, I spun on my heel and dashed toward Mr. Lazzio’s office like it was the last bus out of hell.

“Miss Whitenhouse!” she screamed behind me, her voice echoing down the hallway, but I didn’t have time for that.

Not now.

I had more important things to do, like taking what was *mine*.

With one last surge of adrenaline, I threw open the door to Lazzio’s office with enough force to make the walls shake. The door slammed against the wall.

My eyes scanned the expansive office, taking in its opulence.

Marble floors gleamed under soft lighting, and sleek, black, luxurious furniture filled the space. One side boasted a U-shaped couch around a low, modern coffee table, while the other featured an imposing desk with three computer screens glowing faintly.

The floor-to-ceiling windows showcased the breathtaking New York City skyline, a spectacle of lights and snow drifting lazily against the glass.

From the 33rd floor, the view was nothing short of stunning.

Finally, my gaze landed on the man behind the desk.

Angelo Lazzio.

CEO of Lazzio Entertainment Group and Lazzio Exhibits Inc.

The only son and heir of Carlos and Monica Lazzio, members of one of the three richest families in the West.

He rose from his chair with an effortless grace, his movements slow as he rounded the desk and leaned casually against it, arms crossed.

His dark eyes locked onto mine, his brow arched in mild curiosity, or perhaps disdain—it was hard to tell.

Angelo Lazzio was the epitome of the Italian archetype.

Tall, dark, and frankly, *disgustingly* handsome.

He was the kind of man you'd call unfairly good looking, the sort that makes you question if life handed out certain genes as a cruel joke.

If I weren't still riding the high of adrenaline from shoving his old secretary into the elevator like the star of my own low-budget action movie, I might have felt a twinge of intimidation. *Might have.*

Instead, I drew in a steadying breath, squared my shoulders, and let the faintest smirk curve my lips.

"I'll keep this quick, Lazzio," I began, my voice calm but edged with determination. "I may be young, but don't mistake that for naïveté. You have no idea how much value I can bring to this place—or how I can turn your museum into *the* premier art showcase in the world."

His expression was unreadable.

Still, I pressed on, taking a step closer.

"I've done my research. Your museum opened a few months ago, and the critics were less than kind: too predictable, too cold, lacking *passion*. But passion? Passion is what I bring." My voice softened. "I'll make it unforgettable, Lazzio. I'll make it *glorious.*"

Before he could respond, Grace burst into the room, red-faced and panting, clutching the doorframe.

"I'm ... *so* sorry, sir," Grace huffed, her glare practically drilling a hole through me. "I called security. She *pushed* me to get in here!"

Lazzio's dark gaze slid from Grace to me, lingering as if I were an oddity worth examining. Then, just barely, the corner of his mouth twitched. Not quite a smile, more like the ghost of one.

"It's fine, Grace. Leave us."

Her jaw dropped, her eyes widening in shock. "But, sir—"

He turned to her fully, and when his eyes met hers, the room seemed to shift. There was no raising of his voice, no visible threat, just a look. But it was enough to make Grace snap her mouth shut like a bear trap.

With a curt nod she backed out of the office, shooting me one last withering glance before the door clicked shut behind her.

His eyes locked back onto mine, cold and *far* too intense.

Honey and dark wood draped in silk sheets.

The thought slipped into my head, unwelcome and wholly inappropriate.

I couldn't tell if it was more disturbing or intoxicating, but it hung there, a soft and sinful whisper.

As if he'd plucked the thought right out of my mind, his gaze shifted, starting at my feet.

Slowly—*agonizingly so*—it roamed upward, lingering on the curve of my legs, pausing at my waist before moving to my chest, brushing over the hollow of my throat, and finally landing back on my face.

A strange shiver rippled down my spine.

His hands gripped the edge of the desk behind him, knuckles flexing, the tendons in his arms tightening just enough to draw my attention.

"Come on, Miss Whitenhouse. Convince me."

Oh, now he wanted to play?

Sure. Why not.

Convincing men like Angelo Lazzio was practically a sport, wasn't it? Or maybe more of an art form. Either way, I was not about to crawl or beg.

If anything, *he'd* be the one crawling before this was over.

But the way he leaned back against the desk, all predatory patience and coiled power, made something inside me twist.

Rationality screamed for me to walk away, but that reckless little voice in my head—my ever-loyal partner in crime—whispered. *Stay. Let him see what you're made of.*

This wasn't just about pride or ambition.

No, this was about revenge.

A slow burn that had carried me through sleepless nights and hollow days, sharpening me into something relentless.

And now, standing before Angelo Lazzio, I could feel it thrumming under my skin, urging me forward.

"I'm not here to beg. I don't beg. And I'm not here for charity, either. I'm here because I'm a taker. I take what I want, what I've earned, and what belongs to me."

"And you think a place here is yours?"

I let out a breathless laugh. "I don't think. I *know*. That museum you've poured millions into? It's beautiful, but it's soulless. It's screaming for someone who can make it matter, someone who isn't afraid to get their hands dirty. You need someone with guts. That's me."

He let out a scoff. "A lot of confidence for someone so young."

I stepped closer, the scent of leather and something unmistakably masculine wafting through the air.

"I'm only six years your junior. But unlike you, I don't have the luxury of wasting time. So ask yourself ..." I paused, watching the flicker of something—curiosity?—dance in his eyes. "Will you be the man who lets me walk out, a missed opportunity? Or the one who sees what I can bring to your empire?"

My gaze didn't waver, holding his with the quiet assurance of someone who knew exactly what she was worth—and how to take it.

He nodded slowly, his tongue dragging over his teeth. "See you next Monday, Miss Whitenhouse. Merry Christmas."

My Christmas miracle.

A small smile curved my lips, fire igniting in my chest as I held his gaze for a beat too long.

With measured steps, I turned and strode out of the room, throwing a playful wink at his secretary on my way to the elevator.

The moment the doors slid shut, I exhaled sharply, my composure crumbling.

Then, unable to hold it back any longer, I let out a scream, the kind that only comes when you know everything's falling into place.

My plan was working, exactly how I had imagined.

Every move, every word, hitting the mark.

And this was just the beginning.

CHAPTER FOUR

"Art is the lie that enables us to realize the truth."
— **Pablo Picasso**

Jade

25 years old

Five years ago

"I'll give you five million, take it or leave it, Miss Whitenhouse."

I tilted my head, a smile tugging at my lips as I crossed my legs, letting my new Louboutins catch the light.

His gaze flicked down, lingering for a moment on my legs before returning to my face.

"Simons," I began, "my offer is already generous. Two million dollars for Frida Kahlo's portraits to be displayed in our exhibition next Friday, staying in the museum for just one week. Two million, for seven days. If you ask me, that's a bargain you'd be crazy to refuse."

I raised my caramel macchiato to my lips, savoring the warmth and sweetness as he studied me with those calculating brown eyes of his.

Nathan Simons was New York's golden boy.

At twenty-seven, thanks to his daddy's shrewd investments in art, he was already a millionaire and a darling of the city's elite.

Tall, blond, with freckles dusting his high cheekbones, Simons was an infuriating mix of charming and maddeningly entitled.

Women fawned over him, seduced by his gentlemanly facade and that disarming, practiced smile.

But I knew better.

That smile had probably landed on ten other women before me today, each convinced she was the only one.

We'd worked together before—three months ago, on an exhibition celebrating Latin culture. It had been a massive success. But today he was unusually resistant, more persistent than I'd ever seen him.

And I didn't like the glint in his eye.

"I don't know. I'm not sure I'm feeling this one."

I narrowed my eyes. "What do you mean?"

He shrugged, his gaze darting to my lips before returning to meet mine. "Is it really a bargain? Handing over my paintings just for strangers to ogle? I don't know, it feels ... cold. Transactional."

I raised a brow, setting my coffee down. "So what *do* you want, Simons?"

He leaned back, his smirk widening. "A date."

I coughed, the coffee catching in my throat.

Clearing it quickly, I tucked a loose strand of hair behind my ear—a nervous tic I hated.

"Simons," I began, carefully.

"Jade," he interrupted smoothly. "We've known each other for months now. Don't you think we're past last names?"

I gave him a tight smile. "Nathan—"

"I'll lend you the paintings for free," he cut in and leaned forward, his voice dropping lower. "If you say yes to just one date. Dinner at a nice restaurant. Red wine. Nothing outrageous. And if you liked it ..."

"Tell me."

"Then I'll take you back to my place and give you the greatest night of your life."

I tilted my head, letting the silence hang between us.

My fingers brushed the rim of my cup, tracing lazy circles as I considered Nathan Simons and his audacious little proposition.

A date.

A *greatest night of my life* kind of date at that.

I'd been working for Lazzio for a year now, and as promised, I wasted no time proving my worth. My ideas weren't just good—they were ingenious, the kind that turned his fledgling museum into a place of glory.

Of course that meant working my ass off, hustling to build a network of contacts who didn't just see Lazzio as a billionaire shark out to snatch their precious art, but as someone determined to showcase it to the world.

And let's be honest, it was my beautiful smile and devilish soul that made them believe it.

Most of my negotiations were with men.

And let me tell you, when you're a young woman batting your lashes and gushing about how *lucky* you are to work with them, contracts practically sign themselves.

It's a strategy that's equal parts infuriating and effective.

Flirting works—sadly, it *always* does.

But as our success snowballed and Lazzio's museum gained real credibility, I'd started noticing something. On the rare occasions I saw him—and believe me, he didn't bother with pleasantries—he made it crystal clear where he drew the line.

Flirting to close a deal? Fine.

Sleeping with clients? Absolutely not.

But hell, it's been way too long since I've had sex, and lately, the cravings have been relentless.

The last time? Two years ago.

Some drug dealer who looked *passable* after a few drinks, but the morning after? I'd woken up in the backseat of his car wearing nothing but my T-shirt. Let's just say he didn't age well overnight.

That was my rock bottom—sex-wise, at least.

I had decided then and there: no more drunken mistakes, no more letting my life spiral just because I couldn't handle my own loneliness.

Two years later, I've clawed my way back to something resembling a normal human being. Steady job, no drugs for 18 months, and even a borderline respectable workout routine. Mondays are for yoga; Fridays are for Pilates. Throw in a cute Soho apartment—thanks to Lazzio's fat paychecks—and I'm practically thriving.

Which means it's time to let myself live a little.

Just a *tiny* bit.

And who better to dust off the cobwebs than a golden boy who clearly gets around enough to know exactly where the clitoris is—and *maybe* even what to do once he finds it?

I swept my hair over one shoulder, exposing my neck, and let my fingers graze my skin slowly. His gaze followed, dark and hungry, and when his tongue darted out to wet his lip, I pretended not to notice.

"Sleeping with clients," I said softly, letting the words linger like the taste of forbidden fruit, "isn't exactly part of my job description, Nathan." My fingers slid to toy with the delicate gold chain at my throat. "I'm not sure my boss would appreciate it."

"I'll deliver the paintings myself, Jade. Free of charge. Lazzio never has to know. It'll stay just between us. You like keeping secrets, don't you?"

My eyes roamed over his face, lingering on the curve of his jaw, the slight shadow of stubble there that hinted at a man who knew how to look effortlessly perfect.

I bit my lip, just enough for him to notice, tilting my head as though I were genuinely considering his offer.

"I have a taste for keeping secrets, Nathan," I murmured, my fingers now toying with a loose strand of hair. "But some of them? They don't come cheap."

I let the words hang in the air, letting them sink in, watching him squirm just a bit.

Then I straightened up, grabbed my bag, and got to my feet.

"I'm not here to make deals for free, Nathan," I said, setting my glass down. "You want my time? My attention? You'll have to show me more than a wink and a promise of making me *come*."

I moved closer, dragging my nail along his jaw, then cupping his chin and tilting his face up to meet mine.

His eyes were full of admiration, and I almost laughed at how easily he fell into line.

I pouted. "But thanks for the offer. I'll think about it ... maybe."

I stepped out of the overpriced coffee shop and walked

back to work, the sweet taste of my caramel lingering on my tongue.

The thrill of the chase, though—it was far sweeter.

Nathan Simons would deliver the two portraits by Friday, no question—probably with flowers and a handwritten note dripping with charm. Typical. And when I didn't respond, when I left his little gestures hanging in the void, he'd try again at the exhibition, angling for my attention with the same predictable persistence.

I'd feign innocence, offer a distracted smile, and murmur, "Oh, I must've forgotten about those."

It'd gut him just enough to make him want me more.

That was the fun part—the waiting game, the quiet torment of a man who couldn't stand not being in control.

The playbook was so familiar that I almost felt bad for him. *Almost.*

I could either string him along for kicks or tell him I wasn't interested, which—let's be honest—I've done dozens of times with clients over the last year.

Or I could finally cave and fuck him.

Honestly ... why not?

It's been way too long, he's stupidly attractive, and God knows a one-night stand might actually do me some good.

Something hot, dirty, and with absolutely *no strings.*

Lost in my thoughts, my body moved on autopilot, carrying me through the glass doors of the building. It wasn't until I tapped the elevator button that I even registered where I was.

The smooth hum of the elevator arriving snapped me back to reality.

As I stepped inside, a sly smile tugged at my lips.

Maybe tonight I'd finally decide ... after putting one of my toys to good use.

Nothing like clearing your head the proper way instead of letting it obsess over sex and orgasms I wasn't getting.

I glanced at my watch.

3:35 p.m.

I hummed along to the soft jazz playing in the elevator, my mind blissfully blank for once.

But then reality hit me like a bucket of ice water.

The meeting.

Oh, shit.

I snapped upright, my finger jamming the button for the 18th floor as if that would somehow make the elevator move faster. It paused at the 23rd, *of course*, dragging out my misery before finally starting its descent.

I had a staff meeting that technically started—well—*ten minutes ago*.

It was Wednesday, but because Lazzio was jetting off to Australia tomorrow to charm their Minister of Culture, he insisted we push the exhibition briefing up a week.

Requirements, complaints, demands—it was all going to be in there.

And I was already ten minutes late.

Angelo Lazzio—the reigning king of perfection, punctuality, and micromanaging the air we breathe—was going to murder me. Not figuratively. No, the man had a way of looking at you that could melt steel and make you rethink all your life choices.

I'd seen it happen to others; now it was my turn on the chopping block.

By the time the elevator dinged on the 18th floor my heart was racing, though not entirely from the panic.

Lazzio was intimidating, sure.

His sharp suits, his piercing eyes, the way he could strip you bare with a single look—he was the kind of man who radiated power. But there was something else about him, something that made my pulse stutter for an *entirely* different reason.

I smoothed my skirt and walked briskly down the hall, heels clicking against the polished floor as I rehearsed my excuse.

When I pushed open the glass door to the conference room, everyone's heads turned. My colleagues were seated around the oval table, their expressions a mix of curiosity and amusement.

And then there was Lazzio, standing at the head of the table with his arms crossed, his dark eyes locking on mine the moment I stepped inside.

"Miss Whitenhouse," Lazzio said, his voice like ice. "How nice of you to join us."

I swallowed hard, quickly sliding into the only empty chair —directly across from him.

"Sorry, traffic," I said lightly, my lips curling into a half-smile.

Lazzio didn't respond immediately.

Instead, he leaned forward, his hands resting on the sleek glass table as he studied me. His suit jacket stretched just enough to reveal the crisp white dress shirt beneath, tailored so perfectly it looked like it belonged in an art exhibit itself.

The corner of his mouth quirked, just enough to make me wonder if he was amused or irritated—or worse, *both*.

"Traffic? You don't even drive, Miss Whitenhouse."

"Pedestrian traffic," I said smoothly, crossing one leg over the other under the table. "You know how the streets get this time of day."

"Well," he said finally, straightening to his full height, "now that you're here, perhaps we can continue."

I nodded, ignoring the heat creeping up my neck as he gestured for the team to proceed.

If I thought the hard part was over, I was dead wrong.

The meeting had barely started, and already, I could feel his eyes on me. It wasn't just his gaze; it was the kind of stare that could pin you in place, take the air from your lungs if you let it.

But then again, this was Lazzio.

His eyes *always* had a way of lingering on me whenever we were in the same room.

They weren't filled with anything interesting, though. No desire, no warmth—just boredom. That cold, detached look, like I was some piece of furniture that happened to catch his attention for a second.

The first four months after I signed my contract, he was gone. Off to LA, building some film domain for his entertainment empire. I barely saw him.

Undeterred, I spent my time working with the other colleagues who had no choice but to teach me everything they knew.

Unfortunately for them, I learned quickly.

So quickly, in fact, that I ended up excelling past them all.

When he finally came back, it wasn't the museum or the exhibitions he seemed to care about.

No, it was me.

Always me.

My opinion, my advice, everything.

He always requested *me*.

But something told me that this time, he was paying attention in ways I wasn't sure I wanted him to.

The meeting dragged to its conclusion, the room buzzing as people packed their laptops and papers, eager to escape.

Just as I got up and tucked my tablet into my bag, Lazzio's voice sliced through the air, stopping me cold.

"Sit."

My heart thudded. "Last time I checked, I'm not your pet, boss."

He pushed off from the table and walked toward me with that same smug confidence I hated.

"I never said you were. Sit, Miss Whitenhouse."

I raised an eyebrow. "Or what? You're gonna drag me there by my hair like a caveman?"

His eyes sparkled with amusement, but he didn't answer.

He just took another step forward, closing the distance between us.

"Sit."

I rolled my eyes and did so, but not without showing my annoyance with a sigh. "I was only ten minutes late. I don't think I need a spanking because of it."

"Keep talking like that, and you just might get one."

"Ugh, you're *so* inappropriate."

Crossing my arms, I tilted my head to the side, waiting for whatever urgent thing he needed to tell me. He studied me for a second, his eyes narrowing just slightly.

He was simmering now.

He hated when I pushed him like this, but I loved it.

Annoying him was too easy.

"How's Simons?"

I looked down at my nails. "Good. Saved you two million, by the way. You're welcome."

He didn't look impressed. "Guess your flirting's more effective than I thought."

"Yes. So effective that he's taking me on a date Saturday night."

He ran a hand down his tie. "A date?"

Honey and dark wood draped in silk sheets.

A rush of something sweet and dangerous stirred in my chest. I hated how good he looked, how he could make even the simplest move seem like a carefully calculated play.

I could almost feel the heat rolling off of him, and it made me want to tear my own eyes out.

"Yep, and then he's taking me to his place for, and I quote, 'the greatest night of my life.'" I scoffed. "Bold of him to think I'm that easy to impress."

"Bold of you to assume anyone's still desperate enough to try."

"Wow, insecure *and* cruel. Must be exhausting being you, Lazzio."

He turned and walked to the table, slipping his phone back into his perfectly tailored black pants before leaning against it.

His expression was cold and unreadable, like always, but the way he ran his tongue across his teeth told me he was more pissed than he let on.

Interesting.

"Tell me more, Miss Whitenhouse. Even though you know it's off-limits to screw my clients. Unless you're eager to lose your precious position."

Ah, my favorite part of the day—seeing which one of us could push the other closer to losing their patience.

I crossed my legs, letting my heel dangle lazily from my foot. "You know, maybe we should revisit that policy. Some of our clients are very much my type. Think about it—a little *extracurricular* activity could be great for my mental health. I rake in millions for you, you share the profits, and I get to screw the ones who catch my eye. Sounds fair to me, don't you think?"

Jade: one.

Lazzio: zero.

"Fair? Only if I wanted to start running a brothel. Though, judging by the way you *think*, you'd fit right in."

I tilted my head. "I bet you'd be my most loyal customer."

His jaw tightened, just slightly, but it was enough to tell me I'd struck a nerve.

"Trust me, Miss Whitenhouse, I would never be desperate enough to pay for what you'd be selling."

Ouch. That one had claws.

Jade: one.

Lazzio: one.

A wicked smile spread across my cheeks. "Oh, I wouldn't charge you, boss. I'm not cruel enough to make you admit what you want."

"Ah, and what do I want?"

I remained silent as I stood, moving slowly around the table, my heels clicking against the floor as I made my way toward him.

I stopped just inches away, watching him carefully.

His hands gripped the edge of the table, his eyes narrowing, the tension between us thickening.

I ran a finger along his tie, my touch lingering just long enough to make him flinch before I yanked it—just a little—messing it up, watching his gaze darken.

I could feel it—the urge to snap, to lose control.

Deep down, I knew he wanted to strangle me for it. His obsessively neat, perfectly tailored clothes, his immaculate office, his rigid little world ... and here I was, enjoying every second of destroying it.

I yanked him toward me by his tie, my face inches from his. "Anyway, what is it you need from me, Lazzio?"

When he's requested me alone, it was usually because there was something only I could handle—some negotiation that needed to be taken to the absolute edge.

So I knew exactly why he had asked me to stay after the meeting.

And I was over our little game now.

My heels were killing me, and all I wanted was to take them off, slip into something comfortable, and soak in a hot bath.

I wanted to go home.

He leaned back just a fraction. "As I'm heading off to Australia, you're in charge of this weekend's exhibition. I need you to work some of your magic on James Greg. Get that portrait of Napoleon he's holding hostage. The bastard won't budge if it's me, but for some reason, your pretty eyes seem to do the trick."

I let go of his tie. "Consider it done. Have a safe trip, Lazzio. Try not to get bitten by a tarantula or something—I'd hate to be the one stuck as CEO."

With a sway of my hips I turned to leave, knowing he'd have to get the last word in, as usual.

"Try not to fuck Nathan Simons," he called after me. "Wouldn't want him needing therapy at my expense."

I didn't bother turning around. I just flipped him off and walked out.

Guess I'll be fucking Nathan Simons this weekend then.

CHAPTER
FIVE

"I know it is wet and the sun is not sunny, but we can have lots of good fun that is funny."

— **Dr. Seuss**

Jade

26 years old

Four years ago

On the tips of my toes, my ponytail brushing my cheek, I pinned the picture to the wall. I made sure it stayed in place before stepping back and placing my hands on my hips to admire my work.

Another name. Another picture.

The fourth one now.

I dusted my hands off and sank to the floor, spreading out the two files I'd "borrowed" from Lazzio's office.

The originals? Safely back where they belonged. Files on every one of our clients and collaborators—their lives, weaknesses, secrets, families—everything I'd need for their downfall.

I'd stumbled across Lazzio's little stash a couple of months ago when he left for China for a month.

Grace, his sweet little witch of a secretary, took the week off; she claimed she was "sick".

Me, though? I was snooping.

I found those files tucked away in his desk and spent the whole damn night going through them. That's when I came across the one that made my blood run cold.

James Greg.

A name I knew far too well.

His file was *thick*, filled with all the dirty little details I didn't want to know but couldn't stop myself from reading. Every financial transaction, every shady deal, every little piece of leverage Lazzio had on him.

But it wasn't the business stuff that caught my attention. It was the personal notes—things no one was supposed to see.

Lazzio had a knack for digging up what people wanted to forget, and Greg was no exception. The guy was a mess, just one bad decision away from crumbling, but somehow he'd managed to keep up the perfect façade.

Honestly, I didn't give a damn about his life. I was just looking for something that would tell me if he was the one I was after.

After two years in New York working for Lazzio, helping him build his empire, everything was going smoothly—except for the usual back-and-forth power games between us. You know, the kind that had my pulse racing one minute and my eye twitching the next.

It was the twisted kind of entertainment that kept me on my toes, whether I liked it or not.

I was still thirty months sober from drugs, and honestly? I

was kind of proud of myself. I still drank, though—just a glass or two a week, usually when I was soaking in the bath.

Work, workouts, and my revenge-plotting nights kept my demons at bay.

But exhaustion didn't mean I'd let up.

My apartment's office had become a makeshift headquarters for my plans—a secret room with fingerprint-locked doors, where every lead, every scrap of evidence, and every thread of vengeance was meticulously pinned in place.

If Dr. Morano could see me now, she'd probably say I was wasting my energy clinging to the past. Revenge, she'd tell me, solves nothing, heals nothing. But what she didn't know wouldn't hurt her. And it certainly wouldn't stop me.

I hadn't seen her in three years, though she still emailed me occasionally, asking how I was.

Sometimes, I replied. Sometimes, I didn't.

Either way, her well-meaning concern barely scratched the surface of what I'd become.

A woman with one singular purpose: to destroy the person who had destroyed her.

The doorbell rang, pulling me out of my scheming.

I got up, gave my dress a quick pat-down, and left the room, double-checking the lock before heading for the hallway mirror.

One glance told me everything was in place—hair flawless, makeup on point.

I slipped on my heels and swung the door open.

"Happy birthday, princess," Aussie said, holding out a bouquet of red roses with a boyish grin.

Last year, after Lazzio dared me not to screw Nathan Simons, I went ahead and did it anyway. Call it a mix of horniness and spite. He was gone to Australia, I was feeling rebellious, and Nathan was offering, so why not? Dinner turned into drinks, and drinks led to his bed.

Was it the "greatest night of my life" like Nathan had promised? Not even close.

Was it still enjoyable? Absolutely.

A hot, sweaty man deliciously kissing my neck, his mouth going places no one had in years? Yeah, I had missed that.

Without realizing it, Angelo Lazzio and his infuriatingly smug self had managed to crack open the vault I'd sworn shut.

But let's be clear—I don't sleep with clients.

Nathan was a one-time rebellion.

These days, I stick to men who are safe bets—no strings, no drama, no ties to my job or my boss.

That's where Aussie came in.

My yoga instructor, of all people.

At five-foot-eight with surfer hair and brown eyes, he had a vibe so laid back he practically melted into the floor. He was Australian—hence the nickname—which somehow made everything he said sound charming. He was also very much not part of New York's upper crust, which was a bonus.

We'd met in his hot yoga class two weeks ago.

By class three, I was pretty sure he'd spent more time correcting my form than anyone else's.

By class four, he'd asked me out.

And by date one, well ... let's just say he had made me laugh—a rarity these days—and the next thing I knew, I was in his bed, rediscovering just how fun a good *ride* could be.

I gave him a quick once-over: crooked tie, easy grin, the slightest hint of smugness that I didn't totally hate.

"Thanks, Aussie," I said, taking the red roses.

Not the most original choice, but at least he wasn't empty-handed.

I wished they were red dahlias though.

I set the bouquet on the counter, grabbed my keys, double-checked for my phone and lip gloss, and got out.

The door clicked shut behind me as I turned back to him.

I pouted. “Is this my only present?”

“Well, you’ll have to wait,” he said, his voice smooth, almost teasing. “But first, let me take you dancing, princess.”

And that’s the moment I knew.

After tonight, I wouldn’t be seeing him again.

The way he spat out “*princess*” made my skin crawl.

I almost turned around right there, locked myself in my apartment, and threw up.

But it was my birthday, and I hadn’t been out dancing in so long.

I needed a little fun back in my life, so I decided to follow him—begrudgingly—to the elevator and into the cab.

The whole time, I was silently praying that the club he’d chosen wasn’t as lame as he was.

Aussie may have had a disastrous personality, but at least he had good taste in clubs and women—after all, he was after *me*.

He guided me through the crowd, his hand lingering on my lower back.

People were dancing, singing, and having the kind of fun I hadn’t realized I was missing. *Exactly* the vibe I needed.

When we reached the bar, I leaned against it and ordered a margarita—extra lemony—and Aussie went for a beer. *How original.*

“Have I told you already how fucking hot you are tonight?”

I raised an eyebrow. "Only tonight?"

He grabbed my hand and kissed the top. "Every day, princess. But tonight? You shine brighter than a disco ball."

I glanced down at my dress—sparkly silver, sinfully short, with a perfectly fitting bustier. *Dolce & Gabbana.*

"I mean, I am the star of the night, after all."

I could see his eyes narrow, but his smile only grew wider.

"So"—he leaned in a bit closer—"you gonna let me show you a dance or are you just gonna stand there looking all perfect?"

I took another sip of my margarita, feeling the burn slide down my throat as I grabbed his hand, pulling him into the crowded sea of bodies.

For a random Thursday night in November, this place was packed; honestly, I wasn't mad about it.

I looped my arms around his neck, my hands playing with his hair. His hands slid down to my hips, pulling me closer until we were practically glued together.

The music was infectious, and I could feel it vibrating through my chest.

I pulled back slightly. "What's the name of this club?"

When we exited the taxi, I had barely glanced up. I was too busy focusing on not tripping in these damn heels that somehow made me just a little taller than him.

No comment.

"The Diamond."

Hmm, it sounded familiar, but I couldn't place it.

He turned me around, pressing me to his front, his chest warm and solid against my back. I could feel his breath on my neck, his hands gripping my waist, pulling me closer.

His teeth grazed my ear. "You're trouble, you know that?"

I smirked, biting my lip. "You have no idea."

We kept dancing, and for a moment I let myself get lost in

it—the lights, the music, the intoxicating feeling of a man pressed up against me—

Wait!

The Diamond.

Now it clicked. I had heard the name before.

It was Leonardo Vittori's club.

Lazzio's closest friend—or, as I liked to call him, his *bestie*.

I'd never met the man, but I'd heard enough to know I should avoid him at all costs. Any friend of Lazzio's had to be just as insufferable as he was.

Great. Just fucking great.

Of course I'd end up in the one place where Lazzio's presence lingered like a ghost, even when he wasn't physically there.

And tonight? I didn't want to run into anyone from his circle—or him.

I'd seen enough of him this week—hell, this month—to last me a lifetime.

It was tradition at the office: everyone got their birthday off.

For the last two years, I'd kept mine the same.

Get up, work out, head to the store for a vanilla cupcake with strawberry icing, and FaceTime my mom so she could sing me Happy Birthday while I blew out the candle. Then I'd hang up, order takeout, and spend the day in my vault poring over contracts, digging into our clients' lives. Or, if my heart got too heavy, retreat to a bubble bath with a glass of wine and The Office on a loop for a good laugh.

I'd checked all the boxes today—except the going-out part. That was new.

As predictable as ever, Lazzio had sent his yearly text—"Happy Birthday."

Short, dry, and devoid of any warmth, but somehow still exactly him.

Tomorrow, I'll find an envelope on my desk.

Inside, there'd be a note: *Use this to relax and stop pissing me off*, along with a spa voucher.

The bastard knew me too well.

So yeah, I didn't want to see him. Especially not on my birthday.

I turned on my heel and placed my hands on Aussie's chest.

"I'm bored. Let's go."

Taking a step to leave, I barely got anywhere before he grabbed my wrist. Tight. *Too* tight.

"Wait," he said, pulling me closer, his grip firm on my hips. "Your present's comin'."

My stomach twisted.

The shift in his tone wasn't cute. It wasn't teasing. It was something darker, something I didn't like one bit.

His whole vibe had shifted from charming to something ... off.

I pushed at his chest. "Let me go. I'm getting another drink, then I'm out of here. This birthday adventure? Officially over."

His fingers dug into my hips, hard enough to bruise, and I felt the slow burn of fury ignite under my skin.

"You're gonna stay right here," he growled, his Australian accent cutting sharper than usual, "And you're gonna take the bloody present I forked out half my paycheck for. Then you're gonna shut your damn gob."

What the hell?

He thought he could *manhandle* me? Threaten me? Like hell.

I let out a scoff. "Half your salary? You should've saved your money, *mate*. You're about to spend the rest of it on an emergency room bill if you don't let go of me right now."

His hand shot to my chin, yanking my face closer with enough force to make my jaw ache. "You fucking—"

He didn't get to finish, because the lights suddenly cut out, plunging us into darkness. The DJ, who clearly had no sense of timing, kicked off "Happy Birthday" with cringe-worthy enthusiasm.

The lights flickered back on, but only on *us*.

Out of nowhere, two girls with stripper heels—barely dressed in anything except tiny bikinis—strutted toward us. They were carrying two massive bottles of some ridiculously expensive brand of champagne, and both had firework sparklers shooting from the tops.

Aussie instantly let go of my chin, a fake grin plastering itself on his face.

He tried to laugh it off like nothing had happened, but his eyes betrayed him.

"Happy birthday, princess," he muttered, still not letting go of me entirely.

I didn't say a word, just took the champagne glass one of the bikini-clad girls handed me.

She grinned wide, shaking the bottle like it owed her money. When the cork shot off, champagne sprayed everywhere; the crowd cheered.

She poured the bubbly into my glass—or at least, tried to. Most of it missed and ended up on my new Louboutins. *Fantastic.*

I stared down at the sticky mess pooling around my toes, my grip tightening on the glass.

The crowd kept clapping, phones out, recording every second like this was the highlight of their miserable lives.

Meanwhile, all I could think about was how satisfying it would be to smash the champagne bottle over Aussie's smug head.

The idea wasn't just tempting—it felt inevitable, like fate.

Without hesitation, I grabbed the bottle from Barbie's hands. She blinked, her expression morphing from playful to startled in an instant. "Hey—"

She didn't get to finish.

With one smooth, wide arc, I swung the bottle straight into Aussie's head. The satisfying crack of glass shattering echoed through the air, followed by an explosion of champagne that showered the nearby crowd and my dress.

He collapsed onto the floor, unconscious.

The crowd froze for a beat, then erupted in a mix of gasps, cheers, and horrified laughter.

I stood there for a second, breathing hard, holding the jagged remains of the bottle like it was some kind of trophy.

I sighed. "Happy birthday to me."

CHAPTER SIX

"I might be the villain of this story."
— **Rebecca Makkai**

Jade

I wiggled my feet under the bench, hissing as a sharp jab reminded me that, yep, there was still glass stuck in my toe.

Across from me, some woman was giving me a death stare.

I ignored her, tilting my head back against the wall.

All I wanted was for this night to disappear into a black hole. Was that too much to ask?

The floor beneath me was a sticky crime scene of gum, spit, and God knows what else. Hugging my knees to my chest, I tried to fold into myself, close my eyes, and pretend none of this was happening.

"You a stripper?"

"No," I muttered, not bothering to look up.

"Well, you look like one."

"Thanks." I cracked one eye open. "I'm not."

Blessed silence finally descended, broken only by the faint clatter of keyboards and murmured conversations. My body relaxed for the first time all night, the tension in my shoulders slowly unwinding as my breathing evened out.

"Why are you here?"

Groaning, I opened my eyes and leveled her with a glare. "I killed someone. Now, unless you want to be next, shut up."

She laughed—a loud, snorting, braces-flashing laugh like I'd just delivered the punchline of the year. Shaking her head, she leaned back and crossed her arms, entirely unfazed.

For the first time in what felt like hours—but was probably only thirty minutes—I actually took her in. Hair in a messy bun, a battered leather jacket, and this smug little grin like she'd seen it all and dared you to surprise her.

She looked about forty-five, though the dark spots scattered across her cheeks told me drugs might've aged her faster than life ever could.

"Relax. Just makin' conversation," she said, leaning back in her chair like we were in some shitty coffee shop instead of a holding cell. "What'd he do to deserve it? Cheat on you? Or was he just a bad tipper?"

"I'm not a stripper!"

She gestured lazily at me, head to toe. "C'mon, that outfit? It's a reasonable assumption."

I glanced down at my ruined *Dolce & Gabbana* dress, now smeared with champagne, glass dust, and probably Aussie's ego.

"Why are *you* here?"

She shrugged, unbothered. "Drug dealing."

Of course.

The dark spots on her cheeks, the too-sharp cheekbones, and the jittery energy practically screamed it. The telltale signs of crack addiction were all over her.

"Could've guessed."

She barked out another laugh. "Alright, I like you. Name's Cheryl. You?"

"Not in the mood for bonding, Cheryl."

"Well, that's a shame." She stretched. "You're not gettin' out of here anytime soon, princess. Might as well chat."

That word again—*princess.*

My jaw tightened.

I didn't respond, letting the silence stretch between us as my eyes darted around the police station.

The place looked exactly how you'd imagine a police station at midnight—dingy walls, flickering fluorescent lights, and the smell of burnt coffee mixed with crimes.

After smashing Aussie's head in, I'd done the obvious thing: I took off my heels and ran.

I didn't even grab my bag, just bolted out of the club with adrenaline.

But apparently, you can't outrun karma—or New York cops.

They picked me up a few blocks away, their sirens splitting the night.

I didn't fight them. What would be the point?

Instead, I played the birthday card, throwing in a promise to cooperate if they skipped the handcuffs. They actually went for it—maybe out of pity, or maybe because they wanted to see how ridiculous I looked climbing into the back of their cruiser in a champagne-soaked dress.

Spoiler alert: it was ridiculous.

At the station, they asked if I wanted a lawyer.

I shook my head, but my eyes drifted to the phone.

I needed to call someone, even though the idea left a bitter taste in my mouth.

They waved the phone toward me and I dialed the only person who could untangle the mess I'd gotten myself into.

My stomach churned the entire time.

Now, hours later—or maybe just minutes that felt like hours—I waited.

Sighing, I let my feet swing idly beneath the bench once again.

The background noise of the station barely registered until it stopped. A whistle—or something like it—cut out mid-note, leaving an uncomfortable silence behind.

I tilted my head, curiosity getting the better of me.

Then, I heard my name.

The officer who said it—a small blonde with a high ponytail and green eyes—looked up. Her expression shifted when she saw him. She smiled, her fingers brushing the ends of her ponytail as she adjusted her posture.

Tall, broad shoulders, dark hair.

Honey and dark wood draped in silk sheets.

Angelo Lazzio.

He didn't need to turn around. I'd have recognized his back anywhere.

My name fell from his lips and the blondie nodded, responding softly, her cheeks coloring as she tucked a strand of hair behind her ear.

He didn't even look at her.

Everyone else, though? They couldn't stop looking. The entire room seemed to lean in his direction, like he was the answer to a question they hadn't realized they'd asked. Admiration, lust, envy—you name it, it was written all over their faces.

Lazzio didn't notice—or if he did, he didn't care.

He turned around, and his eyes locked onto mine. Cold. Calculated. Not a flicker of warmth, which honestly felt about right.

His jaw ticked, and he started toward me, blondie by his side.

I stretched lazily. “Well, this should be fun.”

The cell door opened with a beep, the sound loud enough to make me wince. He stepped inside, his eyes dropping immediately to my feet. His lips tugged downward—barely a frown, just enough to indicate he’d noticed.

“Come on.”

I pushed off the bench, brushing off my dress that was now sticky.

As I passed Cheryl, she barely glanced at me. Her gaze was glued to Lazzio like he was the eighth wonder of the world.

“Goodbye, Cheryl,” I said, tossing her a little wave. “He’s gonna help you get out too, don’t worry.”

She didn’t even blink.

If I hadn’t been so annoyed, I might’ve found it funny.

Standing next to him, barefoot, I suddenly felt this weird nervous energy creeping up on me.

I quickly pushed past the officers—whose whispers followed me—eyes still locked on Lazzio, and made my way out.

I blew the smoke out, fingers tight on the cigarette, freezing my ass off while waiting for whatever Lazzio was doing inside.

A cop stood off to the side, puffing away by himself,

looking like he was lost in a deep, soul-crushing moment. I had figured, why not? Might as well ask.

I had asked if I could bum a smoke, and he'd just shrugged, tossing me his pack without saying a word.

I'd lit up and stuck the cigarette between my lips, but he had kept his eyes trained on the cars rolling by, acting like I wasn't even there. It was almost like I had intruded on some sacred self-reflection moment, so I had taken the hint and stepped back, leaving him alone.

Finally, Lazzio emerged from the station, and I could feel his eyes scanning the lot until they found me.

The second our gazes met, the air shifted—dark, stormy.

He stalked over, snatched the cigarette from my lips without a word, and crushed it underfoot.

He didn't even glance back as he turned on his heel, heading toward a black SUV, its hazard lights flickering in the night.

He slid into the vehicle, slamming the door shut behind him.

I followed him, my bare feet tapping softly against the pavement until I leaned down and tapped on the passenger window with the tip of my nail.

He lowered it, and I flashed him a wicked smile.

"Thanks, but I'm gonna walk. See you tomorrow morning, boss."

I didn't even have time to take a step back.

"Get in the fucking car, Jade."

My heart fluttered in my chest like a thousand butterflies.

It was the first time he'd *ever* said my name.

For a second, I debated.

Walk away. Get lost in the night, barefoot and *free*.

But instead, I reached for the handle and pulled the door open.

The moment I slid into the car, the scent of him hit me—rich, smoky, with a hint of something dangerous that made the air feel heavier. It wasn't the luxury of the leather seats that made me uncomfortable, it was the proximity to him—the way the space seemed to shrink, suffocatingly close.

He turned the car on, the engine growling to life as he merged onto the road.

"Tell me what happened."

I yawned. "No."

"Who's the man you knocked out?"

I chuckled darkly, eyes flicking to his profile. "My yoga instructor. Guess I have more strength than I thought."

"What the fuck did he do?"

I let out a sigh and stared out the window, as if the world outside was more interesting than this conversation. "If I knew you'd interrogate me, I would've stayed behind, Lazzio."

His grip tightened around the steering wheel. "What did he do?"

Fine.

Guess he wasn't going to let it go.

I leaned back in the seat. "Hurt me—though, not exactly the kind of pain I'd call *fun*."

His tongue ran over his lower lip. "Where are your shoes?"

"Left them in the club when I ran away." I waved my hand dismissively. "Be a sweetheart and ask your buddy Vittori to send them back to me. They were my favorite Louboutins. Oh, and my bag too!"

"You aren't getting shit back, Miss Whitenhouse. I had to grease the cops with 70K just to get you and your little friend Cheryl out and erase the charges your little yoga instructor tried to play."

I almost told him Cheryl wasn't my friend, that I'd never even met the poor woman before tonight, but held my tongue.

Drugs can strip you bare, leave you a shadow of what you used to be. She was a walking reminder of who I could've been if I hadn't pulled myself together.

So yeah, if I could help her for a minute, I didn't mind—even if it cost Lazzio a little cash. The man's a freaking billionaire. I'm sure he'll cry into his silk sheets later.

I tapped my nails against the armrest. "Well, guess you're not *that* much of a sweetheart then, are you?"

He glared at me for a second.

I pouted. "Consider it my birthday present, Lazzio. No need to waste money on a card or spa vouchers this year. You're welcome."

His eyes flickered with something—dark amusement, maybe irritation?

Hard to tell.

"You're twenty-five, and you still can't get your shit together. Getting drunk, getting arrested ... Do you ever stop and think? Or are you too busy being nothing but a fucking joke?"

I clenched my fists, fury burning in my veins.

Freaking Italian bastard!

"I hate you *so* fucking much," I muttered under my breath. "After everything I've done for you and your little precious Lazzio Exhibits Inc.—how my work literally helped push your shit show to the top—you should be on your knees kissing my feet, not running your mouth like some judgmental jerk."

I didn't care anymore.

If he wanted to tear me down, I'd tear him apart right back.

He slammed the car to a stop, and I realized we were already at my apartment complex. My hands were shaking, but I yanked off my seatbelt quickly, the anger simmering so hot I honestly felt like I might lose it completely and really end up in jail—this time for murdering my boss.

He got out, slammed the door, and walked over to my side, pulling it open.

I ignored him, stepping out onto the pavement, my bare feet hitting the ground.

"You're bleeding."

"And you're an asshole. Now move."

He exhaled sharply, and before I could even process what was happening, he had me hoisted over his shoulder, his hands gripping the bare skin of my thighs.

I gasped. "What the hell do you think you're doing? Put me down!"

He didn't answer, just kept walking, my legs dangling in the air as I wriggled in a mix of embarrassment and frustration.

"You can't just—*ugh,* put me the hell down, Lazzio!" I shouted, kicking my legs like a toddler throwing a tantrum.

His tone was maddeningly calm. "You're still bleeding. You're not walking anywhere like that. I don't need you taking a sick leave and messing up my schedule."

I rolled my eyes so hard I almost got dizzy. "Oh, how selfless of you. Put me down before I puke all over your suit, Lazzio."

"Do it, and I'll make you lick it off."

I froze for half a second. "You're disgusting."

"And you're a fucking child."

"You're lucky I'm too dizzy to fight you properly," I muttered, thumping a weak fist against his back.

He pushed open the door to my apartment complex and set me down roughly.

My feet hit the floor and I immediately winced, hissing through my teeth.

Mr. Jones, my building's concierge—who was the picture of every English grandpa stereotype rolled into one—glared at us. He was always in that tweed cap, even indoors. It was like the thing was surgically attached to his head.

"Everything okay, Jade?"

"Just peachy, Mr. Jones. Could you grab me a first aid kit?"

He stood, setting his newspaper aside, and cast us one last wary glance before heading off.

Lazzio took a step toward me. "Let me carry you to your door."

I held up a hand, stopping him in his tracks. "Oh, hell no. You're *not* coming up."

He looked like he wanted to argue, but Mr. Jones returned with the first aid kit, handing it to me with a kind smile. "Anything else you need, Jade?"

"Just a new life," I muttered.

Mr. Jones chuckled softly, blissfully unaware of the tension curling in the air.

Lazzio didn't reply.

Instead he paused, his eyes falling to my feet—bare, bleeding, pathetic.

Then he wiped his mouth with the back of his hand and, without another glance, turned on his heel and headed for the door. His hands flexed and curled at his sides, restless, like he was trying to shake off something that had burned him.

And that's when it struck me—it was the first time he'd ever touched me.

Skin to skin.

He stopped at the threshold, one hand gripping the handle.

His voice was low, just above a whisper. "Happy birthday, Miss Whitenhouse."

The door slammed shut behind him, and I finally let go of the breath I'd been holding all night. But then it hit me—how the hell did he know where I live?

My whole body ached from the tension, but at least it was over.

Or so I thought.

Morning came too soon, the light filtering through my curtains. I reached for my work phone, more out of habit than curiosity, only to freeze when the screen lit up.

A way-too-familiar face stared back at me from the headline: *Australian Yoga Instructor Found Shot Dead in His Apartment.*

I blinked at the screen, my stomach twisting.

Guess the guy was more problematic than I'd realized.

Tossing the phone aside, I flopped back onto the bed with a sigh.

No more yoga for me, then.

CHAPTER SEVEN

"We are bound by the secrets we share."
— **Zoë Heller**

Jade
27 years old
Three years ago

"Don't you want to come back home, Jadie?" My mama's voice wavered, soft but heavy with the kind of sadness that made my chest ache. "It's been almost three years now since you left, and I ... I need you back home with me."

Her frail, trembling hands rested on the edge of the dining table, and I reached for them instinctively. Her fingers felt too light in mine, like they might just float away if I wasn't careful.

Three years in New York.

Three years of building a life that wasn't tethered to Bay Village.

Back then, we'd agreed—she'd visit every few weeks, stay for a week, then return to her house. It had worked for us. At least, it had ... until it hadn't.

I couldn't call that place home anymore. It wasn't.

But looking at her now—so small, so fragile—I couldn't bring myself to say it.

"Mama, you know I can't do that," I said, my voice quieter than I wanted it to be.

Her grip on my hands tightened. "Why not, Jadie? What's keeping you here? Your ... job?" She said the last word like it left a bitter taste in her mouth.

I pulled my hands back gently, resting them in my lap. "You know why I'm here."

"Jadie—"

"I made myself a promise, Mama. I promised I'd find the person who ruined us. And being here, working for the Lazzios? Every day I get closer. Closer to finding them."

She shook her head. "And what are you going to do when you find them, huh? What, *Jadie*? You think revenge is going to fix anything? You think it'll make the pain stop? Trust me, it won't. It never does."

I leaned back in my chair. "I'll kill them."

Her breath caught. "Jadie! You do not mean that. You can't—"

I cut her off, leaning forward now. "Don't tell me what I can't do. Don't tell me what I don't mean. Because I've been carrying this, *this*"—I gestured at the space between us, the weight of all we'd lost—"for years. And the only thing keeping me breathing is knowing that one day, I'll make them pay for what they've done."

The words left my lips like a vow.

I sat back, my nails digging crescents into my palms as the memories surged.

The abyss I'd spiraled into after the psych ward. The haze of drugs and cheap highs. The arrests. The self-destruction so complete, I almost didn't recognize the version of me that had crawled out of it.

What had saved me wasn't hope, wasn't love, wasn't even survival. It was *rage*.

A cold purpose that had focused me like a razor's edge.

Revenge had become my lifeline, my obsession.

And I'd done a damn good job of it for the last three years.

My vault room back at my apartment? It was filled wall-to-wall with receipts, photos, timelines, connections. A meticulous, airtight roadmap leading me straight to the bastards who had destroyed my family.

Every day, I got closer. Every day, I sharpened my plan to finish what I'd started.

The idea of abandoning it? Of walking away because revenge wouldn't bring them back or soothe the raw ache grief had carved into my chest for the last five years?

That was a joke. A sick, nauseating joke.

I would see this through.

My mama could beg me, plead with me, but nothing was going to change that.

She sighed, her shoulders sagging. Slowly, she lifted her coffee cup to her lips.

Clara Whitenhouse. My mirror.

Same long black hair, same dark eyes. Her skin was so pale you could trace every delicate blue vein along her throat.

When I was little, people used to call me her shadow. Her twin.

And they weren't wrong.

She was my hero. My anchor. I used to follow her everywhere as a kid, mimicking everything she did—the way she spoke, the way she carried herself, even the way she folded laundry.

I had wanted to be just like her.

When my papa died so suddenly, when I was just four, she hadn't crumbled.

She'd held on, held us together.

She'd worked until she was bone-tired, dragging us out of the wreckage he'd left behind. She'd never cried in front of us, not once, but we'd heard her. Late at night, her muffled sobs had seeped through the walls.

And now?

Now, I was the one making her cry.

Not picking up on the frost spreading across the table, our waitress—a petite redhead with a smile so sweet it bordered on saccharine—bounced over and set down our plates like she was delivering happiness on porcelain.

"Enjoy!" she chirped.

Chocolate chip pancakes for me, eggs Benedict on salmon toast for Mama.

The diner, usually alive with weekend chaos, was eerily quiet for a late-August Sunday. No families spilling syrup everywhere, no hungover college kids mumbling orders for black coffee.

Just me, my mama, and the waitress.

I dug in right away, shoveling in syrup-drenched bites like my life depended on it, needing the sugar rush to untangle the nerves crawling under my skin.

Across from me, Mama silently picked at her eggs Benedict.

God, I *hated* silence.

Suddenly desperate to fill the void, I blurted out the first thing that came to mind.

"I'm thinking I'm gonna ask my boss for a promotion."

Her fork paused mid-air.

"I've been working there for three years," I continued, "and I think it's time to level up, you know? I want to be the new COO now."

She didn't even blink.

"Lazzio's a royal pain in the ass," I said, gesturing wildly with my fork, a piece of pancake almost flying off. "But even he knows I'm the one keeping that circus running. So yeah, I'm gonna ask him. And by asking, I mean I'll remind him that without me, his entire empire would collapse faster than his temper when someone uses the wrong font on a report."

Mama tilted her head, a bemused smile playing on her lips. "And if he says no?"

I shrugged dramatically. "Then I'll quit on the spot, obviously. Let him suffer for a day or two while I sip cocktails and binge crime documentaries. Maybe even send him a postcard from my couch—*Thinking of you while your company burns to the ground. XOXO, Jade.*"

She laughed, finally. "You're ridiculous, Jadie."

"And brilliant," I countered, stabbing another pancake slice triumphantly. "Don't forget brilliant."

The day after he bailed me out of jail on my birthday, I walked into my office and found a few things on my desk: a shiny new pair of Louboutins, my bag, the same spa voucher he gets me every year, and a small, unmarked box.

I opened it to find an assortment of bandages, gauze, and antiseptic wipes.

I couldn't help but laugh—*really*?

Ah, and of course, a card.

It read: *"Try not to get arrested again. I won't save you next time."*

After that, things were ... different.

Not in a good way.

Sure, we still had our usual rounds of me driving him insane by spilling coffee on his shoes, stealing his pens, and flirting with the movers who brought in his precious sculptures. But for some reason, he was colder. More distant. Like he'd put up an invisible wall, and I didn't quite know how to knock it down.

He pretended my birthday night had never happened, and I wasn't exactly going out of my way to remind him. Pretending was easier, anyway.

Then he had disappeared. Gone for seven months, off to Latin America—Mexico, Argentina, Brazil. Some business nonsense that I couldn't care less about.

When he had come back, he was even colder.

I'd hoped the sun would've melted the frost off his soul, but it hadn't. Still, he had the same icy glare, the same superiority complex, and the same way of looking at me like I was something beneath his shoe.

As for me? After the Aussie debacle that almost had me in an orange jumpsuit, I had decided one-night stands were a thing of the past.

Well, at least the *no-strings-attached* kind.

Flirting and make-outs though? That was still fair game.

Keeping it light, keeping it fun—no more getting tied up in anything too complicated. Men were too unpredictable—especially in New York.

I'd had enough of the drama.

Less chance of getting arrested, more chance of keeping my sanity intact.

What I hadn't known back then was that a few weeks later, I'd get that promotion—but not in the way I had expected. Not by annoying Lazzio until he finally caved, but by stumbling onto one of his *dirtiest* little secrets.

"You added a butterfly to your necklace?" My mama's voice was soft, her eyes tracing the new charm.

Instinctively, I reached for it, my fingers gently caressing the two little gold butterflies.

"Yeah ... one for Papa, and ..." My words faltered.

She smiled with a wistful, sad curve of her lips. "They're beautiful, Jadie."

With a sigh, we both finished our brunch and caught a taxi back to my place.

The afternoon was spent in the comforting rhythm of cooking lasagna together, the aroma filling my apartment, and then collapsing on the couch to watch *The Notebook*.

We tried to carve out some mother-daughter time, pretending for a few hours that everything was right in the world between us. Even though, deep down, I knew things would never quite be the same again.

CHAPTER EIGHT

"They won't believe you until you succeed."
— **Brajesh Kumar Singh**

Jade

28 years old
Two years ago

"I can't believe it! Me, winning the award for the best art show in New York?"

Lazzio didn't even spare me a glance.

His fingers kept flying over his keyboard. "Not *you*, Miss Whitenhouse. Lazzio Exhibits Inc. You're just the one *collecting* the award."

I threw myself onto his sofa, crossing my arms. "Same thing. Besides, I do own thirty percent of it now. So technically, it's practically mine."

He shot me a look so murderous, I half expected him to reach for the nearest sharp object. But he didn't say a word. Just kept tapping away on his keyboard like I wasn't even there.

I leaned back into the couch, tapping my nails against my chin. "What on earth am I gonna wear to this gala? I need something that screams *I won bitches!* but, like, in a classy way. You know?"

"Get out. You're giving me a fucking headache."

I grinned, lounging deeper into the couch. "Thank God you won't be there tonight. I've seen enough of you for the whole month."

"I've invested millions over the years into that gala. I'm obligated to go. But trust me, knowing you'll be there annoys me just as much."

A bad taste filled my mouth.

"Seriously, what's your deal? You followed me to my meeting with the mayor yesterday, and three days ago you were stalking me at a meeting with one of our investors. If I didn't know any better, I'd say you're a little obsessed with me, Lazzio."

He scoffed. "Ah, obsessed, huh?"

I glared at him. "You heard me."

He leaned back, eyes narrowing as he scoffed. "Don't kid yourself, sweetheart. I'm not obsessed, just making sure you're doing your job and not adding another client to your list of men to fuck. I heard about Nathan Simons." Disgust curled his lips. "You really know how to pick them, don't you?"

My stomach dropped to my toes, but I shoved the feeling down before it could settle.

How did he find out?

For some bizarre reason, every time a man's name came up —whether I'd seen him, dated him, or even just *mentioned* him

—Lazzio's reaction was always the same: disgust, quickly followed by indifference.

It was almost as if the idea of me being sexual made him sick, which frankly was rich coming from someone with his *questionable* kinks I'd accidentally uncovered.

I pouted. "Jealous that you'll never make it onto the list?"

He ran his tongue over his teeth, the muscles in his jaw tightening as his eyes darkened to something almost lethal.

For a moment, I was sure he was mentally calculating how to dispose of my body without anyone noticing.

"Careful, Miss Whitenhouse."

His tone was so ice cold it practically burned.

Yeah, that was my cue.

I wasn't suicidal—annoying him was fun, but even I knew when to quit.

No need to let his bad mood wreck my perfectly good night ahead.

I stood, smoothing my skirt, and made a show of sauntering toward the door, a sway in my hips just for fun.

As I reached the door, I turned just enough to catch his gaze, letting my lips curve into a smirk. "Oh, and just a heads-up—Nathan Simons? Best sex of my life. You could probably take a few notes."

A little white lie, sure, but it hit the mark.

I didn't stick around for his reaction, though the murderous tick in his jaw and the way his hands clenched the edge of his desk spoke volumes.

The door clicked shut behind me, and barely a second later, something heavy crashed against it, rattling the frame so hard I half expected it to splinter.

I bit back a laugh and strutted to the elevator, feeling more alive than I had all week.

My speech lasted thirty minutes—a well-rehearsed string of gratitude directed at the socialites hosting the event, and the Mayor of New York for allowing our space to evolve from a mere museum into a dynamic, living art experience (or whatever term the PR department had spun for it).

I thanked my colleagues for their tireless overtime efforts and—begrudgingly—Angelo Lazzio, my boss, for founding Lazzio Exhibits Inc. and building this empire that somehow made art accessible to people from all walks of life.

I also expressed our profound gratitude for this honor, despite last year's little hiccup—a devastating fire that had momentarily turned the museum into ash and memories.

Officially, the incident had been blamed on an open gas line and an unfortunate cigarette, the perfect cocktail of negligence and bad timing.

Unofficially? It was the handiwork of the enemies of Lazzio's friend, Alexsei Romaniev.

Angelo's precious creation hadn't been the target, just collateral damage in someone else's feud—a messy inconvenience for the rest of us.

After the fire, we'd shuttered what was left of the museum and had embarked on a rebuilding project. That had cost a jaw-dropping $25 million, and had required over a year of work.

Now, we were finally ready to reopen—well, partially. Some levels were polished enough for visitors, though it would still be a while before we were hosting grand exhibitions under the stars again.

Then came the award—shiny, heavy, and with a fat check for $200K.

I decided to donate it to an underground charity for burn victims.

It felt like the right thing to do.

As the host announced dinner, I made my way off the stage with champagne in hand, cursing myself for choosing my brand-new YSL heels—still unforgiving—while my feet screamed for mercy.

I opted for a black silk siren dress, sleek hair, and red lips, my uniform for such occasions.

When I reached the table, a small crowd began to form around me, bombarding me with questions like I was on a late-night talk show.

"Miss Whitenhouse, you look absolutely stunning."

"Who is your date tonight, Miss Whitenhouse?"

"Congratulations on your promotion to COO!"

"Can you do an exhibit on wild animals?"

The crowd swelled to the point where I almost felt suffocated.

"Miss Whitenhouse, I'd love to partner with you on—"

I forced myself not to roll my eyes, plastering on a fake smile that could rival any Hollywood starlet's.

As they continued to throw questions at me, my eyes drifted from one face to the next until I finally managed to escape to my seat and stuff my annoyance down with caviar and lobster.

The second I sat down, my eyes locked on Lazzio; he was relaxed in his chair, glass of water in hand. His attention was completely on the blonde next to him. She was the perfect fit—blue eyes, freckles, sporty, and just his type.

His gaze was warm and amused as it lingered on her like he

was studying a piece of art, that lazy smirk of his never quite fading.

He sipped from his glass, eyes boring into hers as she blushed every time he said something low and leaned in close.

She giggled—God, the sound was unbearable—before lightly swatting his arm.

Then he leaned in again, lips near her ear, and whatever he whispered made her flush with excitement. She downed her champagne in two quick gulps, a grin tugging at her lips as she placed a hand on his shoulder and whispered something back.

With a flirtatious smile, she excused herself and got up.

I couldn't help but let out a quiet scoff, reaching for a shrimp and biting into it. *Hard.*

Lazzio's jaw ticked, but he didn't even bother glancing in my direction.

Then, the words he'd said this afternoon started to echo in my head—heavy, burning, and just as infuriating as before.

You really know how to pick them, don't you?

I glanced around the table, everyone lost in conversation, chattering, and laughing loudly.

Leaning in, I couldn't resist. "You should probably follow her. She doesn't seem too bright—might get lost out there. Wouldn't want her to slip away before you get your *turn*, huh?"

I reached for my champagne glass and took a slow sip, my eyes never leaving him.

I tilted my head, a playful pout curving my lips. "But then again, that's your type, right? Dumb, pretty, and completely self-absorbed. You *really* know how to pick them, don't you?"

"Jealous, *diavoletta*?"

I set my glass down, and leaned back. "Jealous? *Please.* More like bored."

Why would I be?

I couldn't stand the man with his perfectly tailored suits

and that cold, detached persona. It made me think he had never actually lived a day outside of his perfectly curated life.

"Ah, I didn't realize my sex life was your entertainment, Miss Whitenhouse," he said, his voice smooth and dark. "But if you're looking for a show, you'll be waiting a long fucking time. I'm not in the habit of letting anyone watch."

"That's not what I heard, Lazzio."

A couple of months ago, at one of our exhibitions, I overheard some girls in the bathroom gossiping about him. Apparently, he had a threesome with two girls—one had to watch while he did the other, and the other had to do the same.

Absolutely disgusting.

"You've been spying on me now?" he drawled.

"Every day, every night," I sighed, feigning exhaustion. "You're like a parasite. Always there, forcing me to waste my time on your questionable behavior. Honestly, I'd call it a public service to keep an eye on you."

For the first time in the four years I've known him, he laughed.

A dark, earth-shaking laugh that curled between my legs.

I tilted my head. "Women must be not only dumb but also blind to fall for your pretty face and miss the gaping void where your heart should be."

The corner of his lips lifted. "Maybe they're hoping to fill it."

"With what? Cheap perfume, a blowjob, and crocodile tears?"

"You tell me. It's clearly working on you, Miss Whitenhouse."

"Working? *Please.*" My gaze flicked over him, unimpressed. "You'd have to try a hell of a lot harder, Lazzio."

His smirk deepened. "Let me know when you're done lying to yourself."

I didn't get a chance to reply—thankfully—because the butlers arrived with trays of food. Frankly, I was in no mood to entertain him any longer.

I excused myself with a tight smile—three glasses of champagne were working their magic, and nature was calling.

I made my way to the restroom, expertly avoiding anyone who might want to chat.

The last thing I needed was more small talk.

I locked the door behind me with a sigh of relief and went about my business.

But of course, when you go out of your way to avoid gossip, it has an annoying way of falling right into your lap.

"I'm hookin' up with Angelo Lazzio tonight," a girl chanted, her voice practically dripping with excitement.

I could tell it was definitely the blonde girl who had been sitting next to him.

"Stop! You're *so* lucky, Kiara! But I've heard some things ... You have to confirm them tomorrow," another girl gushed.

"Like what?"

A faucet splashed, then cut off abruptly.

"Okay, you know the weird girl with the bob who works at the Chanel store on 57th, Lindsay? She slept with him a few months ago, right after she styled him for that meet-and-greet with the president. She said he's only into it from behind, no missionary or anything like that, and ..."

The words hung in the air. Silence.

I leaned in, pressing my ear to the door, desperate to catch the rest.

"Well, what?" Kiara snapped, impatience lacing her voice.

I didn't blame her. I was dying to know too.

The girl's voice lowered, barely a whisper now. "He doesn't ... you know ... go *down* on women."

I slightly gasped behind the door, pressing my hand over my mouth to stifle it.

What?

What kind of weirdo skips the basic stuff?

No missionary and no oral?

"Are you serious? That's ... that's a red flag."

"Yeah," the other girl muttered. "But apparently he's really, *really* good at other things. Like, *exceptionally* good. The Chanel girl couldn't stop talking about it for days."

With that, the two girls giggled and left, their laughter fading as they disappeared down the hall.

I stood there for a moment, frozen.

Angelo Lazzio doesn't fuck missionary and doesn't like to go down on women.

What a boring man.

I slowly pulled myself together and washed my hands, my mind racing with confusion and curiosity.

If I had thought my boss was weird before, now I thought he was a straight-up sociopath.

How does someone like that function in the real world?

No going down ... yet apparently he was some kind of sex machine?

I sighed and left, heading back to eat dinner in silence, pretending I wasn't a tiny bit obsessed with everything I had just overheard.

CHAPTER NINE

"It is better to be hated for what you are than to be loved for what you are not."

— **André Gide**

Jade

29 years old

A year ago

"What do you want now, Satan? Haven't you annoyed me enough for one day?"

I perched myself on Grace's desk, crossing my legs as I picked up the picture frame she kept proudly displayed—her grinning husband and their army of children.

Honestly, I'd never seen any of them in real life.

The man never set foot in this office, and her kids were apparently too mythical to exist outside holiday cards. Sometimes I wondered if this picture wasn't just some stock photo she'd picked up to fit the mold of a sweet old grandma still working because she couldn't sit still. Blah blah, *barf.*

"What are you even doing here, oldie? It's Christmas Eve, and it's past three. Shouldn't you be, I don't know, grilling your turkey or knitting socks for the grandkids you swear aren't imaginary?"

She snatched the picture out of my hands before she carefully put it back on the desk, dusting it like I'd somehow smudged its sacred aura.

"Not that it's any of your business, but I have things to finish up before the holiday. Unlike some people, I don't run around bothering coworkers like a stray cat."

"*Meow,*" I said dryly, sliding off her desk. "Just saying, Grace—your turkey's going to end up drier than *you.* And I'd hate for your perfect little family to choke on that."

Her scowl deepened, the kind of look that could curdle eggnog.

I smirked, tossing her a casual wave as I strutted off.

But not before I heard her mutter under her breath, "At least I have a family."

I froze for half a second.

At least I have a family.

Something in my chest tightened—hard, ugly, and rough, like barbed wire wrapping itself around my ribs.

I took a shaky breath, forcing myself not to go there.

Not to think about *them.*

About the kinds of memories that could sneak up on you when you least expected it, dragging you underwater and drowning you in a tide you couldn't fight.

I swallowed hard, steadying myself, and made my way to Lazzio's office.

Barging in without knocking was second nature by now—

my default. Maybe because it felt easier to shatter his silence than to sit in my own.

He was at the window, phone pressed to his ear, speaking in that velvety Italian of his. Snow dusted the city skyline outside, and for a moment, I let myself drink in the sight of him: tall, broad shoulders, the darkest of hair, and utterly oblivious to my presence.

His suit caught my attention—light beige.

It was so ... uncharacteristic.

Angelo Lazzio, the self-crowned king of brooding darkness, suddenly giving off espresso at a Tuscan villa vibes? *Interesting.*

I slammed the door shut behind me, loudly enough to make my point.

The point being: I'm here to annoy you, deal with it.

He didn't even flinch. Didn't bother turning around, either.

I leaned against the door. My eyes stayed on him, watching the way he carried himself like nothing could touch him.

For a moment, I hated him for it. Hated the calm he exuded, the way he seemed perfectly in control while I was ... not.

I looked down at my hands clenched into fists at my sides. And I hated that too.

Freaking annoying Grace and her stupid remarks.

A dry laugh escaped me before I could stop it. Of course I'd lose it in *his* office.

The one place where weakness wasn't just unwelcome—it was ammunition.

Feeling like a mess thanks to the holiday nostalgia clawing at my chest, I needed a way to release it all. And for some twisted reason, my pain always found a way to spill over onto someone else.

For the past five years, that someone had been my boss.

The man was too tall, too strong, too thick for his own good—he could take anything life threw at him.

And that made him the perfect target.

Call it toxic. I called it therapy for my nerves.

He was my punching bag, and I didn't even feel guilty about it.

Why should I? It worked.

I walked over to his desk, letting my fingers trail over everything—his pens, the picture frames, and especially that ridiculous picture of his new dog, Georgino, from a few months ago. The little furball was clearly his latest obsession.

I picked up his Rolex, letting the weight of it sit in my hand for a moment before slipping it onto my wrist. The diamond gleamed so brightly I had to blink.

His wallet sat there, just waiting to be tampered with. I flicked it open, casually flipping through the multiple black cards, business cards, and some ID card he clearly took way too seriously.

But what really caught my eye were the three crisp hundred-dollar bills tucked inside.

Without thinking twice, I snatched them, sliding them into my bra.

A little extra padding never hurt anyone.

Just as I finished, I heard the shuffle of movement behind me.

He turned around, hung up the phone, and shoved it back into his pocket, his eyes narrowing with that familiar annoyance that always made me smile.

"Why, hello, boss. You look quite nice today. Off to snatch some poor woman's soul off of the right path and lead her straight to hell?"

"Only Satan herself would know what that feels like."

I chuckled. "Well, if that's the case, maybe you'll be joining me in hell after all. Wouldn't want to let all that potential go to waste."

He strode toward me, grabbing his wallet with an annoyed flick of his wrist, shoving it into the inner pocket of his blazer. "Hell would be a mercy for you, *diavoletta*. If I had my way, you'd be rotting somewhere far worse."

I folded my arms, the Rolex sliding loosely down my wrist.

His eyes darted to it, then back to my face, and I caught the slight twitch in his jaw.

"Far worse than hell?" I mused, tilting my head as if considering it seriously. "Like, I don't know, an eternity in your office—stuck with bad coffee and your dry, soul-crushing ego?"

He didn't answer, just stepped closer. Close enough that the faint scent of his cologne—something expensive and maddeningly intoxicating—wrapped around me. His eyes, cold and dark, scanned me, cataloging every detail like he always did. When they landed on my chest, a flicker of understanding passed through them.

"Give it back."

I blinked up at him. "Give what back? Oh, this lovely watch? Thought I'd borrow it—such a shame to let it sit there collecting dust when it could be, you know, *appreciated*."

"The money, Jade."

A slow, simmering heat unfurled beneath my skin.

It was the second time my name had slid from his lips—a dark caress, cold enough to steal the breath from my lungs.

"Ah, you mean the crisp Benjamins currently keeping me company?" I grinned, letting my hand trail to the neckline of my dress. "Sorry, boss. They're mine now. Call it a convenience fee for putting up with you."

His patience—what little of it he ever possessed—shattered in an instant.

He reached for me, his hand fisting the front of my dress, the fabric twisting tightly in his grip. The neckline slipped, inching dangerously lower.

One sharp tug, and the delicate lace of my bra would be exposed.

I tilted my head, pouting playfully. “You know, for a supposed billionaire, you’re awfully stingy.”

For some obvious reason, he didn’t find it funny.

A low growl rumbled from his chest. “Now.”

I tapped my chin. “Mmm, no. Don’t think I will. But thanks for asking so nicely.”

He stepped in, way too close—close enough that the heat of his body almost made me gasp.

His tongue flicked against his teeth in that way he did when he was pissed, but I couldn’t help but notice how that anger only made him ... deliciously sharper. *Dangerous.*

“Miss Whitenhouse—”

I let out a bored sigh. “If you’re dying for it back, you can fetch it yourself, Lazzio.”

His eyes darkened, and that smile—oh, it was anything *but* friendly.

Without warning, his free hand shot under my dress, fingers grazing my chest as he hunted for the bills. My breath caught, my pulse racing as his gaze stayed locked on my lips. His fingers brushed so close to my nipple I swear I felt the heat of it, teasing me just enough to drive me insane.

For a split second, I thought he might actually go further, and I almost wanted him to. But instead, he jerked his hand back like I was the one burning him, leaning back as if I was the last thing he wanted to touch.

But the look in his eyes?

It was raw, dark heat, and it made my skin ache.

"You're playing with fire, sweetheart. And sooner or later, you'll get burned."

"Maybe I like the burn, Lazzio," I whispered.

His eyes flashed, and without a word, he grabbed my wrist; he pulled me in so close I could practically feel his heartbeat. In one swift motion, he snatched the Rolex off my wrist, his fingers grazing over my skin, sending delicious shivers down my spine.

Butterflies erupted in my stomach, fluttering lower, like they were racing to get somewhere they shouldn't be.

It was the second time in all the years we'd known each other that his hands had touched me.

Fuck. I didn't even realize how much I missed being touched—his touch was like a wake-up call, and suddenly everything felt *alive* again.

The last time I felt this *alive*?

Three months ago, when I was moving into a place just a stone's throw from Central Park. My lease was up, and I had wanted something bigger—somewhere close enough to run every morning before work. A mover had been helping me with the boxes. He'd leaned in, whispered that I'd looked *too* good to be true, and, well ... one thing had led to another.

Lazzio pulled away like he hadn't just manhandled me, slipping his Rolex back on and walking to the coat rack.

He grabbed his jacket and slid it on, moving like I wasn't even there.

"So, what are you doing for Christmas?"

"None of your business."

I smirked, crossing my arms. "Let me guess. Another boring family dinner? I'm sure they all just *love* your charming personality."

He didn't respond, just grabbed his phone from the desk and made a beeline for the door, clearly trying to avoid me.

So, *obviously*, I followed him.

He opened the door with a soft click and stepped into the hallway.

Grace's desk was empty—she must have gone home to her dry turkey and happy, smiling little elves.

Lazzio hit the elevator button with a flick of his finger.

"So, when do I get my Christmas present? Or should I just expect a pair of socks with your face on them, so I can *literally* step all over you?"

He tapped the button again like it might make me go away. If only.

"You know, Lazzio–"

"What are *you* doing for Christmas, Miss Whitenhouse? Let me guess—another lonely night locked in your cold, empty apartment, because no one can stand being around you. I'm sure even your family avoids you. Hell, they probably thought about putting a bullet in their heads just to escape another miserable night with you."

His words hung in the air, too heavy, too mean, and I was frozen—caught somewhere between anger and something far more unsettling.

He turned and his hand—unexpectedly gentle—lifted my chin, forcing me to look up at him. The moment felt too intimate, too charged, and I couldn't tear my gaze away, even if I wanted to.

"Enjoy your Christmas, sweetheart. I'm sure your misery will be the only thing that doesn't ditch you this year."

His thumb slowly traced the curve of my lower lip.

I couldn't breathe, couldn't move.

My eyes fluttered closed for a second, but only for a moment—when I opened them again, his face was so close that his breath was warm against my cheek. His nose brushed lightly against mine.

For a beat, we stood there, suspended in time.

But just as quickly as it came, he pulled back.

He stepped into the elevator, his eyes locking with mine as the door slid shut with a soft click.

And for the first time, I felt it.

The silence. The absence of my usual snarky comebacks.

Angelo Lazzio had made me speechless.

I brought a hand to my lips, the echo of his touch still burning on my skin.

Jesus.

I should've been pissed.

I should've yelled something back, but my mouth? It wouldn't cooperate.

I stood there like an idiot, hands trembling, because deep down, I knew he was right.

The door closed behind me before I gracefully slipped into his chair, the leather creaking under my weight as I leaned forward, fingers already dancing over his ridiculously expensive computer. The one he'd had to buy last year after the old one *mysteriously* ended up in pieces against the wall.

I was still absolutely furious. Still fuming.

I should've just followed him, dragged him into some dark corner, and chopped his head off as the best Christmas present I'd ever give myself.

But no. Instead, his words—those perfectly timed insults—had done exactly what they were supposed to.

They had dug in deep. Poked around in all the places I'd kept hidden.

Places I thought were safely locked away, but now? Not so much.

And honestly? It had worked.

It had *refocused* me.

Reminded me why I was here in the first place.

Because I needed something from his files. Something important. Something called The Cyrus Project.

So, the head-chopping would have to wait for now.

Over the years, I'd learned everything there was to know about New York's elites.

Specifically the big three: the Gregs, the Lazzios, and the Harpers.

The untouchables. The ones who thought they could get away with anything.

I'd spent the last five years perfecting the art of surveillance.

Every public event, every secret meeting, every dinner I had managed to crash—hell, I'd even showed up at their weddings, funerals, *and* engagement and divorce parties. Sunday mornings at church, country clubs, galas, clubs—you name it, I had been there. And no one had noticed. No one ever did. But I saw it all.

I knew everything. Every little secret they thought they'd buried.

I had them all mapped out, connected by red strings on a board—affairs, betrayals, stolen inheritances, secret bankruptcies. Their addictions to drugs, gambling, and of course, power. The whispers of blackmail schemes, quiet bribes, and messy cover-ups painted their twisted world like a masterpiece of sin.

Their vices were my Bible.

I had it all under control.

And I had played my role perfectly.

They had never suspected a thing. They thought I was just a pretty young woman with too much confidence. So they'd talked to me. They had let their guard down. Shared their dirty secrets, their twisted little victories, all the gossip that could bring them down.

And I had soaked it all up.

Because in those moments, I'd held the power.

But there was still one thing missing.

One piece of the puzzle that would make everything fall into place.

And that piece? It had a name: The Cyrus Project.

A few months ago, I'd overheard Angelo Lazzio and his father at one of our exhibition nights. They were talking about Jonathan Cyrus, and how he was still seething over the fact that one of his precious projects had gotten ruined.

That conversation? It had sparked my curiosity.

With a sigh, I stared at the login screen. Time to crack the code.

First try: Angelo's mama's name. *Nothing.*

Second try: his birthday. *Still nothing.*

Third try: his favorite color. Black, of course. *Denied.*

I tried: Satan666. That was good for a laugh, but nope, still no access.

His last fling's name? It was worth a shot, though I had to pause and think—was it Sarah or Sophie? I tried both. *Nada.*

Oh! Maybe his dog? But nope. *Nothing.*

I pouted, drumming my nails on the desk, before laughing at my own ridiculousness. "Why not?" I murmured, typing in my own name.

Click.

Access granted.

I blinked at the screen like it had personally insulted me.

What the actual hell?

Of all the possible passwords—my name? *Why?*

A bead of sweat slid down my back, making me shiver.

Guess my boss was more obsessed with me than he'd ever care to admit.

The thought should've derailed me—should've had my mind spinning off into questions I didn't want answers to—but I shoved it aside.

Focus, Jade. You're in. Now dig.

And oh, did I dig. For hours.

His emails, documents, the hard drive—nothing was safe. Most of it was the usual Lazzio garbage: power plays, back-room deals, and secrets so poorly hidden it was almost insulting.

But then I found it.

His secured second email address. The one he rarely touched. A treasure chest of potential dirt, locked tight. Naturally, I picked the lock.

And there it was.

One email.

Just one email, dated exactly eight years ago, from a blocked, untraceable address:

The explosives are on, sir

My heart sank, and for the first time tonight, I felt the air catch in my lungs.

Because now, I had confirmation of something I didn't want to believe—something I'd thought was impossible.

Angelo Lazzio was the one who had murdered my sister.

And he was going to pay for it.

PART TWO
THE PRESENT

CHAPTER TEN

"I hate men who are afraid of women's strength."
— **Anaïs Nin**

Jade

30 years old
Present time

"I would kill for you, Jade. Just give me one fucking chance. Just *one*, and I swear I'll turn your world so upside down you'd never want to let me go."

I laughed, sipping my margarita, the salted rim a welcome distraction. "Manuel, for the last time—I'm not into you."

"That's because we haven't fucked yet, *guapa*. Once we do, I promise you'll change your mind."

Manuel Ruiz was every indulgence I secretly admired in men: strong, capable with his hands, calloused palms from hard labor, masculine, tall, and that annoyingly sweet smile that could charm anyone ... except me.

He had a mouth that spewed filth and eyes that undressed, yet beneath all the bravado, Manuel was a decent man. Gentle, even.

He never crossed a line, never touched me without consent, never hurled threats or wielded manipulation for my attention—a standard shockingly high in the grimy circles of New York's elite.

But as much as I appreciated him, I didn't want him.

At least not tonight.

I just wanted to dance and relax *alone.*

Turning him down again felt as exhausting as the last dozen times.

"I'm not giving up," he called over his shoulder, his determination thick enough to draw a smirk.

I raised my glass and took another sip of my margarita, letting the sweet tang coat my tongue. My eyes scanned the club, darting past the strobing lights and murmuring patrons.

It was a regular Sunday night for me, a much-needed exhale after yet another wildly successful exhibition Friday night. The New York Times had declared it "the finest display of art and glory." As much as the praise had inflated my ego, the constant buzzing of attention left a strain that only this club, *The Diamond*, could soothe.

Yeah, *that* club—the one where I sent some Aussie guy to the ER for trying to get handsy, then got a free ride in the back of a cop car. Good times.

Owned by none other than Leonardo Vittori, it wasn't just a sanctuary; it was an empire. And tonight, like every Sunday for the past year, I found myself here, savoring the energy, the ambiance, and my carefully curated escape from the world.

That was my Sunday routine.

Wake up well past noon, order takeout—a chicken Caesar salad with a side of fries—then draw myself a long, steaming bath while cracking open a bottle of my favorite red wine to get my blood primed for the night ahead.

Getting ready was a ritual in itself. My wardrobe revolved around what one might call outrageous excuses for dresses, but for me, they were my uniform. Short, scandalously tight numbers—sometimes sparkly, sometimes black, sometimes a riot of color—with necklines daring enough to make anyone blush.

My hair would be my final message: sleek and straight if I was hunting for a fling, or swept into an updo or ponytail if I was simply out to dance and drink the night away.

Tonight, I chose fun over lust.

I had slipped into a pearl-embroidered Balmain dress, a masterpiece of shimmering elegance that clung to me like a second skin. My hair had gone up into a perfectly imperfect messy bun, and I'd painted my lips a deep, provocative red.

The message was clear: *Not tonight, boys.*

But clearly, I had underestimated just how stupid men could be.

I downed the rest of my margarita in one go.

Placing the empty glass on the bar, I winked at the bartender, signaling for another. He nodded, already pouring, and I leaned back on the stool, crossing my legs as I let my eyes drift over the crowd.

People swayed, stumbled, and collided in a chaotic dance of hormones and bad decisions. Some were making out like it was their last night on earth; others seemed a few seconds away from throwing punches.

Directly in front of me, a girl danced with a boy, his hands gripping her hips as her head tilted back onto his shoulder. They moved to the beat of a Spanish song I couldn't name if my life depended on it. She ground against him with enough fervor to make the room sweat, and whatever he whispered in her ear had her blushing and giggling before she grabbed his hand and led him off into the crowd.

I sighed, turning back to my freshly served margarita.

The bartender had even added a little umbrella—cute, but utterly impractical. I flicked it aside, taking a long sip, relishing the tangy sweetness.

At least the drinks didn't disappoint tonight.

My nail tapped against the bare skin of my thigh, keeping time with the rhythmic beat, my eyes lazily drifting across the room.

Then, a loud *pop* shattered the air.

The first scream was a spark, setting off an eruption of panic. People scrambled in every direction, chairs overturned, and drinks spilled as more shots followed, each one cutting through the music like a jagged knife.

I sighed again, gripping my margarita.

Navigating the stampede wasn't easy, but I managed, dodging flailing arms and spilled liquor. My heels clacked sharply as I descended the stairs, weaving past the chaos just as armed men stormed up toward the mayhem above.

The basement was quieter, the muffled sound of screams and gunfire fading into the background as I made my way down a narrow hallway.

Reaching the last door, I pushed it open.

They didn't even glance up from their card game.

I dropped onto the sofa, still holding my margarita. "I don't know if this is one of your kinks, Vittori, but for the love of God, put better security in your fucking club. Your place always attracts weirdos far too comfortable with a gun. I came here to party, not to dodge bullets."

Leonardo Vittori leaned back in his chair, his green eyes

flicking to me with an expression that managed to be both bored and vaguely amused.

Head of the Sacra Corona, he's nicknamed *il senza cuore*, the heartless one. He earned the title after killing his first victim with a dagger straight to the heart, twisting it until the organ fell from the body.

Cute, I guess.

We have a twisted little arrangement, and somehow he'd become a friend—if you could call it that.

I could waltz into his clubs, his restaurants, and his lounges without ever dropping a penny—as long as I listened to his never-ending soap opera of women falling into his bed and the filthy things he did to them.

A fair trade, if you ask me.

"Get your feet off my fucking table."

I rolled my eyes, deliberately tapping the toe of my heel against the polished sparkly wood. "Relax, Vittori. It's not like it's made of gold."

Marco, his youngest brother, sat slouched over his cards, looking like he could barely be bothered to play. Enzo, the middle one, leaned back with that half-smirk of his.

The empty seat in front of them was an unspoken invitation, but I couldn't help but frown at it.

Something felt off tonight.

I couldn't quite put my finger on it, but my gut was telling me this wasn't just another ordinary night with them.

I didn't even have time to say anything before the door opened and *his* gaze settled on the back of my neck, the hairs on my arms rising in warning. I took a long sip of my margarita, the sweetness now replaced with a bitter edge—as if the universe had decided to fuck with me on a whole new level.

His voice drifted to my ears, dangerously close, as he

muttered something to Vittori. I couldn't make out the words. It wasn't like I wanted to hear them anyway. I was too busy trying to ignore him, praying the damn couch would just swallow me whole and put me out of my misery.

But then came the next words, and they sliced through me like ice.

"Hello, Miss Whitenhouse."

For fuck's sake, does the universe have it out for me?

Why the hell do I have to hear that voice, see that face, even *on my fucking day off?*

I leaned back further into the couch. My face buried in my drink, I let the strands of my hair fall forward, partially hiding my expression as I *tried* to avoid looking in his direction.

It wasn't that I couldn't, it's just that I didn't want to.

The room suddenly felt like it was closing in on me; I could practically taste the claustrophobia creeping up my spine.

I inhaled slowly, forced myself to stand, and finished my drink in one go, the bitterness matching the churn in my stomach.

Turning my head, I finally looked at him.

Tall. Dark. And disgustingly handsome.

Honey and dark wood draped in silk sheets.

Mister Angelo Lazzio, or as I like to call him, *Mr. Stick-Up-My-Ass* himself, strode silently through the room.

His broad shoulders were practically bursting through the fabric of his suit, and his wavy, disheveled hair—clearly messed up from running his hands through it one too many times—only made him look more ridiculously handsome.

Ugh, I wanted to vomit just looking at him.

He casually held a cold bottle of water, his eyes flicking over mine—filled with that familiar blend of annoyance and utter boredom—before he sank into the empty chair across from Vittori. His back was now to me.

Guess he was as thrilled to see me as I was to see him.

I got up, empty cup in hand, and sauntered over to the table and stopped at his side, my hip hovering inches from his forearm.

His cards were spread out neatly in his hands, and from the look on his face, I already knew—he was going to win. *As usual.*

I tiptoed and leaned toward Vittori, craning my neck to peek at his cards. He angled them just enough for me to see. Pitiful. Not a single high card in sight.

"Anyway, you men are boring. I'm going back to the party upstairs."

Vittori scoffed, leaning back with his drink. "I had the club shut down for the night. Some guy just got himself killed."

I blinked. "Wait—your men shot someone?"

He shrugged, tossing his cards down. "Nah. Turns out the idiot stole his friend's wife or something, and the friend shot him. Antonio just texted me—dead on the spot."

Marco took a slow sip of his whiskey. "What's his name?"

Vittori picked up his phone, scrolling lazily. "Manuel Ruiz. Never heard of him."

My heart sank for a split second before sarcasm took over.

"Oh no," I said, my voice dripping with fake disappointment.

Well, I guess he wasn't that much of a good guy after all.

Lazzio laid his cards down, his winning hand making the men around the table groan.

"Another one of your admirers, Miss Whitenhouse?"

Lazzio, *of course*, had been an unwilling spectator to my love life since the day I started working for him. Not that I wanted his input, but somehow, every time I was minding my own business—flirting, mingling, or prowling for a one-night stand to scratch an itch—Angelo Lazzio made it his personal mission to be there.

Always watching. Always judging.

Sometimes he'd give me that disappointed look, like I'd just rolled around in trash. Other times, he'd make some snide remark about my "standards." And then there were the worst moments—those rare, infuriating times he'd actually *step in*.

"I have a reputation, Miss Whitenhouse," he'd say, voice dripping with condescension. "I can't have my COO ruining it by parading around with whatever gutter-born stray caught her attention. Keep it fucking discreet."

Discreet.

As if he had any right to tell me what to do, let alone judge my taste.

God forbid Angelo Lazzio ever let me have *fun* without his shadow looming over it.

"Yes," I said, crossing my arms with a smile. "He even said he'd *kill* for me. But I guess now he won't be able to, will he?"

Lazzio's expression didn't change—as cool, detached, and infuriatingly calm as always. Without a word, he lifted his water bottle and drank, his Adam's apple moving slowly, a drop of water dripping to the side of his neck. He didn't stop until the bottle was empty, and when he finally lowered it, he wiped his mouth with the back of his hand.

"Ah, my mistake. It's just so hard to keep track with you."

Vittori chuckled, his whiskey swirling lazily in the glass as he brought it to his lips. His eyes gleamed with amusement, darting between us like a spectator at his favorite sport. He was utterly entertained, clearly used to our fights—the verbal equivalent of cats clawing and dogs barking.

"Keep track of what, Lazzio?"

He leaned back in his chair. "Oh, you know," he said, his tone smooth. "Your ... admirers. Your suitors. The long parade of men who seem to lose their heads—sometimes *literally*—

whenever they get involved with you. Quite the pattern, really."

My lips parted in disbelief. "You have the *audacity* to sit there and—"

He cut me off. "Don't flatter yourself. I'm merely observing. I don't *care* what you do with your life, as long as it doesn't spill into mine."

I scoffed. "Says the man who can't seem to stay out of my sex life."

He tilted his head, his eyes narrowing in that predatory way that always made my stomach tighten. His jaw twitched —just for a fraction of a second.

"If I *really* wanted to get in the way, Miss Whitenhouse, you wouldn't have to wonder. You'd know. Trust me."

My throat went dry.

I threw my empty cup on the table. "Well, I guess we'll never find out, will we, boss?"

I spun on my heel and stormed out, the loud click of my heels against the floor practically screaming my frustration. Their Italian nonsense was still echoing behind me, but I slammed that damn door shut with a force that could've shattered glass.

Great.

My night was officially ruined.

Talk about an overbearing, overstepping, pain-in-the-ass boss.

CHAPTER
ELEVEN

"When I shop, the world gets better, and the world is better, but then it's not, and I need to do it again. (Confessions of a Shopaholic-the movie)"
— **Sophie Kinsella**

Jade

As I brought the bag closer, I eyed its deep emerald finish, tilting it under the light like I was inspecting a diamond and not a purse priced at the cost of a small kitchen remodel.

Chanel or not, I knew the difference between indulgence and outright robbery, and this? This was criminal.

Kelly, the sly fox of retail, read my hesitation like a well-worn script. Her perfectly styled gray hair bobbed as she handed me a glass of champagne, her weapon of choice.

"This bag looks exquisite on you, Miss Whitenhouse. The color is simply *divine*."

Of course, she played the emerald card. My Achilles' heel.

Kelly had me pegged from the first day I'd strolled into this shop four years ago.

Since then, I'd probably funded her vacations, Christmas bonuses, and the "Best Salesperson of the Year" plaque that undoubtedly hung in the back room. And yet, like a moth to a flame—or more accurately, a bag addict to overpriced leather —I kept coming back.

Retail therapy was *still* therapy, right?

Who needed a shrink when a Prada tote or a Givenchy clutch could fix your bad mood for at least 48 hours?

Was it shallow? Maybe.

Should I care? Probably.

Did I? Absolutely not.

I sighed, sliding my black card out of my wallet. "I'll take it."

Kelly's smile stretched wider than the Grand Canyon as she clapped her hands in delight, ushering me to the register like she'd just won a jackpot.

I took another sip of champagne, letting the fizzy sweetness drown out the nagging voice in my head reminding me I'd just dropped 9K on a bag that would likely end up collecting dust next to last month's retail regret.

But hey, at least I'd have something pretty to carry my existential dread in.

"I loved your exhibition last Friday—*Black and White*. The pictures of Werner Bischof and Thomaz Farkas were absolutely stunning. Railways have never looked so alive; I just had to see them in person. Oh, and you looked divine in your Valentino dress. Truly a piece of art yourself, Miss Whitenhouse."

I smiled, warmth blooming in my chest.

Compliments like that made the endless stress worth it, even if just for a moment.

Being COO was no stroll through luxury. Juggling exhibitions every week to match Angelo Lazzio's relentless perfectionism wasn't just exhausting—it was soul-draining. Each new showcase demanded scouring the globe for rare, breathtaking pieces, leaving me creatively hollow by the time the museum's doors reopened.

With the museum closed one week a month, I had to produce three major exhibitions every four weeks, a rhythm designed to drain anyone not fueled by caffeine and sheer spite.

So yes, I earned every single one of my millions and every indulgent penny spent on couture dresses, high heels, and tiny bags that could barely hold a credit card, let alone my unraveling sanity.

"I'm so pleased to hear that, Kelly. You know I trust your taste implicitly. You've never let me down," I said with a wink.

My week was carved out like clockwork: Sundays and Mondays off, Tuesdays and Wednesdays devoured by endless work, Thursdays reserved for exhibition rehearsals, Fridays set ablaze by exhibition night, and Saturdays split between dissecting every detail in staff meetings.

It was a relentless grind that demanded nothing less than perfection.

After last night's circus—the four margaritas that left me with a skull-splitting headache, Manuel's lifeless body I had to step over on my way out of the club, and of course, Angelo Lazzio and his insufferable *everything*—I needed a hard reset.

Today was my escape hatch: buying things I didn't need, indulging at my favorite restaurant like calories were a myth, and scrubbing my brain clean of any trace of my boss.

That man, with his compulsive need to micromanage every

molecule of my existence—and the one I had a personal vendetta against? Not today.

Today was about me, my credit card, and the unshakable thrill of rebellion.

Or so I had thought.

I said my goodbyes to Kelly, promising to come back next Thursday to collect my Versace dress, and left the store. My toes throbbed in my heels, my arms ached under the weight of too many shopping bags, and my coat clung to me like a furnace.

The city heat only made it worse.

As I wandered down 57th Street, debating where to burn more money, my phone buzzed in my bag.

I stopped, juggling the bags cutting into my legs, and finally set them down to dig out my phone.

"Jade Whitenhouse," I answered, pressing the phone to my ear.

A woman's voice, trembling, sniffed on the other end. "Miss Whitenhouse, it's Laura, your mother's nurse. I'm deeply sorry to inform you ... she's gone."

The world tilted.

My heart plummeted, hitting the pit of my stomach like a stone.

"What?" I whispered, barely recognizing my own voice.

"Your mother passed away this morning, Jade—"

I didn't hear the rest.

My head barely registered the words because, at that exact moment, some homeless guy in a baseball cap sprinted past and yanked my Chanel bag right off my arm. I didn't even move. Didn't chase him. Didn't scream. I just stood there, stuck to the pavement like my feet had turned to stone, my tears hot and prickling behind my eyes, refusing to fall.

Three years ago, my mama got sick. Breast cancer.

That's why she had begged me to come home, to stay with her.

But I didn't. I couldn't.

Instead, I'd thrown money at the problem—gotten her the best doctors, the best treatments. I'd brought her to live with me, but she had hated it.

She'd said Bay Village was her home. I had let her go back, thinking it was fine.

I'd called her every day, sent flowers and told myself I'd done enough.

She was the strongest person I knew.

She was supposed to make it. She *had* to make it.

"But ... you said she was doing fine," I choked out.

Laura sighed heavily. "I'm so sorry, Miss Whitenhouse," she said again, her words a distant hum as the city spun around me.

And all hell broke loose.

I screamed—loud, raw, and unforgiving—my phone slipping from my fingers, hitting the pavement with a harsh crack. My throat felt like it was being shredded, the kind of pain that rips through your chest and doesn't stop.

Tears blurred my vision.

I didn't care that I was standing on a crowded street, people walking past me like I was a ghost. The world kept spinning, like nothing was happening, like I wasn't crumbling right there in front of them.

Faces stared straight ahead, eyes glued to their screens, too busy to notice.

My pain was just noise to them, background static they couldn't even be bothered to acknowledge.

Meanwhile, my world shattered for the third time in my life.

CHAPTER TWELVE

"That's what we all want, isn't it? Power without price."
— **Kelley Armstrong**

Angelo

"How are the twins?"

I winced as I heard him laugh, the phone crackling like it was on its last legs. I pulled it away from my ear to save my eardrum.

You'd think that being an ex-Silas member with enough cash to last five lifetimes would convince Romaniev to upgrade his damn phone, but the bastard clung to the same old relic he'd had when he met his wife. He swore getting rid of it would bring bad luck—his words, not mine.

"They're good. Can't believe they're already two," he said with a sigh.

Three years ago, after the mess that had nearly cost Caia and Alexsei their lives—and had burned my fucking museum to the ground—the Romanievs had moved to a quiet house in New York. That's when they'd found out they were expecting twins.

Over the years, Alexsei had become like a brother to me, and all I wanted was for him to be happy, especially after losing his first son.

"Can't believe you're running an all-girl household."

He scoffed, half laughing. "More like they run me. Caia's got her little army trained to strike right where it hurts. And that doe-eyed look they pull? Absolute weaponry. I'm a goner every time. Hopelessly wrapped around their tiny, tyrannical fingers."

Mira and Vera were like little clones of his wife, but had Alexsei's blue eyes and dark humor. The last time I saw them was about a month ago, before they took off on a cross-country road trip. Caia had wanted to expand her work and capture every state through her lens, so Alexsei had made it happen. He bought a $750K tour bus—decked out with a bathroom, bedrooms, a kitchen, and all the luxury you could imagine.

They had left, and were currently somewhere in Washington.

"How's Scar'? Her tour wrapped up last week, right?"

I let out a sigh and sank into my couch, my gaze drifting over the city skyline. New York at night was a beast of its own—sparkling, overflowing, and radiating an energy I still couldn't quite put into words.

Sure, I'd grown up in Florence and spent my summers on the Amalfi Coast, but the moment I'd stepped foot in New York at ten years old, I was hooked. Its dark beauty and shiny facade were unlike anything I'd ever seen.

This place was my second home, my arena.

We had moved here because my father had wanted to expand Lazzio Entertainment Group. He'd bought three Broadway theaters and started another movie company in Los Angeles.

That move had catapulted us into the upper echelons of wealth.

"Yeah," I said, closing my eyes and rubbing my temple as a headache crept in. "LeRoy mentioned she was doing better. Compared to her last tour two years ago, she actually made it through without missing a single rehearsal or fumbling a show. Still, I can't shake this bad feeling."

He hummed. "Scarlett Harper, the biggest pop star in the world right now—and the biggest pain in your ass. Sorry you've got to play her manager while I'm gone, but maybe it's the perfect chance to put the guns away and try to get along. After all, she is your cousin."

Scarlett Harper, daughter of Lucius Harper and Francesca Lazzio—my father's sister.

Born into privilege, Scarlett had spent her entire life as a true Upper East Sider, living the jet-set life most only dream about. Summers in the Hamptons, Cancun, or Tulum, while winters had seen her traipsing through Lapland and Aspen, or strolling through the Christmas markets in Alsace before retreating to the Alps for a taste of winter wonder.

Just like me, she had been raised in a world of excess, where everything came easy, and consequences were an afterthought. It's no wonder she walks around like she owns the place.

Our family time—the Harpers and the Lazzios—had become sacred after we'd moved to the States. Though we'd rarely seen each other growing up, Sunday dinners had become our tradition, where we'd talk about business, family vacations, art, and Lucious' grand plans to make Scarlett Harper a legend of our time—a future EGOT winner with an Emmy, Grammy, Oscar, and Tony to her name.

She was already part way there, having won a Grammy for Best New Artist and a Tony last year for her role as Juliette in *Roméo and Juliette* on Broadway. She'd debuted at our theatre, The Sunflower—a role, of course, cast by my father.

"Cousin or not, she's fucking annoying."

"Just like you are."

"Shut up, *stronzo*."

I hung up a bit later and headed to the bathroom, ready to wash off the day and grab a few hours of sleep before Monday's chaos stormed into my office—decked out in sky-high Louboutins, with fire blazing from her mouth.

"When you said you'd tear down the museum and make it something majestic, I almost believed you'd pull off something worth looking at. But red tiles? That's the big vision? I shouldn't be surprised—mediocrity's kind of your brand, Lazzio."

I instructed the movers to haul the packages up to the third floor. One of them handed me a clipboard and a pen, clearly eager to wrap this up and get out of here.

I glanced at the paper, scrawling my name with a quick swipe.

"Make sure you don't leave any scratches on the floors," I said, barely looking up.

They nodded and got to work.

"The red tiles are for the third floor, Miss Whitenhouse. It's supposed to represent battlefields—red-veined marble from Greece to echo blood on stone, surrounded by sculptures and paintings of real warriors."

I walked toward my office, feeling her trailing in my shadow.

Just before the door, I stopped and turned to meet her pretty gaze.

"Don't *ever* question my taste again. You, of all people, know that greatness is my only standard."

I shut the door firmly, the sound echoing through the room as I made my way to the chair behind my desk. The leather creaked as I settled in, surveying the stacks of paperwork and blueprints sprawled across the polished wood.

I leaned back, fingers steepled as I took a slow breath.

Jade Whitenhouse existed for one reason: to ruin my peace of mind, and keep me tethered to the edge of insanity.

The thirty-year-old stood at five foot eight, her raven-black hair spilling over her shoulders like sin itself, with eyes so dark they seemed to steal the light from the room. Her skin—pale enough to rival Morticia Addams—had an unsettling allure that was both chilling and impossible to ignore.

I should've fired her years ago.

Sure, her work was absolutely flawless—on paper, she was the perfect COO. But that sharp tongue of hers? It chipped away at any shred of respect she managed to earn.

And yet, despite my better judgment, I couldn't get her out of my head.

No matter how hard I tried, my mind had decided that of all the things to fixate on, it had to be her.

More than that, she also carried one of my secrets—a sinful one.

Not big enough to dismantle my empire, but just dangerous enough to threaten my standing in the Lazzio family. One wrong move, and she could knock me down a rung I'd spent years clawing my way up to reach.

So, for now, she stayed—much to my fucking irritation.

CHAPTER
THIRTEEN

"Go to heaven for the climate and hell for the company."
— **Benjamin Franklin Wade**

Angelo

"I need you to do something for me, *mio figlio*."

The butler poured me another glass of chilled white wine as I savored the pasta alle vongole. The rich flavors of garlic and lemon burst on my tongue, mingling with the salty flavor of the clams.

The table stretched out like a display of forced camaraderie —all smiles and polite laughter, masking the simmering tension beneath. My parents sat to my right, with Uncle Lorenzo and his wife, Luciana, beside them.

Across from me, the Harper family sat in an uneasy line: Lucius Harper and his wife Francesca, and Scarlett, who swayed between half-drunken stupor and silent rebellion. Next to her was Kiara, their eldest—calm, detached, like she didn't belong.

At the far end was Uncle Fernando, observing in quiet amusement.

I was placed at the head, my father's symbolic gesture of passing the reins, though he rarely relinquished control.

I met his gaze, a flicker of curiosity in my frown.

He hardly asked for anything these days.

"What is it?"

He moved closer, scanning the room to make sure everyone was lost in their own conversations. "I need you to check the security systems at one of our Broadway theaters—The Sunflower on 42nd Street," he murmured. "There's an actress involved ... you'll see what I mean. I need you to erase the footage, but first, download it to a hard drive and bring it to me." His lips curled into a dark grin. "It might come in handy later. The Gregs can't be trusted."

My mind clouded with confusion. "What do the Gregs have to do with your ... actress?"

He shrugged, taking a slow sip of his wine. "James has been having an affair with her, keeping it under wraps. But last night ... they had a fight. He went to her trailer to apologize, and they ended up fucking in the elevator. Your security called me to let me know."

Interesting.

I arched a brow. "Want me to cover this up?"

"I don't want you to cover it up," he corrected, his voice low and measured. "I want you to fucking take control. The Gregs have been slipping, and I don't trust them to keep things in line. This isn't just about some actress—it's about power. If we don't handle this now, it could come back to bite us. Hard."

The Gregs are meant to be our allies, but we don't mistake that for loyalty.

When we meet, it's never just a handshake—everyone's armed. Knives, guns, whatever they can conceal.

We tolerate each other, pretend to play nice, but the truth hangs in the air: trust is a weakness none of us can afford. We're all just waiting for the other to make a mistake, so we can strike first and claim what's ours.

For James Greg—the king of the Greg empire, the man behind the largest oil company in America—to cross into my territory and mess with one of my employees?

That's not just a threat. It's a trap.

A trap to see how I'd respond.

Because messing with my employees?

Especially one with long black hair and a body that could make any man drop to his knees? That's my fucking job. And I don't like to share.

And I'm sure he had fucked his mistress in that elevator on purpose—just to send a message, to make sure I knew exactly what he was doing and gauge how far I'd go. Or maybe he was so blinded by his own dick he thought I wouldn't notice, or worse—didn't care.

But no matter the reason, he had crossed the line.

And my father wanted me to make it clear: this isn't something we let slide.

I nodded slowly, my gaze drifting to Uncle Lorenzo, his cheeks flushed a deep red—rage mixed with too much wine. I could see the storm brewing, and it wouldn't be long before he exploded and turned his anger onto his poor wife Luciana.

Before that could happen, I rose, glass in hand, and tapped it sharply with a knife to grab everyone's attention.

"I have an announcement," I said. "As you all know—"

"Oh my god, are you getting married?" Aunt Francesca interrupted, clapping her hands excitedly.

A collective gasp swept across the table.

"No, I—"

She cut me off again. "But my assistant told me she saw you three nights ago, with a woman with long blonde hair and a cap. Your chauffeur drove her off. I thought you were finally settling down, Angelo. You're almost forty—"

Before I could respond, my mother groaned loudly. "*Dio mio*, Francesca! My son is only thirty-six, not forty. You'd do well to focus on your daughter, who's barely sober when she performs and threw up on stage again last night. And stop calling my son a womanizer!"

Francesca's mouth dropped open in shock. "Monica! How dare you! You know Scarlett is going through a lot lately. Fame isn't easy, right, *dolcezza*?" She nudged Scarlett, who was half-drunk, her head lolling over the table as a faint snore escaped her lips.

My mother laughed.

Francesca frowned. "Anyway—"

Uncle Lorenzo shot up from his seat, the chair clattering to the floor. He swiveled, eyes darting left and right. "What did Father say about your bitching, Francesca?" His voice was thick with venom. "Lucius, you better teach your wife to keep her mouth—"

Luciana clutched the end of his suit sleeve. "*Caro mio*, please, calm down—"

"Don't talk to me, *strega*! Never speak when I'm talking—"

My father sighed heavily, giving a subtle signal to the butlers.

With practiced ease, the two men moved to restrain Lorenzo as he fought against them, dragging him out of the room.

Luciana pushed herself shakily to her feet, her eyes brimming with unshed tears.

She shot a strained, apologetic glance at the table before mumbling an excuse. "I swear he'll behave next Sunday," she said quietly, her voice heavy with regret.

Without another word, she slipped out, her promise lingering in the air—a weak, futile attempt to clean up yet another mess my uncle had made.

"He needs to be locked in an asylum," Francesca muttered, reaching for a piece of bread.

My mother scoffed. "As if you're a model of sanity."

My aunt's jaw dropped. "Oh, *prego*! Says the woman who dropped 100k on shoes yesterday because a headache apparently required Jimmy Choo therapy!"

The two sisters continued their bickering, and I sank back into my chair with a sigh, my own head throbbing.

As my grandfather had always said, *Non esiste una famiglia italiana senza un po' di dramma.*

There's no such thing as an Italian family without a bit of drama.

I got James Greg's epic sextape dumped onto my drive the day after our family dinner, right after making sure my security crew erased every trace from the memory chips while keeping a neat copy on my end.

I couldn't resist taking a peek, and sure enough, the old man still had some game.

Almost impressive for a sixty-seven-year-old.

Now I faced a bit of a dilemma—what to do about Pauline Dupont.

The French Broadway star was one of our top earners, drawing global audiences. She had even bagged her first Tony for Best Actress, making her a real asset. But I don't tolerate my employees fucking disrespecting me and flirting with the enemy.

That shit just won't fucking do.

But when it comes to one specific, devilish one? Your rules surprisingly bend, Lazzio.

I shut the voice in my head down, burying it deep where it couldn't cause any more trouble.

I reached for my phone and hit the red button to connect with my assistant, Grace.

"Yes, sir?" she answered immediately.

"Grace, set up an appointment with Miss Dupont for Friday night after her show. Tell her it's for a contract negotiation."

"Got it, sir. And may I remind you that you're meeting Leonardo Vittori at *La Piadina* for lunch in thirty minutes?"

Leonardo Vittori, head of the New York outfit, is a close friend, like the brother I never had. But I was a businessman, and he was a mafia don—truth be told, we shared the same line of work, though mine was a little more legal.

"*Sì.*"

"Perfect. I'll have your chauffeur come now. Oh, and I almost forgot—Miss Whitenhouse took the day off. Family emergency."

I frowned.

I thought she had no family.

When Jade Whitenhouse had shown up at my door almost six years ago, fresh out of college and desperate for a job, I hadn't even bothered to meet her. I'd had Grace send her away.

She had been too young, too inexperienced. I hadn't needed some twenty-three-year-old who'd probably spent her teens glued to *Sex and the City*, dreaming of the glamour of New York City and all that fake shit movies and shows peddle about working here.

I had just opened the museum a year before, and I'd had a vision.

This place was going to be *the* new art attraction of New York, not just a museum. I'd wanted it to be a fucking lifetime sensory experience—sight, smell, touch, taste.

I had a fucking vision, and I hadn't been about to let anyone slow me down.

I'd wanted the best of the best, and no young girl was going to measure up to that.

Or so I had thought.

Then, as I had been getting ready to leave, she'd barged into my office. Her eyes had been as dark as night, her face pale as snow, lips blood red. She'd had a frown on her face, but it wasn't one of fear—the girl had attitude. I could tell right away she wasn't the type to take no for an answer, and that had intrigued me.

And damn, the girl had been breathtaking.

The most beautiful woman I'd ever seen.

My eyes had been drawn to her, something unfamiliar and heavy settling in my chest, and when our gazes had met, I'd almost found myself at a loss for words.

Even when I'd threatened her, she hadn't flinched.

Instead, she'd met my gaze with a cool, unwavering stare, as if she welcomed the challenge. That look—that fucking look—had told me all I'd needed to know: She hadn't been afraid of me. And that had made her even more dangerously attractive.

She'd left without saying a word, the air thick with the lingering scent of musk and dark amber. Moments later, Grace had stormed into my office, her face pale, glasses askew, one hand pressed to her chest like she was about to collapse.

"I'm so sorry, sir," she'd stammered, still breathless. "She *pushed* me! I—"

A chuckle had escaped my lips. "Prepare her contract, Grace. She starts Monday."

I'd thrown on my coat, grabbed my phone, and walked out of the office, heading toward the elevator.

"What? But sir, she's ... so disrespectful! No manners! She didn't even say hello or introduce herself properly when she arrived. She just barged in and demanded to see you, as if she were the queen of the world, and she almost killed me! She—"

The elevator doors had slid open, and I'd stepped inside.

"Grace, go join your family. I'm sure your grandkids are dying to see you."

Grace had been in her early fifties, having worked for my father since her twenties, and for me the past fifteen years. She'd known every Lazzio, known our stubbornness, our ruthlessness.

I'd trusted her with my life, and I'd always respected her judgment.

But this time, I hadn't listened to her.

I'd had to trust my gut. And my gut had told me that Jade Whitenhouse was going to make me billions.

The crease in her forehead had deepened. "I don't know, sir. I have a bad feeling about this one."

"We'll see. Merry Christmas, Grace."

With that, the doors had closed, and Miss Jade Whitenhouse had stepped into Lazzio Exhibits Inc. Like a storm, she'd swept through everything, tearing down and rebuilding in her wake, a force that had both thrilled and tormented me all at once.

Over the years, she had become a ruthless shark in our treacherous waters.

Anything she'd wanted, anything she'd *needed*—it was hers. Suppliers, art, contractors—she'd bent them to her will with nothing more than a smile, and it would all unfold before my eyes, like a twisted magic trick.

She wasn't just part of the reason Lazzio Exhibits Inc. was as powerful and prestigious as it was. She *was* the reason. And she knew damn well the grip she had on me and my fucking empire.

As painful as it was for my ego, I had to give credit where it was due.

Jade Whitenhouse was one of a kind.

But over the years, she'd never spoken about herself, her family, or anything that wasn't tied to work.

The only exception? Sex.

She'd made no effort to hide that she was a sexual being, and she didn't give a single fuck about it. But aside from her sex jokes, innuendos, and business talk, she was an enigma—and I liked it that way.

It was exactly what had made her such an indispensable asset and kept my obsession in line.

The less I knew, the better I could control myself.

So, after more than six years of unwavering devotion to this place, for her to suddenly take a day off? And for a *family emergency*? That was fucking odd.

"Did she tell you what kind of emergency that was?"

Grace scoffed, the frustration clear in her voice. "As if this devil would have the decency to explain. She just sent me an email this morning—'Family emergency. Taking the day off.' No explanation. Nothing. I can't stand her—"

"*Grazie*, Grace."

For years, the two of them had been locked in a silent war,

waging petty, calculated attacks with all the subtlety of an open battlefield.

One would spill coffee on the other's desk; the other would toss her lunch in the trash. They'd sabotage each other's phones, swipe sunglasses—anything they could to get under each other's skin.

I'd stopped keeping track of their little skirmishes long ago.

They were like cats and dogs—fiercely loathing each other, but smart enough to disguise it with fake pleasantries and snarky jabs, always one step ahead in their passive-aggressive games.

And I was smart enough to never get in between.

"James Greg? Can't believe his dick can still get hard," Vittori laughed.

I grimaced, raising my glass to my lips. "Don't even fucking remind me. That image is scarred into my brain for life."

"And with a twenty-five year old?" He shook his head, a dark smirk twisting his lips. "You assholes aren't paying the poor girl enough—she's stuck fucking a prehistoric corpse now, because of you."

We were seated in the dimly lit corner of *La Piadina*, Vittori's pride and joy.

The place had that authentic, rustic Italian charm—the kind that made you feel like you were a guest in some old Roman villa rather than a trendy Manhattan restaurant.

But behind the thick walls of Tuscany wine and fresh pasta, he cleaned his money, laundered through every dish served.

The lasagna arrived, served in the same traditional ceramic dishes that seemed as old as the restaurant itself. The layers of pasta, thick with ricotta and rich Bolognese, steam rising from the edges, made my stomach growl in anticipation.

I cut into it, the cheese pulling apart in perfect strands as I brought the first bite to my mouth.

"Nah. She's not fucking him for money. It's something else."

Vittori raised an eyebrow, intrigued. "What else?"

I shrugged. "Maybe she actually fell for him."

He stared at me like I'd just insulted his mother. "*Che cazzo?* Is she out of her mind?"

"Don't know. Don't give a fuck. I just wanted to find out what they're hiding."

His eyes shifted, narrowing as they locked on the window where a cop car rolled by. His gaze lingered there for a beat longer than necessary.

"Think Greg is looking for dirt on you?"

"Why would he?"

He scoffed, setting his fork down with a sharp clink. "I don't know, maybe because you fucked his sister *and* his daughter? You think he's just gonna let that slide?"

I let out a dry chuckle, leaning back in my chair. "That was years ago. Hell, he probably doesn't give a fuck about his sister."

Vittori smirked, taking a long sip of wine. "True. But the daughter? You're still playing with fire, *stronzo*."

I raised an eyebrow. "I've always enjoyed a good burn."

Maybe I like the burn, Lazzio.

I cleared my throat, hoping it would clear my head as well, shaking off the pretty devil that seemed to possess my mind constantly.

"Speaking of fire, I've got my own shit going on. This cop, Detective Alvarez—guy's a pain in the ass. Came sniffing around a while back, asking about some of my more *questionable* shipments. Drugs, you know, the usual. But now he's not just asking for favors—the bastard wants to blackmail me."

I raised an eyebrow, my fork halfway to my mouth. "What does he want?"

"A cut, and he'll let me move my shit without his guys breathing down my neck. Bastard's trying to play with me."

A cold smile crept across my face. New York was a tight circle. Everyone knew who to avoid, and this detective clearly hadn't done his fucking homework.

If he thought he could squeeze Vittori, he was in for a rude awakening.

Leonardo wasn't just impatient—he was ruthless.

He'd settle a problem with a bullet, a blade, or his bare hands, if it came to that. And from the look in his eyes, he was ready for it.

"Anyway," he said, lighting a cigarette, his eyes narrowing as a cop car slowed to a crawl on the other side of the street. "Cyrus called me last night."

Fucking annoying-ass Cyrus.

I took a slow sip of wine. "And?"

He exhaled smoke slowly, a dark grin curling at the corners of his mouth. "Wanted to check if—"

Before he could finish, the restaurant door slammed open, and a wave of feds stormed in, guns raised, shouting orders. Women screamed, men shouted.

Vittori just leaned back in his chair, smirking like he'd

almost expected the whole thing, his eyes dark and gleaming with a sick kind of thrill.

I sighed, glancing at my Rolex. *Shit.*

I was going to be late for my meeting.

CHAPTER FOURTEEN

"Three may keep a secret, if two of them are dead."
— **Benjamin Franklin**

Jade

"I need you to sign these," I announced, barging into Lazzio's office without bothering to glance up.

I dropped the new contract with the Louvre onto his desk —a hard-won deal allowing us to rent up to 25 of their pieces each month.

I was particularly excited about this one. Once the museum's construction was finally complete, I wanted to showcase *Les Ombres de Francesca da Rimini et de Paolo Malatesta.* Nothing screams passionate, destructive love like those two tragic fools.

They were the ultimate story of lust overruling reason, of

two people so consumed by their desire that it led them straight to Hell. *Classic.*

"*Perfetto. Ci sarò tra due settimane. Manda i miei saluti ad Antonio.*"

I fixed my gaze on Lazzio as his smooth Italian accent filled the room.

He stood by the window, casting a long shadow over the chaos of New York City—cars, helicopters, and a million flashing lights below.

Today, he wore his usual tailored Armani suit, a sleek, dark gray two-piece with the vest draped over the back of his chair.

I cleared my throat impatiently, tapping my heel against the marble floor to get his attention.

He turned slowly, a frown deepening between his brows, with that infuriating smirk tugging at his lips—the one I'd fantasized about slapping off more times than I cared to admit.

His gaze slid down my body, taking in the sparkly, violet two-piece blouse and short skirt, paired with my knee-high Hermes heeled boots. The skirt was so short it left little to the imagination, and I knew the thought crossed his mind too, because I saw a flicker of irritation flash in his eyes before they met mine.

He ended his call and placed his phone on the desk.

"If I didn't know you, Miss Whitenhouse," he sneered, sarcasm dripping from every word, "I'd think you were fucking raised in a barn. Knock before you stomp in like you own the place."

I rolled my eyes and grabbed one of his precious framed photos off the desk—his parents looking stiff as ever, and his dog, Georgino, the mutt he spends an excessive amount of time with, in my opinion.

I set it back down with a smirk.

"Funny, I *almost* do own the place, remember? Got thirty percent, so it's practically mine."

He scoffed, dropping into his chair. "I've got the remaining seventy, Miss Whitenhouse. So, I fucking win. Now, what the hell do you want?"

Oh, but not for long, Lazzio.

"I need you to sign these," I said, pointing to the contract. "So I can send them off before I go home."

He flicked through the papers quickly, then scrawled his signature right next to mine, shoving them back at me.

My gaze dropped to his hand, which was covered in freshly bruised knuckles.

I raised an eyebrow. "Burned yourself with your toaster again?"

His expression darkened.

"What?"

"Get out, Miss Whitenhouse."

I laughed, strutting around his desk and perching myself on the edge, thighs brushing against his hand as I crossed my legs. "You've been awfully moody today, Lazzio."

He leaned back, arms crossed, eyes lingering on my bare legs for a moment longer than necessary. "Got raided by the feds yesterday."

"Yeah, heard about that." I took his hand, eyeing the fresh bruises. "Did you take a swing at Vittori?"

He yanked his hand back, standing up abruptly. "*Sì*. Don't you have better things to do than get on my nerves?"

I sighed, swinging my legs playfully in the air. "Sadly, no. Grace left early today, so I needed a new target to torment."

"Ah, I'm the lucky one, huh?"

I pouted. "Kinda. You should feel honored."

In the six years I'd been working for Angelo, nothing got me off more than pissing him off. Watching his eyes darken, his shoulders go rigid, that little flush of rage creeping up his neck—it was almost as good as an orgasm.

Seeing that look on his face, knowing I'd wrecked his mood?

It was the kind of twisted satisfaction that made my day worth living.

"Where were you yesterday, Miss Whitenhouse?"

Shit.

I thought it would've slipped right past him.

My fingers dug into the edge of his desk. "Family emergency."

"Thought you had no family, *diavoletta*."

"I don't."

"Then explain."

"No."

"*Now*."

"A friend of mine gave birth. Back home in Philly. I promised I'd be there."

A total lie.

His gaze sharpened. "Boy or girl?"

"A boy."

Another lie.

"Name?"

I swallowed hard. "... Ronald."

The second it had left my mouth, I regretted it.

Who the hell names their kid Ronald? What was I thinking?

He didn't respond immediately, his eyes scanning me like I was a puzzle he couldn't quite solve.

Feeling a mix of irritation and satisfaction, I stood up quickly, adjusting my skirt and grabbing the contract.

As I turned toward the door, I could feel his eyes on the back of my legs.

Angelo Lazzio had a thing for legs. After all these years, it was as clear as day. I'd caught him staring more than once—whether in private or in public, the man's eyes always seemed to find his target.

The type: blond, short, athletic. Strong legs.

I couldn't resist poking the bear.

Stopping at the door, I turned around and leaned against it. "No date tonight?"

He got up and grabbed his vest, putting it on. "No, Miss Whitenhouse. No date tonight."

"Guess the married women of Manhattan can have one night of peace, for once."

His jaw twitched. "I guess so."

I'd been sitting on a secret for three years now.

One of Lazzio's little *secrets.*

One stormy night—one of those nights that felt like the universe is in a bad mood—I had been working late on a project with a small art dealer in Spain.

He had this rare painting of Louis XIV, and I'd been pushing hard to convince him to lend it to us for an exhibition we were planning.

The exhibit had been called *Kings and Queens of Remorse*, showcasing monarchs who'd lived these glamorous, luxurious lives, but were absolute monsters to their people.

Louis XIV was a prime example: yes, he'd built Versailles and lived in a gilded palace, but at the same time, he had been ruthless, ruling with an iron fist while starving his people. It was a perfect fit.

And I wasn't just talking about Louis XIV.

There was Catherine the Great, who hadn't just ruled Russia—she'd apparently ruled a hell of a lot of men, too. No judgment, but she hadn't exactly been known for keeping things *tame* in the bedroom. A real queen, right?

Then there's Henry VIII, who couldn't make up his mind about wives—he'd married six, killed two, and *still* hadn't gotten the son he'd wanted.

And let's not forget Queen Mary I of England, Bloody Mary, who had executed hundreds of Protestants in her quest to restore Catholicism to England.

If you wanted to make an impression in history, you had to be both glamorous *and* awful.

Anyway, after hours—literally hours—of negotiating, the man had finally caved.

He'd signed the contract and sent it over to me right away.

Grinning to myself, eager to rub my skills in Lazzio's face, I'd taken the elevator up to his office, barging in unannounced like I always did.

What I had walked in on, though, had been enough to traumatize me for life.

Lazzio had been sitting behind his desk, his suit still perfectly in place—at least the parts that mattered. The rest of him had been buried deep inside a woman, her body pressed against his as she rode him, hands gripping the desk for support. Her head had been thrown back, her back arched, and his hands had been tight on her hips, guiding her in a rhythm that looked as though it was designed to destroy her.

The whole scene had been just ... *crazy*.

For a second, I'd just stood there, frozen in disbelief.

Finally sensing my presence, Lazzio had looked up.

His face had contorted in horror as he shot up from his chair, quickly trying to adjust himself. The woman, still in a daze, had finally seen me and had let out a blood-curdling scream before scrambling to hide under his desk.

I'd gasped once my eyes had recognized her.

Of course!

Long blonde hair, timid blue eyes, and that thin, slightly crooked nose—how could I have forgotten?

"Jade, I promise this is not what it looks like," she'd muttered, her voice weak and trembling.

I'd raised an eyebrow, crossing my arms. "Really? Because from where I'm standing, it looks exactly like what it is, Mrs. Lazzio."

Angelo. Was. Having. Sex. With. Luciana. Lazzio.

His uncle's wife. In his office.

I hadn't been able to believe it.

Lazzio's face had twisted into a scowl. "Miss Whitenhouse, get out!"

"Get out?" I'd echoed, mockingly. "Oh, no, I think I'll stay. This is way more entertaining than anything I had planned for the night."

It truly had been.

I'd almost wanted to get on my knees and thank God above for making me witness this. Finally, I had discovered one of Lazzio's little secrets, and breached that thick, impenetrable facade of his.

A tiny baby step closer to my goal.

And it had felt fucking good.

The anger had still been written across his face, but there had been something darker, more dangerous brewing behind his eyes.

"You better get the fuck out of my office, *now*," he'd growled.

My brows had shot up.

I had never seen him this angry. I guess I had really struck a nerve this time.

I'd snorted and turned on my heel, striding out of his office.

As I had made my way to mine, the image of his frantic scramble had still burned in my mind.

For some reason, I'd had a feeling it was just the beginning.

And boy, had I been right.

For the next few years, I'd kept a close eye on Angelo Lazzio's little secret.

He had a kink, but not just any run-of-the-mill kink like roleplay or BDSM.

No, Angelo Lazzio had a thing for married women.

Specifically, women married to men he couldn't stand.

That was his thing.

If he hated someone, I could assure you, he'd be fucking their wife that same night—and the guy would never have a clue.

But fucking Luciana? Even he must have known that was off-limits.

The Lazzio legacy was all about loyalty, family, and keeping the bloodlines untarnished.

This? This had been a betrayal of the highest order.

His uncle would never stand for it—not when it meant his own nephew had dishonored the family's sacred rule.

Lazzio had just handed his uncle a weapon, a reason for vengeance.

If the old man wanted it, he could demand his nephew's head on a platter.

I knew Angelo knew that too.

It's why, as I was about to leave that night, he had slipped into my office without making a sound. He'd pressed his body against the door, his eyes locking with mine.

"Want me to buy you off, or can you keep your mouth shut?"

I had smiled darkly, savoring every second of it. "Nah. I

don't need you to bribe me," I'd said, grabbing my coat and slinging it over my shoulders, my Chanel Boy bag hanging off my arm.

"Good," he'd muttered, turning toward the door.

But I hadn't been done. Oh no, not yet.

"Oh, but there's still something I want from you, Lazzio."

He'd frozen, his hand tightening on the door handle, his knuckles turning white.

"I want fifty percent of Lazzio Exhibits Inc."

"What?" he'd barked, spinning around to face me.

"You heard me."

"You want to own fifty percent of *my* fucking company?"

I'd leaned against the desk, casually tossing my bag onto the chair.

"Yeah, that's right," I had said with a smile. "Fifty percent of Lazzio Exhibits Inc."

His hands had balled into fists as he took a step toward me. "You're out of your fucking mind if you think I'm giving you half of anything."

I tilted my head. "Maybe," I'd said softly, leaning in just a little. "But I'm pretty sure you'd rather give me fifty percent than have your dear old uncle Lorenzo find out his lovely wife is getting fucked by his nephew on a random Tuesday night, while she probably told him she was heading out for Bible study."

He had moved fast, reaching for the gun under his vest.

In an instant, he'd had me pinned hard against the wall, the cold barrel pressing deep into my throat. My nails had dug into the skin of his wrist.

"I'm done with you, Miss Whitenhouse."

My hand had slid up to his face, fingers tracing his jaw, nails leaving a slow, burning trail. "Likewise, Lazzio."

A deep, guttural sound had risen from his chest.

"Get your shit and get out. You're fired."

My smile had only grown wider, darker.

I'd wrapped my fingers tighter around his gun, lifting it to my lips. My tongue had slipped out, dragging along the cold barrel in a sensual tease.

I'd dragged my lips over it—slow and filthy, sucking once, twice, three times—each pull exaggerated. A low, shameless moan had slipped from my throat.

My eyes had stayed glued to his, daring him to look away, and when I'd finally let it slip from my mouth with a loud, wet pop, I couldn't help but let a wicked laugh escape.

"Oh, Lazzio," I had breathed, lowering the gun, letting the tip glide down my throat, tracing my skin until it nestled between my breasts. "You know you could *never* fire me."

His grip had tightened on the gun.

"You think this is a joke?"

"Isn't it?" I'd chuckled darkly, my fingers sliding around the back of his neck, pulling him even closer until my lips had brushed against his skin. "I've got too much dirt on you," I whispered, before my tongue had slowly dragged along his neck. "I could *ruin* you ... so, no, you won't fire me, baby."

He'd stayed silent, his jaw clenched so tight it looked like it might crack.

I'd pushed him off, grabbed my bag, and walked toward the door, but before I could escape, his hand had slammed it shut, trapping me inside.

Damn, he was a one-man broadcast of mixed signals—louder than static, and twice as useless.

His body had been pressed against mine, his scent—dark wood mixed with honey whiskey—had saturated the space between us.

Honey and dark wood draped in silk sheets.

"Ten percent," he'd muttered, his voice low and rough.

I'd turned slowly, pressing myself against the door as his other hand had landed on the wood, caging me in.

His face had been just inches from mine, his breath warm on my skin.

"Forty," I'd said, voice steady, my pulse quickening despite myself.

His jaw clenched. "Twenty."

I'd shaken my head, my eyes wandering over his features—sharp jawline, dark eyes flashing with irritation, and full lips. "Thirty. Last offer."

He had leaned in even closer, his lips brushing the shell of my ear as his voice had dropped to a whisper. "Done. And if I find out you told even one soul, I will kill you with my bare hands, Miss Whitenhouse."

"I promise, Lazzio. I'll *never* tell your secrets," I'd lied.

That night, I had become COO and co-owner of Lazzio Exhibits Inc., and with that had come the freedom to expand my talents across the company.

More than that, it had given me the perfect opportunity to get on every single nerve of Angelo Lazzio—and it was fucking bliss.

"What about you, Miss Whitenhouse? No date tonight? Or should I say, no fucking with a mover, plumber, or—what was the last one again? Oh yeah, an electrician?"

As much as I knew Lazzio was familiar with his own history, I supposed it was only natural he'd know mine too.

After all, he'd occasionally crossed paths with the different men I'd lost myself in for a night—or sometimes more—just to erase the tension that working for him left in my system.

Even if he tried to shame my taste, it would never occur to him to mingle with the lower class.

No, Mr. Lazzio was far too *uptight* for that.

I smirked, checking my nails. "What can I say? I've always had a thing for men who know how to use their hands ... and their mouth." I let my gaze flick up, watching the flicker of annoyance cross his face. "Especially their mouths. Kissing, making out ... and going down. Ugh, I *love* it all. Especially when they go down on me. Only real men do that. The rest? They're just ... boys."

The scowl etched across his face was almost artful—pure rage, with just a dash of offended pride. Angelo Lazzio, king of "no missionary" and "too good to go down," looked like he was seriously considering throwing me out of the nearest window.

As if the very air he was breathing had been poisoned by my presence, he scoffed sharply before storming out of his office.

He didn't even look back, his footsteps echoing down the hall as he made his way to the elevator.

Before the door closed, he shot me a final glare.

"You know," he called out, "It's pathetic how desperate you are for validation from men who can barely afford to wipe your shoes. Guess some people are so used to settling for the scraps, they don't even realize they're eating off the floor."

Freaking bastard.

I saw red.

That fucking smug look on his face was too much to take.

Without thinking, I took off my heel and hurled it toward him, watching it sail through the air with all the force I could muster.

But before it could reach him, the elevator doors slid shut with that cold, final sound, and all I heard was his laugh. That insufferable, arrogant laugh that echoed through the hallway as the elevator descended, taking him from my sight.

I stood there, fuming, my heart pounding in my chest.

Oh, Angelo Lazzio, I can't wait to stand in your ruins and watch you burn.

Kicking the door shut behind me, I made a beeline for the kitchen, the weight of three grocery bags pulling at my arms. I dropped them onto the counter with a sigh.

After shoving everything haphazardly into the fridge, I slipped out of my coat and kicked off my shoes, leaving a messy trail of clothes as I made my way to the bathroom.

I cranked the shower to the hottest setting, steam filling the space almost instantly.

Stripping off the rest of my clothes, I stepped into the scalding stream, letting the water beat down on me like a storm.

It seared against my skin, but the heat couldn't wash away the words echoing in my mind—*settling for scraps, eating off the floor.*

Ugh, I should've killed him on the spot.

My hands pressed against the cold tiles, my head hanging low as the water soaked my hair, turning it into a dark curtain that veiled my face.

I stayed under the spray until it ran icy, my skin prickling with the cold.

Wrapping a black towel around my body and another around my hair, I padded out into the dimly lit apartment.

Lighting the candles scattered around the room, I poured

myself a glass of red wine, letting its warmth bloom inside me as I finally sank into my velvet sofa.

Angelo Lazzio—the devil's thorn buried under my skin.

I took a long sip of wine, savoring its dark, bitter bite before getting up and heading to my office.

My thumb pressed against the cold fingerprint scanner until the door clicked open.

I slipped inside, letting it shut slowly behind me, sealing me into the dimly lit space.

The room remained in darkness for a beat longer before I flicked on the light, harsh brightness revealing the meticulously organized chaos—the blueprint of my revenge.

No one had ever stepped foot in this room but me.

And for good reason.

Because if they did, I'd either end up in a cell or worse—bound and gagged in some dark basement.

This room was my lair, my sanctuary, crammed with secrets and lies, every piece of it a sharpened knife aimed straight at Angelo Lazzio's throat.

I navigated through the sea of scattered documents and photos on the floor, careful not to disturb the mess I had so deliberately set up.

I sank into my crimson velvet loveseat, grabbing the small remote I always kept there.

With one press, the hidden TV slid out from its panel in the wall. I switched to the last channel—the live feed from Lazzio's security cameras at his Broadway theater, The Sunflower.

I'd overheard him on a call earlier, mentioning he needed to speak with one of the actresses, so I knew exactly which camera to pull up.

I scanned through the different camera angles, eyes narrowing as I searched the building.

Finally, I found him—smoking in the back alley, his silhouette framed by the cold, winter air. The smoke from his cigarette mingled with the white puffs of his breath, dissipating into the darkness. He leaned against the brick wall, only half of his face visible; the other half was cloaked in shadow.

One thing I'd learned about Angelo Lazzio—he was a paragon of health.

He worked out every day, ate like a monk, barely touched alcohol, and never smoked ... unless he was absolutely stressed.

Tonight, something had clearly gotten under his skin.

I sipped my wine, savoring the taste as I watched him from my private little theater of his life.

What could possibly be eating at him?

Just then, a figure emerged from the darkness—a woman.

Tall, red-haired, dressed in what looked like a 17th-century costume, her face painted white with bloodred lips. An actress.

She was frantic, her shoulders shaking, hands flailing as she spoke, her words lost to the silence of the feed.

Lazzio stood there like a stone, towering over her. His expression was unreadable, jaw clenched so tight I could almost hear his teeth grind through the screen.

I zoomed in, trying to get a better look at her face.

Pauline Dupont. His prized actress.

Was she another one of his mistresses?

I frowned.

No, she didn't fit his usual pattern. She looked too ... unhinged, too desperate.

I took another sip of my wine, my eyes fixed on Lazzio, as if I could pierce through his skull and read his thoughts.

What the hell was going on in that alley, Lazzio?

Before I could blink, the scene on the screen took a turn so shocking, my fingers slipped, and my wine glass shattered against the floor, red liquid splashing like blood on the velvet.

The actress, her face twisted in terror, screamed something at him.

In response, Lazzio grabbed her chin, his thumb stroking her jaw in a mockery of tenderness. He leaned in, whispering words that made her eyes bulge with fear.

Then, without warning, he pulled a gun from his coat and shot her point-blank between the eyes. Her body crumpled to the ground, blood splattering across his face like a twisted artist's canvas.

A silent scream wrenched out of me, my hand clasped over my mouth, too terrified to even breathe, as if he could somehow sense my presence through the screen.

He calmly wiped a speck of blood from his cheek, then turned—just slightly—toward the camera.

His eyes locked onto the lens, as if he knew someone was watching.

And then—static.

The screen crackled, then turned black.

Someone had just cut the feed.

I stared at the blank monitor, heart pounding, unable to move.

I had just witnessed a *murder.*

I sat there, paralyzed by the dark satisfaction that gnawed at my insides. Angelo Lazzio had just handed me the final weapon I needed.

The perfect moment of weakness. The final piece to destroy him.

And yet, something in me felt cold—emptier than before.

Was I really ready to pull this trigger?

I stood up, my legs shaky, my thoughts fragmented.

I glanced at the shattered wine glass on the floor, the fragments sharp and glistening, like memories I'd long since buried.

The only thing left now was the choice I had to make.

And, God help me, I would make it.

The game had changed.

And I had just turned the final page.

CHAPTER
FIFTEEN

"Never trust anything that a man will not set his reputation and name upon."
—**Jeff Grubb**

Angelo

"*... The thirty-three-year-old actress was found dead in her apartment this morning. Authorities are claiming that the Broadway star and Tony Award winner, half-American, half-French, shot herself at approximately two a.m. this morning. Residues of cocaine and ecstasy were found in her blood, and doctors confirm that the star had been diagnosed with depression and was undergoing medication for the last two years ...*"

I shut the TV off with a click and sank back into my chair, staring at the black screen.

Pauline Dupont had been a problem I hadn't fucking

needed, and now, she was nothing but a mess I didn't want to deal with anymore.

But she'd served her purpose.

That was the problem with people like her—they thought they knew the game, but they don't understand the rules until it's too late.

And now, she was gone.

But the mess she had left was far from over.

My grip tightened around my coffee mug as I swallowed the hot liquid in one go, the scalding burn igniting a curse under my breath.

Then there was a knock at the door.

Grace stepped in a moment later, her face tight with a kind of controlled worry. She shifted from foot to foot, her hands fidgeting as she passed me my morning newspaper.

"Sorry to disturb you, sir, but Channel 5, CNN, Fox News, and other media outlets are all downstairs in the media room, waiting for you."

I set the mug down with a soft clink.

The media circus downstairs wasn't a surprise.

After everything that had just gone down, I had known they'd be itching for answers.

I stood up, adjusting my cuffs. "Let's go."

As we approached the media room, I caught sight of Jade lingering outside.

Her hair, usually loose in wild, dark waves, was pulled back into a tight updo.

It didn't suit her. Too neat, too restrained, like it was suffocating everything that made her, *her*.

The long-sleeved black dress she wore clung to her figure, but covered too much. Too modest. Jade wasn't modest, and seeing her like this felt like looking at a faded version of something vibrant.

Her fake glasses—the ones she slapped on when she wanted to play professional—rested on her nose, but they couldn't distract from what I saw beneath them.

The makeup she usually wielded like a weapon was muted, almost bare, though her lips still held that faint red stain that captured my attention every damn time.

Her Louboutins clicked against the floor, but even that sound felt different, less sharp, less her. And then there were her eyes—dull, tired, refusing to meet mine, not even once.

This wasn't my Jade.

At least, not the Jade I knew, and I hated that it unsettled me more than it should.

"Your lawyers are already in the crowd," Grace said, handing Jade a bottle of water. "When you speak, remember to glance at them from time to time. They've prepared your statement and are already seated at the table on stage."

Jade groaned, clearly annoyed. "I didn't expect to be on TV today. I would've put more effort into my makeup."

Grace rolled her eyes. "Someone just died, Satan. Can you at least act like you care for the cameras?"

Jade crossed her arms. "You're not the one who's gonna have millions of people judging the way you look, oldie."

I ignored their bickering and motioned for Jade to go in first.

She did, and—*fuck*, no.

Her dress dipped scandalously low in the back, revealing the damn dragon tattoo that never failed to ruin my focus. Vibrant reds and blues stretched across her skin, daring anyone to look, and making it impossible not to. It wasn't just a tattoo—it was a deliberate choice to set the world on fire, one glance at a time.

I caught her wrist, pulling her back hard enough to make her stumble.

"Go put on a damn jacket. You're not walking in there like that—unless you're trying to convince people we run a porn studio."

Jade ripped her arm from my grip. "I don't have time to run back to my office and play dress-up."

I stepped closer. "We're about to give a statement on a fucking suicide, Miss Whitenhouse. We need to look like we're mourning, not like you're trying to seduce the viewers."

She rolled her eyes. "Fine. Give me yours then."

I barked out a cold, humorless laugh. "Over my dead body."

She leaned in, her voice a low hiss as a couple of journalists walked by.

"Come on," she whispered. "They'll think you were just comforting me after the news. My poor friend Pauline shot herself, and here you are, being the caring boss."

As much as it made my blood boil, she was right.

The vultures waiting in the room just steps away were here for one thing only: to pin the blame on someone, and dig up a juicy story. Any slip-up, any crack in our facade, and they'd feast on it, twisting it to smear Lazzio Entertainment Group's image into the ground.

I sighed, shrugging off my blazer and tossing it into her hands. "Don't get any ideas. This doesn't mean shit."

Jade smirked as she slipped it on, the oversized fit swallowing her frame. "Of course not," she muttered, smoothing the sleeves. "We wouldn't want anyone thinking Angelo Lazzio actually has a heart."

I shoved the door open and stepped into the media room, ignoring her completely.

The flash of cameras hit us instantly, the sound of murmured questions buzzing like a swarm of angry bees.

I felt her step in beside me, her expression instantly

shifting to a mask of sorrowful composure as the eyes of the world locked onto us.

Showtime, baby.

"David McLoad from CNN," announced a short, chubby man with funky glasses as he grabbed the mic. "Pauline Dupont was one of the most talented actresses in your Broadway productions. How could you not have known she was struggling mentally, Mr. Lazzio?"

"Thank you for your question, Mr. McLoad," I said, letting my gaze sweep across the room, taking in all the journalists with their mics and cameras trained on us.

He nodded.

"We were actually aware that Miss Dupont was having a tough time, which is why we ensured she was under the care of a psychiatrist. She had regular sessions with Dr. Huang every Tuesday and Thursday morning. Additionally, we arranged alternative therapies—homeopathic treatments, traditional Chinese medicine—to give her a more holistic approach in managing her anxiety and negative thoughts."

Lie after lie after fucking lie.

But I knew the press would eat it up.

They wanted a neat little package, something they could twist and sensationalize, and I'd made sure all the sources were legit.

They scribbled furiously, nodding like sheep.

McLoad sat back down, and another reporter immediately jumped up—a petite woman with a cropped pixie cut.

She grabbed the mic with purpose.

"Alexandra Jasper from Fox News," she said. "Miss Whitenhouse, knowing a woman your age, working in the same company, chose to end her life—doesn't that scare you? Don't you worry that the Lazzio empire's relentless pressure might have driven her to this? Are you not afraid you might face a similar fate?"

A collective gasp rippled through the crowd as they turned their eyes to me, waiting for a reaction.

I knew what Jasper was getting at—the implication that the Lazzio name was a curse, a brand of power that crushed the souls of those under it.

And while she wasn't entirely wrong, she was still crossing a fucking line.

Jade offered a small, soft smile. "Thank you, Miss Jasper, for your concern," she said. "Firstly, I want to say that Pauline was a dear friend of mine. She had a beautiful soul, always finding the good in people, and she believed that art should be accessible to everyone, regardless of their background." She paused, taking a shaky breath as if to steady herself. "Waking up to the news of her passing was devastating. Knowing I couldn't be there for her in her darkest moment is something I'll carry with me for a long time."

A tear slid down her cheek, which she quickly wiped away.

A few of the women in the room murmured sympathetic noises, urging her to take her time, as if this wasn't a show being put on for their benefit.

Jade took a slow, deep breath, letting the silence stretch just long enough to make everyone a little uncomfortable.

"Losing someone so close is ... indescribable," she continued, her voice catching ever so slightly. "We all knew Pauline was going through a rough time, but no one could have imagined it would come to this. If I could go back and do things differently, I would. I wish I'd checked in on her more, been there when she needed a friend. But we can't change the past."

She glanced at me, her eyes searching for a silent reassurance.

I feigned it, resting my hand on her shoulder, then slowly trailing it down her back before allowing it to drop back to my side.

She continued, her eyes locking on Alexandra Jasper. "As for me, Lazzio Entertainment Group, and specifically Lazzio Exhibits Inc., where I serve as COO, have been nothing short of the foundation of my dreams and the springboard for my success."

My eyes didn't drift from her.

"This company has been the blueprint for innovation, professional growth, and pushing boundaries. So, no, Miss Jasper. I don't fear that I'll meet the same fate as Pauline. The cause of her tragic end wasn't this company—it was her struggle with mental health. And it's a struggle many face, often silently."

Alexandra Jasper's lips thinned into a line, clearly not satisfied with the carefully polished answer.

She leaned back, folding her arms, but said nothing more.

I leaned forward slightly, catching the room's attention.

"What happened to Pauline was a tragedy," I said, my voice steady. "And while it's easy to speculate and point fingers, the truth is that mental health struggles are complex, and deeply personal. We did everything we could to support her, but sometimes it's not enough. We will be conducting a full internal review to see if there were any warning signs we missed, or if there's more we could have done. Our hearts go out to her family and loved ones."

The room buzzed with whispers, pens scratching across notepads as journalists scrambled to capture every word.

Grace stepped forward, a firm but polite smile on her face as she addressed the crowd. "Thank you all for your questions. That's all the time we have for today. We appreciate your understanding during this difficult time."

Jade gave me a quick, knowing look, a ghost of a smirk playing at her lips.

She knew we'd pulled it off.

I held her gaze a moment longer, the sinful thoughts in my head darkening my every breath.

I could barely keep my focus as I turned and left the room, leaving her behind.

CHAPTER SIXTEEN

"Clowns are respectable only in a circus."
— **Tamerlan Kuzgov**

Angelo

"*Dio mio,* Angelo! I asked you to blackmail Greg, not to fucking kill his mistress!"

I leaned back in the chair, the dim lighting flickering, casting shadows over the concrete walls.

This basement meeting room—accessible only through the parking lot—was a place few were allowed. Only family. Only the ones who had earned their place.

Across from me, my father's jaw was clenched tight. Uncle Fernando sat silently to his right. Vittori leaned back in his chair, his arms folded, flanked by his brothers, who barely made a move. My cousins, Matteo and Richi, sat side by side, expressions unreadable, as always. And the Marvelli brothers, Elio and Aurelio, who had taken their father's place in the family business after his sudden death last year.

The two brothers were the ones who'd helped me with the mess—carrying the body and setting it up in a suicide position, just to make sure the narrative had fit.

A few well-placed bribes to Doctor Huang and Detective Kingsley, the police chief, had made sure the case was closed before it had even begun.

Vittori grinned and flicked the ash from his cigarette. "I admit, *stronzo,* that was fucking stupid," he said, exhaling a cloud of smoke before offering me a cigarette.

I waved it off, irritation creeping in.

"She gave Greg access to the theater's bank accounts," I said, my voice laced with venom. "Both her and the accountant were fucking him, so he had everything right under his nose. That bastard stole ten million from me with their help."

The room went deadly quiet.

For only a second, though.

Vittori's wicked laugh filled the air, like it was the funniest thing he'd ever heard.

My father slammed his fist on the table, cursing loudly.

The truth was, the money meant nothing to me. To us.

It was the principle of it, the fucking audacity of it all. Another attack from that low-life, soul-sucking piece of shit, who seemed to think he could play me.

But this time, it was different.

10 million dollars.

He was clearly pushing for a war. The real question was—why?

I knew it wasn't just because I'd fucked his daughter. That was nothing to him. He had never cared about the women in his family like that.

No, this was something darker. Something more twisted.

Then it fucking hit me.

Boston. Nine years ago.

The Cyrus project.

Or, more accurately, the mess that had almost ruined us ... because of him.

But why the hell was it all resurfacing now?

I sank into the couch, Georgino jumping into my lap as I replayed the interview with Jade and me, trying to see it from an outsider's perspective. His velvety fur brushed against my fingers, as he sniffed and licked them. But my attention kept snapping back to Jade, watching the clip for the third time. There was something in her eyes when she'd spoken—something elusive, unfamiliar, and damn near impossible to place.

I couldn't shake how effortlessly she had played her part. For a second, I almost believed Pauline had been her best friend growing up, even though I knew damn well they'd never met.

She's damn good at lying.

Too damn good.

It made me wonder what lies she had fed me—what else she's kept hidden, buried beneath that perfect facade. And the worst part? I want to dig until there's nothing left to hide.

I grabbed my glass, drained it in one go, and decided it was time to call it a night.

Turning off the TV, I dragged myself to bed, but sleep wouldn't come.

We wouldn't want anyone thinking Angelo Lazzio actually has a heart.

Of course, I fucking didn't.

Grazie a Dio.

If I had, I wouldn't have made it past the age of nine.

The second that thought hit, everything flooded back.

The Hamptons.

My parents, laughing, carefree, the sun burning on our backs. Me, playing with sand, building castles.

Then—darkness.

It had happened so fast, I hadn't seen shit coming.

Neither had my parents.

But the one thing I remembered, the only thing that had stuck—a tissue had been shoved against my mouth, and then ... nothing.

Just fucking darkness.

I'd woken up choking on mildew and blood, shirtless, shivering in an empty basement. My wrists and legs had been tied up, ropes digging into my skin, meant to keep me there.

Forever.

Those fourteen days had changed *everything*.

And now, after all these years, I knew the truth: revenge isn't a sweet release—it's a double-edged fucking sword.

One moment it fills you, the next, it rips you apart.

But it's a blade I've never been afraid to use.

CHAPTER SEVENTEEN

"A girl should be two things: classy and fabulous."
— **Coco Chanel**

Jade

"I've never looked worse in my life, Sofiya. I'm *so* embarrassed," I groaned, popping another hummus-dipped chip into my mouth. "My reputation is ruined! People know me for my bold fashion sense, and on that stage? I looked like a poor homeless woman who wandered off to the food bank but somehow ended up on live TV instead."

The press statement about Pauline Dupont's suicide had been two weeks ago, yet the memory still haunted me—mainly how absolutely wrecked I'd looked on TV.

Turns out, without concealer, I look like I'm on my third round of antidepressants, chasing it with a bottle of Jack.

Maybe that was my real talent: looking like a walking mental breakdown.

Sofiya laughed on the other end of the line. "You looked fine, Jadie, I swear. Just a little tired," she reassured me, her daughter Joy's giggles echoing in the background. "Wait—Joy, put that down! You're going to hurt yourself!"

Sofiya Volkov was my best friend—the only person I ever let close enough to glimpse the real me, or at least as much as I allowed.

We had used to work together when she'd been an art contractor at Lazzio Exhibits Inc., back when she'd moved to New York a few years ago. That was, until her ex—an insanely hot, but maddeningly possessive Russian mobster—had found her, begged for forgiveness, and proposed right there on his knees.

How'd they meet? Let's just say it was too sinful to recount.

Sofiya always claimed it was a string of sinful promises that had pulled them together.

Mikhaïl Volkov.

I couldn't help but hate the man a little—he'd stolen her away, turning our daily hangouts into a long-distance friendship I'm terrible at, but am doing my best to keep alive.

They'd had their first child, Joy, four years ago, and now Sofiya was pregnant *again*—with a boy this time. Volkov chaining her to Moscow all over again only made me curse him harder. We could have been tearing up New York City like we'd used to, but no, he had her playing housewife.

Still, she was disgustingly happy, and I couldn't help but grin like an idiot every time we caught up over the phone or on Skype. I missed her like hell. They only make it to New York a few times a year, and it was never enough.

I popped another chip into my mouth, half listening as

Sofiya scolded her little devil, who was proudly yelling, "Papa lets me do *whatever* I want!"

"Yeah? Keep talking, and your papa's getting punished with you," Sofiya shot back. "And trust me, he won't like the kind of *punishment* I have in mind."

I snorted. "He deserves it for knocking you up again. That's for sure."

She laughed. "Shut up."

From the corner of my eye, I caught sight of Grace sprinting through the entry lounge, clutching two white bags sporting a logo I knew all too well. *Bagels & Jo.*

I guess murder works up an appetite.

"Uh, sweetie, I gotta go," I said, munching on one last chip before standing and tossing the rest into a nearby bin. "Time to annoy Lazzio for a bit."

I headed toward the elevator, hitting the button for his office floor.

Sofiya sighed dramatically. "Poor guy. You were put on this earth solely to make his life a living hell, weren't you?"

I chuckled. "Exactly. Love you. Talk soon!"

Hanging up, I stared at my reflection in the mirror, inspecting every detail. No food between my teeth. The dress —a brazen red with dramatic, poofy sleeves and a plunging V-neck—was sinful, framing my gold butterfly necklace.

I smoothed down my hair, letting the sleek black strands fall like a curtain of midnight, my lips painted the same bold red as my dress.

This was how I should've looked on TV—a red goddess draped in power and sin, wearing the metaphorical blood of my boss's latest kill like a badge of honor.

The click of my heels echoed against the polished tiles as I walked.

Passing Grace's desk, I caught her gaze for a split second.

With her glasses—straight out of a wicked fairy godmother costume from *Shrek*—she shot me a disapproving once-over, her eyes dragging from the top of my head to the tips of my heels, punctuated by a shake of her head.

As I walked past, I shot her a wink, catching her barely audible mutter: "The devil really does wear Prada, huh?"

I didn't bother responding.

Instead, I stormed into Lazzio's office, slamming the door behind me with a satisfying thud.

"*Voglio sapere tutto. Ogni singolo, maledetto dettaglio della vita di quel bastardo. Cosa diavolo sta facendo adesso? Dove cazzo si trova? Con chi cazzo è?*"

I walked to his desk, his back turned as he talked on the phone, standing in his favorite spot by the window, eyes scanning the New York skyline.

He didn't even bother turning around—he knew it was me.

I dropped onto his desk, legs crossed, and grabbed one of the Bagels & Jo bags Grace had left behind, rifling through it casually.

"*Voglio una lista di ogni amante che ha avuto, ogni donna con cui è stato. Lo stesso per sua moglie—ha qualche amante? Trova tutto. Ogni sporco segreto. Voglio sapere tutto*," he ordered.

Oh, he was pissed.

Very pissed.

I kept digging through the bag, my fingers brushing past crumbs and paper until I found what I was looking for—a vanilla cookie, topped with blueberry buttercream frosting. His favorite, and mine too.

The second my fingers brushed against it, with some sort of cookie-detecting radar, he whipped around, phone still glued to his ear. His brows furrowed as he stalked toward me, snatched the cookie right from my hand, and took a bite.

"*Perfetto,*" he muttered before hanging up and slouching back in his chair with a sigh.

He carefully placed the cookie on his desk, but not before laying a napkin under it, as if the desk might suddenly sprout a deadly virus.

Such a germ freak.

"The two new floors have been done for a week, yet you're still dodging the one thing I need—a date for the exhibition, so we can announce the opening," I said, arms crossed. "This isn't like you, Lazzio."

He reached into the bag, his fingers brushing my thigh just enough to make me pause, then pulled out a bagel, unwrapping the foil. Salmon, green onions, and spicy cream cheese—his usual.

He bit into it without even glancing my way, acting like I didn't exist, while his eyes locked onto the computer screen.

I leaned in closer. "You know, it drives me *crazy* when you ignore me." I let my fingers slide slowly up my leg. "Makes me want to push your buttons even more."

He stayed silent as he scrolled through his emails.

The longer he pretended I wasn't there, the more I wanted to make him *see* me.

I shifted closer, letting my leg brush against his hand.

His jaw tightened. His eyes remained glued to the screen, though I noticed the muscle in his neck twitch.

"Lazzio—"

His desk phone suddenly chimed, cutting me off, and he tapped the red button, his jaw working as he took another bite of his bagel.

"Sir, the security crew just called. James Greg took the elevator up and is on his way to see you. He'll be here any minute. Should I tell him you're not in?"

James Greg.

Founder and CEO of Greg Oil Inc., the biggest oil company in the West.

His son, Liam Greg, had become the COO after he'd married Katie Kingston a couple years ago. We had been invited to Tulum for their wedding, and it had been by far the most extravagant, over-the-top display of wealth I'd ever witnessed.

I'd never forget the hotel, the crystal-clear waters, the over-the-top luxury—those buff waiters with their chiseled abs ...

"*Sì*, you can let him in."

My brows shot up.

Lazzio *hated* the Gregs.

Scratch that—*loathed* them.

They were nothing more than a power play, a fake friendship forged for appearances, but I knew the truth.

Lazzio couldn't stand the sight of Greg, and I was certain he'd rather drag his nails across a chalkboard than entertain him.

So for him to let Greg walk in here *unannounced*?

That sent warning bells ringing in my head.

"The next exhibition is in two weeks, *Power and War*, just like you titled it," he said, finishing his bagel, and casually tossing the foil into the bin under his desk. "Go check the different floors—art's all here, except *Guernica* by Picasso. Their museum is still jerking around with the contract. I just sent it to your email."

He rose to his feet, his dark eyes finally locking onto mine.

There was no warmth there, but something else—something dangerous.

That was the aura of a murderer.

I stood, crossing my arms with a smirk. "Good. Watching you sulk for two weeks was getting old. Impressive, really—

how you manage to be such a monumental asshole and still get things done."

"Funny, coming from someone who thinks running her mouth counts as productivity."

Anger flared in my chest.

Stepping closer, he brushed a strand of hair behind my ear, his voice dropping to a cruel whisper. "Keep flapping that pretty mouth, though—it's entertaining. Probably the only thing it's good for anyway."

His face was so close I could see the faint flecks of gold flickering in his dark eyes—something I'd somehow missed in the six years I'd known him.

His long lashes brushed his cheeks as he blinked, and the olive undertone of his skin looked almost too perfect under the harsh office lighting.

That jawline could have cut glass, and his lips—*so* full—held a tiny beauty mark on the upper edge, a detail that suddenly seemed all too distracting.

He was too close. Too goddamn close.

My finger drifted to his jaw, my freshly painted black nails grazing his skin, leaving a thin red line in their wake—just enough to tease, just enough to sting.

When my finger reached the corner of his mouth, I found a trace of blueberry frosting he'd missed.

With the tip of my nail, I swiped it, a wicked smile tugging at my lips.

My finger grazed his lips, lingering just long enough to leave them tinged with a hint of heat. Then, slowly, I brought it to my mouth.

My lips closed around it, circling deliberately, eyes locked on his the entire time.

I let the sweetness linger on my tongue, savoring it, before pulling my finger free with a soft *pop*.

"Too bad for you, you'll *never* know the kind of surprise my mouth's really capable of, Lazzio."

His eyes flicked to my lips, and for just a split second, I saw a faint flicker of desire pass through them—barely enough to be sure, but I saw it.

That brief flash of weakness.

It lasted no more than a microsecond though.

He opened his mouth, probably to say something crude, and I couldn't help the flutter of excitement in my stomach, eager to hear what else he'd throw my way.

But of course, three soft knocks on the door interrupted him.

He stepped back, wiping his mouth with the back of his hand, but before Grace could open the door, I closed the space between us. My towering Prada heels gave me just the edge I needed, finally bringing me eye to eye with him—a rare feat against his 6'5" frame.

For once, he didn't loom over me. We were equals, if only in height.

Reaching up, I grabbed his black tie, letting my fingers skim the sleek fabric as I slowly undid it.

His dark eyes followed every move, his lips parted just enough to betray the breath he was holding.

He stayed quiet though, perfectly still.

I didn't just untie his tie. No, I played with it, letting it slip through my fingers, the cool silk brushing against my palm. It was slow—painfully, deliciously slow.

And God, his scent.

It wrapped around me, heady and intoxicating, like expensive cologne and something distinctly him. A scent that made it hard to think straight, let alone remember why I had come here in the first place.

Fuck, when had he started smelling so damn good?

When I finally tied the knot back, I tugged it snug against his throat, tightening it just a little too much. The pulse in his neck jumped, his jaw clenching as my fingers lingered for a second too long.

"Wouldn't want your enemies seeing any weakness in you," I whispered, the ghost of my breath brushing against his lips. "Or would you?"

His tongue ran over his teeth, and his lips trembled ever so slightly.

"*Sí*, Grace," he said sharply, the sudden loudness of his voice breaking the moment.

The door swung open, and Grace stepped in, her eyes snapping between us, her frown carving deeper as she tried to piece together what she'd just interrupted.

Smirking, I tugged on Lazzio's tie again, pulling him closer as my fingers teased the silk, twisting it around my wrist. My nails grazed along the collar of his dress shirt, dipping just low enough to scrape against the warm skin beneath.

The red line I left there was faint, but satisfying, especially with Grace's scowl deepening by the second.

Shifting forward, I let my chest brush lightly against his. His gaze dropped instinctively, flicking to the faint freckles scattered across my décolletage.

His breath stuttered, subtle, but telling, and it made my grin widen.

Grace cleared her throat loudly.

But Lazzio didn't move. He just stood there, silent, watching me with that tightly wound restraint that was starting to crack. Then, suddenly, his large hands gripped my wrists and pulled them away.

"Enough, Miss Whitenhouse," he said almost breathlessly.

I pouted.

Guess the fun's over.

Grace's voice wavered slightly. "Mr. Greg is here to see you, sir."

Lazzio still didn't look at her. His focus was locked on me, dark eyes tracing every inch of my face slowly.

"Let him in," he said finally.

She stepped aside, waving the man in, and I took it as my cue to strut out of the room.

My job here was done.

I'd pushed Angelo Lazzio to the edge of his control—exactly as planned.

I didn't bother looking back; I didn't need to. The heat of his gaze burned against my skin, unmistakable and furious.

No doubt he was already running through a dozen calculated ways to make me regret every teasing second of this.

Good.

Let him stew.

The man could use a lesson in loosening up, even if it killed him—or better yet, drove him mad first. Besides, I'd be lying if I said it wasn't downright delicious to leave the man who had destroyed my life smoldering like that.

James Greg entered, nearly bumping into me.

At sixty-seven, the silver in his hair and the lines on his face didn't make him look old—just more intimidating.

His suit was impeccable, his gaze even more intense, and there was a flicker of mischief in his eyes as he took me in. Like he knew my deepest, darkest secret, and couldn't wait to use it against me.

He took my hand, pressing a kiss to the top of it.

"Beautiful Jade Whitenhouse," he said smoothly. "Always a pleasure to see you. Shame it doesn't happen more often."

"The pleasure is all mine, Mr. Greg."

The playful spark in his eyes dimmed for a beat, his voice lowering to something more serious.

"I'm here to offer my condolences on Pauline Dupont," he said, softer now, but with an unsettling calm that prickled under my skin. "I heard you two were close."

My posture stiffened, the mention of Pauline's name tightening something inside me.

I forced a tight smile. "We were ... close enough, yes. Thanks for the kind words, Mr. Greg."

His eyes lingered on me for a beat too long, a flicker of something unreadable passing through them.

"I know loss can be ... complicated. But I'm sure you know how to handle it. After all, you're a strong woman, working for the explosive Angelo Lazzio."

Lazzio's dark gaze flicked to him.

"I can handle a lot more than you think, sir."

"Oh, I have no doubt about that, Miss Whitenhouse."

I excused myself with a smile that was polite but didn't quite reach my eyes, casually mentioning that I had work to finish. It was a subtle, yet clear signal that the conversation was over.

I added that I hoped to see him and his wife, Laurie, at the upcoming exhibition in two weeks, though it was a total lie.

But just as I hit the threshold, his voice stopped me.

"And I hope to see you on Friday for our Thanksgiving celebration in Aspen," he said. "Angelo's coming, after all. It'd be a shame if his precious little diamond of a COO didn't make it."

Before I could respond, Lazzio's voice slid in.

"Miss Whitenhouse has plans this weekend—"

"Yeah, I do," I cut him off. "But I can make time. I'd love to come, Mr. Greg."

If Lazzio could've shot daggers with his eyes, I'd be six feet under by now.

"Perfect, see you on Friday then."

With a nod, I spun and sauntered out, the smile still playing on my lips.

As I passed Grace's desk, her glare could've burned a hole in me.

She hissed out, "Satan."

I smirked, enjoying the fire in her eyes.

Let her burn. It only made my little victory sweeter.

CHAPTER
EIGHTEEN

"A thing is not necessarily true because a man dies for it."
— **Oscar Wilde**

Angelo

"To what do I owe this visit, Greg?" I asked, gesturing toward the cream, L-shaped couch in the corner of my office, my voice dripping with annoyance I didn't bother to hide.

He followed my lead without a second thought, settling into the seat across from me.

I sank back into the couch, the tension between us thick enough to choke on. The kind of silence that would make anyone squirm—except James Greg. He looked right at home in it, like he thrived on the discomfort.

Just then, Grace entered, balancing coffees, tea, and a tray of pastries with the deliberate clink of porcelain slicing through the oppressive air. Her eyes flicked to mine for a moment, the anger there clear as day.

She was pissed, and for the life of me, I couldn't figure out why.

Without a word, she left as quickly as she'd come.

James leaned forward, reaching for his cup.

"For my condolences, of course," he said. He took a slow sip of coffee, his eyes narrowing with faux sympathy. "I heard about your little actress, Pauline Dupont. Tragic, really. Suicide, right?" He shook his head, his lips curling just slightly. "Such a sad story."

I barely registered his words.

The memory of Jade pressed up against me just minutes ago, her body barely a breath away, her tits brushing my chest, her nails digging into my skin—it kept me fucking speechless.

Her dark eyes? *Fuck.*

They were a drug, pulling me in until the world blurred, and all that remained was her. Her body. Her voice. Every fucking inch of her.

This woman—she had gotten under my skin in ways I should've never allowed.

But damn, I hadn't been able to shake it for the past six fucking years.

"I reckon I should be the one to offer my condolences," I said, grabbing a cup and taking a long, slow sip. "You two were lovers, after all."

His smirk didn't falter, but there was a brief flicker in his eyes.

Wrath.

He set his cup down, eyes narrowing slightly as he leaned back in his chair.

"I only fucked the poor woman once. Wouldn't exactly call her that."

"Well, you won't be calling her *anything* anymore. She's gone. Gone for good."

The amusement in his eyes flickered out like a candle in the wind.

I'd clearly hit a nerve.

"Yeah," he said, rising to his feet. "Never thought a bright little thing like her would take the easy way out. Suicide's a hell of a thing."

"Guess it's a quick fix for a permanent mess."

His eyes hardened, the cocky mask slipping for a second, replaced by something darker. "Yeah. I suppose so, Lazzio."

He turned and walked to the door. As his hand hovered over the handle, he paused, glancing back at me with that smug grin that made me want to punch his ugly face.

"See you on Friday, right?"

Friday. Thanksgiving in Aspen, same predictable shit every year—Lazzios, Harpers, Gregs having a weekend getaway all together.

But I could feel it, deep in my gut.

This year wasn't going to be like the others.

James Greg wasn't here for small talk. He was playing something far uglier.

"See you on Friday, Greg."

Grace slipped into the room after three soft knocks, and I waved her in, my phone still pressed to my ear.

"È venuto nel mio ufficio con le condoglianze per Pauline. Non ci credo nemmeno per un secondo—sta tramando qualcosa," I

muttered, keeping my tone low, even though Grace wouldn't catch a word of Italian if her life depended on it.

After all these years, her fluency stopped at *buongiorno, ciao,* and *grazie.*

Vittori's laugh rumbled through the line. "Gotta hand it to him—the old bastard's still got balls."

Still seated on the couch, I watched as she hurriedly cleaned the coffee table, her movements frantic. Her brow furrowed so deeply it was practically carved into her face, and she was moving so fast she nearly dropped one of the cups.

What the hell's wrong with her today?

"*Devo andare,*" I muttered, before hanging up.

She didn't meet my eyes as she crouched to grab a spoon that had slipped from her tray.

"Grace—"

"Please, be careful, sir."

I raised a brow. "Careful?"

She didn't know a thing about the shit James Greg had stirred up, or the black cloud hanging over Pauline's death.

She couldn't.

But this wasn't about Greg walking out of my office.

No, there was something else buried in her tone—something far more personal.

Suddenly, she shook her head, like she was trying to clear something from her mind. She walked toward the door, her steps quick, as if fleeing the words she'd just spoken.

"Grace."

She stopped, her hands tightening on the tray.

After a long pause, she finally turned around.

"You're probably going to think I'm crazy, but ..." Grace paused, inhaling deeply as if the words weighed on her. "Please, be careful with Miss Whitenhouse. I've had a bad feeling about her for years. There's something ... off about her. Too ... evil."

I didn't answer right away, just furrowed my brow.

For years, I'd brushed off the tension between them as a personality clash—Grace's quiet, measured demeanor fighting against Jade's bold, relentless attitude.

But now?

Now, Grace sounded genuinely scared.

I brushed it off with a laugh. "Grace, you've been holding a grudge for six years. Let it go. She's fucking crazy, I'll give you that. But you can't deny she gets the job done."

Crazy's an understatement.

I winced, my fingers brushing over the fresh cuts on my jaw from her nails.

"It's more than that! After six years, we still don't know anything about her. She never talks about her family, her friends, or ..." She shook her head as if struggling to fit the pieces of a puzzle. "Her hobbies. She's far too ... mysterious. I feel like she's hiding something. Something dangerous, sir."

I lifted a shoulder. "Frankly, I like the way she is. She does her job. Works hard. Goes home. What's the big deal?" I got up and grabbed the tray from her hands and dropped it on my desk. "Any boss would kill to have someone like that."

I knew I'd kill to keep her by my side, whether I wanted to admit it or not.

"So, you don't believe me? I'm almost sixty, sir. Time teaches you to trust your instincts. And that girl"—she pointed at the door—"She's got the devil's mark on her."

With a bitter glance, she stormed out, slamming the door behind her.

Merda.

CHAPTER NINETEEN

"Being a woman is a terribly difficult trade since it consists principally of dealings with men."
—Joseph Conrad

Jade

"I'm *so* excited! It's been years since I've been to Aspen! I can't believe you actually tried to ditch me for this trip. You're such an asshole, Lazzio."

The jet gleamed in front of me—navy blue and crisp white, as if it had just rolled out of a billionaire's dream. Angelo Lazzio's dream, to be exact.

The crew stood in perfect formation—stewardesses in deep navy uniforms, their tight buns and forced smiles completing the look. The men were just as pristine in tailored jackets and white shirts.

Lazzio, as usual, ignored me.

He walked right past, his long stride eating up the stairs like he owned the thing—which, of course, he did. A nod to the crew here, a grunt there, and he disappeared inside without a word.

I handed my bag off to a waiting stewardess and climbed the stairs, taking the pilot's offered hand.

"I can't wait to go skiing, eat some fondue," I said, shrugging off my fur coat and tossing it onto the seat. "Hit the sauna—"

"Sit down, Miss Whitenhouse."

The command hit me, a twist of nerves and something far darker simmering under my skin.

Ah, he was pissed. And damn, I loved every second of it.

He'd called last night, trying—yet again—to convince me not to come.

Something about James Greg being dangerous.

Please.

As if I didn't know the kind of company I kept. Angelo Lazzio lecturing me about danger was like a wolf warning a sheep about the dark.

The man was a freaking murderer, after all.

But to be completely honest, I had almost bailed.

A weekend alone sounded amazing—hot bubble baths, red wine, maybe even a club or two to find someone ... fun. It had been far too long since I'd had sex, and lately, even the slightest flirtation felt like foreplay. Like the pilot standing a few feet away— blue eyes, broad shoulders.

But then I'd remembered one very important thing: Lazzio didn't want me here.

Which meant, obviously, I *had* to come.

I dropped into the plush leather seat across from him, and

his eyes locked on me, unflinching. His fingers brushed along the faint scratches on his jaw—scratches I'd left there.

I bit back a smirk.

Guess I'd underestimated how sharp my nails were.

Today, for some reason, he looked like sin wrapped in designer fabric—the kind of polished Armani perfection that made women forget their own names. Those glasses—the ones he only wore when he had a headache—made him look like he belonged on the cover of a magazine. Except no model looked like they could crush you in a bear hug—or worse—without breaking a sweat.

My gaze lingered on his arms, the fabric stretching just a little too tight over his muscles. For a second, I wondered what it'd feel like to have one wrapped around my neck—

Jesus Christ, Jade.

Pull yourself together.

The man had killed my sister.

That was Angelo Lazzio—my nemesis, my tormentor, the one who had wrecked my life.

I slouched further into the seat, forcing myself to look away.

Only a few months of celibacy, and I was already losing my damn mind.

"Let me be clear, *diavoletta,*" he said, leaning in just enough to invade my space, his eyes flicking briefly to my lips. "This flight is five fucking hours, and I don't want to hear another word out of your mouth. *Capiche*?"

Okay, Mister Dictator.

"Guess that means I shouldn't ask if you want to join the mile high club, huh?"

His expression didn't even twitch. Not even a flicker of amusement.

Instead, he shot me a dark look before grabbing his phone and burying himself in it like I didn't exist.

Well, wasn't he just a ray of sunshine?

I leaned back in my seat and crossed my legs, the leather creaking faintly beneath me.

He wanted silence? Fine. I could give him silence.

But I wasn't about to sit here bored out of my mind, either.

My eyes wandered over him again, tracing the strong lines of his jaw, the way his dark hair curled just slightly at the ends, and those damn glasses perched on his nose.

God, he looked insufferably good, which only made me want to annoy him more.

"Lazzio."

He didn't look up, but I saw the faint twitch in his jaw.

"Is that a yes or no on the mile high club? Just so we're clear."

The phone lowered slowly, and those cold, dark eyes met mine with a promise.

Not the kind that came with roses and chocolate—the kind that came with blood and bruises.

"Miss Whitenhouse." His voice was quiet, *too* quiet. "If you don't shut up, I will throw you off this plane. At thirty thousand feet."

Yep. Silence it was.

I plastered on my best fake smile and stood, making sure to drag it out just enough to irritate him.

I sauntered to the bedroom at the back of the jet, my heels clicking against the polished floor, the sound echoing in the quiet cabin.

The door shut behind me with a soft click, and I flung myself onto the oversized bed, releasing a sigh that was half frustration, half surrender.

After everything—and having to deal with him—I figured I'd earned a nap.

And if I just happened to dream about a certain someone with dark eyes and a sexy Italian accent being thrown off the plane without a parachute, well, that would be a little secret between me and my devilish subconscious.

Aspen in November? It felt like stepping into a snow globe made of fairy lights and overpriced hot cocoa.

The snow, the twinkling lights, the trees—I half expected some poor town guy to show up and sweep me off my feet. He'd beg me to leave the city and marry him, promising a cozy life in a cottage surrounded by animals. Every Christmas, we'd kiss under the mistletoe where we'd first met, with our twenty-something kids trailing behind us.

Honestly, I couldn't decide whether to laugh or swoon at the thought.

After sleeping through the whole flight—apparently, dealing with Lazzio's constant bad mood had drained me—I woke to the stewardess gently shaking my shoulder.

"We're about to land," she said softly.

I dragged myself to the restroom for a quick refresh: a touch of makeup, a swipe of gloss, and I was ready. Back at my seat, I buckled in, ignoring the weight of Lazzio's gaze drilling into the side of my face.

The jet landed smoothly, and as we stepped off, workers were already loading our luggage into a sleek black Range Rover.

Lazzio opened the rear door, giving me a look that screamed, *hurry up.*

I slid inside without a word, and he followed, immediately absorbed in his phone.

"Hello, sir. I hope you had a pleasant flight," the driver greeted warmly. He was middle-aged, bald, and had the kind of smile that could disarm even the most jaded traveler.

"Good to see you, Thomas," Lazzio muttered without looking up.

I rolled my eyes. *Asshole.*

"Hi, Thomas," I said, leaning forward with a smile and offering my hand. "I'm Jade, Mr. Lazzio's COO. Thanks for picking us up."

His handshake was firm, and he returned my smile with genuine warmth.

Unlike some people, I wasn't about to let my bad mood spill over onto everyone else.

As Thomas steered us through Aspen's snow-blanketed streets, the city glowed with lights. Couples strolled hand in hand, their laughter muffled by the snow. Kids dashed around, building lopsided snowmen.

It was all disgustingly wholesome.

"Enjoy the view," Lazzio muttered. "We won't have time for it later."

"God forbid you let me have a second of enjoyment," I shot back, folding my arms as I turned to the window. "Wouldn't want to disrupt your *schedule of doom.*"

Thomas chuckled softly from the driver's seat, his eyes briefly meeting mine in the rearview mirror. "Aspen really does shine during the snowy months. Have you been here before, Miss Jade?"

Yeah, when I was eleven, with my mom and my sister.

Best Christmas ever.

"Years ago. I almost forgot how magical it looks under all this snow."

And it really was beautiful.

For a split second, I wished time would freeze—just long enough to soak in the snow, the lights, the postcard-perfect town—before reality came crashing back, dragging me into my usual mess.

"There's something my father always used to say," Thomas remarked. "In Aspen, love either wraps you in warmth or leaves you frozen, wishing it had never touched you at all."

There it was—the classic talk about love, redemption, and tragedy.

It was almost ... adorable.

"Well," I shrugged, pulling my fur coat tighter around me. "I'm expecting neither of those. Just some skiing and a whole lot of ridiculously fattening, oily food to stuff my face for the next three days."

I hadn't had fondue in a while, so I was practically buzzing with excitement.

My mouth was watering just thinking about it.

Lazzio shot me a look.

He put his phone back in his pocket and leaned back in his seat.

"I doubt love could ever find its way into your cold heart, Miss Whitenhouse," he whispered.

The words dripped from his lips, sweet but *deadly*.

I smiled.

He wasn't wrong.

"That's what makes us equals, Lazzio. Only a heart as frozen as mine could recognize how hollow yours really is."

"Your family and the other guests are waiting, Mr. Lazzio," a butler greeted us, opening the mansion door.

With a practiced smile, he took our coats and handed us champagne.

I sipped mine, the bubbles tickling my throat, while Lazzio gave a brief nod, checking to see if I was following before striding through the grand entrance. Above, a massive chandelier hung like a jewel, casting a soft glow.

The hallways were lined with thick carpets and taxidermied animals—deer, bears, boars. Guess James Greg had a thing for hunting.

After what had felt like an eternity of over-the-top decor, two butlers opened the door to a dining room that could swallow a small village.

A long table, draped in a white cloth worth more than my rent, was adorned with an overabundance of flowers and wood decor. The spread was a feast—shrimp salad, caviar with crème fraîche, turkey with stuffing, baked and mashed potatoes, pumpkin soup, lobster mac & cheese, and foie gras. And, of course, gnocchi, arrabbiata pasta, and lasagna.

This wasn't a dinner; it was a spectacle.

Looking at all of it, I'd almost believed I'd died and gone to heaven.

Then I remembered—*hell,* I'd probably never make it that far.

"Angelo, you're here, finally!" Monica Lazzio exclaimed. His mama practically bounced in her seat, waving him over like a dog begging for attention.

The room fell silent, all eyes on us.

"Angelo, Jade," James Greg nodded, lifting his glass in a lazy toast. "Welcome. Please, take a seat and enjoy the food after your long flight."

Lazzio's hatred for him made perfect sense now. Greg was dripping with fake kindness, passive-aggressive enough to make even *me* uncomfortable.

I followed Lazzio and slid into the empty chair beside him.

Scarlett Harper, Lazzio's cousin and international pop star, sat next to me. The woman behind *Hate the Way I Live*—one of my favorite songs ever.

Her eyes were empty, her fiery red hair as untouchable as ever.

I barely glanced at her, feeling the chill rolling off her, thick enough to freeze the air around us. Not that I blamed her. Fame's a bitch, especially when you're stuck in a room full of people who call you family, yet stab you in the back the second you turn.

But I wasn't here for her.

I was here because, like some other people in this room, I wanted to see Angelo Lazzio fall. And if there was anything to learn from watching a man burn, I was ready to take notes.

I took another sip of champagne, watching as his mother's gaze sharpened on Spencer Greg, one of James' daughters.

"What about your husband, Spencer?" Monica asked, feigning interest, though there was a sharp edge to her tone—like she was probing for something to use.

"Don't know," Spencer replied, her voice cool. "Probably off avoiding this dinner."

"This dinner, or just ... you?" her twin sister, Sarah, asked with a smirk.

Laughter rippled around the table.

I leaned back in my chair, my gaze flicking between the twins.

They didn't look like twins—not even close. One had sleek blonde hair, the other fiery copper. Their features were similar, but hardly identical.

Memories flashed in my mind—the names of Lazzio's lovers.

Right, he'd slept with both of them.

I downed my champagne in one go.

The taste hit me strangely, leaving a bitter aftertaste.

Lazzio caught my eye. His expression was unreadable, detached, but I saw that flicker of amusement before he turned back to the conversation. *Asshole.*

The dinner dragged on, full of dark glances and even darker remarks.

To my surprise, I was the only one actually eating—everyone else was too busy drinking and pretending to be civil.

After dessert, the men retreated to the library for cigars, while the women slithered off to the sitting room to gossip.

Exhausted despite the plane nap, I excused myself with a fake smile, said goodnight to the ladies, and started hunting for a butler to escort me to my room.

It took nearly ten minutes to find one—standing frozen like a statue in this absurd mansion.

The man straightened. "Miss Whitenhouse, may I help?"

"Yes, I need to get to my room," I said. "The night's not getting any younger, trust me."

He gestured for me to follow.

After what felt like forever walking down a hallway of 17th-century portraits—kings, queens, and a lot of frilly collars—we stopped in front of an elevator.

He pressed the button, and the doors opened.

"You'll be staying in the *La Belle Nuit* suite. Your bags are already in your room." He hit the number fifteen on the panel and handed me a card. "Only people with this card can access the suite. Don't lose it."

I grabbed the card, fighting an eye roll, and stepped inside.

"Good night, Miss Whitenhouse."

The doors closed before I could respond.

The elevator ride was short, but it gave me enough time to brace for the over-the-top extravagance waiting for me.

When the doors opened, I walked straight into a room that screamed *royalty*—the Marie Antoinette kind.

Everything was excessive. The chandelier above looked like a Versailles knockoff, dripping with crystals that caught the light. The walls were pastel pinks and creams, with delicate gold moldings and floral designs.

It was a Parisian fairy tale ... minus the rats.

Across the room, the little salon sofa looked like it belonged in a museum—faded velvet, untouched, meant for some frail aristocrat who wouldn't dare sit on it.

But my eyes went straight to the real showstopper: the bed.

The baldaquin king-sized bed was a monster of dark wood and golden drapes. Four towering posts held thick, golden curtains, making the bed look like the perfect place to pretend I was royalty—or someone's expensive secret.

I sighed, tossing the card on the marble table before heading for the bathroom, stripping off my clothes and throwing them around the room.

In nothing but my underwear, I pushed open the bathroom door, desperate for a long, hot shower to erase the grime of the flight.

But nothing could have prepared me for what I walked into.

I screamed, the sound ripping through my chest, sharp enough to make my own heart skip a beat.

There he was.

Angelo Lazzio.

Naked.

Completely, shamelessly, *devastatingly* naked.

In the shower.

Rubbing his chiseled body with soap, the bubbles slipping over his skin.

His eyes shot wide the second my scream hit him, his hands fumbling desperately to cover up what was definitely *not* meant for anyone else to see.

Oh. My. God.

He was packing ... way more than I'd ever expected.

"Get out, Miss Whitenhouse!"

I froze, my brain scrambling to catch up with what had just happened.

But how the hell was I supposed to think straight after that?

I stood there, my eyes locked on him and his ... *big* situation. My brain was barely processing anything, but my eyes? They were glued.

I couldn't look away.

No wonder all the married women in New York practically begged to sleep with him.

Hell, even I—*almost*—wanted a taste.

"NOW!"

That snapped me out of my trance.

I looked down and realized I was standing there in nothing but my underwear. My face went up in flames as I scrambled to get out, slamming the door with a little too much force, my heart pounding like I was sprinting for my life.

What the hell is wrong with you, Jade?

I couldn't even make it through *one* night without embarrassing myself.

I yanked on my jumpsuit, practically ripping it as I stormed out to the balcony.

Throwing open the windows, I let the cold winter air slap me in the face.

It didn't calm me, but at least it distracted me from the image of his naked body scorching my mind.

CHAPTER TWENTY

"I want bad girls to win."
— **Mark Strand**

Jade

"What the fuck are you doing in my room, *diavoletta*?"

There were two ways to handle this.

I could demand answers, throw a fit, and pin this disaster on James Greg—the meddling, unbearable bastard behind it all.

Or, and this was *far* more entertaining, I could make Angelo Lazzio wish he'd stayed naked in that shower.

My revenge would be a slow burn.

I'd make him fall for me, and consume him with obsession until he couldn't tell where desire ended and madness began.

Then, once I had him exactly where I wanted, I'd tear his

world apart—just like he'd done to my sister, but with more exquisite cruelty.

My eyes drifted over him—barefoot, gray pajama pants hanging low on his hips, a white T-shirt clinging to his chest. His damp hair framed his face, water droplets tracing the sharp angles of his jaw and neck.

He looked like sin carved from marble—Abercrombie gone rogue.

"Well," I drawled, letting my gaze linger, "you turned down my mile high club offer, so I figured *La Belle Nuit* might catch your attention. Most men don't say no to a wild night with me, Lazzio. So, what is it? Playing hard to get?"

"Why would I play hard to get when you're already so difficult to want, Miss Whitenhouse?"

What a liar.

I pouted, pointing to the obvious bulge in his pants. "You might want to tell him that, because he looks *very* interested right now."

He glanced down, swore, then glared at me. "Jade, I'm seconds away from throwing you out the fucking window. Out. Now."

I tilted my head. "You seem stressed. Maybe you should've stayed in the shower longer. Let the bubbles work their magic."

"Get. Out."

That rough, commanding voice—the way he had bitten out my name—sent heat curling between my legs. Almost made me want to drop to my knees and ...

Focus, Jade.

I sighed dramatically, sprawling on the bed like a cat claiming the best spot in the sun.

"You're the one in *my* room, Angelo," I said, dragging his name out just to irritate him. "So why don't *you* leave? I'm sure there's no shortage of women desperate for a taste of Mr. Stick-Up-My-Ass. Though, let's be real, you've probably worked through half of them already—"

"Jade!" he barked, his voice a mix of rage and ... guarded desire.

A delightful cocktail of both.

For a moment, I swore I saw a vein twitch in his temple.

God, he was so easy to rile up—it was almost unfair.

"Relax, Lazzio. The butler probably gave you the wrong room." I shrugged, sinking deeper into the bed. "You could call him and throw a fit, or, you know, just stay and enjoy the view. I am pretty irresistible, after all. I'll try not to break you ... too badly."

His scowl deepened, and I had to bite back a laugh.

This was just too easy.

He grabbed the phone, dialing who-knows-who, while I stretched like a lazy cat, enjoying the show. I grabbed my bag, made my way to the bathroom, and locked the door behind me.

As I peeled off my clothes, I couldn't stop the image of Lazzio's body—those muscles, that *thickness*—creeping into my mind.

Dammit, Jade!

I tried to focus on the water, but all I could think about was him.

I was in *big* trouble.

Three days of this? Oh, hell.

When I stepped out of the shower, towel wrapped around me, hair braided, I was relieved to find the room blissfully empty.

Thank God. No sign of my boss with the permanent stick up his ass.

Smiling to myself, I let the towel drop without a care in the world, pulling out my black velvet nightdress—the one that barely grazed my thighs.

I slipped it on and collapsed onto the bed, letting the tension of the night finally slip away.

I slept like the dead until the sunlight barged in through the curtains I'd completely forgotten to close.

Groaning, I dragged myself out of bed, still half asleep, and stumbled across the suite. I made my way past the sofas to pull the curtains shut and—

What the actual hell?

There was Lazzio, passed out on the world's tiniest sofa, his ridiculously long legs dangling off the edge like a broken mannequin. His mouth was slightly open, and even unconscious, his face had that trademark scowl.

Who frowns in their sleep?

Wait.

Creepy, overbearing asshole!

Without a second thought, I marched over and pinched his arm hard, nails digging in with zero mercy.

"Ouch!" He shot upright, wincing, rubbing at the spot where I'd just assaulted him. His eyes snapped open, the shadows under them showing how little sleep he'd had. "Are you fucking insane?"

"Insane? Insane is *you* sleeping in my room like some creepy-ass stalker!"

His hair was a tangled mess, and for some irritating reason, he still looked disgustingly good, even like that.

He groaned. "*Dio mio.* There were no fucking extra rooms. The west wing's under construction. So I ended up here. On this"—he made a disgusted gesture toward the tiny, pathetic excuse for a sofa—"*furniture* they somehow managed to shove into this place. Trust me, Miss Whitenhouse, this was the last place I wanted to crash."

I jabbed a finger at him. "First choice or not, how about a little heads-up? You know, knock-knock, 'Hey, I'm crashing here for the night, hope you don't mind my snoring?'"

His jaw locked as he stood, towering over me, like he was trying to intimidate me.

Honestly, it only worked because he was ridiculously tall.

"I don't fucking snore."

"Yeah, yeah, sure. Keep telling yourself that, big guy."

Before he could come back with something even more infuriating, the phone on the nightstand rang. I took that as my cue to escape to the bathroom, leaving him to stew in his own frustration.

I needed to get ready for the day—and away from all that testosterone and that *morning wood* situation his gray pants were doing absolutely nothing to hide.

If anything, they had made it deliciously worse.

In typical Greg fashion, the breakfast buffet was a feast of indulgence—French pastries, Italian coffees, and American classics. My bottomless morning appetite was thrilled.

I worked the room, playing the effortlessly chic guest while feigning interest in the dull conversations around me. Everyone was dressed like they were heading to a gala at nine a.m.

I fit in perfectly, of course, in my plaid vintage Chanel skirt, Le Temps des Cerises jumpsuit, sheer tights, and Prada boots. My hair cascaded in sleek waves, makeup glowy, matching the fake festivity.

To my relief, Angelo Lazzio was nowhere to be seen.

"*Dio mio*, Jade, you look ravishing," Monica Lazzio said, kissing my cheeks before pointing to the seat next to her. "I can't believe someone like you is wasting her time with my son. You should be on runways, in commercials—you're every man and woman's fantasy, *dolcezza*."

I smiled.

Monica was surprisingly kind—a rare thing in this world. Despite her occasional superiority, she'd always been gracious to me.

"Flattered, Monica, but I think my talents lie elsewhere."

Like tormenting your son for fun.

She laughed warmly. "Always modest. You must come shopping with me this afternoon. I'll find you something spectacular."

Before I could respond, she added, "Then we'll hit the spa. I can't imagine a better afternoon. We could use some pampering, don't you think?"

Perfect.

Every piece of the puzzle was falling into place. I had everything I needed to make my revenge sting—everything that would tear him down, piece by piece.

The proof? Hidden away, locked tight in my little cage of secrets. Every bill, every contract, every security camera video. I had it all—his empire, the very foundation of his existence, ready to crumble into dust.

But that was just the icing on the cake.

No, I needed more.

Something deeper.

I needed to sink my claws into something so personal it would destroy him from the inside out. Something that would leave him a hollow shell of the man he thought he was.

And who better to spill that truth than his mother? The

woman who couldn't keep a secret if her life depended on it. She was like a child with a candy bar—always ready to drop whatever juicy tidbit she thought was harmless.

His empire might crumble, but his soul?

That would shatter into a thousand pieces, and I'd be the one to grind them into dust.

No redemption. No fucking escape.

"I would love to, Monica."

CHAPTER
TWENTY-ONE

"You not only are hunted by others, you unknowingly hunt yourself."
— **Dejan Stojanović**

Angelo

I had known she was going to drive me insane on this trip.

Yet every damn time her pretty mouth had pouted, whatever fight I'd had left drained right out of me.

Every. Single. Time.

When she was near, all I could do was cling to the last threads of my control—fighting the demons clawing at me, barely resisting the urge to shut her up, to make her choke on every venom-soaked word ... or shove her to her knees and fill that wicked mouth and see those sharp eyes soften, surrendering completely to me.

And now, the little devil had seen me naked.

When her eyes had locked on me—wide with admiration and fucking lust—I'd almost lost it.

I was *this* close to letting go and taking her, after years of fighting it.

Maybe I should've taken her up on that ridiculous mile high club offer after all.

As much as it killed me to admit, she was the perfect distraction from the rage clawing at me, begging to tear Greg apart right here, right now.

I brought the cigar to my lips as we sat in his library, the black leather couch surrounded by shelves of books and trophies.

My father sat across from me, glaring.

He was pissed. Had wanted me to deal with Greg yesterday.

But I was patient. My revenge was slow—something far more satisfying than just pulling a trigger.

Kilian Greg, Spencer's husband, was slouched next to my father, still drunk from last night. The guy had probably skipped dinner to gamble away his money at the casino. Addict. I almost felt sorry for him—but some messes didn't clean up easily.

"What about a hunt tonight?" Greg said, smoke curling from his cigar. "Perfect weather to track boars or bears. Something that might actually put up a fight."

The words left his mouth, but all I could hear was the blood rushing in my ears.

I knew he was talking about me. The bastard probably thought I'd given up on punishing him—not just for stealing from me, but for the trouble of having the actress' blood on my hands.

Hunting didn't sound good, especially with him.

My hands itched—not for a rifle, but for the look of terror in Greg's eyes as I tore his life apart, piece by fucking piece.

"I'm down," Lucius Harper said, stretching and leaving.

The others trailed behind, too lazy for the hunt.

It'd be just me, Greg, and Harper. My father bailed without a word.

Now it was just the two of us, the room thick with cigar smoke and barely contained hate.

"She was a good fuck," Greg finally said, like it meant nothing. "Got too clingy, though. You'd think a woman her age would act her damn years. Still, you killing her? That shit's been bugging me."

There it fucking was.

I took a slow drag, letting the smoke burn in my lungs before exhaling toward him. "Ah, my bad."

Why stop there?

"If it can make you feel worse," I said, leaning forward just enough, "she was crying for you right before I put a bullet here." I tapped my forehead.

He scoffed. "Poor girl."

But the way his jaw tightened? That crack in his mask? I saw it.

He wasn't as unaffected as he wanted me to believe.

It almost made me smile.

Almost.

I leaned back, letting the cigar burn between my fingers.

"Should've kept her in line. Might've saved her life."

He leaned forward just a fraction, eyes narrowing. "And what's gonna save yours?"

I let my smirk deepen. "Nothing, Greg. Just like nothing's fucking saving yours."

I extinguished the cigar with a deliberate twist, the embers fizzling out like the last shreds of mercy I'd ever had.

Rising, I towered over him, fists clenched tight—like I was holding back something far worse.

I didn't spare him a glance as I walked out, but the words still burned my throat.

I'd tear him apart, piece by fucking piece.

And when I was done, he'd beg for death to take him—because it would be the only mercy left.

CHAPTER
TWENTY-TWO

"Man is not what he thinks he is, he is what he hides."
— **André Malraux**

Jade

I sighed, feeling like I'd just completed a marathon in heels. My feet were screaming, my back drenched from hours of parade-walking through luxury stores with velvet ropes at the entrances.

We'd tried on enough outfits to open a boutique, and my arms were about to fall off from hauling all the bags.

Don't get me wrong, I love a new wardrobe, but Monica Lazzio?

A shopping machine.

Almost sixty, and still outpacing me like she's training for the Olympics.

"After all that, we definitely deserve some coffee. Don't you agree, *dolcezza*?"

I slumped into my seat, feeling like I'd been hit by a truck.

The butler handed me my caramel macchiato, and when it hit my lips, I almost moaned loud enough for the whole mansion to hear.

"Definitely," I muttered, clutching the warm cup.

Forget the bags—this was the real treasure of the day.

"You know, after all these years working for Angelo, I still can't figure out why you two never got together."

I almost spat my drink out, coughing like I was choking on air, blindsided by her bluntness.

Well, Monica, maybe because your son is the reason I'm hollow inside, and I'm still working for him just to get my revenge.

"What do you mean?"

She gave a little laugh, adding sugar to her coffee, her spoon spinning like she was stirring up a magic potion. "You know exactly what I mean, *dolcezza*. You two would make a great pair. You're exactly the woman he needs. Someone who won't kiss his ass, and can keep him on his toes."

I snorted. "Monica, I really like you, I do, but if I were dating a man like your son, I'd end up in prison or a psych ward. Just working for him is more energy than I can give."

That, and maybe the knife I'll eventually stick in his heart.

She shook her head, eyes narrowing as if she saw something I didn't. "You don't see Angelo for what he really is. Under all that brooding mess, he's a good man," she sighed, almost fondly. "Life forced him to become heartless at a very young age."

And there it was.

Come on, Monica. Tell me your son's darkest secret.

I leaned in slightly. "What do you mean, Monica?"

For a moment, I saw hesitation in her eyes—a storm of doubt, like she wasn't sure she could trust me. But it faded just as quickly.

"No, I shouldn't ..." she trailed off, shaking her head, clearly torn.

Shit.

I slid my hand over hers. "What is it? You're freaking me out."

She sighed, breath shaking.

Her hands trembled so badly that she had to set her coffee cup down with a soft clink. Her eyes scanned the room, checking for anyone listening.

The other women? Gone. Off to the spa or lunch.

It was just her and me now—alone.

The perfect setup for something I was ready to hear.

"Okay," she whispered, voice so low I had to strain to catch it. "I trust you, Jade."

Big mistake.

I nodded slowly.

"When Angelo turned nine, Carlos and I planned a surprise for him. A weekend in the Hamptons—just the three of us."

She swallowed, unable to meet my gaze.

"We wanted him to have our full attention for three days—no interruptions, no work. We locked up our phones, stashed them in the safe. It was supposed to be perfect. Mid-August, warm, sunny. We rented a private house with its own beach." She sighed, her voice softening. "It was beautiful, Jade. A weekend that was supposed to make everything right."

"That sounds like a wonderful birthday surprise."

She nodded, lips pressed tightly together. "It was. We ate, laughed, painted together. But on the last day, Angelo wanted to stay on the beach. He was so content, building sandcastles, lost in his little world." She stopped herself, and the smile faded. "Everything happened so fast, Jade ..."

I leaned in, instinctively holding my breath.

A few seconds ticked by, Monica sitting there like she

was carrying the weight of the world in her hands. Her lips were pressed together so tightly, I thought they might disappear.

For a split second, my cold little heart started to ache for her.

But I snapped myself out of it, quick.

"Carlos and I decided to go for a swim. Just a few minutes. Nothing too long," she said, her breath unsteady. "We thought it would be fine. It wasn't like we were leaving him alone. He was just playing, building his castles by the water. We were right there—just a few hundred feet away. But when we came back ..."

She paused, swallowing hard, as if trying to force the words out.

I could see the pain flash across her face.

"When we came back ..." Her voice dropped to a whisper, barely audible. "He was gone."

"Gone?"

Monica nodded, eyes unfocused. "We searched *everywhere*, Jade. We screamed his name. We ran up and down the beach, asking everyone if they'd seen him. But no one had. And then, after what felt like forever, we called the police. The moment we reported it, I knew—it wasn't just some prank. No. It was too quiet, too calculated. He'd been taken."

Nothing on my bingo card of Angelo Lazzio's secrets could have prepared me for this.

Stolen money? Yeah, maybe.

Hooked up with a teacher? Sure.

But *kidnapped*?

"Who took him, Monica?"

Her eyes flickered to mine. "That's the thing, Jade. We never found out. They took him, and we spent days in hell—no ransom, no contact. Just gone. For fourteen days. Then, one day, we got a call. A man on the other end told us Angelo was safe ... but he was different. Changed."

She wiped her eyes quickly, trying to hide the tears that had fallen.

"When we finally got him back, he was never the same. He was scared, withdrawn, haunted by things I could never understand. And that's when Carlos started changing too. The people who took him, Jade—they didn't just take Angelo. They took something else from all of us. Our happiness."

Angelo Lazzio—kidnapped.

The man who controlled *everything*, who crushed anyone who dared to cross him, had once been a helpless child, taken without a trace.

How the hell did that fit into the puzzle of who he was now?

I couldn't speak.

My brain was racing, but my mouth? Useless. Stuck in neutral, unable to process the bomb she'd just dropped.

Monica sniffed. "You know ... he never—he never talked about what happened during those fourteen days. Not once. Not to me, not to Carlos, not even to the therapists we forced him to see. All he ever said was that he was fine. That he didn't want to talk about it."

He'd never told anyone?

Why?

Monica reached into her purse, fumbling as she pulled out a tissue and wiped her eyes. "The only thing left from that time are the scars on his back. Just a few, but ... deep. And he's never explained how he got them. Never."

Scars.

My throat tightened.

Angelo Lazzio, the untouchable kingpin, carrying scars no one dared to ask about.

For a moment, I just stared at her.

The guilt she must carry as a mother—it had to be crushing. To have looked away for just a few minutes and lost her son. To have spent those fourteen days picturing every unthinkable horror, only to get him back as a silent, shattered version of the boy she'd known.

And just like that, Monica Lazzio had given me exactly what I needed—served it up on a silver platter.

The perfect way to shatter Angelo Lazzio.

"You're not coming. End of discussion."

I rolled my eyes, crossing my legs as the mattress dipped under me.

He yanked off his shirt, and my irritation took a quick detour south. My gaze, uninvited, traced the sharp lines of his chest, those unfairly sculpted abs, and the faint trail of dark hair leading down into the waistband of his double-lined pants.

Without a word, he gestured toward the bed.

I handed him his jumper, but not before inhaling it deeply. "Mmm," I hummed, stepping closer.

His eyes narrowed, dark and burning, as he snatched the fabric from my hands. He slipped it on, the movement quick, but his eyes still locked with mine.

"I promise I won't annoy you," I said, tilting my head, lips curling into a sweet, innocent smile. "Not a word, not a peep. I'll be like your shadow."

He sighed, grabbing a belt and threading it through the

loops of his pants. That belt buckle gleamed—fuck, it would definitely haunt my dreams tonight.

"Hunting isn't a safe space for a woman like you, Miss Whitenhouse. I wouldn't want your Louboutins to get dirty."

I took a step toward him, fingers tangling in his hair as I yanked his head back.

His breath caught for a second.

"Oh, I can get dirty," I whispered, my thumb tracing the line of his jaw. My fingers slid down, cupping his face as I leaned in, lips grazing the shell of his ear. "Wanna find out?"

He shoved me back hard, and I ended up sprawled across the bed, bouncing once like a ragdoll.

I couldn't help it. I laughed.

A deep, breathless chuckle that came straight from the dark, twisted part of me.

He glared down at me. "You're seriously twisted."

You know what?

I *was* feeling twisted, and in a reckless mood, and those two never really got together—never really *fit* together—without me itching to play with fire.

"Oh, boss," I whispered, slowly crawling forward. "I think what's really missing in your life is a bit of fun. A little sinful adventure."

I yanked the hem of my jumper up, the fabric dragging over my skin as I felt his eyes scorch me. The sparkly emerald bra clung to my chest—tight, teasing, daring him to look closer.

I watched his jaw tighten, that small twitch of irritation in his eyes.

Good.

My boots? Gone in an instant, tossed aside like they were nothing.

The skirt? Yeah, that hit the floor as I stood, leaving me in nothing but black lace stockings and a matching green thong.

I turned my back to him, arching just enough to give him a full, taunting view of the tattoo crawling across my spine—the one I knew he hated.

"You know, Lazzio," I muttered, "You're too predictable. Always trying to be in control. But you wanna know what I think? I think you need to let go. Just a little. I think it's time someone showed you what it feels like to get *really* dirty."

I bent forward, watching his eyes follow every move, every inch of me, as I hooked my thumbs into one of my stockings.

Slowly, I slid it down, making sure to drag it over my skin.

When that one hit the floor, I did the same with the other.

Straightening up, I met his stare.

Dark eyes, furrowed brows, and the unmistakable heat creeping across his skin—whether he wanted to admit it or not, Angelo Lazzio was turned on.

With a wicked smile, I slid the bra off, tossing it aside carelessly, and it fluttered to the floor. My chest was bare now, nipples hard, practically aching for attention.

His eyes were glued to them, not moving an inch.

"What do you think? Still think I can't *come*?"

I couldn't suppress the smug smile creeping up as his gaze flickered between my chest and my eyes, caught in the pull of both.

Then he moved closer.

I settled back onto the bed, supporting myself with my arms as I opened my legs to let him in. He didn't hesitate, following me as I slowly sank onto the covers, my bare back pressing into them, arms resting at my sides.

To my surprise, he leaned down, each of his fists planted beside my head as he hovered above me, his face inches from mine.

"You can come, Miss Whitenhouse," he murmured, his hot breath making my lips tingle. I couldn't resist licking them, tasting the wrath in his words. "But if I hear one fucking word from you, I'll dig a hole in the woods and bury you in it."

I smiled. "Is that a promise?"

His breath danced across my skin before his lips brushed against my ear.

I felt his hand curl around my throat, his fingers digging into my flesh.

"*Sí, diavoletta*. And just so you know ..." He moved even closer, my tits now pressed against his chest.

For a split second, I was consumed by the heat of him—until I noticed the fabric of his jumper separating our skin. It suddenly pissed me off. I wanted to feel his naked chest pressed to mine.

Honey and dark wood draped in silk sheets.

"I'm not just your fucking boss, Miss Whitenhouse," he said slowly, his hand tightening around my throat. "I'm a man first—and you'd do well to remember that before you strip in front of me. Next time, I won't hesitate to take you."

With that, as if his skin were burning, he released my throat roughly, causing me to bounce on the bed slightly.

He grabbed his coat and stormed out the door before I had a chance to blink, let alone process what the hell had just happened.

CHAPTER TWENTY-THREE

"Don't wait to be hunted to hide, that was always my motto."
— **Samuel Beckett**

Angelo

I checked my hunting rifle, making sure it was loaded before slinging the strap over my shoulder. The deeper we trudged into the snowy forest, the thicker the sludge of mud and snow clung to our boots, leaving a messy trail behind us—like some fucked-up version of Hansel and Gretel.

It was cold. Too fucking cold.

I glanced back to make sure Jade wasn't turning into an ice sculpture, but she seemed fine. Silent, as promised, wrapped up in a fur-lined coat, thick pants, and chunky winter boots. Winter boots—an actual first.

She wasn't teetering around in heels, for once.

I shook my head, a bitter laugh threatening.

Maybe I should just leave her out here to freeze. It'd make my life easier, especially after that little stunt she pulled earlier—stripping right in front of me, showing off the most perfect tits I'd ever fucking seen.

The image of her nipples—

"*Cazzo*," I muttered, shoving a branch out of my way harder than necessary.

Snow tumbled from the tree, crashing to the ground like the forest itself was mocking me.

My jaw tightened as I moved forward, the cold gnawing at my skin with every step.

Another branch snapped under my grip—this one done with intention.

Greg and I had split up for the hunt—him and Harper off one direction, while I was stuck with Miss Little Nudist tagging behind.

I knew exactly where this was headed. Greg thought it was a test of who was the better hunter, but he didn't fucking get it—I wasn't out here to hunt animals.

Suddenly, a low, deep grunt split the air, freezing every muscle in my body.

Jade bumped into my back, stumbling slightly.

"Ouch!" she hissed.

"Shh," I whispered, my hand shooting up to silence her.

I dropped to the ground, grabbing her arm and dragging us both behind a thick wall of branches.

Our bodies collided, the heat of her so close it almost shattered my focus.

Every muscle in my body fucking trembled, like it always had when she was near—when her touch brushed against me, even just for a second. I couldn't fucking stop it. I couldn't control how she twisted me up, how her mere presence undid everything in me.

I pressed a finger to my lips, my eyes darting through the trees.

That sound wasn't the wind.

We weren't alone.

Then, a rifle crack—three quick shots that echoed through the woods, too fucking close.

I clenched my jaw, my brows pulling into a deep scowl.

"Lazzio—"

"Shut the fuck up," I muttered, my grip tightening on the rifle, eyes slicing through the trees.

The silence pressed in around us, heavy, suffocating, broken only by our unsteady breathing. She edged closer, her body brushing against mine, her breath warm against my neck as she tried to figure out what had my attention.

Then it came—a guttural, ear-splitting grunt that cleaved through the stillness.

My head snapped up, and there it was—a massive boar, eyes glowing red, charging straight at me like it had been sent by hell itself.

"Oh my God, Lazzio!" Jade screamed, spinning to run.

Her foot caught a branch, sending her face-first into the snow.

For one goddamn second, my focus wavered, watching her fall like a fucking idiot. But then the boar shrieked, a high-pitched wail that sent a jolt through my skull.

I didn't think.

I raised the rifle and fired.

The first shot hit its side, blood splattering across the snow.

The second tore through its neck. It staggered, but kept charging.

The third shot dropped it, its massive body skidding across the bloodstained snow, leaving a red streak as it slid to a stop inches from me.

The stench of blood and wet fur filled the air as I lowered the rifle.

I stared at the beast, steam rising off its blood-soaked body like it was still alive—still fucking raging.

"Well, that was fucking close," I muttered, smacking the snow off my pants.

I turned, and—

Che cazzo.

You've got to be fucking kidding me.

Jade was still facedown in the snow, sprawled out like some moron trying to make a snow angel. Arms wide, legs splayed, completely frozen.

I let out a breath through gritted teeth, glaring at her limp form.

"Miss Whitenhouse now is not the time to play fucking dead. Get up."

Nothing.

No twitch, no smart-ass comment—just dead weight in the snow.

"You better be out cold, Jade, because if you're not, I swear to God—"

Still nothing.

"I said, *now*, Jade!"

Silence.

Thick, gut-twisting silence, the kind that settles in your chest and squeezes.

No fucking way.

She knocked herself out. Had to.

I dragged a hand down my face, fighting the urge to lose it.

This is what I got for bringing Miss Little Nudist into the damn woods.

Just my fucking luck.

I knew it. I knew she should've stayed back, lounging at the spa or sipping overpriced drinks somewhere warm like the high-maintenance princess she was.

But no—here we were.

Her, unconscious in the snow. Me, stuck babysitting.

I dropped to my knees beside her, gripping her shoulders. I gave her a firm shake, not hard—just enough to jolt her—but nothing.

No movement.

My throat tightened.

"Jade," I tried again, as I brushed the snow off her face.

Still nothing.

My stomach churned, my pulse hammering in my ears as I turned her over, hands shaking like I'd lost control of them. Her head flopped back, and that's when I saw it.

Blood.

"Fuck!"

A dark, wet streak ran down her forehead, sharp against her pale skin.

"Jade!" I barked, shaking her harder this time, panic clawing up my throat. Her lips twitched, but no sound came out.

My chest tightened, breath coming short as I leaned in close.

She was breathing. *Barely.*

"Goddamn it," I hissed, brushing her cheek with my knuckles, fingers trembling. "Wake up, Miss Whitenhouse!"

Her body was limp, dead weight, when I slid my arm under her knees and another behind her back. Pulling her to me, her head dropped against my shoulder, blood soaking into my collar, smearing hot and wet against my neck.

Her skin was freezing.

"Stay with me, Jade! You don't get to fucking check out on me. Not here. Not like this."

I tore through the forest like a madman, branches clawing at my face, snow dragging at my boots. The wolves were howling somewhere out there, their cries slicing through the night.

And then there were the gunshots—closer, louder, like thunder in the still air.

Greg.

A chill shot down my spine that had nothing to do with the freezing cold. That bastard was getting closer, and I felt it in my gut—the kind of certainty you couldn't ignore.

I wasn't the hunter anymore.

I was the fucking prey.

"*Cazzo*," I muttered, tripping over a buried root.

I barely kept us upright, my grip on her tightening like she might slip right out of my arms. Her face was still pressed to my neck.

"Stay with me, Miss Whitenhouse," I hissed.

She felt heavier with every step.

Blood was still seeping from the gash on her head, soaking into my shirt, warm and slick against my skin.

The snow wasn't helping—it clawed at my boots, dragging me down. Branches slapped at my arms and face, but I didn't give a fuck.

Let the forest take its best fucking shot—I wasn't stopping.

"Breathe, *amore*," I whispered, my voice rough, cracking. "Keep breathing, goddamn it. Don't make me drag your stubborn ass all the way back for nothing!"

Gunshots ripped through the trees again, closer this time.

I stumbled, and nearly went down, but forced myself forward, gripping her tighter.

Her head lolled against my shoulder.

"Shit," I muttered, pressing my lips to her forehead. "*Mi dispiace*. I promise we're almost there." My voice cracked, but I didn't stop, eyes locked on the faint glow of the hunting lodge ahead.

Then it came.

A gunshot, loud and vicious, ripped through the air behind me.

Pain. A brutal, fiery explosion to my leg.

It hit like a sledgehammer—white-hot, searing, and savage—driving me straight to my knees.

I collapsed, my leg giving way beneath me, the force of her weight dragging me down. The freezing snow bit into my skin as I slammed into the ground, a cold, sharp contrast to the burning agony ripping through my body.

My vision blurred, the world spinning. My breath came out in short, jagged gasps, the cold air stinging my lungs.

The lights of the lodge blurred, dimming behind the edges of my vision.

I sucked in a ragged breath, my arms locking tighter around her.

"No. No fucking way," I groaned, forcing my head up, ignoring the searing burn radiating through me.

We were getting there.

Or I was dying here with her in my arms.

CHAPTER TWENTY-FOUR

"All you need is love. But a little chocolate now and then doesn't hurt."
— **Charles M. Schulz**

Jade

The ground beneath me shook like I was teetering on the edge of a cliff, just a step away from plummeting into something far worse than death.

The darkness wasn't the usual kind you get when you shut your eyes. It was worse—a thick fog of bad decisions, and something far too sinister.

The air felt like cement, crushing my chest, suffocating me with each breath. My head spun as if I'd been drinking whiskey straight from the bottle. The whispers—*God*, the whispers—

clawed at my mind, twisted and dark, as if they knew every fear I ever had, and relished each one.

They didn't even try to hide the poison in their voices.

I twisted my head, desperate to escape this nightmare, but it was like running in quicksand—every movement a struggle. The fog, thick as tar, pressed in on me, and I could feel eyes on me, unseen, but so damn present.

Then, out of nowhere, something warm pressed against my forehead, a stark contrast to the cold gnawing at my bones.

I froze.

My heart slammed in my chest.

As I sank deeper into the abyss, my breath turning shallow and desperate, I heard five rough words whispered into my ear.

"*Sei al sicuro ora, amore.*"

Then everything went dark—nothing but darkness, as if the world itself had decided to swallow me whole.

I cracked my eyes open, surprised at how heavy they felt. The faint sunlight crept in, brushing against my skin.

Those damn curtains again?

What's the point of being a billionaire if you can't even splurge on proper blackout curtains, James stupid Greg?

I tried to sit up, but pain shot through my head—high and brutal. I winced, bringing my hand to my forehead, and immediately noticed the bandage wrapped around it.

My eyes scanned the room, expecting *La Belle Nuit*'s usual over-the-top Marie Antoinette decor, but instead, I was met with ... something else.

The room was spacious, modern, with dark hues and deep green accents, and creamy, fluffy covers. Matte black tiles lined the floor, and the walls were adorned with a huge abstract painting by Helen Frankenthaler—green, velvety tones that matched the oppressive mood in the room.

Where the hell was I?

My eyes flicked to the nightstand beside me, where my phone sat next to a glass of orange juice, a cold bottle of Fiji water, two aspirins, and—oh, a vanilla cookie topped with blueberry buttercream frosting from Bagels & Jo.

My mouth felt dry as hell, like I'd been chewing on cotton. I grabbed the bottle of water and slammed it back in one go, barely giving myself a second to breathe. My head throbbed, like a drumbeat behind my eyes. I pressed my hand to my forehead, hoping the aspirin would take the edge off.

The orange juice was calling my name, so I took a few sips, the sweet, fresh taste sliding down my throat, hitting just right.

Then, I grabbed the note.

Drink.

I frowned, recognizing Lazzio's handwriting.

Then it hit me.

I was in Lazzio's apartment. In his bed. His scent hit me, as if to confirm my theory, and I couldn't help but pull the covers tighter, inhaling deeply.

Yep, unmistakably his. No question about it.

Wait.

I looked down at my body, a flash of panic hitting me. Please tell me we didn't ...

But nope, still in my green thong, no bra, and a long, black Fendi T-shirt—definitely his.

I grabbed the cookie and took a bite, hoping the sweetness would calm my headache and the weird disappointment gnawing at me—that I hadn't had sex with Lazzio.

Okay, no. No! I was seriously lying to myself.

Why the hell would I be disappointed about not having sex with that murderous asshole?

That must be this damn headache talking.

I touched the bandage around my head again, frowning.

What had happened to me?

A knock on the door broke the thoughts swirling in my mind.

I put the cookie down and scrambled to pull the covers up to my chin, pretending to be asleep, hoping my terrible acting skills would save me. My heart was practically trying to escape my throat.

The door creaked open, footsteps drawing closer. The bed dipped next to me, and I tensed, hoping he'd just leave.

But no, of course not.

A warm hand brushed my cheek, sending a shiver down my legs.

"Jade?"

I stayed perfectly still, eyes closed, trying to make my breathing sound like a sleep-deprived dying animal.

"I know you're awake, Jade," he said, as I felt the cool touch of his finger at the corner of my lips. "You've got a bit of frosting right here."

Asshole.

I opened my mouth and bit his finger, hard.

He laughed, the sound dark and amused, and it made my pulse skip a beat.

I finally opened my eyes.

To say he looked like shit was an understatement. His face was a mess of cuts and bruises; his eyes were so swollen I wasn't sure how he could even see. And his hair—well, let's just say he looked like he'd been dragged through a storm.

There was a roughness to him now, like he'd been through hell and had barely made it out alive. But despite all of that ... he was still so freaking handsome, heat bloomed low in my stomach.

I thought I might pass out again.

Six years of working with him, and I had never fully admitted what he was—a walking, breathing, hot magnet.

And now? I couldn't look away, and honestly, I didn't even want to.

"There you are," he said, his voice rough and gravelly, but there was something soft in his eyes—relief, maybe.

Or maybe I was just imagining it.

I swallowed hard. "What happened?"

He sighed and brushed his hand over my cheek. "How are you feeling?"

I straightened up. "Amazing. I could run a marathon."

His lips twisted. "Little liar," he murmured, his voice rough.

Butterflies spread between my legs.

"What happened to your face, Lazzio?" I asked, my hands reaching up to grab his face, my fingers grazing over the cuts. "You look—"

"Magnificent?" he interrupted, a cocky grin pulling at his lips.

I rolled my eyes, trying to hold back a smile. "You look like shit."

He chuckled darkly. "Ah, my mistake, Miss Whitenhouse."

I reached for my orange juice, the glass cool in my hand, more to distract myself than to actually drink it. His gaze hadn't left me, fixed and heavy, like he was studying me.

I turned my head toward the window, needing to escape that stare.

The NYC skyline stared back, all glitter and steel.

My brows furrowed.

"Wait," I started, still looking out. "Weren't we just in Aspen?"

He sighed. "What do you remember?"

I closed my eyes, searching through the chaos in my head. My skull throbbed in response, like my brain itself was protesting the effort.

Please, aspirin, work your magic.

Flashes came back in fragments, scattered and blurry.

Then one hit me so vividly I opened my eyes.

The suite came back to me in flashes—dim lights, plush carpet, and ... him.

I'd stripped right in front of him, the cool air prickling my nipples, his body pressing into mine like he couldn't help himself. His hand had circled my throat, and my heart had pounded against his palm, not from fear but something else *entirely*.

And then I'd begged him—actually begged—to take me hunting.

What the hell had I been thinking?

That's where my memory fuzzed out, like a scratched DVD skipping over the good parts. Everything after that? Gone.

"I remember ... the forest. Snow. That's it."

He nodded slowly. "We were hunting. A boar charged us. You panicked, fell, and hit your head on a rock hidden under the snow."

I stared at him, stunned. "A boar?"

"Big one. Ugly bastard."

"That's ... humiliating."

He smirked. "You're lucky I was there to carry your dramatic ass back to safety."

"Dramatic?" I snapped, gripping the glass tighter. "I hit my head on *a rock*, Angelo."

His name left my lips, unfamiliar, yet dangerously intimate.

I never called him by his name—too personal, too much of a temptation. But now, the way it slid off my tongue, making my lips ache for more, I couldn't stop myself. I wanted to say it over and over again, just to feel it linger.

"Exactly. Next time, leave the hunting to me."

I set the glass back on the nightstand. "And what about you? What's your excuse for looking like you took on a bear?"

"Nothing," he said, dismissively, reaching for his phone. "Anyway, I took you to the hospital. They patched you up, said it was just a bump to the head. Then we flew out—jet, helicopter, and now here we are."

My jaw dropped. "And I just slept through *all* of that?"

"You've been out for two days, Miss Whitenhouse," he said with a wicked glint in his eyes. "Guess that rock wasn't a fan of yours."

I squinted my eyes, frustration bubbling up as I reached for something, anything, to throw. My fingers brushed against a pillow, and without thinking, I hurled it at him. It was a weak, half-hearted attempt, but of course, he dodged it effortlessly.

He straightened up and coolly gave me a look. "If you've got enough energy for theatrics, you've got enough to freshen up."

He turned on his heel and walked out, leaving me there, alone and fuming.

Wait ... had he just insinuated that I *stank*?

CHAPTER
TWENTY-FIVE

"A friend may be nature's most magnificent creation."
— **Ralph Waldo Emerson**

Jade

"He called me dramatic and theatrical! Can you believe that? Honestly, that boar had one job, and it failed spectacularly."

Sofiya practically cackled, her laughter echoing through the call. "He said that?"

"Yes!" I waved my hands like a lunatic. "He's absolutely *insane*. I gathered what little energy I had left, called a taxi, and went straight home. And then—get this—he still sent me a text, demanding I take the rest of the week off until the big exhibition on Saturday. Like he's doing me some kind of favor!"

"Jadie—"

"Oh, and he *also* had the audacity to insinuate that *I stank*! Me! The woman who carries six different perfumes, two deodorants, and enough scented creams to moisturize an army!"

Still fuming, I shot up from the couch, snatching my phone as I stormed to the fridge.

A bottle of wine practically threw itself into my hand. I poured a glass so full it was practically obscene, then took a long, satisfying sip.

Not only had this man turned me into a petty, vengeful little devilish monster, but he was also going to turn me into a full-blown alcoholic.

For the past three days, I'd been stuck at home, lying low and letting my head heal. The bandage had come off this morning, revealing a tiny, barely-there scar. No stitches, thank God.

Physically, I was as good as new.

Mentally? A disaster.

Now that I felt somewhat human again, I avoided my home office like it was cursed—a haunting reminder of my three-day tantrum. Every photo of Lazzio I'd ever printed had been vandalized with devil horns, absurd mustaches, and captions like *Not Even That Hot* or *Overbearing Boss of the Year.*

Today, I doubled down on my childish antics, burying myself in Twilight marathons and inhaling enough takeout to make my delivery guy assume I was running a one-woman pity party.

But now? Now I was ready to rejoin society.

Back to work. Back to throwing verbal darts at Lazzio's perfectly chiseled face.

This whole fever dream of wanting to seduce him just to ruin him more?

It was over—or at least, that's what I told myself.

I'd stick to the destroying part; there was no need to have him buried between my legs.

Sofiya snorted. "Wow, someone's extra salty today."

I groaned, grabbing my wine glass and collapsing onto the couch like the drama queen I apparently was. "I am! I mean, sure, I *know* I've got issues. Maybe I shouldn't poke the bear or, I don't know, strip naked in front of him, but still—"

"You did *what*?"

The glass froze halfway to my mouth as my brain short-circuited.

Crap. Crap. Crap.

Jade, you absolute idiot!

I sipped my wine as casually as someone who had just launched themselves off a cliff, pretending Sofiya's face wasn't now practically glued to the screen, her wide eyes full of judgment, her jaw on the verge of unhinging.

"Nothing."

"Did you seriously strip naked in front of your *boss*?"

"No."

"Jade."

"... Maybe?"

"Are you insane?"

I sighed, swirling my wine. "Look, I think we've known that for a while."

"Jadie, I love you, but I cannot—*cannot*—defend you on this one."

I plunked my glass down on the coffee table, slid even deeper into the couch like it might swallow me whole, and pulled a cushion over my face to muffle the dying sounds of my dignity.

"I know! He's just so—ugh! He's infuriating! Always so tightly wound, so smug, so perfectly in control. I just wanted to see him sweat, to make him lose it for once! I'm going straight to hell for this. First-class ticket. Window seat."

"Forget first class, Jade. They're naming the gates after you. Welcome to *Jadieland: Eternal Damnation Edition*."

I peeked out from under the cushion, glaring. "Not. Helping."

She lifted a shoulder. "Hey, I'm just saying, it's bold. You really stripped naked in front of Angelo Lazzio? The man who could probably intimidate a brick wall into crumbling?"

I groaned again, flopping back. "It wasn't some grand plan, okay? It was the heat of the moment. I got carried away."

"Heat of the moment," she repeated, arching a brow. "So ... did it work? Did you break him?"

"A bit." My voice was barely above a whisper. "He was pissed. Like *really* pissed. He said I'd better remember he's not just my boss, but a man first. And next time?" My breath caught. "Next time, he wouldn't hesitate to fuck me."

The silence was deafening.

When I glanced at the screen, Sofiya's expression was frozen—wide eyes, parted lips.

"What?" I snapped.

"Oh my god, Jadie," she whispered, leaning closer. "Angelo Lazzio wants to sleep with you."

I rolled my eyes, dismissing her with a flick of my hand. "No, he doesn't. He said it to scare me, to assert control or whatever ridiculous power play he thinks he's running."

Her brows shot up. "Stop lying to yourself. He said it because he meant it. Men like him don't bluff when it comes to things like that."

I buried my face in the cushion again, my words muffled and pathetic. "Why are you even my friend?"

"Because I love watching this trainwreck you call your life," she shot back without missing a beat. "And because, somehow, you're even funnier when you're spiraling."

Peeking out from the cushion, I glared at her, but it only made her smirk widen.

"Jadie," she drawled, "he wasn't joking. He said it because he wanted you to know exactly what he's capable of." Her grin turned dark, conspiratorial. "And because he's probably thought about it more times than he'd care to admit."

"Shut up."

"You shut up. Or better yet, admit it—you liked it. Maybe not his words, but the way he looked at you when he said it."

Heat flared across my cheeks.

"You hate how much it's gotten under your skin. Admit it, you can't stop thinking about it."

"I hate you, Sofiya."

"No, Jadie. You hate how much you want Angelo Lazzio to mean it."

I walked through the museum's quiet halls, heels clicking against polished floors, heading for my office. After days of wallowing, it was time to reclaim my dignity—or at least fake it convincingly.

I showered, then slipped into my finest—an emerald Jacquemus dress with a plunging V-neck, sheer sleeves, and a daring slit up my right leg. My Kate Louboutins added power, and my black serpent Bvlgari necklace, earned by securing 30 percent of Lazzio Exhibits, gleamed at my throat.

Work was my anchor, grounding me when everything else felt like chaos.

With the exhibition a day away, nothing less than perfection would do—every detail had to scream *success*.

Each floor stood as a testament to battlefields and centuries of war. The exhibits were precise, flawlessly curated. I stalked through them, hunting for a flaw, something to tear apart. But, to my annoyance, there was nothing.

The artifacts gleamed under expertly angled lights, the arrangements immaculate.

Everything was infuriatingly flawless.

I sighed, frustration bubbling.

Perfection shouldn't bother me—but today, it did.

Pivoting, I headed to the café in the restaurant wing. It was closed to the public, but a few staff lingered. The moment I walked in, the room fell into silence.

It wasn't the usual awe-filled quiet—it hummed with curiosity.

Eyes darted away the second I glanced their way, but whispers continued, buzzing in the background.

My jaw tightened.

I passed them, pretending not to notice, and ordered my caramel macchiato with extra sugar.

Settling into one of the overpriced couches, I wrapped my fingers around the warm cup.

Normally, I thrived on this—on the way people shrank under my gaze, fumbling over their words. But today? It grated.

Every glance, every smirk, every murmur felt like it was about me.

"I can't believe you have the audacity to show your face here today."

I turned slowly, raising an eyebrow as Grace glared at me,

her venom darker than ever. Arms crossed, face crimson, eyes burning with pure fury.

"What do you want, oldie?"

"For you to burn in hell."

Her words hit like a slap, but she didn't stick around to see the damage. Spinning on her heel, she left me standing there, stunned.

In all the years of fake smiles and petty jabs, this wasn't her. She wasn't blunt—she was a snake. But today? She went straight for the throat.

I set my coffee down, blood simmering, and stalked after her.

"What the hell is your problem today?"

Grace stayed silent, tapping the elevator button with manic precision.

When the doors slid open, she stepped in, stabbing Lazzio's floor number.

Too stubborn to let her stew in silence, I followed her in.

"You know, oldie, you should come shopping with me sometime," I said, giving her outfit a deliberate once-over. It was actually cute, but that wasn't the point. "Who even wears dresses like that anymore? It's not the '60s."

She ignored me, eyes fixed on the blinking numbers above the door.

When the elevator opened, she bolted out like I was toxic air.

I groaned, patience slipping. "Grace—"

She spun so fast I stumbled back.

"In all the years you've worked here, I've begged Angelo to get rid of you," she spat. "To fire you. You're the devil's little soldier, making his life hell. And God knows, he's suffered enough!"

My mouth opened, but she cut me off, voice trembling with animosity.

"But because you're *good* at your job—because somehow, you made his life easier—I respected his decision." She stepped closer, eyes blazing. "But he should never have been in danger because of you. The man was shot, for God's sake! Shot! Saving your ungrateful ass. He lost so much blood the doctors said he's lucky he didn't lose his leg!"

My chest tightened as her words cut deeper.

"He can barely walk properly now," she hissed, eyes flashing with something close to grief. "And here you are, prancing around like nothing happened. Like he didn't almost die because of you!"

My stomach twisted.

Shot.

Lazzio had been shot.

The forest.

The bastard hadn't told me.

Not a damn word.

The nerve. The audacity. The gall of him!

He saved me, dragged me out of there, and didn't think to mention he was bleeding out while doing it? Or that he almost lost his leg?

My fists clenched. "That self-righteous, controlling son of a—"

"You're angry?" Grace hissed, cutting through my thoughts. "He gets shot, and *you're* the one who's angry?"

Oh, I was furious.

But not at her.

And definitely not because I thought I deserved his silence.

No. I was angry because Angelo Lazzio made the choice to swallow all that pain—his pain—and keep it hidden, just to make sure I was okay.

I didn't know whether to scream, or kill him. Probably both.

"Where is he?"

Grace scoffed, barely sparing me a glance as she strutted toward her desk, slumping into her chair. "Like I'd tell you."

I stepped closer, lowering my voice. "You're going to tell me where he is, or I'll find him myself. But trust me, it'll be a hell of a lot messier if I have to do it the hard way."

She tilted her head, eyes narrowing. "He doesn't need you storming in and making a scene."

"Grace."

Her lips pressed into a thin line.

Finally, she sighed, frustrated, muttering, "The Lazzios' meeting room. But you won't get far. You don't even have clearance to get to the—"

I didn't wait for her to finish.

My eyes darted to her desk, catching sight of her keys—the set with the elevator pass I needed.

Without a second thought, I lunged.

"Jade!" Grace shrieked, scrambling up as I snatched the keys, pushed her out of the way, and bolted for the elevator.

Yep, second time I've knocked the poor old lady to the floor.

At this rate, Satan's probably drafting me for a TED Talk in Hell on how to be the perfect villain.

The doors slid open, and I jabbed the button with more force than necessary, willing them to close faster as Grace's heels clicked furiously behind me.

She almost made it. *Almost.*

But the doors sealed shut just in time, cutting off her furious shouts.

I leaned back against the cool metal, clutching the keys, adrenaline surging.

"Guess I'm doing this the messy way after all."

CHAPTER TWENTY-SIX

"If you can make a woman laugh, you can make her do anything."
— **Marilyn Monroe**

Angelo

"The bastard's hiding. No one's laid eyes on him since that night," my uncle Fernando grumbled, voice thick with frustration. "Probably shitting himself knowing you made it, and figuring you'll be tearing after his worthless ass."

Vittori leaned in. "He's not hiding. He's sitting back, waiting for you to find him. He knows you'll come, and he's betting it'll end his way—his last pathetic move, all for that dead whore of his."

My father slammed his fist against the table. "He stole ten fucking million, Angelo! Ten million! And he's still breathing?

That piece of shit should've been rotting in the ground days ago! What the fuck are you waiting for?"

I grabbed my coffee, just to have something in my hands. The burn as it slid down did nothing to numb the fire gnawing at my head, the same goddamn image looping in my mind, no matter how hard I tried to erase it.

Jade fucking Whitenhouse.

Mia diavoletta.

That raven hair, always looking like it was begging to be grabbed, her dark eyes that dared me to do it—dared me to lose control. That pale skin, the kind that bruises too easily, marking every damn reminder of who's been there. And those fucking freckles, scattered across her chest like a goddamn map, begging to be followed.

Her tits. Perfect, maddening, and so fucking full I swore they were made to bring me to my knees. Pink nipples I wanted to bite, suck, and turn red under my teeth. And her waist—small enough to snap if I wasn't careful, curving just right into those hips I knew would fit perfectly in my hands.

Then those legs.

God, those fucking legs. Long and sleek, wrapped in those fucking heels, like a wet dream built to destroy me.

And the dragon. That fucking tattoo. Colorful ink carved into her perfect skin, coiling down her back like it was made to taunt me.

Every line, every scale, every inch stopping just above those dimples on her lower back—dimples I wanted to sink my teeth into.

Her ass? *Fuck me.* I closed my eyes, gripping the edge of the table as I tried to shove the thought down, but it was already too late.

Six years.

I'd been battling this fucking obsession for six goddamn years.

And until now, I'd kept it under control.

I had promised myself I wouldn't give in to the pull of Jade Whitenhouse, knowing she was the one who could break me, make me lose every ounce of control I had left.

But for some reason, my mind had stopped working, and my heart was too tired of waiting, too tired of denying what it was feeling.

Jade Whitenhouse wasn't just under my skin; she was in my blood.

And it was fucking poison.

Exactly why I'd never given in—because I knew the second I did, I'd never let go. I'd force her into submission, make her survive on me, depend on me, until she couldn't help but feel the same.

For two days, she had been out cold in my bed, her hands clinging to the covers like they were the only thing keeping her from falling apart. Her skin had been flushed with fever, damp with sweat. I'd cleaned her off every hour—hadn't been able to help myself.

She'd twisted and turned, tangling herself in the sheets, her face buried in my pillow.

The first night, after the doctor had checked my leg for infection—the bullet wound throbbing like a reminder of all the ways I'd fucked up—I'd tried to keep my distance.

I'd given her the bed, and settled in the guest room.

But past midnight, I'd heard it—her screams, raw and jagged.

I had been in the room before I'd even had time to stop myself.

She had curled into a ball, shaking so hard it made my chest ache, her breath coming in broken gasps.

Her voice had been wrecked as she whimpered one thing: "Please don't kill me too, Angelo."

I hadn't had time to question her.

She'd broken down completely, sobbing like her world had shattered.

Without thinking, I'd climbed into the bed and pulled her against me, locking her in my arms to stop the shaking, to stop whatever the hell was hurting her.

She'd clung to me. Like it wasn't a choice—like she had needed to. Her head had buried into my chest, tears soaking through my shirt as her breath had hitched and finally, *finally* started to even out.

I had stayed there the whole night, listening to her breathing steady while my own head spun. By morning, I'd already made the call—Grace could handle things at the office.

I wasn't going anywhere. I'd needed to stay beside her.

So, I'd stayed.

And I fucking shouldn't have.

The second night, she'd found her way to me again. Not with words or screams, but with the way she'd shifted closer, her face pressed into my neck, her leg thrown over mine like she couldn't sleep without feeling my body against hers.

And by the third night?

She didn't have to reach for me—I had already been there, lying awake, feeling her breathe against my chest, and hating every part of me that didn't push her away.

Because it had felt ... too fucking good.

For six years, I'd been dreaming of this, fighting to keep it at bay, convincing myself I didn't want what I could never have.

And now that it was mine? There wasn't a chance in hell I'd let it go.

Three nights. That's all it had taken.

Three nights, and now every part of me was hooked—addicted, obsessed, *ruined.*

My body had made up its mind, and all it wanted was Jade fucking Whitenhouse.

Now.

I wanted her on her knees, mouth open and ready, so I could fuck that sharp tongue of hers into silence. I wanted her riding me, those perfect tits in my mouth, her pretty face softening as she fell apart. I wanted her on all fours, her back arched, that dragon tattoo daring me to trace it with my tongue.

I wanted to fuck Jade Whitenhouse until she forgot her own name and only remembered mine.

And I hated her for it.

The pretty woman had been a thorn in my side for six years, a walking disaster designed specifically to drive me insane. She didn't listen. She touched my shit just to piss me off. She always had a comeback, always a smirk that made me want to throttle her—and now?

Now I needed her more than I needed my next breath.

And the worst part?

I already knew I wouldn't stop myself. Not anymore.

And for a man who thrived on control, this was crawling under my skin and pissing me off.

"I'll find him. Just got other shit to deal with first."

Like ripping this fucking obsession out of my veins, like a junkie going through the worst kind of withdrawal.

My father pushed himself up from the chair. "Waiting makes you look fucking weak, Angelo!"

I opened my mouth to fire back, but before I could, the door slammed open.

Jade stormed in like a fucking hurricane, breath ragged and

heavy, and the entire room froze—every single man locked on her.

She moved fast, too fast.

In the blink of an eye, she was at Vittori's side, her hands a blur, snatching the gun from under his vest.

Without missing a beat, she fired.

The shot screamed through the air, so close to my head that I felt the rush of wind before I dodged it.

The men scrambled to their feet, their guns already out, all of them pointing at her, ready to turn the room into hell.

"You get shot and keep it from me? What the fuck are you playing at, Lazzio?"

I sighed, wiping the irritation off my lips like I had just tasted something rancid.

"Damn, Beatrix Kiddo," Vittori muttered, half laughing as he lit a cigarette, looking like he was watching the best damn show in town.

He was the only one still seated.

My father looked so pissed, I thought smoke was going to start shooting out of his ears. "Miss Whitenhouse, what the hell is wrong with you?"

She didn't budge, gun still aimed high, eyes colder than a deep freeze.

"Your son, sir. That's what's wrong."

Uncle Lorenzo took a step forward. "He shouldn't've saved your ass. Should've let you die in the snow like a popsicle, you fucking bitch."

Before he could blink, she turned and shot him in the leg.

I almost laughed.

He screamed, clutching his thigh.

Uncle Fernando slid his gun back under his vest. "Bastard deserved it."

Yeah, he fucking had.

My father's eyebrows shot up. "Miss Whitenhouse, you've crossed the fucking line!"

She took a step toward me, her eyes seething with rage—and something else.

Guilt.

"I never asked for your help, Lazzio."

Her voice cut through the air, dark and venomous, masking the faint crack that betrayed her.

She'd been fending for herself for so long, the thought of someone stepping in and caring was almost offensive to her.

"Leave us."

The men all holstered their guns and filed out, one by one, my father glaring at me with a look that could've burned a hole through stone—pure disappointment.

Vittori, of course, was the last one to move.

He strolled over to her, holding his hand out for his gun.

She rolled her eyes and shoved it into his palm.

He gave me a half-amused chuckle, his eyes glinting with that "good luck with this one" look, before strolling out.

"How's your head, Miss Whitenhouse?"

She crossed her arms. "Good. How's your leg?"

I scoffed, pushing myself up and striding toward her, doing my best to hide the grimace that tried to break through the facade.

The pain in my leg throbbed, but I shoved it down.

"Good," I said, my voice flat.

She shook her head, eyes narrowing. "Liar."

I closed the distance between us, moving slowly, until we were inches apart.

Her angry eyes, blazing with fire, softened for the briefest moment, and I knew—she felt it too.

That spark, that tension, or whatever the hell it was hanging in the air between us.

My hand slid to her chin, fingers curling gently as I tipped her face upward.

She sucked in a breath, and I leaned in close, inspecting the scar on her forehead.

My lips brushed over the mark before I pulled back just enough to catch her eye again.

"Next time you try to kill me, *diavoletta*," I muttered, a smirk tugging at the corner of my mouth, "aim lower."

She jerked my hand away, shoving it off her chin like I'd burned her.

"Why didn't you tell me about your leg?"

I took a step back, arms folding across my chest. "Why didn't you tell me about your nightmares?"

Those three nights had felt endless, and each time, I'd caught her—twisting, muttering like she was running from something, or someone.

And that name ... *Stella*.

Her face drained of color. "What?"

"I've spent three nights next to you, Miss Whitenhouse. And every one of them, you screamed for someone—Stella."

Her eyes flashed for just a second—too quickly for her to hide it—but I saw it.

Panic.

Real panic.

"I don't know what you're talking about."

I raised an eyebrow. "Really? 'Cause I heard you. Who's Stella?"

She froze, her lips parting like she had something to say, but nothing came out.

I let out a dry chuckle. "What's the matter, Miss Whitenhouse? Did I finally succeed in making you speechless?"

She cleared her throat. "It wasn't Stella, it was Bella ... you know, like Bella from *Twilight*," she said with a small laugh.

"The woods probably reminded me of all that brooding vampire drama—"

"Stop lying, Jade."

Her eyes snapped to mine, wide for a second before narrowing in that stubborn defiance I knew too well. "I'm not."

I took a step forward, and she mirrored it, stepping back, keeping that damn distance between us.

"All you ever do is lie, Miss Whitenhouse."

She snorted. "Well, you should already know that, Lazzio. You've known me for more than six years now."

I moved again, another step closer, forcing her to retreat just a fraction.

"Who's Stella?"

She tilted her head, ignoring my question again. "Who shot you?"

Another step forward.

She took another step back, but this time, her back hit the wall.

Trapped.

"James Greg."

She nodded slowly, but there was something in her gaze—like she'd already known, like she'd been expecting this answer.

"Who's Stella, Miss Whitenhouse?"

"Why does he want you dead?"

I lifted a shoulder, casually stepping closer.

My arms framed her face against the wall, caging her in.

"I took something from him."

She didn't budge, just let her arms fall at her sides, her eyes tracing every inch of my face.

"Miss Whitenhouse—"

She leaned in, close enough that I could feel the heat of her skin.

Her pretty face was just inches from mine now.

"Who kidnapped you, Angelo?"

My blood ran cold, a chill so deep it sank straight to my bones.

My heart thudded erratically in my chest.

How the fuck did she know? Only my parents and Grace knew about that—something they never spoke of, not once since it had happened.

I moved faster than I thought possible, grabbing her by the throat.

"Don't play with fire, *diavoletta*," I breathed out.

She giggled, her dark eyes lighting with amusement. "You've never looked hotter than now, Angelo."

My grip tightened as I brought my face closer, lips hovering above hers.

"How the fuck do you know?"

She smiled, fingers slipping into my hair, tugging me closer, teasing me with the briefest brush of her lips against mine. "Your mama's very easy to crack."

I scoffed, feeling her lips graze mine again, noses brushing, her tongue touching my lips ever so slightly.

Cazzo.

I pressed her body into mine, a deep groan slipping from my throat.

The heat between us was unbearable, and at that moment, I had two choices: kill her with the gun tucked under my vest, or ...

Fuck it, who was I kidding?

I tightened my grip around her throat, pulling her closer, my mouth crashing onto hers hard. She gasped, and her faint moan was all the confirmation I needed—this was what she wanted, too.

Her fingers dug into my jaw, and her teeth grazed my lips, rough and hungry.

I let go of her throat roughly, shifting my hands down to her hips, grabbing a handful of her ass. Her dress clung to her body like a second skin, and I pressed her harder against me, feeling my dick harden.

Fuck, yes.

Fucking finally.

She yanked at my hair, nails scraping my scalp, and I dropped my mouth to her neck, licking a path up to her jaw before finding her lips again.

She moaned louder, her body writhing against mine like she couldn't get close enough.

I tried to find the zipper of her dress, desperate to strip it off, but she shoved me away.

My breath was ragged, chest heaving.

I looked at her, confused, and she smiled—an evil fucking grin that made me want to kiss it right off her face.

"Let's play a game."

What?

"Let me fuck you first," I muttered, stepping forward, but she side-stepped me, an amused glint in her eyes.

Looked like she was the one playing hard to get now.

"Two truths and a lie."

She walked toward my chair, her hands caressing the table. Each movement was measured, sensual.

When she finally reached the chair, she sat on it with effortless elegance, crossing her legs with a flick of her ankle.

She looked like an evil queen, waiting for her subject to kneel before her.

And for a second, I almost fucking did.

"If you can spot the lie, I'll let you fuck me right here, right now," she said, her voice low, almost playful. Yet her eyes were darker than the night itself. "But if you don't ..." She tilted her head, her gaze sharpening. "You'll tell me what happened during those fourteen days you were kidnapped when you were nine."

Every muscle in my body tensed, a knot twisting deep in my gut.

She was playing a dangerous game, and the stakes—fuck, the stakes were higher than I'd expected.

My instinct screamed to take her, right then, right there. To fuck her, and make her regret ever starting this twisted game. The thought of punishing her, making her feel every ounce of my fury, was too good to ignore.

I could already see her squirming beneath me, clinging to whatever power she thought she had, only for it to shatter under me.

"Shoot."

Her eyes flickered in surprise, like she hadn't expected me to just play along.

"Okay." Her finger brushed her chin, her gaze heavy with mischief, like she was plotting something twisted. "Well ... I'm fluent in Italian, I've studied a dozen ways to poison your coffee, but to my damn luck, Grace is the only one allowed to bring it to you ... and ..."

She stood up and walked toward me, giving me *that* look.

The kind that made my chest tighten and blood burn.

She closed the distance between us.

Her finger traced the edge of my vest before pressing her hand against my chest, right over my heart.

"And last but not least," she whispered darkly, "I've already touched myself thinking about you."

I let out a rough chuckle, my hand tightening on her wrist as I pulled her closer.

"Is that so, Miss Whitenhouse?"

Her finger traced my jaw. "It's for you to figure out, buddy."

I released her wrist, my other arm tightening around her waist as I lifted her with ease. Carrying her toward the big oval table, I set her down on the edge, her legs dangling freely.

She spread them wide, inviting me in.

"Judging by how you get off on fucking with me," I muttered, "I'd say you've been busy planning ways to poison me."

Her breath caught as I grazed my hand over the exposed skin of her thigh. She braced herself with her arms behind her, silent—her eyes locked on my hand as it slid higher, teasing, until it disappeared beneath the edge of her dress.

I felt the lace of her underwear.

A dark smile spread across my lips. She was already fucking soaked.

I pushed aside the fabric, leaning in closer as my lips brushed her neck, kissing and sucking at her skin.

Her scent hit me—dark oud, with a hint of caramel. It was fucking intoxicating.

"And with how fucking wet you are right now, Miss Whitenhouse," I growled, letting my finger glide through her folds, watching her drop her head back, her moans thick with desperation. "I'm sure you've been imagining me buried deep inside you."

I slid a finger inside her, feeling her pussy clamp down, tight and eager.

"Am I wrong?" I whispered.

I pushed my finger deeper, her breaths coming in short, ragged gasps.

Then I added another, fucking her hard and fast, her slick coating my hand as I bit down on the curve of her neck.

My free hand tangled in her hair, gripping tight as I yanked her head back. She gasped, her body arching into the pull.

When she tried grinding against my hand, desperate for more, I tightened my grip, jerking her head back harder.

"Don't fucking move," I said, my fingers working faster, deeper.

Her pussy clenched around me, impossibly tight, her body trembling as she neared the edge.

"You're close, aren't you?" I muttered, my lips brushing her ear.

"Yes," she breathed out, breathless and needy.

I let out a low, dark chuckle. "That's my girl."

Leaning in, I kissed her hard, and she responded with equal hunger, her hands flying to my face, her tongue plunging into mine. She kissed me like she needed me more than air.

Her body went rigid, a broken cry tearing from her as she came, nails sinking into my scalp, yanking at my hair like she wanted to tear it out. She bit down on my lip, her teeth digging in, pulling a growl from deep in my chest that rumbled against her mouth.

I didn't stop—my fingers still fucking her, slick and tight, until her body stopped shaking.

"Fuck," I muttered against her lips, grabbing her jaw to hold her in place as I pulled my fingers free, dripping with her. I brushed them over her lips. "Suck."

Her mouth parted eagerly, her tongue flicking out to lick them clean, eyes never leaving mine, as if daring me to look away.

I pushed my fingers in deeper, and she sucked them with a desperate intensity, her lips pulling tight, her cheeks hollowing out.

"Guess I won, Miss Whitenhouse."

Honestly, it felt too damn easy.

I couldn't help but think she'd picked those three just to make sure I'd fuck her.

A wicked smirk curled at the corners of my lips.

My finger slid out of her mouth, and before I could react, she shoved me back, stood up, and kissed me—a quick, teasing peck on my lips.

I reached for her hips, but she stepped out of my grasp, her body moving with purpose.

She walked slowly toward the door, hips swaying. Stopping at the door, she glanced back at me with a smug grin.

"*Grazie per l'orgasmo,* Angelo," she chuckled softly. "*Ma non, ho vinto io.*"

She didn't wait for a response.

With a wicked laugh, she was gone.

Che cazzo.

CHAPTER TWENTY-SEVEN

"Success is getting what you want, happiness is wanting what you get"
— **W.P. Kinsella**

Jade

"Congratulations, Jade, you've truly outdone yourself," Francesca Harper said, leaning in to kiss my cheeks as I handed her a glass of champagne.

I took a sip of my own, letting the bubbles fizz on my tongue as she continued.

"This exhibition?" She paused, her gaze sweeping the room as she savored her drink. "Simply exquisite. Who would've thought war could inspire such breathtaking beauty?"

The room buzzed with murmured compliments and the

clinking of glasses, the kind of noise people made when they cared more about being noticed than noticing anything else.

"I wasn't sure what to expect," Francesca continued, her tone dripping with the kind of sugar that rotted teeth, gesturing to the towering centerpiece with her champagne flute. "But this? It's ... ambitious. Raw, even."

Ares, God of War, stood eight feet tall, carved with sinful precision. His body was a masterpiece of muscle and dominance, the kind that made you question your morals. His massive sword gleamed as if it had tasted blood, while his shield bore the scars of battles fought long before anyone in this room had been born. The fury in his face could bring armies to their knees—or, more likely, leave someone breathless for *entirely* different reasons.

I took another sip of champagne, letting my gaze wander over him with a smirk.

"It's meant to be, Francesca. War isn't polished, or pretty. It's raw. Unforgiving."

Her eyes didn't leave the sculpture, though a faint smile played at her lips. "Quite the statement," she said, tilting her head. "Ares himself would be impressed."

Over the years, Francesca Harper—Scarlett's mother—had become a fascinating specimen for me to quietly analyze. The woman was every bit a Lazzio: strong-minded, exuding the kind of Italian timeless class and beauty that could make even the boldest stare.

But it wasn't just her elegance—it was that Lazzio fire in her eyes.

The unspoken warning that if you crossed her, she'd ruin you in ways you wouldn't even comprehend until it was too late.

Like any proper Italian mama, she didn't need to yell to

make her point—she was the storm, calm and deadly. That's why she had my respect.

In a world where women of her status wasted their days gossiping, shopping, and draping themselves over men for attention, Francesca Harper stood out like a hawk circling above the chaos.

After telling her to enjoy the evening, I left her side and moved through the museum, winding my way through each floor.

I greeted attendees, exchanged meaningless pleasantries, and made sure every piece of the night had fallen into place as planned. But the further I went, the harder it became to ignore the weight pressing against my chest, that familiar gnawing feeling creeping up my throat.

This would probably be one of the last exhibitions I'd direct here. Next week, hell would ignite, and when the smoke cleared, my time in New York would be done. It would be time to go back to my old life.

I caught myself wondering about the old house—what it looked like now, who the poor souls living in it were. Maybe I'd drop by, knock on their door, see if—

"No gun tonight?"

I turned around.

Leonardo Vittori, dressed head to toe in black, his eyes glittering with amusement.

Of course, it had to be him. As if Lazzio wasn't enough of a headache, his best friend had to be just as insufferable.

I'd spent years unraveling their unlikely alliance—a mafia boss of the Sacra Corona, and a nepotism-bred heir to an entertainment empire.

Turns out, the two weren't so different. Both thrived on stealing, manipulating, and ruling like the world owed them everything.

Match made in hell, really.

I let my gaze rake over him. Six foot four, buzz cut, green eyes sharper than broken glass. His cheekbones could cut stone, and under his left eye, those two infamous tear tattoos marked him as a family traitor—a man who'd killed his own blood.

"Why, Vittori? Hoping I'll aim for you next?"

"Oh, Jade," he drawled, his Italian accent wrapping around the word like silk dipped in venom, "if I were Lazzio, I'd have shot you the second you barged in to disrupt my meeting. Right here"—he tapped his temple with two fingers—"between your pretty little eyes."

"If you were Lazzio," I chuckled, leaning closer, "you wouldn't need to hide behind empty threats. You'd have the balls to do it instead of flapping your mouth."

His smirk deepened, lazy and taunting. "You're lucky I like my women with a bit of bite. Makes taming them so much more ... satisfying."

I rolled my eyes, stepping back.

"Taming, huh?" I snorted. "Get out of my way. Some of us actually have work to do."

As I moved past him, my eyes flicked over the crowd.

People were tipsy, mingling, laughing, their voices blending into a soft hum beneath the awestruck gazes that lingered on the art. It all felt distant, a background murmur to the heat building in the air.

Vittori's scoff pulled me back. "I see it now."

I glanced back, brow raised. "See what?"

His eyes landed behind me before closing the space between us, his fingers brushing a strand of hair from my face. "Why Lazzio's obsessed with you."

Even before I turned, I could feel Angelo's eyes on me, burning my skin.

A spark of an idea flickered, dangerous and wicked.

I stepped closer to Vittori, flattening my hands against his chest, tilting my head just so, letting my eyes soften. "Really? Why is that?"

His smirk didn't falter—if anything, it deepened.

He knew exactly what game I was playing, and the bastard was enjoying it, probably feeling Angelo's murderous stare drilling into his face as much as I could sense it.

His hand cupped my face, thumb grazing my cheek.

He leaned down, his breath brushing my ear as he spoke. "Cause you're the kind of devil that makes men beg for pain."

A quiet laugh slipped past my lips as I let my hands fall and stepped back.

"Then I guess you'd better hope he likes to suffer."

Vittori's laughter echoed through the room, but it was abruptly interrupted by a shrill scream—"Fire!"

The entire room froze, people scrambling for the exits, their heels clattering against the marble floors in a mad rush. Glasses fell, drinks spilled, and for a moment, panic reigned.

And then, through the chaos, Angelo appeared like a storm. His eyes found me immediately, and the fury in them was almost palpable.

Without a second thought, he aimed a fire extinguisher at me and blasted it, coating my dress in a white, misty fog that left a chill in the air.

My hands instinctively flew up, trying to shield my face from the blast of spray that had soaked my dress.

The room went deadly silent.

Angelo's gaze, now fully possessive, held mine for a moment too long before his eyes threw daggers at Vittori.

I blinked through the smoke, pushing the mist away, still processing what had just happened.

My heart sank as I realized what had just triggered him.

Jealousy.

But it wasn't just jealousy—it was something darker, something possessive.

Vittori let out a low chuckle, his eyes flicking between me and Lazzio.

"What the fuck, Lazzio?" I snapped, brushing the mist off my arms.

"I apologize, Miss Whitenhouse, but I thought I saw a flame on your dress. Seems like it's just the one burning between your legs."

Bastard.

He was pissed that I'd dared to flirt with Vittori in front of him.

My eyes scanned the room.

The crowd had vanished—probably too embarrassed for me—or maybe they were just eager to spread the drama, running downstairs to share the spectacle with everyone else.

Either way, they had enough juicy material for their gossip.

I could practically hear the whispers now: *Did you see how Angelo Lazzio fired that fire extinguisher at his employee?*

Ugh, I couldn't believe he had just ruined my favorite Givenchy dress.

The one that had taken me weeks to get my hands on.

But, of course, Angelo Lazzio couldn't let me have a goddamn thing.

Fine.

If he wanted to play this game, I'd play too.

I reached for the zipper and slid it down. The dress, so perfectly tailored, dropped off my body and pooled around my feet in a whisper of silk.

I kept my eyes on him, savoring the way his gaze darkened—his expression shifting into something I recognized all too well.

Wrath.

I shrugged. "Don't worry, Lazzio. I hated this dress anyway."

Now, I stood in nothing but a tight black bra that clung to my breasts like a second skin, and a thong that didn't leave much to the imagination.

Vittori whistled low.

Lazzio, on the other hand, didn't bother with subtlety.

A curse escaped from his lips, a string of words I couldn't quite make out.

He quickly shrugged off his blazer and threw it over my shoulders.

The fabric was heavy, but oddly intimate against my skin.

I raised my hand, flashing a playful wave over my shoulder. "*Ciao*, Vittori."

But the moment was short-lived. Angelo's hand shot out, swatting mine down with a snap.

He strode toward the elevator, dragging me along by my wrist. I stumbled, trying to catch up, my heels clicking furiously against the floor.

His grip was tight, but his focus?

It was all on the elevator button, which he tapped over and over with an almost obsessive energy.

"Let me go, Lazzio, I've got other guests to entertain."

The elevator doors slid open, and without a word, he shoved me inside. He tapped the button for the parking floor, the doors closing with a soft whoosh.

He stood there, his back to me, but something in the air shifted.

He was frozen, his breath coming fast, and the energy around him turned so dark that, for a split second, I actually felt a jolt of fear.

Something told me I may have crossed the line with this one, but ... oh well.

"Lazzio—"

"You let him *touch* you, Miss Whitenhouse," he cut me off, his voice dipped in a dry, humorless chuckle. It sounded more like disbelief wrapped in rage. "You let him put his *fucking* hands on you."

I rolled my eyes, crossing my arms. "Yeah, well, you blasted me with a fire extinguisher and ruined my entire night. So, if we're keeping score, I'd say we're even."

He turned around slowly.

His jaw tightened. He took a slow step closer, closing the already narrow space between us.

"Even?" he repeated. "You think this is about keeping score?"

I lifted my chin. "Well, what else could it be? You ruined my dress, my night—hell, my *life*— and *now* my patience. What's next, my sanity?"

He laughed, but it was hollow, a sound that made my stomach twist.

He took another step forward, and I found myself backing up until the wall kissed my spine.

"You're the one screwing with my fucking sanity, Miss Whitenhouse."

I pressed back against the wall, as if it could swallow me whole, but there was no escaping him. His hand shot up, planting beside my head, his body caging mine, suffocatingly close.

"You've ruined my reputation in front of my men with your fucking arrogance," he bit out. "You've dragged ghosts out of my past I swore I'd buried for good." He pressed his body against mine, his breath brushing my cheek. "You make me feel things I've spent my entire life killing. Things I *don't* want to feel. Things I *can't* afford to feel, Jade." His voice wavered, and for a split second, I saw the cracks beneath the anger. "You've lit every corner of my mind on fire, and now, all I can fucking think about is *you*."

The breath I was holding left my lungs.

"Are you happy now? Happy to have ripped my life apart, piece by fucking piece? Happy to know I can't stop thinking about you, even when I hate every damn second of it?"

His chest heaved.

Yes, Angelo.

That's what I was supposed to do.

Break you, dismantle you, make you hate me, make you suffer for ruining my life.

That was the plan.

But something deeper twisted inside me, something bitter and shameful.

Guilt.

I swallowed hard, my throat thick with words I couldn't say.

He dropped his face into the crook of my neck, exhaling like he was fighting to hold himself together.

"Do you even realize what you're doing to me?" he muttered, voice all raw and rough, like he couldn't believe the words were coming out of his mouth.

His hands slipped from the wall, wrapping around my waist and pulling me closer, like he was trying to make sure I wouldn't slip away.

There was something else in how he held me, something deeper, like if he let go, he might actually break.

"I fucking hate you, Jade. But *Dio mio*, I can't stay away."

Neither can I, Angelo.

CHAPTER
TWENTY-EIGHT

"Every man has his secret sorrows which the world knows not; and often times we call a man cold when he is only sad."
— **Henry Wadsworth Longfellow**

Angelo

"You could've just dropped me off, you know. I think we've chewed each other out enough for one day—I don't need you gnawing on my nerves any further."

I tossed my keys onto the counter, kicked off my shoes, and went straight for the wine cellar. This girl was going to be the death of me—if I didn't kill her first.

She followed, of course, like a storm cloud that had decided to park itself in my living room. By the time I turned around with the bottle and two glasses, she'd already made herself at home.

High heels discarded, legs tucked beneath her, she lounged on my cream couch like it was custom-built for her. Her eyes scanned the room, lingering on the dark, earthy walls, the Persian rug, and the piano in the corner—untouched since my grandfather's hands had last graced its keys.

I poured the wine and handed her a glass. She downed it in two unceremonious gulps, and placed the empty glass on the table.

I sat down beside her, nursing my own drink.

My head hit the back of the couch as I sighed.

"I woke up chained in a basement. On a chair. A masked man sitting across from me, waiting for me to wake up."

Her posture shifted immediately. Legs pulled in, hands fidgeting.

"I'm a man of my word. I owe you the story. Every miserable, blood-stained piece of it."

She didn't move, didn't speak, but her breath caught—just enough for me to notice. She pulled her legs tighter, curling into the corner of the couch; she braced herself, but still, her eyes didn't leave me.

I drained the rest of my glass, slamming it down.

My jaw clenched, and for a second, I debated stopping—locking it all back where it belonged.

"He didn't speak at first. Just stared, like I was some animal he'd caught, and was deciding how to carve me up." My voice dipped low, jagged, as I stared at the wall. "He finally stood. Took his sweet fucking time walking around me, like a vulture."

She hugged her knees tighter.

"It lasted fourteen days," I said, voice flat, as if saying it out loud would make it less real. "The first few days, he didn't ask me anything. He just hurt me. Blades, mostly. Small, shallow cuts—nothing fatal, just enough to make me bleed, make me feel every inch of it. And when that got boring? He got … creative."

Her face twisted with fear.

"By the fourth or fifth day, I lost track. All I could feel was the pain. That's when the questions started. He wanted everything—Lazzio family secrets, my grandfather's dealings, my father's stash of dirty money. He wanted names, locations, every skeleton the Lazzio family had buried, and where they'd buried it. He was patient, I'll give him that. Made it a game. But he said he wanted to know everything and I …"

She leaned in slightly. "And you didn't, did you?"

My laugh came out bitter, scraping the raw edges of my throat. "Of course not. I didn't know anything—not really. I was just a fucking kid. But even if I did …" My voice trailed off, the memory so vivid it made my hands curl into fists. "I'd rather have died on that chair than give him the satisfaction."

She looked unsure, like she didn't know whether to stay or run.

Smart girl.

"I haven't been the same ever since," I said, my voice quieter. "No one walks away from shit like that and stays whole. He took pieces of me—pieces I'll never get back. And some nights? Some nights, I still hear his voice. Feel his fucking knives."

Her eyes softened just a fraction, and I hated it.

Pity.

The last thing I wanted from her was pity.

"So now you know," I said, standing abruptly.

"Did you ever find out who he was?" she whispered, pulling my blazer tighter around her body.

"Nah," I scoffed, the sound bitter, harsh. "The Lazzios tore the city apart looking for him. Turned over every rock, burned down every lead. But he left without a trace." My jaw clenched.

"He hit me hard on the head before he dumped me. I was out cold. When I came to ..."

I paused, the words sticking in my throat.

"It's okay—"

"I woke up on a beach, blood crusted over my head, disoriented as hell. Didn't know where I was, or how I'd gotten there. Some old man walking his dog found me there at six in the morning."

She didn't say a word, and maybe that was for the best.

I stood abruptly, as sharply as the thoughts running wild in my head.

Sitting there, drowning in her eyes while my past clawed its way to the surface—it was too fucking much.

My chest was too tight, my skin too hot, my thoughts too loud.

I needed distance. I needed out.

I nodded toward the spare room, barely glancing back as I moved past. She could figure it out. Hell, she could sleep on the couch for all I cared.

I just needed to get away from her—away from those pretty eyes that saw too much.

When I got to my room, I slammed the door and let my head fall against the wood, a deep breath forcing its way out of me.

What a great fucking night.

I felt her energy the moment she entered, the pull impossible to ignore.

The floor creaked under her weight as she moved, and her breath—soft, measured—hung in the air between us.

Then, the mattress shifted as she slid in beside me.

Guess she couldn't sleep either.

Time dragged, as I wondered how long she'd wait before making a move.

Not too long.

Her fingers brushed my back, tentative at first, tracing the scars like they were something she needed to understand, some map to a place she shouldn't be.

I froze.

Her touch was light, almost innocent.

I turned quickly, grabbing her wrist and halting her. Her breath caught, but she didn't pull away, didn't fight me. I held her there, her hand pressed flat against my chest, my heart hammering under her palm.

For a moment, I let it linger, her fingers too close to something I didn't want her to touch, but couldn't stop from wanting.

I brought her hand to my lips and kissed her knuckles.

"How the hell are you fluent in Italian?" I muttered, the question slipping out before I could stop myself. It had been gnawing at me ever since that flawless Italian had rolled off her tongue.

A little smirk played at the corner of her mouth. "What do you mean?"

"Don't play dumb," I chuckled darkly, still holding her hand. "Six years. Six fucking years, and you were sitting on that little secret?"

"I learned it so I could make sure you weren't talking behind my back, Lazzio."

"Hmm," I muttered, narrowing my eyes. "What have you heard, then?"

She shrugged, slipping her hand free from mine, only to let it dance freely on my chest, her fingers lazily tracing patterns against my skin.

"That you think I'm very smart, the shadow haunting your dreams, way too attractive to be gracing your life, and that you cry into your pillow every night wishing you were worthy of me."

I couldn't help it—I laughed.

A low, genuine laugh rumbled from my chest.

"Cry? I don't think I've ever encountered someone so outrageously in love with themselves."

Leaning in, her lips just barely brushed mine, her hand sliding to cradle my cheek.

"It's okay, boss," she whispered. "You're only human. No one can escape falling for me—not even you."

Then she pressed herself against me, and—

Jesus Christ.

She's naked.

Gloriously fucking naked.

A groan slipped out before I could stop it, deep and guttural, and my hands instinctively circled her waist, pulling her closer.

Her bare chest pressed against mine, and it was like we were two puzzle pieces, perfectly designed to ruin each other.

She let out a soft breath as my fingers skimmed over the delicate curve of her back, and her lips parted wider, inviting me in.

My mouth dropped to hers, hungry and rough.

I leaned back, brushing a strand of her hair.

"You're right, *amore*, I'm only human."

I pushed her away slightly because I knew exactly where this could go if I let it, and it wasn't just sex.

No, it was something darker, heavier—a truth I wasn't ready to face yet, not with her. Not with anyone.

Maybe not ever.

"Let's play again, Jade."

She giggled. "Still bitter about losing?"

"No. Two lies, one truth. You find the truth, and I'll do whatever you want for an hour—*anything*. But if you lose ..." I let the pause linger. "You owe me a big secret. Something real, something you've never told anyone."

Her fingers threaded into my hair, tugging sharply, forcing me to meet her gaze.

The heat in her eyes burned, but it was the curve of her lips —a sinful, taunting thing—that nearly unraveled me.

"Brave words, Angelo. After the way you've humiliated me tonight, I could *ruin* you. You sure you're ready to hand me that kind of power?"

"Try me, *amore*," I rasped.

"Okay, I'm in."

"Perfect. So, I have a house in Milan, Italy. Where Dante Alighieri's lover, Beatrice, used to live. My biggest dream was to travel to the moon, and ... I found Georgino in the streets of Prague a couple of years ago, and decided to take him with me. Don't ask why."

She pushed herself up, her arms braced on the mattress, the covers slipping down to her waist, her full tits just *there*, bare, right in my fucking face.

"Wait, where's Georgino? You never leave that little monster alone—"

"My mama took him for the night."

She hummed and laid back down, and I couldn't help myself—I leaned in, kissed the skin between her tits, my eyes locking with hers.

The faint light from the city barely illuminated her face.

Her hand found the back of my head, her breath catching in a quiet sigh.

Don't do it.

Don't you fucking do it, Angelo.

But hell, I couldn't stop myself.

I leaned in and teased her nipple with the tip of my tongue, a low growl rumbling in my chest as I sucked gently. Her skin tasted like fire, like everything I shouldn't want, but craved anyway.

My hand worked the other nipple, pinching it just enough to make her gasp.

"How am I supposed to focus, Angelo?"

I grinned against her skin and bit down on the other nipple, hard enough to make her arch into me.

"Come on," I murmured. "Find the truth."

Her hand shot to my face, fingers curling against my jaw as she pulled me up, her lips crashing into mine. She kissed me slow but deep, her tongue teasing the edge of my lips before she pulled away.

"Easy," she whispered, a smirk curling her lips. "I think you found Georgino in the streets of Prague. That dog might look like royalty, but with the way he acts? He's a dumpster-diving stray in disguise."

She moaned softly as my lips began trailing down her neck.

"And your house is in Florence, not Milan. You've been there every summer since I've known you."

Her fingers threaded into my hair as I bit harder.

"And let's be real," she went on. "A man like you, who practically owns the world, dreaming of leaving it behind to float around the moon? Highly unlikely."

I moved to her ear, my breath brushing against her skin as her hand trailed lower, resting on my back.

"You lost, *amore*."

She froze, her body tensing as she pulled back to glare at me.

"Are you seriously telling me you didn't find that over-pampered demon dog in the streets of Prague?"

"*No*," I replied, stealing a quick kiss as she glared harder. "And yes, I own the house in Florence. Good guess, though."

Her jaw dropped. "You ... wanted to be a moon traveler?"

"Astronaut," I corrected softly.

She shoved me, hard, and I rolled onto my back, laughing as she leaned over me, her eyes blazing with betrayal.

"You—the man who can't handle turbulence without cursing in three languages—wanted to ride a rocket into space?"

I caught her wrist and pulled her down. "I was seven, Jade. Big dreams, limited logic."

She groaned, throwing herself back against the pillows as she yanked the covers up to hide her face.

"Come on," I drawled, as I tugged the blanket down. "I won. Tell me one of your darkest secrets."

She peeked out, her hair a wild halo around her flushed face.

"You're not going to let this go, are you?"

"No."

She sighed, her lips brushing against mine in a fleeting kiss before she pulled back, her eyes darting away like she was searching for an escape.

"I lied," she muttered, her voice quieter now. "I do have family back home. I just ... don't talk to them. Haven't in a long time."

In the six years Jade Whitenhouse had worked for me, not once had she mentioned a damn thing about friends or family. The only exception had been when Sofiya Melov—Volk's wife

—had started working for me, and the two of them had hit it off.

Best friends ever since, like two sides of a coin I couldn't flip.

"Why?"

She exhaled sharply, her fingers brushing her lips like she was trying to shove the words back in.

"It's complicated," she said, her gaze fixed somewhere just over my shoulder.

"A few weeks ago, you left for a 'family emergency.' Was that about them?"

Her head snapped toward me, her eyes narrowing, but there was no real fire behind it. Just exhaustion.

"You noticed that, huh?"

"I notice everything about you, *amore*."

She hesitated, her lips parting like she wanted to argue, but then she closed them again, her shoulders sagging slightly.

"It was my mama's funeral," she finally admitted, the words barely above a whisper. "She passed away."

"From what?"

Her lips quivered, and for a moment, she didn't speak.

Then a single tear slid down her cheek.

"A broken heart."

In all the years I'd known her, she'd been untouchable—unshakable.

She hadn't cried.

She hadn't cracked.

Seeing her like this was a punch to the gut, the kind that lingered long after the blow.

A thousand questions clawed at my throat, but I swallowed them down, my mind stuck on the fact that she was breaking right in front of me.

Without a word, I pulled her to me, her body stiff before it collapsed into mine. She buried her face in my chest, her tears hot against my skin.

Her leg slid over mine—possessive, desperate.

I just held her tighter, one hand buried in her hair, the other tracing calming circles on her back.

She cried like she hadn't let herself in years, like every sob tore something out of her that she couldn't afford to keep anymore.

And I let her.

I let her break down, even though it ripped through my chest—because she was mine to hold together, even in pieces.

CHAPTER TWENTY-NINE

— DEAN CAVANAGH

"We can depend on nobody in this world, and sometimes we even betray ourselves."
— **Dean Cavanagh**

Jade

Disgust exploded inside me, sour and burning, crawling up my throat like bile.

I hated myself. Like, really, *seriously* hated myself.

I couldn't even glance at my reflection without wanting to hurl—or better yet, smash the nearest mirror, and pretend I didn't exist.

I stormed into the Jimmy Choo store like a woman on a mission, my heels clicking loudly enough to warn everyone to get the hell out of my way.

Retail therapy was the goal, but not just any kind of retail therapy.

I needed something expensive. Something with an edge. Something high enough to make me forget how spectacularly I'd just embarrassed myself.

The shoes gleamed under the lights, practically singing my name. One pair, a killer black stiletto with enough sparkle to blind an entire nation, caught my eye.

Perfect.

I could already imagine wearing them to my own funeral—the one I'd arrange after jumping off the thirteenth floor of my apartment. Because clearly, being this dumb wasn't survivable.

Ugh.

I can't believe I let a world-class, ego-driven, murderous asshole, overbearing jerk crawl under my skin.

Worse, I had broken my damn promise.

The one I had sworn on my soul, my sanity, and maybe even my favorite pair of heels.

The one that had said, "Jade, don't let anyone—especially *him*—mess with your head, and make you lose focus on your revenge."

And yet, here I was, standing in the wreckage of my own boundaries, feeling equal parts furious and disgusted.

Honestly, someone should slap me.

Or better yet, shove me into traffic, because clearly, I've lost all sense of self-preservation.

Just thinking about how I had stripped for him, *again*—after he had humiliated me at the exhibition, solidifying the horrifying realization that I might actually have a degradation kink—and all he had done was ... hold me.

And the bastard hadn't even tried to take advantage of it!

Then, because I had the self-control of a toddler on a sugar high, I had opened my big, dumb mouth and almost spilled my real secret. My *mama*? Seriously? If he started snooping, knowing him, he'd piece together my entire life story before his espresso cooled.

And let's not forget—I had *cried.*

In front of *him.*

After years of swearing to myself that I'd never, ever let it happen again. No tears, no cracks, no giving in to that soul-crushing, gut-twisting feeling. But then he had just ... he'd opened the damn floodgates, cracked my heart wide open, and let every single demon crawl out.

I groaned out loud, earning a few glares from the women around me.

Perfect.

Now half of New York thinks I'm unhinged.

The other half probably already knows, anyway.

I hated that his story had stirred something in me—something I thought I'd buried a long time ago. *Empathy.*

That childish, useless thing I usually didn't have the time or energy for. But the way he'd said it, the raw edge in his voice, what he had gone through *so* young ... I couldn't help but picture a little Angelo Lazzio, scared, alone, and enduring a hell no child should ever face.

It had made my stomach twist in ways I despised.

He murdered your sister, Jade!

No empathy for him!

My gaze locked on the pair of black heels adorned with crystals so dazzling they could probably guide ships home. They'd look killer with that black YSL dress Monica Lazzio had gifted me in Aspen.

I was already imagining the heads I'd turn when I started walking toward them, eyes glued—so much so, that I didn't notice the human roadblock in my path until I had slammed into them, stumbling like a fool.

"Oh my God, I'm so sorry—wait ... Jade?"

I glanced up, my eyes narrowing.

Long blonde hair, tiny frame, and those icy blue eyes that could probably freeze you in place if you weren't careful.

Luciana Lazzio.

Lorenzo Lazzio's wife—Angelo's uncle's wife.

The woman he had used to have a fling with.

Of course. Perfect timing.

Here I was, trying to get him out of my head, and now I'm face to face with his ex-mistress. Because why not, right?

"Hey, Luciana," I said, hoping she'd get the hint that I wasn't in the mood. "Look, I really have to go—"

I turned, but she was quicker, her hand catching my arm.

"Wait, Jade," she said, her voice softer this time. "I'd really like to talk to you. Please, let's grab some coffee together. Just for a few minutes."

Her fingers tightened, almost pleading.

"Luciana ..." I started, but she cut me off.

"Please, Jade. Just five minutes."

I hesitated, glancing down at her hand still on my arm.

I didn't know what to make of this, but something in her voice made it hard to walk away.

"Fine. Just a few minutes," I muttered.

Guess I can kiss my new Jimmy Choos goodbye.

"I guess we're not here to critique your taste in shoes ... or men," I said, raising an eyebrow over my coffee cup.

Luciana chuckled softly, but it didn't reach her eyes.

She took a slow sip of her matcha latte, her fingers trembling just a little as she set the cup down. “No, Jade. I … I wanted to apologize,” she said, her voice dropping. “For that night, years ago.”

Ah, *that* night—the one burned into my brain, where I had walked in on her and Angelo in his office, doing things that didn’t exactly scream “family bonding.”

“Angelo and I … we never …” She exhaled sharply, like she was trying to force the words out. “We were never together. What you saw—” Her gaze darted away. “It was the first, and only time we ever … did that.”

I stayed quiet, letting the coffee warm my hands.

She must’ve sensed my skepticism, because she leaned forward, her voice trembling. “That night, Lorenzo and I had a huge fight about his drinking. He … hit me.”

Her words stopped me cold.

“I panicked. I didn’t know where to go, so I ran to Angelo. His family has always been kind to me, and I thought maybe —” Her voice cracked, and she looked down at her lap. “Maybe he could help me feel safe.”

I stared at her, trying to process the bomb she had just dropped.

For someone I’d mentally labeled as a snake, she suddenly looked … human.

And I hated it.

“I’m the one who seduced him,” she said, her voice shaking just enough to make me pause mid-sip of my mocha latte. “I stormed into his office, a complete mess. He was kind, promised me he’d make Lorenzo pay. You know how the Lazzios are about family; they don’t tolerate that kind of thing. Angelo was furious that his uncle had laid a hand on me.”

I held my cup a little tighter, my silence urging her to keep going.

"I don't know what came over me," she whispered, her gaze dropping. "I kissed him. He tried to push me away, but I think ... I think he could feel how much I needed someone. Just someone to make me feel like I wasn't falling apart. He let it happen. And then ..." She hesitated, her eyes lifting to meet mine.

"And then I walked in," I finished softly.

She nodded. "It wasn't what you think, Jade. It wasn't an affair. It wasn't love. It was ... a desperate, stupid moment. And I'm so sorry you had to see it."

"Luciana, why are you telling me this?" I asked. "I mean, I have no interest—or care, for that matter—about what Angelo does, or who he does." A sharp, annoying twinge in my chest begged to differ, but I shoved it down where it belonged. "So ... why now?"

She sighed, her perfectly manicured nails drumming against her cup. "Because I'm leaving, Jade. I'm running away."

What?

She continued, her voice softer now. "Angelo's organized everything. A new home, a new name ... even a job. Far, far away from all of this." Her lips curved into a faint, almost wistful smile. "You're never going to see me again. But before I go, I needed to make amends—and ask you for a favor."

I tilted my head. "A favor? From me?"

"I know I'm not in a position to ask, but ... please, Jade. Take care of him. I know you argue like cats and dogs, but anyone can see how smitten he is with you. The way he looks at you, it's not just lust. It's something deeper. And you—"

"Luciana," I interrupted, holding up a hand.

But she pressed on. "He doesn't deserve to suffer any more, Jade. He's suffered enough for ten lifetimes."

With that, she stood up, her hand brushing my shoulder in what I assume was meant to be a comforting gesture.

"Goodbye, Jade," she murmured before walking away, her heels clicking against the tile as she disappeared through the café door.

And in that moment, I knew—really knew—I'd never see her again.

I realized she'd done the impossible: she'd cranked up the guilt I'd been trying to suffocate all morning into a full-blown, suffocating bubble.

Thanks a lot, Luciana. You've really outdone yourself.

How the hell am I supposed to kill him now?

CHAPTER THIRTY

"Men should think twice before making widowhood women's only path to power."
— **Gloria Steinem**

Angelo

"Greg's back in Aspen. Hiding in his mansion. I checked his phone bill—he's called the same number twelve times this week."

I nodded, barely hearing him over the steady tap of my pen against my chin.

Tonight was Christmas Eve.

My parents' mansion in the Hamptons was prepped for the family dinner—a house I'd forced them to buy, not out of love or tradition, but to carve out my own space to face the demons that had refused to die.

A battleground disguised as a home.

The city didn't control me anymore. Nothing did.

I was supposed to catch the helicopter in an hour, but the day had been a grind—putting the finishing touches on Scarlett's Times Square show for tomorrow, ensuring everything was flawless.

Hell, I had even wasted time playing Santa for my family.

"*Mio figlio–*"

"I know where the bastard is," I snapped, not bothering to look at him. "I just don't have time to drag his miserable ass out of hiding today. Let him sit in his gilded cage and have one last Christmas with his family. Let him pretend he's safe for one more fucking night."

My father stayed silent, smart enough not to push further.

I should've dealt with Greg weeks ago—I knew that.

The bastard had fucking shot me, for fuck's sake.

But even he had barely registered in my mind these days, shoved aside by someone far more dangerous.

A pretty demon with long black hair, and eyes so haunting they should've come with a goddamn warning label. Every time I looked into them, it felt like they burned deeper, pulled harder—like they were made to drag me into hell and make me savor every second of the fall.

Last night, I'd fought like hell not to fuck her.

Every second had been a war because, for once, it wasn't just about wanting her body—though God knows I did. I had needed her to see that opening up, baring something raw and buried deep inside, wasn't just a ploy to get her into my bed.

I didn't want her vulnerable for my gain.

I wanted her to *need* me—really need me.

This wasn't a fucking game for me.

I wanted the damned woman in ways I couldn't even put into words.

I wanted her so badly it ached, like an itch I couldn't reach no matter how hard I tried.

My father let out a heavy sigh, the kind meant to convey some profound disappointment I couldn't fucking care less about.

"I'll see you tonight."

He turned and left, shutting the door behind him.

Good.

Now I knew exactly what I needed to do.

But first, I reached for the phone on my desk, and pressed the red button.

"Yes, sir?" Grace answered promptly.

"Miss Whitenhouse left for the day," I began, leaning back in my chair. "Send her a voice message. Let her know a chauffeur will be waiting for her downstairs in thirty minutes. Tell her it's a last-minute emergency."

Grace didn't respond right away.

The silence was long enough for me to picture her on the other side of the door, her lips pressed in that disapproving line she thought I didn't notice.

"Of course, sir. I'll handle it and head home. Merry Christmas."

"Merry Christmas, Grace."

I leaned back in my chair, fingers steepled under my chin as my smirk widened.

The little devil has no idea what was coming her way.

"Aren't you ashamed of yourself? Dragging me out on Christmas Eve? I tolerate your psychotic tendencies all year, Lazzio. The least you could do is let me drink hot cocoa and bask in the Christmas spirit for one freaking night, like a normal human being."

Ah, there she was—back to her usual pain-in-the-ass self.

I suppose pretending she hadn't been naked in my bed, pressing her body against mine, was just part of her twisted little holiday denial.

Fine. Let her act innocent.

We both knew the truth—her body had spoken a whole different language when my hands had been on her.

I extended a hand to help her out of the car, but she swatted it away like I'd offered her a dead rat.

She stormed off toward the elevator, her heels stabbing into the floor.

I lingered for a moment, saluting the chauffeur and slipping him a generous tip for putting up with her attitude.

"Merry Christmas," I muttered, smirking before catching up.

Stepping into the elevator beside her, I watched her finger hover over the button for her office floor. Before she could press it, I leaned in, brushing past her hand to tap the one marked "Rooftop."

Her brows knit together. "Where are we going?"

"Making sure this isn't the most boring Christmas of your life," I said, leaning casually against the wall.

A flicker of curiosity in her eyes betrayed her.

When the elevator doors opened, the rooftop greeted us with freezing wind and the roar of a waiting helicopter. She pulled her fur coat tighter, and for once, she let me guide her into the seat without throwing a tantrum.

I climbed in after her, slipping the ear protectors over her head, securing her seatbelt with care before fastening my own.

Then, with a tug, I slammed the door shut, sealing us inside.

The ride to the Hamptons was quiet.

She stared out at the glittering New York skyline, her profile lit by the city's glow. Every bump of turbulence made her hand shoot out to grab mine, her fingers clinging for a heartbeat before she snatched them back.

After forty minutes, we landed on my parents' estate.

I stepped out, unbuckling my seatbelt before opening her door and offering my hand.

Naturally, she ignored it.

Instead, she sat there, arms crossed, her cheeks blazing red.

"To your parents' house, Lazzio? Are you insane? If I walk in there, they're going to think we're together!"

"Maybe they should."

Her eyes went wide, disbelief etched into every line of her face. "Excuse me, what the hell does that mean?"

"We'll talk about it inside. Later."

She wagged her finger in my face. "Oh no, Lazzio. There's no 'this,' no 'us,' no whatever twisted fantasy you're cooking up—"

I leaned in, cutting her off mid-rant. "Get out of the fucking helicopter, Miss Whitenhouse. Or I'll bend you over right here, right now, in front of everyone, and make sure they all know exactly who you belong to."

She gasped. "Ugh, you're *so* inappropriate."

"I prefer efficient. Now, out."

Her eyes narrowed dangerously. "I have nothing to wear, Lazzio."

"Four dresses are waiting for you upstairs, along with

everything else you'll need for the next two days. It's all taken care of."

With a groan, she unbuckled her seatbelt, shoved past me, and stormed toward the house without another word.

Let the Christmas spirit begin.

CHAPTER

THIRTY-ONE

"Good girls go to heaven, bad girls go everywhere."
— **Mae West**

Jade

One red. One gold. One black. One green.

Of course, the bastard had thought of everything.

The dresses weren't just hanging there—they were *waiting*. Perfectly arranged, paired with sparkly shoes and enough jewelry to make a princess weep.

It was the kind of setup little girls dream of—the fairytale fantasy brought to life.

But standing there, all I could think about was how satisfying it would be to rip them all to shreds.

I shrugged off my coat, tossing it onto a chair before flopping onto the bed.

Grace's call earlier should've been the red flag. "Mr. Lazzio has an emergency," she'd said.

Emergency, my ass. It was a setup.

He'd been pulling me back into his orbit, like a planet trapped in his relentless gravity, no matter how hard I tried to escape.

Didn't the man get it?

I'd been avoiding him for a reason—a list of reasons, actually—but mostly because if I let him drag me any closer, I'd lose the one thing I'd been clawing to hold onto: control.

And now, this? His family thinking we're together?

He was delusional. Certifiably insane.

I'd dealt with egotistical maniacs before, but Angelo Lazzio didn't just take the cake—he smashed it in your face, and expected you to thank him for it.

I stared at the ceiling, fists gripping the comforter like it was the only thing keeping me tethered. Enough was enough.

After this getaway, my plan would finally fall into place.

By the end of the weekend, Lazzio Entertainment Inc. would be nothing but ash.

And Angelo Lazzio? He'd be lying in a pool of his own blood.

It was the only way.

The only way to break free of his claws, and finally claim the revenge I'd been craving for years.

But for now, I had to play the part.

I had to pick a dress.

Not just any dress—one that screamed, *I don't want to be here, but you'll damn well worship at my feet for gracing you with my presence.*

The red one. Obviously.

An Elie Saab gown dripping in gold sparkles, its bustier

mermaid silhouette tailored to perfection. Black velvet gloves to match.

And the pièce de résistance? The black Jimmy Choo heels I'd almost bought before Luciana had forced me to have coffee with her.

Must be fate for them to have appeared here.

I swept my long black hair into a sleek updo, a few loose tendrils framing my face. For makeup, I went with a soft smoky eye—light, airy, but edged with just enough menace to whisper danger. Nude lips, polished to a degree that practically oozed condescension, completed the look.

The result?

A walking masterpiece. The kind that turned heads and stopped hearts.

Yes, I was ready.

Ready to make Angelo Lazzio choke on his arrogance and regret every single second of forcing me into this night.

"Jade, *Dio mio*, every time I see you, you somehow look better than the last," Monica Lazzio drawled as she leaned against the bar, her Roberto Cavalli suit tailored within an inch of perfection.

A dry martini dangled from her fingers like it was part of her outfit.

"Well, what can I say, Monica? I guess it's a gift," I winked, reaching for the champagne flute waiting for me.

Next to her, Francesca Harper gave me a once-over, her red Chanel dress hugging her curves like it had been made for no one else. She didn't need to say anything; the little tilt of her head and the ghost of a smile were enough to declare she approved—begrudgingly, of course.

Lazzio stood by the massive window, framed perfectly by the darkness of the beach outside. He looked ridiculously good, as usual—black shirt, black suit, and a red handkerchief casually tucked into his blazer.

And then it hit me—we matched. Without even trying.

His eyes slid over me, like he was savoring every inch of me in that dress. The way his eyes darkened, like he couldn't decide if he wanted to devour me or just keep me in his head for later, made something in my chest tighten.

Stronzo.

"I must say, I'm delighted Angelo brought you tonight. It's the first time he's *ever* brought a woman to a real family dinner—let alone Christmas." Monica swirled her martini, before she took a slow sip. "I think my son is falling for you, Jade."

Before I could muster up a response that was equal parts polite and insulting, a butler appeared out of nowhere.

"Dinner is served in the dining room," he announced.

I didn't need a second invitation.

With a tight smile at Monica, I followed the butler, Lazzio falling into step beside me. His hand grazed the small of my back—just a whisper of contact, but enough to light my nerves on fire.

I ignored him, and instead let my eyes sweep the house, because, God help me, *this* deserved attention.

If the Gregs' house in Aspen had been majestic, the Lazzios' estate in the Hamptons was straight-up divine intervention.

Every corner of the place sparkled like it had been prepped for a Vogue Christmas special.

Christmas trees? Everywhere.

Not just random ones thrown together either—each was

its own little masterpiece, dripping in gold ornaments, and dusted with fake snow perfectly.

Then there was the dining room.

Oh, the dining room.

It was a fever dream of decadence.

A marble table so long it could probably double as a runway stretched down the center, laden with enough food to feed a small country. Roasted meats gleamed under the soft glow of a massive gold crystal chandelier, its cascading crystals dripping with opulence.

Crystal bowls held colorful side dishes arranged so artistically it almost felt rude to touch them.

I guess that was the highlight of the night—definitely better than the dinner I was *supposed* to have alone in my apartment.

You know, the usual: a sad chicken sandwich and some chips.

The chairs were jet black, high backed, and so dramatic they could have been thrones.

I hesitated for just a second in the doorway, taking it all in. "Wow."

Lazzio moved in closer, and I swore the room got even warmer.

He took my hand, his lips brushing over the glove. "I had the same reaction when you walked in, Miss Whitenhouse—my heart nearly stopped," he murmured. "You're the real Christmas miracle tonight, *amore.*"

My cheeks heated. "Stop it, Angelo."

"I can't help it. You look too tempting tonight—impossible not to stare."

His hand didn't just touch mine—it *lingered,* as if he were savoring the feel of it.

My pulse skipped, but I fought the urge to yank it away.

Instead, with a sigh, I let him guide me to the table.

He then reached for a chair, pulling it out like a gentleman.

"Sit."

I sank into the chair, despite every nerve in my body screaming at me to slap that smug grin off his face.

He sat next to me, *too* close, his leg brushing mine.

I forced my focus away.

The butlers moved around the table, refilling glasses, replacing plates, and ensuring the Lazzios were well catered to.

I grabbed another glass of champagne. The bubbles hit my tongue, and I let the glass linger in my hand, swirling it absently.

I studied the people around me—every laugh, every side-eye, every whispered comment. The familiar faces, and the ones I hadn't seen before. The ones who would laugh with me, and the ones who wouldn't hesitate to slit my throat if it suited them.

But no Luciana or Lorenzo.

Their absence was loud, even if no one else seemed to acknowledge it.

She was really gone, then.

Interesting. Never expected Angelo Lazzio to play the hero.

From time to time, I felt it—his eyes on me.

His knee brushed mine under the table, almost on purpose, sending a little spark up my leg. His hand would brush mine when I reached for something—salt, champagne, whatever the hell it was.

And each time, that spark shot through me again, *hotter* than before.

Then suddenly, Carlos Lazzio rose from his seat, tapping his glass.

"Every Christmas, we share what we're most grateful for. And this year, as always, it will forever be *mia famiglia.*"

Glasses lifted, the chorus was loud and proud: "*La famiglia!*"

My throat tightened, and I could feel that stupid burn behind my eyes.

Yes, *family*.

Family was everything.

Or at least, that's what people said when they actually had one.

I tucked my hands under the table, pressing my nails into my palm until it stung, trying to ground myself. The ache in my chest wasn't playing fair, squeezing harder with every laugh, every smile, every toast around me.

Two deep breaths in. Two out.

I could do this.

Just blend in, Jade.

But, of course, the universe hated me.

Because when I dared to glance up, Angelo was watching me.

Great. Of all the people to notice, it had to have been him.

His hand found mine under the table, before I could yank it away, his fingers wrapped around mine.

"What's wrong?"

I swallowed hard, staring at him, trying to force the words out, but they stuck in my throat.

No way was I breaking down here. Not in front of him.

But then my chest clenched again, my vision started to swim, and—*no, no, no, not now, Jade, come on!*

He let go and stood up. "I invite you all to the ballroom. *The Nutcracker* awaits, along with some early gifts for the children."

The room erupted into movement, chairs scraping, glasses

clinking, everyone laughing and talking as they made their way out.

No one had noticed me, and I should've been relieved.

But *he* had.

Of course, he had.

"Jade—"

I didn't wait.

The chair screeched against the floor as I bolted for the window, hands fumbling with the latch. My fingers shook, desperate, and when it finally gave, the night air hit me like a slap—icy, unforgiving.

I climbed through without thinking, drawn to the crash of the waves like a moth to flames, knowing they'd burn, but unable to stop.

The sand swallowed my heels the moment I landed, clinging and dragging me down with every step. Anger flared, and I yanked them off, hurling them somewhere behind me into the shadows.

Barefoot, I ran.

The beach shifted underfoot, treacherous and endless, until freezing water swallowed my feet and climbed to my ankles. It cut through me, as relentless as knives, but I didn't stop. Not until my legs gave out, sending me to my knees, the shoreline's cold rush soaking through my dress and skin alike.

My chest clenched, air slipping through in shallow, useless gulps. I clawed at it, but each breath was a betrayal, jagged and fleeting. The world blurred—edges smudged with shadow, darker with each blink.

I couldn't move. Couldn't fight it.

My body was turning on me, every muscle locking up as fear roared louder than the ocean.

I dug my nails into my thighs, anything to ground myself, but it wasn't enough. Darkness crept closer, heavy and unrelenting, until the thought struck like lightning—this was it. This was how it ended.

Waves kissed my legs, cold and cruel, as if mocking my struggle. My lungs burned, ribs caving under invisible hands, and all I could do was surrender to the pull of the void.

And then—footsteps.

Heavy. Steady. Cutting through the sand like they belonged to someone who wouldn't stop until they had reached me.

Before the void could take me, Angelo's voice cut through the storm—a beacon, raw and unrelenting, pulling me from the abyss.

"Jade!"

He didn't waste time with empty words or pointless reassurances.

Instead, he crouched, his knees sinking into the wet sand beside me.

The silence between us was deafening, broken only by the crash of the waves and the shallow rasp of my breath.

I felt his hand hover near my arm, unsure, hesitant—like he wasn't certain if his touch would calm me or not.

"Breathe, Jade. In through your nose, out through your mouth. You can do this."

I shook my head violently, the freezing water clawing at my legs.

"I c-can't—"

"Focus on me. Just me."

I tried.

God, I tried. But the air caught in my chest, refusing to obey.

My ribs locked, caging me in, each failed breath a punishment.

And then, I crumbled.

The cold water took me as I fell forward, the waves biting,

the sand pulling. The icy grip numbed my body, but it couldn't dull the terror. Salt water kissed my lips, streaked my face with ruin, makeup mingling with tears, hair plastered to my skin.

I still couldn't breathe.

This couldn't be the end.

Not like this.

Not now. Please, not now.

"Jade, stop!"

The cold only made it worse, the tremors rattling through me as I sank deeper into the panic.

He cursed sharply. Then he moved.

His hands were on me, rough, pulling me up, dragging me out of the water.

His heat was searing, melting the ice in my veins as his arms wrapped around me.

I clung to him, my nails digging into his skin, my face pressed against his neck.

"You're freezing," he growled, carrying me. "Fuck! What the hell were you thinking?"

I didn't answer. Couldn't answer. My chest still burned, my breaths coming in stuttering gasps, but his warmth steadied something deep inside me.

He didn't stop. Not until we were inside—past the echoing crash of the door, up the elevator, and into the bathroom in his room.

The sound of rushing water filled the space as he cranked the shower, steam billowing into the room. He held me upright, his arm locked around my waist like I might disappear.

My gloves went first, his fingers brushing mine as he peeled them away.

Then came the zipper on my dress.

The fabric fell, and so did the rest—bra, underwear, every barrier stripped until I stood bare under his gaze.

But it wasn't lust in his eyes.

It wasn't pity either.

It was something worse. Something that made my throat tighten with guilt.

It was worry.

Angelo Lazzio was worried about me.

He guided me into the shower, the warm water cascading over me in waves, rinsing away the salt, the sand, the night.

He didn't look at me like I was broken.

He didn't say a word about the wreckage I'd become.

His clothes were still on, soaked through as he stepped in with me.

I opened my mouth to protest, but his voice cut through the steam.

"Shh. Let me take care of you, *amore*."

And I let him.

Not because I couldn't fight, but because for the first time, I didn't want to.

His hands moved over me—not rough, not rushed, just careful.

Each touch was gentle, washing away more than the ocean's remnants.

It wasn't control, or power, or even guilt.

It was care—jagged and unguarded, a blade wrapped in silk.

And it made me feel something I wanted to bury.

Angelo Lazzio.

My boss. My tormentor. My savior.

The man who had stolen my sister's life, yet had saved mine three times over.

How could this man be my poison and cure in the same breath?

CHAPTER THIRTY-TWO

"Never love anyone who treats you like you're ordinary."
— **Oscar Wilde**

Jade

"It's the third time I've saved your life, Miss Whitenhouse. Starting to think you've got a death wish," Angelo drawled, handing me the tea like a peace offering.

The first time was years ago, pulling me out of jail.

The second was in the woods.

And now, tonight.

I rolled my eyes, wrapping my fingers around the cup just to steady the tremor in my hands. The steam curled against my skin, but it was the burn in my throat that anchored me.

"Did it ever cross your mind that *maybe* I didn't want to be saved, Lazzio?"

He didn't answer immediately. Instead, he dropped onto the bed, sprawling like a king reclaiming his throne. His bare chest caught the low light, infuriatingly perfect.

"Oh, I've thought about it," he said. "But then it hits me—only you could tear me to pieces like this. One minute, I'm sure I've lost you for good. The next, you're kissing me like I'm the only thing keeping you alive. Then you vanish, leaving me with this fucking hole, wondering if this is the time you'll never come back."

His gaze locked on mine.

"Tell me, Miss Whitenhouse—do you enjoy seeing how far you can push me? Watching me claw at the edge of my sanity just to keep you next to me?"

I set the cup down carefully, the soft clink of porcelain against wood the only sound between us.

Standing, I let the silence stretch as I walked to the bed, feeling his stare burn into my skin.

"Complaining, Lazzio?"

"Not even a little. In fact ...I'm starting to think you might kill me, Jade. And you know what?"

I tilted my head.

"I'd let you."

My heart sank.

If only he knew.

"Don't start with the sweet talk. For all you know, I might want your head on a stick—for every damn headache you've ever given me."

"Bet you do."

The corner of my mouth twitched despite myself. Damn it.

I crawled onto the bed.

His hands found my hips when I straddled him, his grip rough.

His breath warmed my skin as I brushed my fingers along his jaw, the stubble rough under my touch.

I let my lips hover over his. "Thanks. For tonight."

"Anything for you, *amore.*"

Before I could process the words, his hand was at the back of my neck, pulling me in, his lips crashing against mine.

Oh, for the love of—

I grabbed his face, deepening the kiss, swallowing any trace of doubt or reason.

This was the kind of numbness I needed—the kind only he could give.

For just a moment, I wanted to forget everything: who he was, who I was, the blood on his hands, and the wreckage I was planning to leave behind.

I wanted him, needed him like a drug—in me, on me, every messy, broken inch of him.

As if he knew exactly what I needed, he flipped me effortlessly, his weight pressing me into the bed as I found myself beneath him, my legs instinctively wrapping around his waist.

He lingered above me. "I need to know what happened outside before I can fuck you, Jade."

"Stop trying to be sweet, Lazzio. That's not what I need from you."

"What is it you do *need* then, Miss Whitenhouse?"

I let my nails scrape lightly down his skin, just enough to make him shiver, before letting my hands drop to his waist.

"You," I breathed, pushing my hips up against his. "You, inside me. Right now."

My fingers made quick work of his belt and zipper, shoving his pants down just enough before pulling him closer.

The truth of what happened tonight?

It couldn't slip from my lips.

Not yet, not until I did what I needed to do.

How the hell could I explain the panic attack that had nearly swallowed me whole?

That every Christmas for the past six years, I spent it alone —curled up in my bed with a bottle of cheap wine, a sappy movie on the screen, all to help me forget.

To help me forget that they were gone.

That I'd never see them again.

And that the only thing left to look forward to was this cold, empty existence.

Alone.

And it was all because of *him*.

The fact that my body betrayed me, craved him—every single time, it made me sick.

It made me want to take a blade to my own heart for allowing myself to need him, for feeling this twisted hunger for a man who wasn't supposed to exist in my world.

A man who—whether I wanted to admit it or not—had become my weakness.

But I just need it *once*.

Just once to fall into the abyss of lust, to give in to him fully, so I could take everything I needed from him.

Once I had him out of my system, then killing him would be easy.

"You sure?"

I nodded. "*Sì*."

Angelo's fingers toyed with the hem of my T-shirt—*his* T-shirt—and in one smooth motion, he pulled it over my head.

I wasn't wearing *anything* underneath.

The cool air hit my skin, but his eyes set me on fire.

He didn't rush.

Of course, the bastard didn't.

His hands found my hips first, calloused palms burning trails into me as he leaned in, his lips brushing my neck. Soft at first, maddeningly so, before he kissed me, deeper, hungrier.

Then he went lower.

My breath hitched, sharp and shaky, as his lips hovered over my nipple.

He didn't dive in right away; no, he had to be cruel about it.

A flick of his tongue, a soft circle, and then his mouth closed around it, and my brain short-circuited.

His voice was low, rough against my skin. "Say it again. Tell me how much you need my dick inside you."

Bastard.

Hot, overbearing, sexy, evil bastard.

"I want your dick inside me, Lazzio. So *deep* I feel it every time I move. So deep it's all I can fucking think about." I tilted my head. "Happy now?"

His grip tightened, and the way his eyes darkened told me I'd either won ... or doomed myself entirely.

"Oh, happy doesn't even begin to cover it."

Hell broke loose, and it was way better than I could have ever imagined.

He flipped me, tits squished against the mattress as his knee wedged between my legs, spreading them.

He yanked down his boxers and drove into me in one rough, unrelenting thrust that knocked the air right out of my lungs.

"Oh—"

His hand slapped over my mouth, cutting off my scream. "You wanted it, *amore*," he growled against my ear, his voice dripping with that infuriating mix of arrogance and sin that made me hate how much I loved it.

My muffled gasp turned into a moan as he pulled me back, my teeth grazing his palm.

His other hand slid down to my hip, holding me in place as he set a pace that made me see stars, or maybe the devil.

My fingers clawed at the sheets, desperate for something to hold on to as he took me apart.

My eyes rolled back, my body arching involuntarily with every thrust.

I could feel him *everywhere.*

He was way too big for me.

"Deep enough for you, Miss Whitenhouse?" His voice was a little breathless, the sound of it shooting straight between my legs as his hips slammed into mine, his hips smacking against my ass.

Yes.

Yes, oh fuck, yes.

I shook my head, biting down harder on his palm to stifle the needy noises crawling up my throat.

He chuckled darkly. "No? Wrong answer."

Before I could blink, he pulled out, his cock leaving me achingly empty.

A desperate whine escaped me as I tried to push back, but his hand came down hard on my ass, the crack of the slap echoing in the room.

Tears blurred my vision as the sting spread, sharp and electric, but before I could so much as curse him out, I felt his tongue. Warm and wet, dragging up the length of my spine like he wanted to devour me.

"Fuck," he groaned. "I've dreamed of licking this tattoo for *years,* Jade. But you already knew that, didn't you?"

His tongue swirled over the ink, tracing every line like he was worshipping it.

"That's why you wore all those fucking backless dresses," he whispered, his breath hot against my skin. "Strutting into my office like a little slut, like you didn't fucking notice me staring, like you didn't *want* me to fantasize about this—about you."

His mouth trailed *lower*, his tongue tracing the curve of my ass, his teeth grazing the soft flesh there before his head dipped further.

And then his tongue was between my legs.

Wait, I thought he didn't go down on women?

One, two, three strokes of his warm tongue delved deep into my pussy.

I gasped his name, half a curse, half a prayer. "Angelo—"

Before I could catch my breath, he yanked my hair, forcing me up onto my knees.

My back arched sharply, head thrown back as his grip on me didn't falter. His face hovered above mine, upside down and full of something primal, his mouth crashing onto mine in a messy, savage kiss.

It wasn't soft. It wasn't cute.

It was him *owning* me, taking whatever I had left to give.

He pulled away just enough to spread my legs wider, his knee forcing them apart as he lined himself up again. And then —*God*—then he slammed into me, *so* hard and *so* deep I screamed.

Loud. Raw. For the entire damn world to hear me.

My body betrayed me completely, any shred of control gone.

I moved with him, faster, rougher, meeting every thrust, every punishing slam of his hips, like I couldn't get enough.

"*Sì, amore*," he said. "You fucking love that, don't you? Taking me like this—letting me ruin you."

His teeth scraped my neck as his hand dug into my hips

"Tell me, Jade," he hissed. "Tell me how much you fucking love being mine tonight."

I closed my eyes, the sensation being too much. "Yes, I love it *so* much, Lazzio."

I bit my lip, choking on a sob as his hand left my hip to wrap around my throat, pulling me up against his chest.

"Look at you," he whispered against my ear. "Screaming for me. Is that what you needed?"

"Yes," I gasped.

My head lolled back onto his shoulder, his hand tightening just enough to make me dizzy.

"I thought you hated me, *amore*," he murmured, biting down on my shoulder hard enough to make me cry out. "You hate me, and yet here you are, begging for my cock. *Needing* it."

His other hand slipped lower, finding my clit and teasing it in time with his thrusts.

Tears blurred my vision, a sob tearing from my throat as he pushed me further.

"I'll give you everything you need, *amore*. I'll ruin you so thoroughly you won't remember how to breathe without me."

And he did.

Over and over.

Until there was nothing left of me.

As my orgasm ripped through me, my scream was swallowed by the mattress beneath me. My body trembled uncontrollably, my nails clawing into the sheets as Angelo didn't let up—not even for a second. He kept pounding into me, relentless, dragging every ounce of pleasure from me until I thought I'd break in two.

And then, just as the aftershocks of my orgasm left me boneless, he pulled out, letting me collapse forward, my entire body flat against the bed.

I felt the heat of his gaze on me before I even turned my head, my cheek pressing into the mattress as I looked over my shoulder.

There he was, standing over me, his cock gripped in his hand—slick, hard, and oh *so freaking* big.

His eyes locked on mine, dark and ravenous.

"Stay just like that."

Him jerking off just above my ass? Best fucking show I've ever seen.

I couldn't move, didn't even want to.

His gaze dropped to my back, following the curve of my spine, right to the ink etched on my skin.

"You drive me fucking insane, Jade," he growled, teeth gritted, his hand working faster. "This tattoo, this body ... all of it."

I let a breath out, running my tongue over my lips. "Then come on it."

He cursed under his breath, and I felt it a second later—hot and thick—as his cum coated my skin. It dripped over my tattoo, marking me.

He gasped, chest heaving, but his eyes never left mine.

"*Bellissima*," he muttered, almost to himself, his hand gliding over my lower back, smearing his mess into my skin.

For a moment, as I lay there, breathless and tangled in something dangerously addictive, I realized I'd just made a fool of myself.

Now that I'd had a taste of what it was like to be fucked by him, there was no going back.

All I could think was—*more*.

I wanted it all.

"Do you get them often?"

I sucked in a shaky breath as his fingers traced lazy patterns down my back.

My head was on his chest, right over the steady rhythm of his heartbeat.

So *annoyingly* calm. Meanwhile, I was trying not to spiral.

Our legs were tangled, and there wasn't a single part of me that wasn't pressed against him.

We fit together too perfectly, like he'd been cut from the exact mold to fill the hollow ache in my chest. But instead of fixing it, he just made me hyper-aware of how broken I actually was.

By *them,* I knew exactly what he'd meant—my panic attacks.

Great. My favorite topic.

I closed my eyes as his hand slid up to stroke my hair, and for a second, I pretended he wasn't waiting for an answer.

"Rarely," I finally muttered. "Only certain things set me off."

"Like thinking about your family."

"Yeah."

"Ever considered that talking about them could set you free?"

I snorted, burying my face in his chest. "Set me free? I don't think talking is going to *magically* fix me, Lazzio."

I couldn't.

I wouldn't.

I just wanted to stay like this, safe in his arms.

God, I hated this—hated how those ghosts hovered. Always there, reminding me of how much of a disappointment I was.

His arm tightened around me, pulling me closer.

His hand kept moving slowly, stroking my hair, his breath steady against the top of my head. I felt his chest rise and fall beneath me, the rhythm so solid, so dependable, that for a moment I let myself match it.

"Did you ever try to find the man who kidnapped you?"

He let out a low, humorless chuckle. "Ah, so you get to ask the questions, but I don't?"

I tilted my head, smirking as he shifted, propping himself up on one elbow. His arm rested on the pillow, his hand lazily cradling my face.

"Yes."

His finger traced the curve of my jaw, sliding down my neck.

It was slow—*intoxicating*.

He hummed softly. "And why's that, Miss Whitenhouse?"

"Because you dragged me on this trip. The least you could do is keep me entertained. Answering my questions seems like a good place to start."

His finger trailed lower, skimming over my chest, my stomach, before slipping between my legs to the sensitive flesh there.

"Entertained?" he murmured, his voice edged with mockery. "I thought the orgasm I just gave you—the one you screamed loud enough for every Lazzio in the mansion to hear—was proof you've been enjoying your stay, *amore*."

His finger circled my clit.

"Nah," I breathed out, fighting to steady my voice. "I was faking it."

His hand stilled. "Oh, really?"

I shrugged, grabbing his face and pulling him closer until my lips brushed his, the barest hint of a kiss. His finger stopped moving entirely, replaced by the grip of his other hand on my chin.

"Then you're a better liar than I gave you credit for, Miss Whitenhouse."

He didn't give me a chance to say anything else. His lips slammed into mine, making me lose my breath.

I shifted, straddling him.

I was itching to test that stupid rumor.

Eating me out? Check.

Though I was slightly disappointed it had lasted only a few seconds.

It was time to see if that "only fucks from behind" thing held up.

I wanted to see if he'd stop me.

He was already thick and hot against his stomach, and I ground down onto him, the slickness between my legs coating him as I moved slowly, my hands pressed flat against his chest, my tits tight and aching.

He released me, arms folding behind his head, watching with a lazy look in his eye.

I threw my head back, a hot, tight feeling spreading in my stomach, my hair falling behind me.

"You look *so* fucking good right now," he muttered, voice rough.

I shot him a smile, the heat in my cheeks growing as I picked up the pace, my pussy grinding against his cock *so* deliciously I almost saw stars.

"Answer me, Lazzio."

His tongue flicked across his lips. "Why do you wanna know?"

"Because I want to feel *close* to you."

I grabbed his cock, yanking him to my entrance, and sank down slowly, taking every inch of him deep inside me.

That position? One of my favorites. Men at my mercy, eyes wide with desperation as I took what I wanted, pushed them to the edge of their control. I fucking loved it.

There was something about knowing I held the power.

I rode him, my tits bouncing wildly, my body slapping against his, and his curses lit the fuse on my own insanity.

His hands gripped my hips, digging in, pulling me harder against him.

"Isn't *this* close enough, Jade?"

"No," I breathed out. "It isn't."

His eyes sparkled with mischief as he grabbed my waist, flipped me onto my back, and slammed into me missionary style, his lips crashing against mine.

"And what about this?"

I let out a moan, my nails digging into his back, legs wrapped around him.

He was so close—*too* close—that I could see the tiny gold specks in his eyes.

Missionary and cowgirl? Check.

Yeah, that rumor? Total bullshit.

I couldn't keep control any longer.

Cursing under my breath, I came; my eyes squeezed shut, and I sank my teeth into his lower lip.

He groaned into my mouth, his tongue brushing against my lips before he pulled away and came all over my thigh.

He grinned, watching me prop myself up on my arms as his finger scooped up some of his release and smeared it across my lips. I licked it off like it was the best treat I'd ever had.

He grabbed my chin and kissed me deep.

Pulling back, his voice low just above a whisper. "I just know one thing, Jade. The city where he held me hostage ... was Boston."

CHAPTER
THIRTY-THREE

"If you have a sister and she dies, do you stop saying you have one?
Or are you always a sister, even when the other half of the equation is gone?"
—**Jodi Picoult**

Jade
19 years old
Eleven years ago

"Do you know why I love Boston so much?"

She looped her arm through mine as I brought my ice cream to my lips, savoring the taste of vanilla. My eyes wandered around the Harvard Square Mayfair Festival. I took in the crowd, the mouthwatering smell of pizza and street food, the smooth jazz music spilling into the air, and the way people danced together on the small stage. It was mid-spring, and after yesterday's argument about who was supposed to do the laundry but hadn't, Mama had grounded both of us.

Yes, grounded.

At nineteen, I could still get grounded. Humiliating.

Turns out, it had been my turn to do the laundry. To make it up to myself, and to Stella, I asked her if she'd wanted to come with me to the Mayfair Festival. Now, what fourteen-year-old wouldn't jump at the chance to follow her big sister to enjoy a day of fatty food, good music, and cute boys?

She said yes, and just like that, all was forgiven.

"Why?" I asked.

"Because it reminds me of New York, you know? Like, the way the lights sparkle at night, the busy streets, and all the cute boys walking around in suits. One day, when I'm all grown up, I'll move there, get a cute little apartment overlooking Central Park, and ..."

I was mid-lick, savoring my ice cream, barely listening to her as she rambled on about Boston and New York, probably working her way up to something straight out of a rom-com. Vanilla dripped dangerously close to my fingers when a man with devil-red paint smeared across his face stepped right in front of us, forcing me to stop.

"Which one of you *bellissima* ladies wants to uncover what fate has in store?"

I stared at him blankly, his Italian accent strongly tickling my ear, then followed his dramatic gesture to a small, dark tent tucked between two vendor stalls. The fabric was a mix of black and gold, with a crooked wooden sign propped outside that read, "Fortune Teller." Underneath, in bold, uneven letters: "$5."

"Not me, buddy," I said, waving him off.

I went back to licking my cone, already halfway down the

street when Stella grabbed my arm, practically yanking me back.

"Jadie! Oh my god, please, let's do it!"

I turned, groaning. "Seriously? You want him to tell you your future?"

"It's only five bucks!" She clutched my arm like her life depended on it, wide-eyed and practically bouncing. "What if he says something cool? What if he knows something?"

"What's he gonna know? That my ice cream's melting? Because same," I muttered, licking the drip off the side.

"Jaaaadie." She dragged out my name like a five-year-old. "Please!"

"Stella, it's a scam. A five-dollar scam!"

"Please, Jadie. Just five minutes," she whined, clasping her hands in petition now.

I groaned, glaring at the devil-painted man, who was watching us with a smug grin, clearly sensing he'd won. "Fine! But if he tells me my soulmate is a Capricorn, I'm leaving."

Stella squealed and dragged me toward the tent, already beaming like her future had just been written in the cards.

The inside of the tent was even darker than I had expected, the air heavy with the faint smell of burnt sage and something sickly sweet. Fake skeletons hung in the corners, their hollow eyes staring at us, and cobwebs—probably real, knowing my luck—draped the ceiling like some low-budget haunted house.

A single wooden table sat in the middle, draped in a deep-red velvet cloth, its edges frayed like it had seen better days. Fat, black candles were scattered across it, their flames flickering low, casting jagged shadows on the walls. A crystal ball sat dead center, the light catching its surface and refracting eerie streaks of blue and green.

The man gestured toward two stools—old, creaky ones made of rough, uneven wood. I sat gingerly, half expecting it to collapse beneath me. Stella, of course, plopped down like this was the best day of her life.

The second we were seated, a chill ran down my arms, and I instinctively rubbed them. It wasn't cold exactly, but something about the atmosphere made my skin crawl, like the tent itself had secrets it wasn't planning to share.

The man slid into the chair across from us.

Without a word, he extended his hand, palm up, the universal signal for money first.

I sighed, digging into my bag, and slapped a ten-dollar bill into his palm.

He pocketed the bill and leaned forward, resting his elbows on the table. His gaze shifted between us, the flickering candlelight making his painted devil face even more grotesque.

"*Allora*," he said, his voice dropping to a raspy whisper, "which one of you ladies is brave enough to go first?"

Stella raised her hand. "Me!"

The man grabbed a deck of cards, and with a flick of his wrist, they spun between his fingers in a blur of black and gold. His hands moved quickly, fluidly—like he was performing some dark magic, or maybe just trying too hard to be dramatic. For a solid two minutes, all we could hear was the rustle of cards and the eerie hum of distant chanting. It was low, like a dark lullaby, the voices of both men and women blending together.

And then, just as the air grew thick with that strange energy, the music abruptly cut off.

The man stopped, placed the deck in front of us, and spread the cards out in a fan. "Choose three cards, my child."

Stella's eyes lit up like a kid in a candy store, and I could practically see her pulse quicken. She giggled, pointing to three cards.

The man reached for the cards, slowly turning each one over.

As he laid them out, my stomach dropped.

The first card was the Two of Cups.

Then came The Lovers, reversed.

And finally, the last card - a depiction of a corpse pierced brutally, unmoving - the Ten of Swords.

A chill ran down my spine.

The man's eyes darkened. "You were blessed on this earth to have the deepest connection with someone—*la tua anima gemella*, your soulmate."

"That's you, Jadie!" Stella beamed, squeezing my hand with a smile so wide it was contagious.

The man's expression shifted, his tone more serious. "You're going to fall in love—hard. It will be your first, and only lover. You'll love him deeply, deeper than love itself." His eyes narrowed as if the next part was something he didn't want to say, but he had no choice. "But this love ... will be your doom, *dolcezza*."

I blinked, waiting for him to continue.

He pointed to the last card—Death—and my skin prickled. "This love will kill you. Figuratively. Spiritually. Physically."

I stood up, throwing my hands in the air. "That's it? We pay you five bucks each just for you to spout random crap like this?" I shook my head, already over it. "Come on, Stella, we're leaving. Told you it was a scam."

Stella laughed. "Hold up—me? Falling in love? Having some tragic, dramatic love story like Romeo and Juliet? That's so cool!"

I shot her a look.

"Sit, *dolcezza*. I'm not done."

I stopped in my tracks, irritated, but also weirdly intrigued.

"You've gotta be kidding me," I muttered, but reluctantly plopped back down.

Stella was grinning now, practically vibrating with excitement. "Jadie, you have to admit, it's fun. Maybe it means something!"

"Yeah, it means I just wasted ten bucks," I muttered, crossing my arms.

The man's gaze went ice cold. Without saying a word, he grabbed the cards and shuffled them, his eyes locked on mine, like he could see straight through me.

Then, he spread them out, face down on the table.

"Pick three."

I pointed to three cards, my foot tapping impatiently on the wooden floor, just wanting this nonsense to end. Stella grabbed my hand again, her grip tight with excitement.

The man turned the cards slowly, one by one.

The first was the Two of Cups again, then the Five of Cups, and finally, Temperance.

"You are blessed ..." he began, his voice taking on that weird, mystical tone again, "You were blessed on this earth to have the deepest connection with someone—"

"Yeah, yeah, we already know about that," I interrupted, rolling my eyes. "Change the disc, buddy."

His brows furrowed, clearly unfazed. He pointed to the Five of Cups. "You're going to lose someone you love. Someone who is closest to your heart. And the grief will take everything from you. You'll spiral ... almost lose your life."

I stared at the card.

Then he pointed to the angel on the Temperance card, his voice softer now. "But someone is going to save you. Balance you. This angel will be your salvation, your savior. Your guardian angel. *Tuo angelo*."

Silence fell over us.

I glanced over at Stella, her eyes wide with wonder, completely wrapped up in whatever the man had just said. I couldn't help but roll my eyes. The man's expression was blank as he sat there, unmoving.

"Wow, so original," I scoffed, shaking my head. "Thank you so much, Satan."

I stood up, gesturing for Stella to follow me.

As we made our way out of the tent, a cobweb brushed my hand, and I winced in disgust. "Ugh, seriously?" I muttered, shaking it off as we stepped back into the sunlight.

The bright rays hit my eyes, making me squint. Stella circled her arms around mine, her grin still plastered across her face.

As we turned, his voice stopped us cold. "You called me the devil," he said, his grin razor-sharp. "But it'll be the same thing people call you soon—*Diavoletta*."

With a wink that chilled more than charmed, he slipped back into the shadows of his tent.

What the hell?

I turned to Stella with a sigh. "You owe me ten bucks now."

She laughed, clearly unbothered. We kept walking, the absurdity of the whole fortune-telling thing fading from our minds as we neared a hot dog food truck.

The sound of the sizzling grill and the smell of mustard and onions filled the air, replacing the weird energy of the reading with something much more satisfying.

Her arm wrapped around mine, and for a moment, the world felt perfectly normal again.

CHAPTER
THIRTY-FOUR

"The past beats inside me like a second heart."
—**John Banville**

Jade

Dropping my coat to the floor and kicking off my heels, I winced as the icy floor shocked my toes.

Ignoring the chill, I headed straight for the kitchen. I yanked open the fridge, and stared blankly at its contents before grabbing a drink—or ten.

My mind was a mess, the whispers of a thousand devils cackling and mocking me, each one louder than the last. I needed to shut them the hell up.

I poured myself a glass of wine, leaned back against the fridge, and took three generous gulps.

I sighed, long and heavy.

This wasn't supposed to have happened.

None of it.

After that night with Angelo ... the night I had let him fuck me—"let" being a laughable word, considering I'd practically begged for it—I'd ridden him until my legs were sore, wrung out from more orgasms than I'd had all year combined.

The way he'd bit my neck each time he'd come, the growl in his throat when he'd—

Stop.

I'd always loved my independence.

Loved making my own rules, doing whatever I wanted, whenever I wanted, and inviting company strictly on my terms. But now? Now I had a problem.

Because my boss—my goddamn boss—had awakened a side of me I hadn't even known existed. A new, sex-starved, ravenous creature who only wanted him. Needed him.

And no one else would ever be enough.

But hey, at least I had finally gotten the answers to all those little questions I'd been obsessed with for years. Guess some rumors are worth testing after all.

I finished my wine in one go, poured another glass, and made my way to my secret room. My fingers hovered over the scanner, the lock clicked, and the door creaked open.

My heart plummeted to my toes.

I hadn't stepped foot in here in too long, and that's exactly why I'd lost my damn mind. If I had, if I'd taken a minute to ground myself, I never would've let myself sleep with him. Not even those manipulative, dangerously gorgeous eyes of his could've convinced me—no matter how hard they begged.

Oh, Jade ... what the hell did you do?

Careful not to crush any of the scattered documents or photos littering the floor, I put my glass down among them, the soft thud drowned out by the buzzing in my head.

Sliding to my knees, I started rifling through the mess—papers, photos, whatever.

And then, I found it.

A photo.

I snatched it up, my stomach twisting the second I recognized it.

Tears burned at the corners of my eyes.

My fingers trembled as I stared at it, the memory tied to it ripping through me like a jagged blade.

I flipped the photo over, and my breath caught.

There it was—J & S, *Harvard Square Mayfair Festival*, Boston, '14.

A heavy knock echoing at the door caught my attention, followed by the sharp ringing of the doorbell.

Padding across the floor, I reached the door and swung it open.

A delivery guy stood there. "Where do you want these?"

I frowned, but gestured to the kitchen island. He nodded, dropped the boxes there, and started heading back down the hallway.

But then, he paused and grabbed one last package to hand to me—a bouquet.

A hundred red dahlias—my favorites.

"Thanks," I muttered, my gut twisting.

He said his goodbyes, and I shut the door behind him.

I sniffed the bouquet, and despite myself, a smile crept onto my face, soft and almost giddy. My fingers grabbed the note, tearing it off.

Merry Christmas, Miss Whitenhouse.
I couldn't bring your gifts with us to the Hamptons, so I delivered them to you.

See you next Monday, amore.

Freaking annoying, amazing, overbearing, sexy Angelo Lazzio.

I wanted to be angry.

Hell, I was angry.

But all I could do was laugh bitterly, feeling that familiar rush of heat in my chest.

Amore.

God, I couldn't decide if I wanted to slap him, or kiss him until I forgot my own name.

This angel will be your salvation, your savior. Your guardian angel. Tuo angelo.

My Angelo.

"Say that again, my child."

"I had sex with the man who killed my sister—the same man I've spent six years working for, collecting every scrap of dirt to ruin his life, tear apart his empire, and end him exactly the way he ended her."

The words poured out like a confession on fast-forward, but I couldn't stop.

"But now, for reasons beyond human comprehension, I think I'm *falling for him*. It wasn't supposed to be like this! I can't fall for the man who destroyed my life and left me so ... so *alone*! But he's so"—I threw my hands up—"*infuriatingly* attractive! And he makes me feel things I didn't even know existed, and it's like the devil himself is squatting in my brain."

I finally stopped, panting like I'd just finished a marathon.

Dead silence.

I squinted through the screen, willing the priest to say something, *anything*.

"Hmm. Father Harrison? Need me to explain your job to you? You're supposed to *help me!* This is your moment—this is why they gave you the collar!"

He cleared his throat, but his voice was cautious, like he was trying not to set me off. "Miss Whitenhouse ... I believe even I can't help you."

My jaw dropped. "What? No, no, no! You better find a way, Father, because I am not walking out of here without some soul-saving, or a blessing, or—I don't know—a *factory reset*! Purge me! Throw some holy water on me if you have to! I'll even take a manual reboot!"

In my frantic rush, I stood up, forgetting about the low ceiling of the confessional. The top of my head smacked into the wooden frame with a loud thud.

Father Harrison cleared his throat. "Miss Whitenhouse," he began slowly, like he was trying to talk down a wild animal, "I'm not sure ... confession works that way."

I slumped back against the wooden bench, my hands covering my face. "I *knew* I should've never come here! What was I thinking? 'Oh, let me just unburden my sinful, borderline-psychotic love life on a *priest*. That'll totally solve my problems.'"

"Miss Whitenhouse—"

"No, no, it's fine. You've made it clear. I'm beyond help. I'll just ... I don't know, find an exorcist or something." I waved my hands around like I was banishing a swarm of invisible demons. "Because clearly, there's a little devil in me throwing a rave, and you're just not equipped for that kind of insanity."

I heard him cough—no, choke? Was he laughing? *Father Harrison*?

"You know what? I think we're done here," I said, standing up a little too quickly and—whack!—smacking my head against the confessional roof, *again*. "Ouch! Great. Add a concussion to my list of sins."

On the other side of the screen, there was no mistaking it this time—a definite snicker.

"Seriously?" I hissed, glaring through the wooden divider. "You're laughing? Real professional, Father. Very holy of you."

"I'm sorry," he said, his voice tight, but I could tell he wasn't sorry at all. "Go in peace, Miss Whitenhouse. Maybe ... consider therapy."

I scoffed, "Next time, I'm googling 'sin forgiveness for dummies.'"

I stormed out of the confessional, my heels clicking against the church floor like divine retribution had landed in stiletto form.

The whispers had started before I'd even passed the first bench, and by the time I was halfway down the aisle, someone had the audacity to *shush* me.

"Oh, *spare me*!" I snapped, spinning on my heel to face them. "You think God can't hear you gossiping about me from the pews? Newsflash, Brenda, he knows about that box of Chardonnay under your sink too!"

A collective gasp rippled through the crowd, and I swear I saw one nun clutch her chest like I'd struck her with lightning.

"And you," I pointed at a man polishing his glasses, "don't think I didn't see you giving me side-eye. You spent thirty years skimming off church donations, didn't you, Harold? Go pray for *yourself*!"

More gasps.

Someone actually dropped their rosary, beads scattering across the stone floor like they were fleeing the scene.

I didn't realize I'd interrupted the weekly game of Who's the Biggest Hypocrite.

Reaching the massive church doors, I shoved one open with more force than necessary, the sunlight streaming through as I stepped outside like I'd just made my Broadway debut.

But I wasn't done.

I turned back, propping the door open with one foot, and gave the crowd my best condescending smirk.

"By the way—Father Harrison? If God wanted me to *stay* pure, maybe he shouldn't have made my boss so damn *hot*. Just saying!"

The door slammed shut behind me, cutting off the collective gasp from inside, and I strutted into the sunlight like I was walking a runway straight to hell.

CHAPTER
THIRTY-FIVE

"I have loved the stars too fondly to be fearful of the night."
— **Sarah Williams**

Angelo

"How was Christmas, Greg?"

The bastard turned, that wicked grin spreading across his ugly face as he brought his cigar to his lips.

After our weekend in the Hamptons—one of the greatest fucking nights of my life—who would've guessed that screwing my gorgeous, annoying-as-hell employee, whose pussy almost made me lose my mind, would lead to me coming on her tattoo and nearly passing out?

The morning after, I'd fucked her in the shower, pinning her against the wall, hands gripping her ass as I'd pounded into her. Hot water had streamed over us, her head thrown back, nails raking my skin as she'd gasped for air.

We'd spent the rest of the day eating, playing Uno, and watching the kids tear into their gifts. My eyes had never left her—not for a second.

When the kids had screamed with joy, her laugh had almost joined them—but her hand had tightened around her glass, and her eyes had drifted toward the ocean like it held all the things she couldn't say out loud.

I couldn't read her fully, but when her eyes had locked with mine, I'd seen it: *sadness*.

Later that night, in the helicopter on our way back to New York, I'd grabbed her hand, kissed the top of it, and asked, "What's wrong?"

"I don't wanna go home."

When I'd asked her why, she'd shrugged like it didn't matter, and told me to forget it.

Like I could ever forget something like that.

We'd landed on the museum's rooftop, and I'd driven us to her favorite Japanese restaurant. Over the years, I'd learned about her obsession with sushi, and knew she often would order takeout from this place.

We had eaten, and she had been back to her snarky self, making fun of me every chance she got—how I had held my chopsticks, how I'd used too much wasabi, or not enough soy sauce.

She'd said I was embarrassing her, but it had only taken a minute before I'd had enough.

I'd slid into the booth beside her, wrapped my arm around her shoulders, and whispered, "Then feed me."

She had, wordlessly, avoiding my eyes.

I'd leaned in, kissed her neck, then turned her face toward me, catching her lips with mine. She had let me—just for a second—deepening the kiss, her tongue flickering against mine before pulling back, breathless.

"I want something sweet now," she'd said.

I'd smirked. "Me too."

She had shot me a glare. "I meant ice cream, Lazzio."

I had gotten her some vanilla ice cream, drove her home, and we'd made out in my car until she'd slightly pushed me off, breathless.

I had let her go.

She hadn't invited me up.

She'd just opened the door, given me one last look, and left.

It'd been a week since that night.

The employees had the week off for the holidays, and I hadn't seen her—hadn't needed to, or at least that's what I told myself.

But the truth? I couldn't stop thinking about her.

Not even for a fucking second.

The minute I'd stopped seeing her face, I had felt the burn of withdrawal, and it pissed me the fuck off. I should've been focused on other things, like Greg.

The bastard needed to be put in his place. But even with all the shit I had to do, I couldn't get her out of my head.

The way she'd looked at me, like she had fucking known exactly what I had been thinking. The way her body had felt against mine. The way she had moaned my name. The way she'd tasted—fuck.

So fucking sweet. So fucking mine.

Tomorrow, I'd see her again. New Year's prep.

She'd be there, acting all annoying and sassy. And I couldn't fucking wait.

So, for now, I focused on Greg—figuring out how to finally get rid of him.

I flew to Aspen, and found him exactly where my father

had said: in his favorite casino, smoking cigars and playing poker.

"How's your leg?" He gestured lazily to the chair across from him. "Sit, Lazzio. We have much to discuss."

"Yeah, like the fucking ten million you stole from me—which, by the way, is pathetic for a supposed billionaire."

He leaned back in his chair, puffing out his cigar.

"Stole? No, Lazzio. I took back what was mine. A little overdue repayment, if you ask me."

I stepped closer.

"I doubt your actress's life was worth that much, Greg. So tell me—what did I really take from you?"

His smirk faltered for just a second before he masked it with another puff of his cigar.

"Sit. Let's play."

I pulled out the chair, the legs screeching against the floor as I sat down. Greg pushed a fresh stack of chips toward me, his smirk returning as he shuffled the deck.

"You remember Lucius's project in Boston?" he asked, dealing the cards.

I dragged my thumb across my jaw.

I fucking knew it.

That project should've been mine—mine to build, mine to control, mine to turn into a gold mine. But Carlos Lazzio, in all his infinite wisdom, had decided his son wasn't "ready."

Instead, he'd handed it off to Lucius, his friend—the one he'd trusted more than his own blood, apparently.

I could've fixed that problem the simple way—one bullet, one body. But Lucius wasn't just some guy. He was like family, and killing him would've been suicide. My father would've made sure I didn't see the sunrise.

So I had let it go, grudgingly.

But days later, the whole site had gone up in flames. Mines

buried beneath the soil had detonated, ripping through the foundation like the wrath of God Himself had hit Boston.

It had been obliterated. Steel twisted into jagged ribs, concrete reduced to ash, and the mayor scrambling to assure the public there weren't more mines waiting to blow. The contract had been canceled. The land rendered useless. A legacy turned to ashes.

Now that cursed patch of dirt sits there, untouched and unbuildable, because no one's brave—or stupid—enough to dig and risk unearthing the rest of the mines.

"The one that burned to the ground?"

Greg laughed, a deep, nasty rasp, puffing out his cigar. "Yeah, that one. Funny, huh? A project that was supposed to be yours got fucking torched the second someone else laid their hands on it."

I leaned back. "If you've got something to say, Greg, then fucking say it."

His grin widened, cocky and slimy. "That project wasn't just Lucius's, Lazzio. It was mine. He was just a front, a little lapdog to wave at your old man. But me? I was the one calling the shots. I'm the one who told Carlos you weren't ready—too young, too volatile, too much of a ticking fucking time bomb. And he believed me. Gave it to Lucius, just like I planned."

He slapped his cards down—a king, four aces, and a queen.

"But then, one night, your dear father called me and said he'd decided to give you a chance—hand you the project." He exhaled a puff of smoke, his grin turning venomous. "It pissed me the fuck off, so I destroyed it. Burned it to the ground."

Jealousy truly is the devil's favorite sin.

"That project would've brought me ten million. So yeah, boy, I took back what was mine. Call it overdue payment."

I'd have killed anyone else on the spot for pulling this shit

—for daring to run their mouth like they weren't begging for a bullet.

But Greg? He wasn't stupid.

I didn't do messy. No crowds, no witnesses, no loose ends.

That's why he sat there so fucking smug, lounging in that chair like it was a throne.

He knew I wouldn't paint the walls with his blood—not here, not now.

But what Greg didn't understand was that patience didn't mean mercy.

I slapped my cards down—three aces.

Game over.

"The dog in all of this is you, Greg. Ten fucking years to pull this weak-ass stunt? That just proves one thing—you're even more pathetic than I thought."

His face twitched, the fake grin faltering just for a second.

I rose from my seat, ready to leave, but then he said something that stopped me cold.

"Turns out, the Lazzios are just pathetic cowards after all."

I froze, then slowly turned back toward him.

Ain't no fucking way.

A bucket of freezing water slammed into my back, jolting me awake with a shock that rattled my bones. My body jerked violently, teeth chattering as I gasped for air, trying to recover from the cold that clawed its way through me. My wrists were bound tightly behind my back, raw from the ropes, and my legs were lashed to the chair's legs, making every movement a struggle. The cold burned, biting into my flesh, making my teeth rattle uncontrollably.

I couldn't move. Couldn't do a damn thing except sit there, the ropes digging into my skin, my muscles stiff and sore.

A man appeared in front of me, his face hidden under a hood. He grabbed a fistful of my hair, yanking my head back so hard my neck screamed in protest.

"Good morning, little Lazzio," he sneered, his voice cold and cutting. "I hope that freezing water wasn't too much. It's mid-August, after all. Don't want you dying from the heat, do we?"

His laugh was hollow and dark, the kind that made your skin crawl. It wasn't a joke—it was a taunt, a reminder that he enjoyed seeing me like this. He plopped into a chair, legs spread wide, arms crossed as though he were in charge of everything, controlling the very air in the room.

Today, he wasn't shouting, wasn't ranting in fury. He was calm. Too calm. It made the fear scrape deeper under my skin. There was something about his stillness, the way he carried himself, that made my stomach tighten in a way his anger never had. It was worse, so much worse.

I glanced around, searching the room for anything that could help me, anything that could be turned into a weapon, something, but it was hopeless. There was a rickety table in the corner, covered in dry bread, a bruised apple, and a nearly empty water bottle. On that table sat the Japanese knife they'd been using on me for days. The blade gleamed, cruel and sharp. Every time it cut, the pain only seemed to get worse.

It didn't even feel like it was my body anymore—just something they were using, something to break, to destroy.

I met his eyes again, still grinning that twisted, predatory grin. He wasn't going to stop. I knew that now. Not until he got exactly what he wanted.

He leaned in closer, his breath hitting my neck, sour and stale from cigarettes.

I fought not to gag.

"You're tougher than I thought, little Lazzio," he said, his voice low, like a promise of more pain to come. "But that doesn't matter. They all break. You will too."

I swallowed hard, the dry lump in my throat nearly choking me.

"You think your papa's coming to save you?" he mocked, his fingers twitching as they reached behind him. "No one's coming. You're just a scared little boy. And scared little boys don't last long."

I wanted to scream at him, wanted to tell him he was wrong, but my voice wouldn't come. My lungs burned, each breath a struggle as the weight of my fear pressed down on me, squeezing all the air from my chest.

He took a step closer, boots thudding against the cold concrete floor with every step. I could feel him closing in on me, his presence suffocating, making my heart race faster, like it was trying to escape from my chest.

"Where does Carlos keep his dirty money? His contracts with the FBI?"

"I—I don't know," I stammered, my words weak and broken. I didn't know. I didn't know anything. My body was too sore, my neck aching where he'd yanked it back, my hands raw and useless against the ropes.

He sneered, his voice dripping with disdain. "Of course, you don't. You don't know shit, do you?"

His face was so close now I could feel his breath, rancid and suffocating against my skin. My neck tightened, but I couldn't pull away. The cold steel of the knife grazed my skin, light at first, teasing, before it pressed harder, a promise of pain.

Before I could even react, the blade cut into my neck.

The pain exploded through me, sudden and blinding. A scream tore from my throat before I could stop it. It felt like fire had been poured onto my skin, like my flesh was being torn apart. I couldn't think—only scream.

"Tell me where it is," he repeated, his voice chillingly calm, but there was something darker underneath it. I could feel how much he wanted me to hurt. "Or I'll make it worse."

I shook my head, tears streaking down my face, mixing with the blood flowing down my neck. "I don't know! I don't know!" I choked out, my voice trembling.

But he didn't stop. He didn't flinch. The knife pressed deeper, and the agony was all I could feel, the world spinning around me. My chest heaved with sobs, my body shaking from the force of it.

"Turns out, the Lazzios are just pathetic cowards after all."

And then the knife sank deeper, driven into my back.

The pain was unbearable, a fire that burned through every nerve in my body. I couldn't breathe, couldn't scream.

Everything was a blur of agony, of darkness closing in.

And then nothing.

CHAPTER
THIRTY-SIX

"Life is more fun if you play games."
— **Roald Dahl**

Jade

I didn't know who the hell had pissed in Lazzio's morning coffee, but damn, they must've hit the jackpot.

The man was fuming over *everything*.

The account manager had messed up the guest list and ordered way too many champagne bottles. Lazzio hadn't wasted a second hanging up on him—except to tell him that if he hadn't fixed it by noon, he would be fired.

Grace had brought him a tuna sandwich, and he'd groaned like she'd handed him a dead rat. He always hated tuna. Even his dog, Georgino, ate better than that.

His words, not mine.

Carlos Lazzio had come for coffee, but Angelo had sent him packing too, claiming there was no time for drinks when his employees were screwing everything up.

Normally, watching him blow a gasket was my favorite thing—like scoring the perfect pair of heels on clearance, or finally landing those concert tickets I'd been dying for.

Pure joy.

But today?

My chest tightened every time his eyes darkened or his hands twitched.

There was something in the air, something off-kilter, and I didn't like it.

I was determined to figure it out.

Ignoring Grace's ice-cold glare, I pushed open the door to his office and made sure to lock it behind me.

Angelo was hunched over his desk, papers scattered like a hurricane had torn through. His jacket was abandoned on the chair, leaving him in just a white shirt—three buttons undone, no tie. His hair was a mess, sticking out in every direction, like he'd been dragging his hands through it for hours.

And somehow, he'd never looked better.

The way that dress shirt clung to his chest, his sleeves pushed up just far enough to tease at the strength beneath, and that chaotic hair? It was the kind of wreck you wanted to dive headfirst into and make even worse.

If I wasn't about to demand answers from him, I might've let myself stare just a little longer.

But not today.

I'd known the man for six years, and I'd never seen him this tense. Ever.

I walked over to his desk and perched on the edge, crossing my leg.

He didn't even glance up, just kept flipping through paperwork like I didn't exist.

God, I *hated* being ignored.

I cleared my throat, louder than necessary. "I never thought you'd be the type to screw me and then act like I'm invisible, Lazzio."

"Never thought you'd be the type to whine after a good fuck, Miss Whitenhouse. But I guess there's a first for everything. Now get out. I've got a Zoom call to Paris in five minutes."

Ouch.

"Rude," I muttered, snatching a random piece of paper off his desk and pretending to study it like it held the secrets of the universe.

Two seconds later, I tossed it back down, bored out of my mind.

"Seriously, what's wrong with you today?" I asked, narrowing my eyes. "Did someone steal your parking spot, or —God forbid—did the cleaning lady forget to empty your trash?"

He stayed silent.

I sighed. "You look like someone slapped your coffee out of your hand and then set your dog on fire, Lazzio."

"Leave Georgino out of this."

Him and that dog—an inseparable duo.

His future wife was gonna to have to accept being second place to a slobbering, tail-wagging soulmate.

I hummed softly, a smile tugging at my lips as I fiddled with the edge of my dress.

"Thanks for the flowers and the dress. It'll be perfect for the masquerade ball tomorrow night."

He nodded absently, his eyes glued to the computer screen.

Frustration simmered in my chest.

"How can I thank you, Angelo? I'm not one to let someone spoil me without giving something in return."

His eyes flicked toward me, barely. "It's a Christmas gift, Miss Whitenhouse. No need to thank me. Now get out. I've got work to do."

I circled his desk, stepping close until I was behind him. My hands rested on his shoulders, and the tension there practically radiated through my fingertips.

I started to massage the knots in his muscles.

"You're too wound up, baby," I murmured, my voice soft against his ear. "More locked up than the sculptures downstairs. You really should learn to relax."

I leaned in, my breath brushing his neck.

"Maybe I can help with that?"

"Jade—"

My name left his lips just as my hands wandered lower, fingers tracing the open collar of his shirt. I didn't stop, sliding my hands beneath the fabric, my palms skimming the solid planes of his naked chest.

Heat radiated off his skin, tension coiled beneath it, and I pressed into him, my nails dragging just enough to leave a faint trail of fire behind.

My hands ventured further down. "Don't worry, I won't bite ... unless you beg me to."

"I'm the one who'll make you beg, Jade. But trust me, you won't like it."

I snorted softly.

"Let's play again," I said, the words slipping out before I could stop them.

He let out a dry chuckle. "No."

I inched closer, my nose brushing his ear, my lips grazing his skin. "Please?"

"No."

"Two truths, one lie. C'mon, it'll be fun."

"Miss Whitenhouse—"

"If you win," I interrupted, my lips curling into something wicked, "I'll let you do *whatever* you want with me for an hour. But if I win, you're telling me what happened. Deal?"

He grabbed my hands, pulling them away from his shirt, and leaned away.

"I don't need to win anything to make you do whatever I want, Miss Whitenhouse."

Asshole.

Though, unfortunately, he wasn't exactly wrong.

For some twisted reason, my body seemed to have an inconvenient obsession with Angelo Lazzio.

Guess I do have a soft spot for assholes.

I leaned in closer, "*Per favore*?"

He sighed, checking the time on his Rolex like I was wasting his precious minutes.

Which, in a way, I knew I was.

"Fine, but make it quick."

I grinned, flipping his chair so he was facing me.

I straddled his lap without thinking twice, arms wrapping around his shoulders.

"Alright, here it goes. I'm lactose intolerant, I had a pet bunny in high school, but it randomly died one night, and ... I've already won the lottery."

He raised an eyebrow. "The lottery, huh?"

I giggled, leaning in a little closer, my lips brushing against his neck as I whispered, "Why don't you try to find out?"

"I've watched you drink that sickly-sweet coffee for six damn years—caramel macchiato with whole milk. So, no, you're not lactose intolerant." He raised an eyebrow. "And when you had your ice cream the other night, your lips swelled up a little. But I knew it wasn't the ice cream."

Yep, he'd kissed me so damn good, so deep that night, my lips had deliciously swelled from it.

My fingers trailed over his jaw, lightly grazing his stubble, moving down to his full lips, and then slowly back up again. I leaned in, brushing a barely-there kiss against his lips, before pulling back.

"I never realized you paid that much attention to me, Lazzio," I murmured softly.

His gaze softened slightly, the dark intensity melting into something deeper, something that made me blush. His fingers brushed against my cheek.

"How could I not? You're the only thing I see."

The words wrapped around me, sinking into my skin.

You're the only thing I see.

Angelo's phone had barely rung before Grace's voice slithered into the room through the speaker.

"You can connect to the Zoom call now, sir. Mr. DuMarrais is waiting for you."

I groaned so dramatically you'd think someone had just told me the Jimmy Choo sale had been canceled.

"Seriously? *Now?* Of all times? Can't Mr. DuMarrais wait another five minutes while I save your soul from corporate monotony?"

Angelo didn't even look up, just pinched the bridge of his nose in that infuriatingly calm way that told me that now, I was really getting on his last nerve.

"Miss Whitenhouse, not everyone has your flexible relationship with time."

I gasped. "Flexible? I'll have you know I'm a *paragon* of punctuality when it matters."

He finally glanced up. "When does it ever matter to you?"

"Wow, harsh," I shot back, digging a hand in his hair. "You

wound me, Lazzio. I was *this* close to calling you my favorite workaholic."

"Get out, Miss Whitenhouse."

"But we didn't finish the game," I shot back, spinning his chair just enough to make the desk dig uncomfortably into my back.

He wasn't amused.

Before I could blink, his hands had gripped my hips and pushed me to my feet.

"Later," he muttered, his focus already drifting toward his computer.

A malicious idea bloomed in my head.

The kind of idea that would absolutely make him hate me —just a little.

Which, obviously, made it all the more irresistible.

"Fine," I huffed, circling his desk. "But for the record, you would've lost anyway."

His eyes flickered to me, sharp as ever, before he redirected his focus to the screen.

"Bonsoir, Monsieur DuMarais," he said, smooth as sin, his Italian accent somehow getting thicker when he switched to French.

"Bonsoir, Monsieur Lazzio," came the Minister of Culture's voice, rambling on about the Louvre and expanding museum contracts or whatever.

Blah, blah, money, blah.

Angelo's eyes shifted back to me for half a second.

A warning. *Don't push me.*

So, of course, I pushed.

Placing a single finger against my lips, I dared him to stay silent as I reached for the zipper of my dress.

His jaw tightened, and for a moment, I thought I heard his teeth grind.

I moved slowly, dragging the zipper down until the fabric slipped over my shoulder, pooling at the curve of my arms.

His hand, which had been so confidently clicking away at his mouse moments ago, froze completely.

"*... et en plus, nous pourrions envisager un partenariat avec le château de la Loire ...*" DuMarais droned on, blissfully unaware of what was happening behind the computer screen.

Angelo's knuckles flexed against the desk.

His eyes, dark and unreadable, locked onto mine.

Honey and dark wood draped in silk sheets.

The dress slid further, exposing the curve of my collarbone.

I tilted my head, letting my hair fall to one side.

He blinked, once, twice, before snapping his attention back to the screen.

Victory tasted sweeter than I'd imagined.

I wasn't sure whether I wanted to laugh or combust.

Probably both.

The dress crumpled to the floor in a heap of defeated fabric, and I stepped out of it with deliberate ease, leaving me in my favorite sparkly navy Agent Provocateur set—the one that screamed *trouble*—and a pair of glossy black Louboutins so sharp they might as well have been weapons.

If the dress was surrender, the lingerie was a declaration of war.

Angelo didn't even blink.

His eyes stayed glued to the screen like his life depended on it, but the tightening of his jaw gave him away.

DuMarais' voice dragged through the speaker, some nonsense about expanding accessibility to provincial museums.

Fascinating stuff. Really.

"*Forse questo attirerà la tua attenzione, capo,*" I whispered.

His brow arched.

Without a word, I dropped to my knees, crawling under his desk.

Sliding between his legs, I nestled in as his chair pulled back, giving me the room I needed.

His gaze lowered, tracking the way my hands skimmed over his thighs.

"Madame Jean, propriétaire du château de Chambord, accepterait de vous louer ce château emblématique de l'histoire des rois de France ..."

He snapped his attention back to the screen as I pressed my lips against his groin through his pants, dragging my tongue slowly, already feeling him harden.

He inhaled deeply. *"Merci beaucoup, Monsieur DuMarais."*

I yanked his zipper down, quiet but swift, as he wiped his mouth with the back of his hand and cursed under his breath.

My finger slowly traced the shape of his bulge before I reached for the top of his boxer briefs and lowered them, freeing his cock.

"Je vous en prie, Monsieur Lazzio. Examinons ensemble le contrat que votre employée, Madame Whitenhouse, m'a envoyé hier."

I leaned in, my lips just brushing his cock, my voice low. "That'd be me."

Angelo remained silent as I let my tongue lick him slowly from base to top, his pulse growing under my tongue.

I heard his breathing change ever so slightly as I did it again, this time reaching the top and circling it with my tongue before taking it between my lips, my eyes fixed on his face.

"Nous aimerions renégocier le contrat, non pas pour 30 millions de dollars, mais pour 28."

My hands gripped his cock, a low groan rumbling in his chest as his eyes shot me a dark look.

I shook my head and mouthed, "Do not negotiate."

I took him back in my mouth, sucking slowly, and feeling him deliciously hit the back of my throat. His hand tangled in my hair, pulling me back up briefly before lowering me down again.

His dick throbbed even faster, and I rolled my eyes as he slipped from my lips just long enough for me to catch my breath before I quickly sucked him down again.

"*Le contrat est non négociable, Monsieur DuMarais. Donc, à vous de décider si vous souhaitez continuer avec nous,*" Angelo said, his voice a tiny bit breathless, which *almost* made me giggle.

"*Très bien. Nous acceptons alors votre proposition,*" Monsieur DuMarais said, his voice smooth and assured. "*Je vais vous envoyer le contrat signé par mon secrétaire. Au revoir, Monsieur Lazzio.*"

As soon as the meeting wrapped up, Angelo tipped his head back, fingers digging into my scalp as he shoved my mouth down on him harder.

"Fuck, Jade, that feels too damn good," he groaned.

I finally let out a throaty moan I'd been stifling through that dull meeting, feeling him pop out of my mouth.

Without missing a beat, I took his balls in my mouth, my hands expertly stroking his shaft as I sensed his thighs start to tense.

"Where can I—"

He barely had time to finish before I dove back down, taking him deep in my throat, and sucking like my life depended on it.

A loud groan tore from his lips as he came in my mouth.

Fucking glorious.

I swallowed every drop, then teasingly licked the tip a few times before pulling him back under his briefs, planting soft kisses on the fabric before zipping him up with a satisfied grin.

"Feeling better now?" I asked, raising an eyebrow.

He laughed incredulously.

I gave his chair a playful shove, sending him rolling back just enough for me to stand.

As I bent down to grab my dress, I felt his hands circle my waist, pulling me back onto his lap.

"Not so fast," he murmured, his lips finding their way to my neck.

I chuckled, trying to wiggle free. "Wow there, Romeo! Just because I gave you a blowjob doesn't mean I'm giving you a free pass to push my buttons again. I, too, have a meeting—a really important one. You're not the only one working hard around here, you know."

"I thought we were just getting started with our productivity, Miss Whitenhouse."

I giggled but finally freed myself from his grip and snatched my dress from the floor, pulling it back on with flair.

"As much as I love your dedication to my sexual well-being, I really do have to run. I'm all about that professional vibe today."

"Of course, nothing screams more professional than sucking your boss' cock."

I grabbed his pen holder and flung it in his direction, watching it crash to the floor as he laughed. He quickly stood up, grabbing my face in his hands and kissing me deeply, which caught me completely off guard.

I pulled back, breathless.

"How about this—dinner at my place tonight? I'll cook, you can relax. We can discuss all your hard work and the many ways I plan to *promote* you for it."

"Hmm, dinner at your place ... This *promotion* better be something spectacular. I'm talking over-the-top, mind-blowing, passing-out-from-pleasure good."

He winked. "Oh, I assure you, it will be the best kind."

I turned around, unlocked the door, and left, feeling Grace's glare burning into my back. I couldn't resist—I dragged a slow finger across my lips, wiping them clean, watching as her eyes widened when she realized exactly what had just gone down.

By the time I hit the elevator, I was feeling ... suspiciously cheerful.

Who'd have thought that giving my boss a blowjob could do wonders for my mood?

CHAPTER THIRTY-SEVEN

"The best secrets are the most twisted."
— **Sara Shepard**

Angelo

"When are you back in New York? I'm up to my neck in bullshit. Scarlett's throwing a tantrum—LeRoy called me this morning because she's threatening to cancel her New Year's show in LA tomorrow. Meanwhile, I've got the ball here to handle. I swear, it's like babysitting drunk toddlers."

Romaniev snorted. "Next week. Chill out, Lazzio. I'll deal with her later—don't blow a gasket."

The doorbell cut through my rant.

I made my way to the door, grabbed the food from the delivery guy, handed him a generous tip without a word, and carried the bags to the kitchen.

My phone stayed pinned between my shoulder and ear as I dumped the bags on the counter and muttered, "I swear, I need a New Year's miracle or a straitjacket. One of the two."

As I unloaded the bags, the sound of giggling and little feet racing echoed through the phone. Romaniev's voice followed, halfhearted and already resigned to his fate.

"Girls, be careful with the vase," he said, like he already knew they wouldn't be.

Sure enough, a loud crash came next, followed by a chorus of Russian curses.

I scoffed.

Romaniev might be a fucking monster, the kind of man you wouldn't dare cross, but when it came to his daughters? They ran him like a puppet on strings.

The guy followed their every move like a whipped puppy, all bark and no bite.

"Gotta go, Caia's gonna be pissed," he muttered before hanging up.

I focused on dinner—Italian from Vittori's restaurant—because there was no way I'd risk poisoning the poor woman with my cooking.

I didn't care about much, but Jade dragging out food poisoning for the next decade? Yeah, that was a level of misery I wasn't signing up for.

I transferred the food into casserole dishes and popped them into the oven to warm. Plates, silverware, glasses—the works—got laid out on the table. She'd take the wine; I'd stick to water.

Someone had to keep their head clear, and it damn well wasn't going to be her.

As I set the table, my mind betrayed me—again.

The image of Jade on her knees, her lips wrapped around my cock, tore through my thoughts for the hundredth time tonight. My jaw tightened, my groin stirred, and I cursed under my breath.

Over the years, I'd seen every shade of Jade: impatient, spoiled, and maddeningly bitchy, especially when the world had the audacity to spin on its own timeline instead of hers. When I didn't give her the attention she demanded, she always found a way to force my hand.

Spilling her coffee on my desk "accidentally."

Leaving her makeup in my office, then tearing the place apart to find her precious lipstick.

Calling my desk phone relentlessly, detailing every irrelevant second of her day and hanging up only when I stayed silent—boycotting me for a week if I dared to cut her off.

Then there was the Hermes stunt—dropping $120K on the company card "by mistake." Or eating my lunch in front of me, claiming she was starving and I was "built to survive without it."

The woman had worn down every ounce of my patience and shredded every last nerve.

And still, she was the one person who truly knew me—knew exactly how to push every button and get what she wanted. Things no one else would even dare to ask for.

And fuck, if I'd known how sweet her pussy would taste—how it would feel wrapped around me—I would've had her years ago.

But all that waiting?

Goddamn, it was worth every fucking second.

A dark laugh escaped me as I finished setting the table.

The woman was insane.

Completely insane.

And undeniably, irrevocably *mine.*

I was consumed by her—her wicked mouth, those dark

eyes that dared me to come closer, her body that looked like it had been carved just to ruin me.

I was obsessed.

Fixated on claiming her, and it was working.

She could throw all the insults she wanted, but her eyes had betrayed her every single time.

They'd burned with desire, flickered with longing she was too proud to admit.

She had been fighting it, sure, but she was losing.

And tonight?

Tonight, I'd break her.

I'd take her, ruin her, and make her mine. Mind, body, and soul.

"I thought you were the one cooking, Angelo," she said, twirling a forkful of linguine *cacio e pepe* into her mouth.

She dumped so much Parmesan on top that, as an Italian, I almost had a heart attack.

Alongside the pasta, there was bruschetta and chicken Parmesan.

For dessert, I kept it light with lemon tiramisu, a little sweetness to balance all the cheese.

"I did."

She shot me a look. "Liar."

"I told you I have many tricks up my sleeve, Miss Whitenhouse. You might see me as just your boss, but trust me, I'm a man of many talents."

She raised an eyebrow. "Really? What's one?"

I leaned back. "Thought four orgasms in one night was already overdoing it," I said, letting my voice drop low. "But I guess I underestimated you. You're harder to satisfy than I thought."

"Hmm ... is that so?"

"Trust me, you haven't even come close to getting what you really want. But I'm more than happy to keep proving it."

"Prove it, then, Lazzio."

I stayed quiet, a sly grin tugging at my lips.

She has no clue what's coming for her.

Dinner dragged on, but my focus was shot.

We talked about the masquerade ball tomorrow—paintings instead of sculptures—but honestly? I didn't care.

All I saw was her.

The way her lips parted with each bite, the quiet hum of satisfaction as she savored her food.

It wasn't just her beauty—though, *fuck*, she was stunning.

It was the way she carried herself: effortless, confident, impossible to ignore.

And that *fucking* dress.

Black lace, sheer enough to tease, clinging to every inch of her body with ruthless precision. No bra, no shame—just bare skin and a challenge that dared me to look and lose.

That dress wasn't sexy; it was sinful.

Jade Whitenhouse was the devil put on this earth to test me.

And boy, did I fail.

She didn't just step into the darkness—she commanded it, a queen of something wicked and dangerous, ready to ruin me with a single glance.

Jade wasn't my type. She wasn't soft, wasn't sweet—she was fucking impossible.

But impossible was exactly what had me hooked.

Those dark eyes, bloodred lips, every calculated move—she was destruction wrapped in lace. And I wanted every piece of her, even if it killed me.

When dinner ended, I handed her a slice of lemon tiramisu and a cup of sweet mint tea to help her relax.

"I'm quite sad Scarlett couldn't perform for our party tomorrow night," she said, taking a slow sip. "I really love her songs."

I leaned back on the couch. "She's talented, but she's a fucking mess, too. Don't get me wrong, she's my cousin, and I'm protective as hell, but damn, she's a handful."

She hummed, crossing her legs. "Maybe that's why her songs are so beautiful. Broken souls are the most creative, in my experience."

Her eyes flickered to mine for half a second—just long enough to light a fire in my chest—before she dropped them to her cup, setting it down on the coffee table.

Broken souls are the most creative.

Something in my head snapped into place.

"What's the story behind your tattoo?"

Her eyes, heavy and half lidded, met mine. "A broken heart."

"Who the fuck broke your heart?"

She smirked, as if for some reason she found it funny.

"Why were you in such a shitty mood this morning?"

"When did you get your tattoo, Jade?"

She sighed, clearly bored. "Seven years ago. What happened today, Lazzio?"

"A year before you applied to work for me."

She nodded, her eyes tracing every inch of my face, like she was mapping me out.

"Who broke your heart, Jade?"

The words burned my chest.

Whoever did it, I'd rip him apart, piece by piece.

"An Australian. Tall. Dark hair. Just like you."

The lie in her voice wasn't hard to spot.

I could practically taste it.

"Jade—"

"What happened today, Lazzio?"

Bitter amusement twisted in my throat.

No one had ever brushed me off like that before.

She was put on this earth to humble me, and fuck, she was doing it damn well.

"Are we playing twenty questions now?"

She crossed her arms, her tits pushing up so fucking high I had to fight the urge not to stare. "Why not? You're the nosy one—"

"Greg is the one who kidnapped me."

She gasped. "What?"

When I left Aspen and landed in New York, I'd headed straight to the gym in the penthouse. I had to burn off the rage, the nerves, that ticking bomb inside me. I'd run for what felt like fucking hours, my feet pounding the treadmill, sweat pouring down my face.

But it hadn't been enough. Not even fucking close.

I'd grabbed the heavy weights, slammed them onto the walls, and sent glass flying everywhere, shattering the gym.

Everything had clicked when his words had come rushing back.

He had been in the Hamptons when my parents took me for my birthday, staying a couple houses down.

His fucking house, the one he'd bought because his spoiled daughter Spencer had liked it.

When my parents had called the cops, he'd played the good friend—had helped them search for me, all while hiding the truth: he was the one who had fucking kidnapped me.

All these fucking years, he had been right under our noses, slithering around us, poisoning everything he touched with his venom.

The bastard who had scarred me for life.

Jade must've felt the heat of my anger, because she moved closer, her knees pressing into the couch, her hands grabbing my face.

"How did you find out?" she asked.

"A feeling."

"What are you going to do?"

"Kill him."

"Like you killed his mistress?"

My eyes locked onto hers, brows furrowing.

How the fuck did she know?

She read me like an open book, her hand threading into my hair, pulling me just close enough. Her lips brushed mine.

"I put two and two together, Lazzio. I told you I'm *very* clever."

Her lips grazed mine again, her breath warm.

"*Sì,*" I rasped. "*Lo uccido, come la sua amante. Senza pietà.*"

"*Senza pietà,*" she repeated, her tongue sliding over my top lip, a deep groan tearing from my chest. "No mercy."

I grabbed her hips, pulling her closer until she was straddling me, her sweet body pressing into mine. Her arms wrapped around my shoulders, fingers digging into my skin as she leaned back, giving me just enough room to see the way her chest moved with every breath she took.

My hand moved up, brushing her hair out of her face, the soft strands slipping through my fingers.

"Would you kill me too, if I betrayed you?"

I grabbed her throat, my fingers tightening just enough to feel the delicate pulse beneath my palm.

I pulled her closer, until her lips were a hair's breadth from mine.

"No, *amore*. I could never kill you."

Just the thought of her lifeless body on the floor, void of her soul, made my stomach twist in disgust. It was a vision so wrong, so fucking unnatural that it churned something deep inside me.

She smiled, the curve of her lips brushing against mine. "Why?"

"Because you're everything I never knew I needed."

Her pulse quickened beneath my fingers.

She swallowed hard, her chest rising against mine as her eyes softened.

"If you died," I murmured, "I'd burn the world to get you back. Tear it apart, piece by piece, until nothing was left. Then, I'd build it all over again, just for you, Jade."

Her hands slid across my chest as she dipped her head.

Her tongue dragged along my neck.

"You're getting soft, Lazzio," she murmured. "Never thought I'd see the day."

I gripped her chin, forcing her to look at me.

My thumb tugged at her bottom lip.

"Obsession isn't softness, Jade. Learn the difference."

Her smirk was infuriating.

She leaned closer, her eyes dipping to my mouth.

"Obsession, huh?"

Her fingers found the first button of my dress shirt, popping it free.

I caught her lips with mine, swallowing the sound that escaped her throat. Her nails dug into my chest, dragging heat through my skin as another button came undone, then another.

"Why don't you go down on women, Angelo?"

I blinked, taken aback.

"Don't act surprised, boss. Word gets around. Seems the ladies just can't wrap their heads around a so-called Don Juan who avoids eating pussy and hates missionary."

I kept quiet as her lips trailed along my neck, biting and sucking before she licked her way up to my ear.

"But don't worry," she whispered, her breath hot against my skin, "your reputation as a sex god is still somehow magically intact. Even with all those ... little limitations."

I ran my tongue over my teeth. "I don't do it because I don't like it. Eating pussy? Too fucking personal. I fuck from behind because I like being in control, and take what I want."

Control was everything to me.

Part of me knew it stemmed from what had happened when I was younger—being tied up, powerless. That shit sticks with you. The idea of losing control again? It felt like drowning.

But yet ... with her, I didn't mind at all.

Actually, it was, for some fucking reason, almost *freeing*.

I wouldn't tell her though—that she's the only woman I'd ever eaten out. Not because I thought it was shameful, but because I liked knowing that she was the only one whose taste I'd known.

That secret? It was fucking delicious. Just like her.

She tilted her head. "But why do you do it with me, Angelo?"

"Because I want to give you *everything*, Jade—everything you need, everything you crave—even if it means being at your mercy."

She'd hinted enough over the years what she loved, and I had known the second I touched her, all my boundaries would vanish.

I was so fucking desperate to be hers—aching, losing my mind wanting it.

I wanted her to fucking claim me.

"I wanna try something," she whispered against my lips.

I arched a brow.

She worked each remaining button free, her lips never leaving mine.

When the shirt was gone, her nails scraped across my chest.

Her tongue followed her hands, tasting, claiming, biting down just enough to make my dick tighten.

I grabbed her hair, twisting it in my fist, and pulled her head back so I could see her properly.

Her lips glistened, her eyes dark with something between mischief and lust.

She didn't falter, leaning back in to press her mouth to my neck, her teeth grazing my jaw.

Just when I thought I'd take her right there, she pulled away, stood up and held out a hand to me.

Her heels clicked against the floor as I followed her.

She didn't glance back, just grabbed her bag and tossed it onto the kitchen island.

Then she dragged a chair into the center of the room.

"Sit."

I sank into the chair, the wood creaking under my weight. "Jade—"

She didn't let me finish, her arms sliding around my shoulders from behind. Her lips brushed my ear, her breath teasing my skin.

"I'm going to help you let go of something."

My muscles tensed. "What?"

But I already fucking knew.

I pushed against the chair, ready to stand, but her hands clamped down on my shoulders.

"Please, Angelo," she murmured, circling around to kneel in front of me.

Her knees pressed into the floor as her palms settled on my thighs.

"No," I growled, my hands gripping the edges of the chair.

Her fingers moved, her nails scraping the fabric of my pants.

"*Please.*"

"No, Jade."

She leaned in closer. "Do you trust me?"

"This has nothing to do with trust," I bit out.

Her eyes bored into mine. "Do you trust me, Angelo?"

My laugh was low, and laced with frustration.

I wanted to rip her apart for even asking, to remind her that she already fucking knew the answer.

For six years, she had been my shadow, my weapon, my solace.

She knew every dark corner of me, every fractured piece of the man I was.

"With my life."

She stepped back and unzipped her dress. It slid down her body in a whisper, pooling at her feet.

My stomach twisted, a raw ache clawing at my chest as I stared.

No fucking bra.

Nothing but a scrap of black velvet between her thighs and those sharp-as-sin heels.

She moved around me like a predator, her finger trailing along my chest, shoulder, neck. Then it was gone, and the sound that followed made my gut clench.

A click.

Handcuffs.

My heart slammed against my ribs.

She was tying me to the chair.

Just like he fucking did.

Her voice cut through the haze of my spiraling mind. "Let it go, Angelo. That night, that pain—it doesn't own you anymore. I'm here. Let me give you something else to hold on to."

Her hands were on my wrists, the cold bite of steel snapping against my skin as she secured one, then the other.

"I want you to feel something else tonight. I want to replace that darkness with *me*."

A crack ripped through my chest.

The memories came flooding in like a tsunami.

Blood on the floor. Knives glinting under dim light. The rancid taste of bile. The muffled screams in my own throat. The fucking sound of their footsteps on those stairs—heavy, unstoppable.

I thrashed against the cuffs, the chair groaning under the force.

My vision blurred with fury and disgust, the haunting weight of my past pressing down like a goddamn vice.

"Jade," I snarled, my voice breaking, raw. "Take these off. *Now.*"

Her hands settled on my thighs, grounding me, and when I finally looked at her, her eyes burned with something I couldn't name.

Something that cracked me wide open.

"You don't trust me?" she murmured, her lips brushing against my jaw, her nails sinking into my skin.

"I trust you," I choked out. "That's not the fucking point—"

She crushed her mouth to mine, swallowing every curse and protest before I could spit them out.

Climbing onto my lap, she pressed herself against me, her bare tits warm against my chest, her nails scraping my skin.

"A few years ago," she rasped, her teeth tugging at my ear as her hips rolled against me, "you shot down one of my ideas. Turning the museum into a nightclub for a night." Her nails dug into my back as her breath skimmed my jaw. "I was fucking *livid*."

I yanked at the cuffs again, the metal biting into my wrists.

But her voice dragged me back to her.

"I went home that night, spent hours pacing and cursing you out in my head, and finally passed out," she said, leaning back.

Her hands gripped my shoulders, her tits inches from my face as she rocked against me harder, her breath hitching, soft moans spilling from her lips.

"In my dreams, we had the same argument. But instead of telling me to leave, you shoved me over your desk and fucked me from behind. Hard, rough, until I forgot what we were even fighting about. You made me come *so* violently my own scream woke me up—your name on my lips, my sheets soaked, my nipples so tight they hurt."

I let out a harsh curse, the raw image hitting my mind.

She grabbed my chin, her tongue darting out to trace my lips, before sucking my tongue into her mouth and biting down.

The kiss that followed wasn't gentle—it was all teeth, heat, and wet desperation.

She pulled back, her chest heaving as she caught her breath, her lips swollen and glistening.

"Ever since that night, I've imagined you fucking me," she moaned, her hips grinding down harder, her head falling back.

"Every man I've ever met has been a pathetic excuse for you. None of them could even come close."

"Jesus, Jade," I groaned, my cock throbbing, trapped against the soaked fabric between us.

Her head snapped forward. "I've imagined you bending me over every goddamn surface, ruining me until I couldn't walk straight. In my mind, you've fucked me in your office, in your car, in your private jet, even on top of the Lazzio family dining table."

I hissed through clenched teeth as she leaned in, her tongue dragging along my bottom lip before biting it hard enough to make me taste blood.

"Years, Angelo," she whispered, her lips brushing mine. "*Years* of wanting you to use me, fuck me, ruin me, make me yours so completely I'd forget where I ended and you began."

Her tits pressed into my face, and I bit down on her nipple, hard enough to make her scream, her nails raking fire down my chest.

I licked over the welt, my jaw tightening as her body trembled against me.

Her hand gripped my chin, forcing me to look at her.

"Please, don't stop this, Angelo. I've waited too fucking long."

Her breath was ragged, her body a vision of a beautiful, dark dream.

She stood up, her skin flushed, chest heaving, and that wicked smirk curling on her lips as her tongue slid along her bottom lip.

She took off her thong, her juices running down her thighs, glistening.

She turned slowly, deliberately, letting me see every inch of her body, her back arched just enough to reveal that fucking tattoo etched along her spine.

It disappeared beneath the curve of her perfect ass, and I couldn't fucking breathe.

She lifted one leg and placed it over mine, her hands gripping my knees for balance. She lowered herself onto my lap again, pressing her back against my chest. Her ass ground against my cock, teasing me.

She tilted her head back, her lips brushing my ear as her hand snaked around to rest on my throat. "Wanna taste me, Lazzio?"

I pulled against the cuffs hard enough to feel the skin of my wrists split, the sting barely registering over the heat of her body grinding against mine.

"Fuck, yeah."

She laughed softly, the sound a dagger to my sanity, her hips rocking harder, her slickness soaking into me.

She turned her head just enough for her lips to brush against mine. "Your wish is my command."

With that, she placed her hands firmly on my knees.

Then—*fuck.*

She leaned forward, her pussy practically dangling in my face.

I didn't need a second invitation.

I dove in, my tongue lapping up her sweet juices, savoring every drop.

So fucking delicious.

I sucked on her clit, feeling her soft body respond beneath my mouth while her nails dug into my skin. Then I bit it, hard.

"Ouch!" she gasped.

"Get closer," I growled, sinking my teeth into her ass cheek.

She shifted backward without a word, her legs trembling as I buried myself between her thighs.

Her body locked up, thighs trembling violently as my tongue thrust deeper, drawing out a strangled cry. She bucked against me, grinding harder. Her taste was addictive, bitter and sweet, dripping down my face as I fucked her with my tongue.

She shattered—hips jolting, gasps turning ragged, her nails clawing my knees as she gave in completely.

For the first time in years, the ghosts in my mind didn't get through.

She had burned them out, erased them with the way she fell apart.

No darkness.

No memories.

Just her.

"God," she muttered, barely able to breathe as she slumped backwards on my lap.

A second passed before she turned her head, looking at me with a wicked smile.

"I hope you'll remember that forever," she rasped. "Every second of it."

I couldn't even respond, still choking on the fact that she'd managed to make me forget.

Actually forget.

She stood, unhooking the cuffs. My wrists burned as she rubbed them. Then, without hesitation, she climbed back onto me, her legs locking me in place, her mouth crashing down on mine.

I fisted her hair, yanking her head back. "I should punish you for this. Or maybe just fuck you until you can't even stand."

Her grin widened. "Do both."

I didn't waste another second.

Grabbing her ass, I stood, carrying her like a trophy, her legs locking tight around my waist. Her nails scored down my back, her teeth grazing my jaw as she whispered sinful promises that seared straight to my core.

I threw her onto the bed and fucked her until she passed out, soft snores breaking the silence. Her body, flushed and tangled with mine, felt like it had always belonged there—as if the universe had been rearranged just for this.

For the first time in years, the ghosts didn't claw at my mind. They didn't even dare show their faces. She hadn't just quieted them; she'd annihilated them, erased their existence, left only herself in their wake.

Jade Whitenhouse wasn't my salvation; she was my damnation. My curse. And somehow, that made her perfect.

She owned me in ways no one ever had, in ways I hadn't even thought were possible.

I wasn't just hers.

I was now *ruined* for anyone else.

CHAPTER
THIRTY-EIGHT

"The one kiss that was stolen, was given in a lie."
— **Anthony Liccione**

Jade

I woke up in Angelo's bed, the sound of water running from the shower filling the silence. The curtains still couldn't do their stupid job, letting the sun creep in and caress my skin.

I groaned, squinting at the clock on his nightstand. Noon. *Great.*

Dragging myself upright, I leaned against the headboard, wincing as my body protested. Angelo had wrung every last drop of energy out of me last night, like he was trying to leave an imprint of himself under my skin.

And judging by how I felt now? Mission accomplished.

Another groan slipped from my lips as I buried my face in the pillow, letting out a scream into it.

I'd crossed the line. Again. And again. And again.

Each time, I had sworn it was the last. That I'd slam the brakes, stop letting him twist me up inside. But every time, it had been the same. One touch, one look, and I had caved like a fool.

It was maddening, infuriating, and worst of all ... *addicting.*

Because I want to give you everything, Jade—everything you need, everything you crave—even if it means being at your mercy.

Honestly, who could resist that?

The first time I'd woken up here, weeks ago—after that godforsaken boar had ripped through the woods—I'd bolted. I hadn't even looked back. I hadn't been able to stand the suffocating weight of this space, how it had made me feel things I didn't want to feel: self-loathing, a flicker of gratitude I hadn't deserved, and something darker, stickier.

The second time had been no different.

But this time?

This time, I wasn't running.

My legs screamed as I stood, the soreness between them raw. I limped to his dresser and yanked it open. Everything was lined up, ironed, and folded, like he was auditioning for a cleaning infomercial. *Of course. Neat freak.*

I grabbed a long-sleeved shirt and tugged it over my head. It hung loose, the fabric heavy with his scent, wrapping me up in him even when I didn't want it to.

I waited until the sound of the shower filled the house before slipping out of his room. The door clicked shut behind me as I padded down the hallway, my bare feet brushing the icy tiles.

My destination was clear: the last door on the right.

The knob turned without resistance, and I slipped inside, my heart pounding like it might betray me. His office was ... unexpected. A world away from the sterile perfection of the museum. This was a shrine to chaos: dark wood shelves crammed with miniature sculptures of Greek gods and goddesses, a massive portrait of Cleopatra and Caesar glaring down from one wall, and above the desk, a Rembrandt—*Retour du Fils Prodigue.*

I was here to find what I needed—to finish this.

No more crossing lines.

No more games.

No more sex, even if I wanted—*desperately* wanted—to.

Just the end I'd been chasing.

I let my eyes sweep around the room, taking in his library. The bookshelves were lined with thick, leather-bound volumes, each spine *perfectly* aligned. I dragged my fingers along the edge of the shelves, pretending I wasn't imagining what kind of secrets might be hidden behind the neatly stacked rows.

But my focus didn't last.

My gaze slid across the room and landed on his desk—bingo.

There it was. The black burner phone. Its screen was ever so slightly cracked.

Four inches to the left sat his laptop, sleek and closed. Four inches to the right, a picture frame stood with a photo of Georgino and his parents, smiling.

I hovered by the desk, fingers grazing the phone like it might bite me back. My stomach churned, not with guilt—that would've been too easy—but with this gnawing, sickening fear of being caught.

My fingers closed around the phone. The old, cracked case practically mocked me, the jagged edge biting into my palm like it had teeth. Perfect. Because God knows I deserved the sting.

Time to move.

If I stood there any longer, I'd start thinking—*really* thinking—and that was never a good idea.

I slipped out of the room, carefully and silently closing the door behind me. Walking on the tips of my toes, I made my way down the hall, the soft patter of my steps swallowed by the lingering quiet. The sound of the shower had long since faded, leaving only the hum of my own nerves for company.

Pausing just before the living room, I leaned into the shadows, scanning the open space for any sign of movement. Empty. *Good.*

With quick, measured strides, I reached the kitchen counter where I'd left my bag the night before. My hands worked fast, opening the zipper and slipping the phone inside before tugging it closed again.

Mission accomplished.

Or so I thought.

Two strong arms wrapped around my waist out of nowhere, locking me in place.

I screamed, my hand flying to my heart as it thundered against my ribs.

Angelo's laugh rumbled against my back, deep and infuriatingly amused, before he dipped his head into the curve of my neck.

"There you are."

I exhaled shakily. "You scared the hell out of me! I thought you were some crazy stalker about to kidnap me."

His teeth grazed the sensitive skin of my neck. "Don't tempt me," he murmured, his hands sliding down to rest firmly on my hips. "I've been told I'd make a *very* convincing kidnapper."

"Really? Because I'm not impressed. No van? No chloroform? Your execution needs work."

He chuckled, pulling me even closer. "Who needs a van when I can carry you over my shoulder? You'd be halfway to Stockholm Syndrome before I even reached the front door."

"Bold of you to assume I'd make it easy."

"Bold of *you* to assume I wouldn't enjoy the fight, *amore*."

Infuriating.

Absolutely infuriating.

And yet, my body was ready to hand over all my common sense and let him win.

I moaned as his lips kissed the sensitive spot behind my ear.

"See?" He whispered. "You're already warming up to the idea."

I huffed out a laugh, my pulse still unsteady.

Grabbing my bag, I dropped it onto the kitchen stool and turned to face him, already preparing some sharp remarks—only to lose my train of thought entirely.

He stood there, shirtless, wearing nothing but a pair of low-slung black pants that clung to his hips in a way that should've been illegal.

He was barefoot, with water droplets clinging to his still-damp hair, falling in lazy trails down his temples and cheeks. The soft curls were messier than usual, as though he'd barely run a hand through them after his shower.

And that V. The sharp cut of muscle disappearing beneath his waistband. The faint trail of dark hair leading my gaze exactly where it shouldn't go.

Life's unfair. Completely, brutally unfair.

I pressed my palms against his chest. Rising onto my toes, I captured his lips, kissing him with a desperation I couldn't seem to suppress.

This man. This annoying, beautiful, *addictive* man.

He was going to be the end of me.

The universe must really get a kick out of watching me suffer.

His hand slid to the back of my neck.

His tongue brushed mine and the stupid butterflies I swore I didn't have for him?

Yeah, they were staging a coup. Between my legs.

"*Buongiorno, amore*," he murmured against my lips.

"Hi," I whispered back, my voice embarrassingly soft.

I pulled away before I could embarrass myself further, turning to the sink like I had a purpose. Opening one cabinet, then another, pretending to look for a glass when really, I was just stalling.

When I finally found one, I filled it, stared at it for a second, and then left it untouched on the counter.

His gaze scorched my back.

"How'd you sleep?"

"Good," I said, turning to face him, crossing my arms like I was trying to protect what little dignity I had left. "And you?"

He didn't answer right away. Just took a slow, measured step toward me.

Then another.

By the time he stopped, he was close. *So* close.

His hands gripped the edge of the sink on either side of me, caging me in.

I tilted my head up, my heart hammering against my ribs. His nose brushed mine before his lips found me again—this time softer, slower, leaving me aching for more.

"What's wrong?"

"Nothing," I said, too quickly, and way too unconvincingly.

"Jade," he said, his lips ghosting over the shell of my ear

now. "I've known you for six years. Do you really think I can't tell when something's off?"

I exhaled shakily. "I'm just stressed about tonight. It's the first time we're hosting a ball, and—"

"Stop lying," he interrupted, as he kissed me again, harder this time, his teeth catching my bottom lip and tugging just enough to make me gasp. "What's wrong? Tell me."

And God help me, because I wanted to.

But how do you tell the man you'd been *sleeping* with—your walking disaster of an obsession—that tonight you were going to destroy him? That you'd spent six years weaving a web of lies so intricate even *you* couldn't remember where the truth began and the deception ended?

You don't.

Because there's no way to casually slip into conversation that you'd been lying for six years, pretending to be nothing more than his loyal, slightly-too-mouthy employee, when in reality, you'd been plotting to ruin everything he had ever cared about. And maybe it wouldn't be so bad—if it weren't for the fact that you'd also somehow managed to fall in love with him along the way.

Ironic, really.

Instead, you'd stand there, half-naked in his kitchen, wondering why you ever thought it was a good idea to fall for the man who had killed your sister.

And the worst part? I couldn't even blame him for being so ... *him*.

"Jade—"

"I'm just ... processing, you know? You're still my boss, Lazzio. And, well, I never expected to be the girl fucking with her boss. *Repeatedly*. What's next? People whispering that I blow you in the elevator and let you bend me over your desk for raises?"

He laughed, the kind of laugh that made my chest clench with equal parts fury and betrayal.

Because, of course, only Angelo Lazzio could find my existential crisis *hilarious.*

"You say that like it's a bad thing," he said, kissing the tip of my nose.

"You're insufferable," I muttered, smacking his chest—not that it fazed him in the slightest.

He caught my hand effortlessly, brushing a kiss across my knuckles. "Don't worry, Miss Whitenhouse. That's the beauty of being the CEO—if anyone so much as whispers, I'll make sure it's their last word."

And just like that, I hated him even more.

Not for his arrogance, or his power.

But because, in that moment, I almost wanted to believe him.

Almost wanted to trust that he could protect me.

From whom, though?

From himself? From me?

No.

Not even he could save us from what I was about to do.

"How do I know you're not lying, Miss Whitenhouse? You lied on national TV, claiming you were best friends with Miss Dupont and swearing her death was a tragic suicide. And now, out of nowhere, you're telling me Angelo Lazzio murdered her? Forgive me if I'm having a hard time keeping up with your fairy tales."

Alexandra Jasper wasn't just a journalist—she was a predator. The kind who didn't chase stories; she built careers off the wreckage of others' lives. And as the reigning queen of Fox News' prime-time slot, she had the claws to back it up.

She leaned back in her chair, her legs crossed, her perfectly manicured nails tapping against the table between us, a deliberate tick designed to unnerve her prey.

She called herself an investigative journalist.

I called her a vulture.

She circled the dead and dying, ready to pick their bones clean and call it "reporting."

And if she smelled your weakness? God help you.

She'd rip through you before you even realized you were bleeding.

Her eyes glinted with curiosity, like she could already taste the Pulitzer—or the severance package big enough to buy a private island—if she broke this story.

Exposing Angelo Lazzio—the king of New York's high society and CEO of the biggest entertainment empire in the West—as a murderer?

That would make her untouchable.

And she knew it. That's why she was testing me.

I'd come here to betray Angelo.

To carve out a piece of his soul and hand it to this woman on a tarnished silver platter.

And the worst part? I wasn't even sure why anymore.

Revenge? Justice? Or was it just that I hated myself enough to destroy the only person who had ever made me feel seen?

No.

I was avenging *her.*

"Let me guess—you're here because you're scared. Scared he's going to find out about your little mess, huh? Your skeletons? Or maybe ..." She leaned in closer. "You're just a bitter ex, trying to burn him down because he fucked you, used you, and then tossed you out like the disposable little thing you are. You thought you were different. Thought he'd choose you over his other toys. But you were just another warm body to fuck and forget. And now you're what? Trying to get revenge? Or just whining because he moved on and left you scrambling for scraps?"

Stupid bitch.

God, I wanted to hit her.

Or maybe myself for coming here in the first place.

"Keep it up, Jasper, and I might just have to remind you where the line is. You're lucky I'm in a good mood, but push me just a little more, and I might show you just how much I enjoy shutting people like you down. I'll just take my story elsewhere."

I stood, watching her squirm for a second before I made my move to leave.

As expected, she panicked.

"Okay, wait, Miss Whitenhouse, please sit down. I apologize for being ... disrespectful."

I didn't even glance back at her, but I knew I had her exactly where I wanted her.

I turned back to her slowly. "Are you sure about that? 'Cause, I'm perfectly fine taking my story to David McLoad over at CNN. Oh, and just so you know, I'm aware you two are fucking. Makes things a bit more ... fun, don't you think?"

Her eyes went wide for a split second, her smug façade cracking. She was trying to figure out how the hell I knew, but honestly, I wasn't here to explain myself.

I, too, had my ways of digging up dirt, even if it wasn't my full-time gig.

I sat back down slowly, crossing my legs, my nails digging into my palms to keep myself from shaking.

"So tell me, Miss Whitenhouse, how do you know that Angelo Lazzio murdered Paulina Dupont?

I swallowed.

There it was.

My truth, unraveling, ready to tear through everything I'd built up to this point.

It was time.

"I know he did because I have proof," I said, voice smooth, like I wasn't about to rip my own world to shreds.

I reached into my bag, pulling out the hardware CD—the one with the footage from the surveillance cameras in the alley behind his theater, The Sunflower.

Her eyebrows shot up. "You have it on tape?"

I slid the CD onto the table.

Then, I reached into my bag again, pulling out Angelo's backup phone and dropping it next to the CD.

I knew he used that backup phone for his shady dealings—something the FBI could easily use to trace every little detail.

I didn't hand everything over to Alexandra Jasper without purpose. She was the best at what she did, and I also knew her deep ties to the FBI. Her twin sister, Alia Jasper, ran the local division. So, the second I walked out of that office, I knew Alexandra would be on the phone to her sister, giving her all the details.

"I also have proof that Angelo killed two other people."

Her eyes narrowed. "Who?"

I took a breath, letting the weight of it settle in my chest, feeling the burn of it.

There was no going back.

"Nine years ago, Angelo Lazzio murdered my sister, Stella, and her boyfriend, Thomas ... and I watched it all happen."

CHAPTER THIRTY-NINE

"The meaning of life is that it stops."
— **Franz Kafka**

Jade

21 years old
Nine years ago

"Happy birthday, Jadie!"

I smiled, leaning over to blow out the candles while keeping my hair clear of the flames—a precaution born from my thirteenth birthday disaster when half my hair went up in smoke. Let's just say the night ended with a burn on my neck, a chunk missing from my head, and the title of Worst. Birthday. Ever.

"Can't believe my baby's twenty-one," Mama said, hugging

me with enough force to crack ribs. Tears streamed down her face. "Time sure flies, don't it?"

Uncle Jake, a walking beer advertisement in his forties, let out his signature wheeze of a laugh and popped open another can. "Twenty-one, darlin'! Now I can take ya to my spot and teach ya how to drink like a real lady!"

Before I could respond, Aunt Krissy swooped in with a grin that could only mean trouble. Her bleached-blonde hair defied all odds by still existing, and her bedazzled teeth caught every light in the room.

"Well, honey," she drawled, "now that you're legal, it's time to make some real bad decisions. When I was twenty-one, I—"

Sparing myself and everyone else, I scooped up a forkful of cake and stuffed it in her mouth before she could regale us with the saga of her tequila-fueled stadium streaking.

She laughed, still chewing, and handed me a foil-wrapped gift. "Happy birthday, birdie. Just don't expect me to bail you out."

Inside was a $100 nail salon voucher. "Thanks, Aunt Krissy," I said, grateful her mischief had come with a practical upside.

The room hummed with chatter as everyone settled in with their cake, but my focus drifted to the window. For the sixth time, I scanned the empty street.

"She's coming," Mama reassured me, catching my gaze. "Thomas and she had a fight last night, but they're meeting to talk it out."

Uncle Jake snorted, swirling the amber liquid in his glass. "Told her that boy wasn't good enough, but she doesn't listen."

Mama's glare could've melted steel. "Leave Stella alone, Jake. She's young and in love."

Stella. My little sister, and polar opposite. She was all

golden hair, hazel eyes, and rosy cheeks—a walking fairy tale—while I played the dark-haired witch lurking in her shadow. We spent most of our childhood either fighting or plotting each other's doom, but she was still my favorite person.

Until I left for college, anyway. Somewhere between studying marketing and bringing home my first boyfriend—a mistake as regrettable as my bangs phase—we'd drifted apart.

She had cried when she'd met him. "He's going to take you away!" she'd wailed. Spoiler alert: he hadn't. He'd cheated three months later—with multiple girls.

Over time, Stella had come to me for advice, but then Thomas had come along. A charmer from her math class who had turned her life into a loop of teenage chaos. Mama had let her date him at sixteen, claiming it was a "good age to start." Sure, if constant breakups and tearful reconciliations counted as "good."

Two months ago, she'd dumped him in a melodramatic tear-fest after he'd forgotten their anniversary. She'd cried in my arms until she'd fallen asleep, only to forgive him the next day when he'd showed up with flowers. The cycle was as predictable as the sunrise.

But today had felt different. When she'd left earlier, her eyes had been glassy, her smile brittle. My stomach had twisted in a way it rarely had.

The empty street mocked me, and I snapped. Muttering an excuse, I escaped to my room, phone already in hand.

Flopping onto my bed, I dialed her number. It barely rang before she picked up.

"Where are you, Stella?"

Her sniffle cut through the line like a knife.

"At Lake Kendrick," she whispered, her voice fragile. "Thomas left me here. He's gone."

My heart dropped.

I bolted upright, head spinning. "What? *What?* Why didn't you call me?"

"I just ... I wanted to think," she said, sniffling again.

Oh no.

When Stella said she needed to think, it usually meant she was sinking—spiraling into that dark place where self-loathing, doubt, and unrelenting disgust with herself took over. A wave she never seemed to able to outrun.

"How long has he been gone?"

"I don't know ... maybe ten minutes?"

I groaned, already storming out of my room and down the stairs. "Don't move. Stay right where you are. I'm coming."

"Okay," she murmured, her voice barely a whisper before the line went dead.

I grabbed my sneakers from the hallway, yanking them on, and threw on my coat.

As I rushed out the door, I shouted over my shoulder, "I'm going to get Stella! Don't even think about finishing all the cake!"

Mama called something after me, but I wasn't listening. I snatched her car keys from the kitchen counter and pushed open the door.

The November air hit me like a punch to the face, cold enough to freeze my breath mid-air as I rushed to the driveway. My fingers went numb on the car door handle, but I yanked it open and climbed into the driver's seat.

The drive there was silent and fast, the only sound was the hum of the engine and the rush of my thoughts.

When I finally pulled up near the entrance to Lake Kendrick, I was expecting to see Stella sitting by the water, waiting for me. But instead, I stopped short, staring in surprise. A huge chunk of trees around the lake had been cleared, and in their place were bright yellow warning signs—"Private Property" and "No Trespassing."

The area that used to be peaceful and untouched was now marked off with harsh, glaring signs.

I cursed under my breath, staring at the barricades, unsure of what to do.

But I wasn't about to let a few signs stop me.

I threw the car in park, slammed the door, and walked toward the entrance. I crawled under the yellow tape, my heart pounding as I glanced around.

The area was eerily quiet, the kind of stillness that felt off.

I kept walking, determined, until I reached the old picnic area at the edge of the lake.

There, just where I expected her to be, was Stella. Sitting alone by the lake, her back to me, looking like she was trying to disappear into the scenery. Like the world could swallow her whole, and she wouldn't care.

I stood there for a second, taking in the scene, trying to swallow down the lump in my throat.

Seeing someone you love in pain was a kind of agony that gnawed at your soul. It was the kind of ache that stretched deep, because you knew, no matter how much you wished it were different, there was nothing you could truly say or do to make it better.

I took a step closer, my voice barely a whisper as I called out, "Stella?"

She didn't answer, just stared out at the water, the tears still there in her eyes, even though she was trying to hide them.

I sat down next to her, the cold of the ground seeping into my jeans.

"I messed up, Jadie. I thought he was different," she whispered. "I thought he was it. And now ... he's gone. I feel like I'm falling apart."

I let out a dramatic sigh, flipping my hair over my shoulder, playing the part of the older sister who had everything figured out—which, let's be real, I totally didn't. "Look, honey, love is like high heels. You think it's going to be all elegant and fun, but then your feet start hurting, and you realize you're just doing it for show. And I'm sorry, but sometimes the guy you thought was the perfect fit turns out to be the guy who's about to break your toes."

She chuckled a little, but the weight in her eyes didn't go away.

I leaned in, tapping the butterfly pendant around her neck. The one Mama had gotten her for her birthday a few years ago. "You know, you're like this little butterfly," I said, my voice softening, but still laced with that biting edge. "You're meant to fly, not be stuck in some boy's messy web of drama."

Her eyes flickered up at me, confused, unsure.

"You can't wait for someone else to make you happy," I continued, tracing the curve of the pendant. "You control your own wings. You control your own flight. No one else can cage you, not unless you let them."

She looked at the pendant, her fingers brushing over it. "What if I don't know who I am without him, Jadie?"

I sighed, my voice a little softer than usual. "Stella, you're sixteen. You're still figuring it out, and that's okay. You'll have a lot of versions of yourself—some you'll love, some you'll hate, and some you'll barely recognize. But that's part of growing. This boy? He's just one tiny piece of the puzzle. The rest of it is all you, and it's yours to figure out."

Stella let out a soft sob, her blonde hair sticking to her tear-streaked cheeks as she suddenly launched herself at me, wrapping her arms around me in a tight hug.

"Happy birthday again, Jadie!" she choked out between

sobs. "I'm so sorry I missed your cake, and I haven't even given you your present."

I squeezed her back tightly. "It's okay. Let's go home."

We walked around the land, bulldozers not too far off, trucks scattered around like forgotten toys. It was a Sunday, so the place was ghostly empty.

Stella stopped dead in her tracks, her hands flying to her hips. "Did you know?" she said, her voice dripping with disbelief. "A big company from New York bought the whole damn lake—and the twenty acres around it! They're turning it into fucking useless hotels, casinos, tourist traps. Everything I love about this place? Gone."

"Language, Stella," I muttered.

She whipped around, practically on fire. "Sorry, Jadie, but I'm so fucking mad! I hate billionaires and how they don't care about anyone but themselves! All they care about is more, more, more—taking and taking until there's nothing left! They can't even let nature be!"

I stood there for a second, watching her rage, and honestly, I couldn't blame her.

We'd spent so many summers here—swimming in the lake until our fingers were pruny, tossing together picnics on the grass, riding our bikes through the forest, and pretending to be explorers.

This place was *us*. It was everything.

And now it was getting sold off, like some meaningless piece of property.

"You know—" I started, trying to say something to calm her down, but before I could finish, a shout cut through the air.

"Stella! Please, I need you! Stella!"

We both froze.

My heart skipped a beat.

I knew that voice.

Stella's face went pale, like she'd seen a ghost.

It was Thomas.

"Help! Please!"

I glanced at Stella, and I saw it—the panic flashing in her eyes.

Before I could even blink, she was already running toward the voice.

I froze for a second, cursing under my breath, watching her blonde hair disappear behind the trucks. It felt like the world stopped moving for a moment.

Then, like a switch flipped, I snapped out of it. My legs moved before my brain caught up, and I shouted her name again, my voice tight with fear.

I ran, each step through the mud slowing me down, my sneakers slipping with every move. I cursed under my breath but didn't stop.

"Stella!" I screamed again, my voice hoarse, but there was no answer.

Finally, I reached a big white truck with a name starting with a C. I slammed my hand against the cold metal, gasping for air, trying to steady my breathing. My ears rang, the world muffled as I looked around. All I saw were bright yellow warning signs—"Private Property" and "No Trespassing"—taunting me, telling me to turn back.

But then, I saw her.

She stood still, just a few feet away from Thomas, her hands at her sides like she couldn't move. Thomas was the same, frozen, his face drained of color.

When his eyes met mine, they widened in shock.

"Jade! Don't move! Stay where you are!"

Stella's face snapped toward me, tears streaming down her cheeks as she sobbed uncontrollably. "Jadie, don't move! Please!"

I stood there, confused, wiping the sweat off my forehead, my heart pounding in my chest. "What's going on?" I called out.

Stella's hand flew to her mouth, and she cried harder, the sobs shaking her entire body.

I took a step toward them, but before I could move any further, Thomas screamed, his voice raw with panic, cracking through the air like a gunshot.

"I stepped on a mine! Stella too! Everything's going to explode!"

My blood went cold.

I couldn't move. I couldn't think. It was like time had frozen around me. All I could hear was the blood rushing in my ears, the deafening silence that followed, and then the absolute terror in Thomas's voice.

The ground beneath me suddenly felt like it could swallow me whole.

I forced myself to speak, my throat tight. "A mine? Are you sure?"

"Yes," he choked out, his voice shaking. "I—I called Stella to come help me, to get the cops here, but ... but she ... she stepped on one too. I didn't—I didn't mean for this to happen. I'm so fucking sorry, Stella. So sorry. Please, I'm so sorry ..."

His words broke off into a sob, raw and guttural, like a piece of him was being torn apart. His hands were shaking as he ran them through his hair, his face twisted with guilt.

"I swear to God, baby, I never wanted this. I should've kept you away. I should've—" He stopped, his voice cracking, tears streaming down his face.

Stella cried harder, her hands pressed to her sides like she was holding herself together, but it wasn't enough. Tears streamed down my face too, feeling completely useless.

She looked at Thomas, her eyes wide with pain—so much pain—that it felt like my heart was breaking for both of them.

"Stop ... Stop, Thomas. The police—they're gonna help us. They're coming, okay? It's gonna be okay," she whispered between sobs, trying to hold herself together.

Thomas shook his head. "I'm so sorry for lying, Stella. I never should've dragged you here ... I—I love you, baby. Please, forgive me."

I couldn't watch them anymore. It felt like I was falling apart.

I snapped. "Stop! Stop talking like that! Nothing is gonna happen. The police are gonna come and help you, and everything's going to be okay!"

"Jadie, please," Stella sobbed, her voice so small, so broken, it didn't sound like her anymore. "Tell Mama I—I love her, okay? Tell her I'm sorry for everything—"

My chest tightened. "No! No, Stella, I'm not doing that! You'll tell her yourself!"

"Jadie, I'm so sorry. I love you too—so much, so much."

"Stop it, Stella! Stop!" My own voice cracked, and I didn't even care anymore that I was crying. "You don't get to say goodbye! You don't get to quit on me, do you hear me?"

She whimpered, her whole body shaking. "I don't want to die, Jadie. I don't want to die!"

"You're not going to die!" I screamed, my nails digging into my palms. "Neither of you are gonna die! We're gonna get you out of this! But you have to stay still—do not move, Stella, not a single move, do you hear me?"

Her sobs were louder now, broken gasps that shattered every word. And all I could do was watch, my hands useless, my heart in pieces. I wanted to grab her, hold her, shake her, make her believe me—but I couldn't.

I was stuck here, on the edge of a nightmare, watching my sister crumble before my eyes.

Stella's breath hitched, and she looked at me, her face pale. "Jadie ... do you remember when I was five, and you taught me how to ride a bike after school?"

I swallowed hard, my heart pounding in my throat. "Yeah ... yeah, I remember."

Her lips trembled, and she let out a shaky laugh, her voice cracking through her tears. "I fell, like, a hundred times, and you said ... you said that when a little star falls from the sky, she becomes dust and shines on everything she touches. You made it sound so magical, like falling was just part of something bigger."

"Stella, don't. P-Please don't do this."

"You are my star, Jadie," she whispered, her voice trembling. "You always have been. You've always been the one shining on me, even when I messed up, even when I fell. You made everything better."

"Stop it," I begged, my voice barely audible, knees threatening to give out under me. "You don't get to talk like this. Not now. You're gonna tell me this later, okay? You're gonna tell me this when we're sitting in the kitchen, eating the rest of my birthday cake, and opening the gift you got me. You hear me?"

But she just shook her head, her wide, shimmering eyes breaking me, piece by piece. "I'm so scared, Jadie ... I don't wanna die. I don't wanna leave you. I'm not ready."

"You're not going anywhere!" I shouted, my hands trembling as I pressed them to my mouth, trying to choke back the sobs clawing at my throat. "You're not gonna die, Stella! I swear it—I swear to God, you're staying right here!"

Her mouth opened, like she wanted to argue, but the words caught in her throat. And all I could see was the little girl who used to follow me around, her wild blonde hair and those big brown eyes full of trust, looking at me like I could fix anything.

And now, for the first time, I couldn't.

Stella let out a hollow, broken laugh, the sound rattling in her chest. "Jadie ... your birthday present, the one waiting at home," she whispered. "It's a photo album. All the pictures we've taken over the years. Mama helped me put it together. I wrote under each one—where we were, what happened that day, all the stupid little memories. I wanted you to have something to remember everything."

"Stella, stop!"

She paused, her voice faltering as she forced a smile. "And I got you a new keychain, too. With our initials on it. 'Cause you're always losing your keys. Thought it might help."

"Good way to spoil the surprise, Stella."

A heavy silence stretched between us, the kind that made the world feel impossibly quiet, even when everything inside you was screaming.

"Jade," Thomas rasped, his voice shaking, "tell my mom that I love her, and—"

"No!" I cried out, cutting him off, my voice breaking as tears poured down my face. "Not you too, Thomas! Please! You're going to be fine, both of you! Stop it! Stop talking like that! I swear—nothing is going to happen!"

But the thing about promises is that they break as easily as hearts—quietly, suddenly, and completely.

The sirens howled in the distance, slicing through the thick air like cruel knives. Closer. Louder. Mocking us.

Stella froze, her tear-streaked face turning toward me. For one fleeting moment, her eyes met mine—full of fear, love, and something else I couldn't bear to name. Something I didn't want to understand.

Then another siren blared, so loud it rattled my bones.

And in that single, devastating instant, it happened.

A tiny, terrified step back.

"No!" My scream tore through the air, but it was already too late.

A blinding flash swallowed everything—a force so violent it tore the breath from my lungs, the ground shattering beneath me. The air erupted in chaos, in heat, in nothingness.

And then—silence.

The ground, the air, them—gone.

Just gone.

Forever.

CHAPTER FORTY

"The meaning of life is that it stops."
— **Franz Kafka**

Angelo

"The bastard's here."

I handed Vittori a glass of champagne. He tossed it back in one rough gulp, his eyes glinting with silent judgment as I pressed my back against the wall. My gaze drifted across the crowd, the decadence swallowing us whole.

We stood nearly hidden, half concealed by the bloodred curtains that framed the ballroom—dark and opulent, as if the devil himself had curated the place. New York's finest played their parts to perfection. The elite, draped in feathered masks and carnivalesque silks, blurred like mirages—Venetian dreams brought to life. Women in vicious gowns strutted like queens; men in polished suits radiated smug power.

It was impossible to distinguish friend from foe. But enemies? You always recognized enemies.

That's how I saw him.

Greg.

Descending the grand staircase like it had been carved just for him. An elaborate mask hugged half his face, but I'd know that bastard anywhere. His arm was locked firmly around his wife's, his words slipping like poison into her ear as they descended. At the bottom, she drifted away—a pawn released—but him? His gaze cut through the crowd and found me, piercing straight into my goddamn soul.

"So, what's your plan?" Vittori murmured.

I sipped my champagne. "Not killing him tonight."

Vittori scoffed, unamused. "Why not? Bastard kidnapped you, stole from you, and now he's got the audacity to show up at your event, rubbing it in your face."

"Because it's Jade's night."

The words stilled him. I caught the flicker of surprise, even behind his mask.

"And?"

"And I want her to enjoy it. She worked fucking hard for this."

Vittori's lip curled, disbelief painted across his face. "Lazzio—"

"I love her, Leonardo."

"Does she know?"

"She will. Tonight."

If the room hadn't been filled with murmuring socialites and orchestral violins, I knew he would have laughed in my face. Me—Angelo Lazzio—admitting something so reckless, so fucking weak. But the truth had a way of escaping when you least expected it.

I was in love with Jade Whitenhouse.

So wholly, so relentlessly in love that the mere thought of her being upset or disappointed tonight made me want to raze the whole damn ballroom to the ground.

"Finally," Vittori muttered, snatching another glass of champagne. "Took you long enough. Six years obsessed with this girl, and you're only just figuring it out."

Annoyance clawed at the back of my throat. "*Stai zitto.*"

I shoved my empty glass into his hand and turned to leave—but, fuck it. A hard punch to his stomach silenced him faster. He doubled over with a groan, laughter bubbling in its wake.

"By the way, touch her again, and I'll make you swallow your teeth, *stronzo*."

He straightened with a wince, a grin splitting his face. "Noted."

I left him there, weaving through the crowd like a man possessed. I smiled, shook hands, greeted old partners and investors, but none of it mattered. None of them mattered. My soul itched for her—the only person worth seeing.

A flick of my wrist revealed the time on my Rolex.

An hour since the ball had begun, and Jade wasn't here. That wasn't like her. She called me a control freak, but on nights like this? She was the one who demanded perfection—every detail, every corner, every step orchestrated to her vision.

I glanced at my phone. No calls. No texts.

Then, it happened.

The shiver.

The fine hair at my nape rose.

She was here. I fucking *felt* her.

My eyes snapped to the top of the staircase.

Jade Whitenhouse.

Mia diavoletta.

Emerald silk poured over her curves—-*the one I gifted her for Christmas*—black hair swept sleek and regal, her mask catching the light with glittering green flecks—like shards of a dangerous jewel. Her hands trembled against her small bag, those sharp eyes darting over the crowd as though the weight of the room itself might crush her.

I moved.

The violins faded, everything muffled as I pushed my way through the throng until I stood at the bottom of the stairs, waiting.

She froze when her gaze met mine. Just for a second—her hand clutching the banister tightly, her lips trembling, before she forced herself forward, one step at a time.

When she reached me, I held out my hand.

Slowly, her fingers slipped into mine—warm, delicate, her nails grazing my skin like fire. I lifted her hand to my lips.

"Your beauty is a ruinous thing—enough to bring empires to their knees, mine included."

Her lips curled faintly.

I stepped closer, sliding my free hand around her waist.

I dipped my head, brushing my lips against hers—a fleeting taste before she startled, cheeks flushed.

"Angelo," she hissed, pushing me back gently. "Stop. People are watching."

"And?"

"They'll think we're ... *together*."

I traced my thumb along her cheek. "Aren't we, *amore*?"

She inhaled deeply, her resolve cracking as she chewed her bottom lip.

"Angelo–"

"I can still feel how tight your pussy was around my cock

the other night. We can skip the pleasantries and admit it—you're mine, Jade."

"Ugh, you're *so* inappropriate."

I inched closer, "Only when I'm with you. Let's get you a drink."

I took her hand again, unwilling to let go, and guided her through the crowd.

I found a nearby butler, snatched a glass of champagne, and pressed it into her hand.

She finished it off in three gulps.

"Angelo—"

"Mr. Lazzio! There you are!"

A man approached with a woman under his arm—young enough to be his daughter.

"Congratulations on a stunning night. It's our first New Year's Eve in New York, and there's no better way to start the year than with a Lazzio exhibition."

I released Jade's hand, forced a polite smile, and shook his.

"It's me. Cillian Mondeor."

Cillian Mondeor. Europe's golden architect. The man who had turned Paris into a modern masterpiece. A man whose work had made him the envy of the world.

"Welcome, Cillian," I said smoothly. "It's an honor."

"No, the honor's mine. What you've done here—renovating the museum after that fire ... It's extraordinary. You'd never know it burned to the ground."

Smoke. Screams. Flames devouring everything in sight—the memories clawed at me, but I shoved them down.

"Thank you, Cillian. Allow me to introduce my COO, Jade Whitenhouse. She's the mastermind behind tonight—"

I turned.

She was gone.

The spot where she'd stood only seconds ago was empty, swallowed whole by the sea of masks and glittering chaos.

My fingers itched at my side, empty without hers in them.

I moved—cutting through the crowd with purpose, my jaw set tight as I scanned the room.

She was nowhere in sight.

The ballroom, with all its gold and velvet excess, suddenly felt suffocating. The violins hummed something dramatic in the background, people laughed a little too loudly, and I caught glimpses of feathers, lace, and painted eyes that meant nothing to me.

Where did you go, Jade?

My hand itched to pull out my phone again, but I didn't.

Instead, I slipped through the crimson curtains lining the ballroom and into the quieter sculpture room.

The change hit me instantly. The air was cooler, the crowd thinner, voices softer—low murmurs, like secrets shared in shadows.

People lingered in small groups here, sipping champagne as they admired the sculptures. Even the marble statues were dressed for the occasion, Venetian masks perched on cold faces, their stone gazes as lifeless as the men who'd put them there.

But I didn't stop to admire them.

The flicker of candlelight guided me as I walked deeper into the room until I reached it: *Samson and Delilah*, brought all the way from Italy.

I stopped.

The sculpture loomed in front of me—Samson's body draped in defeat, his strength stripped away, the betrayal carved into every perfect line of his ruined form.

Delilah stood poised, beautiful and merciless, her hand hovering above him like a silent goddess.

Their story was simple.

She had loved him. Or at least had pretended to.

And when it had mattered most, she'd betrayed him—had sold his secret for silver, and had let the world tear him apart.

A man so strong, brought to nothing because he had put his trust and love in the wrong woman.

I stared at it for a long moment, something heavy settling in my chest.

"Lazzio."

The voice came from behind me, and I didn't bother to turn right away.

"Great night," Greg began, his champagne swirling in the glass, the faint fizzing sound underscoring his smugness. "Congrats on the party. Though ... I heard the masks are all falling tonight."

I turned to him. "Is that so?"

"That's the rumor."

My eyes landed back on Samson and Delilah—power undone by love, betrayal immortalized in marble.

"They say every rumor has a thread of truth, Greg." I took a step closer, towering over him. "And tonight, your mask isn't just falling. It's shattering. Along with you."

He took a measured sip of champagne. "Or maybe yours, Lazzio."

He gestured lazily to the sculpture.

"Betrayal is the cruelest of acts. That's why no one should trust *anyone*—not their allies, their lovers, not even their family." His eyes locked onto mine, darker now. "That's why your parents should've never trusted me."

A wave of nausea coiled in my gut as his words dragged me back—back to that fucking basement.

The damp stench of mildew and iron. Ropes biting into my wrists, each movement ripping the raw skin underneath.

Blood streaking my arms and pooling on the cold, filthy concrete.

And his voice echoing in the darkness.

How the hell did I not recognize it sooner?

My brain must've blocked it out, wiping it away, trying to erase those fucking memories.

Greg tilted his head, studying me. "Those fourteen days in that basement … I suppose you think of them as your worst nightmare, don't you?" He gestured to the glittering room, the chandeliers above catching the fractured light. "But without them, would you be here now? The grand Angelo Lazzio? Nah. You'd be just another rich little shit. Soft. Entitled. *Worthless*."

A glass shattered across the room, a woman's laughter following, cheeks red with embarrassment as butlers rushed to clean up.

"I was supposed to kill you," he said casually, as if recounting the weather. "I thought, *what's the best way to dismantle the great Lazzio dynasty?* Take out their heir, of course! Their only miracle child after years of trying. Angelo. Heaven's little angel." He sneered. "If I took you from them, they'd *never* recover. The mighty Lazzios, ruined forever."

I took another step forward, my fists loose at my sides.

Calm. Controlled. Deadly.

The air in my lungs turned jagged as my nine-year-old self flashed behind my eyes.

"Careful, Angelo. You wouldn't want to cause a scene."

A low growl rumbled in my chest. "You fucking–"

He leaned in slightly. "But you didn't die. That's what pissed me off the most. You fought to stay alive, even at nine years old. Through the blood, the blows, the insults—you clung to life. Stubborn little thing. I knew you wouldn't know a damn thing about your father's business back then. Too young, too green. But I wanted to watch you sweat. To watch you break. So I kept going, days and nights, cracking that little mind of yours, until even I got fucking bored."

I ran my thumb over my lips, fighting to stay in control.

Killing him here, with all these people watching, would ruin Jade's night—and she deserved better than that.

"And so I let you live. I thought, *let's see what this boy becomes after the scars heal.*" He drained his glass. "Turns out, you became something worth killing after all. And when I come for you again, Angelo, there'll be no pity left in me. Oh, and say hi to Jade for me. Hope tonight doesn't end in another explosion of your wrath like it always does."

A flicker of unease crossed his features as he finally noticed the corner of my mouth curl into a smile—cold, merciless, and fucked up enough to tear him apart.

"I'm counting the seconds, Greg."

With that, I turned and walked off, the fire in me only burning hotter.

I needed to find Jade, make sure she was safe, before I came back to end Greg once and for all.

I searched every fucking room, but she wasn't there—just faces I had no interest in. I called her phone, but no answer. I didn't even think, just took the elevator up to my office, desperate for a glimpse of her.

The hallway was quiet, lifeless without Grace's smile and the comforting smell of coffee. The place felt cold, empty. But then, a faint light from under the door caught my eye. Someone was in there. It must be her.

I pushed the door open, and closed it behind me.

She stood in front of the window, her back to me, arms tight around her waist like she was holding herself together. I leaned against the door, my eyes roaming over her body, taking in every curve. Her hair—so long, so dark—was the first thing that hit me the moment she'd burst into my office six years ago.

All I had been able to think about was running my hands through it, twisting it around my wrist, pulling her closer, feeling it slip through my fingers.

It was so fucking long, sometimes when she'd pissed me off, I'd pictured myself grabbing it like a leash, yanking her around until she fucking listened to me.

I took a slow step forward, my eyes tracing every movement of her body, watching the way she tensed, her breath faltering.

And then, she turned.

She crossed her arms, her gaze heavy with a sadness that twisted inside me.

She'd been different yesterday too—avoiding my eyes, pressing against me in bed like she couldn't stand the thought of being apart, but at the same time, it was like my presence burned her.

I'd asked what was wrong, twice, and both times she had lied.

I could see it—the flicker in her eyes, the way her face paled just a shade.

I knew what it was.

We'd spent so many years hating each other that she couldn't grasp the truth: I had never hated her. I'd always fucking wanted her. But I'd never believed she'd want me in return.

Six years in her shadow—taking care of her, protecting her,

loving her in the dark, never knowing if she felt the same. But her hate? I knew that well. So I had let her give it to me—insults, barbs, petty little jabs. It hadn't mattered. Because it meant she was close. Her pretty face inches from mine, her eyes locked on me, her voice a soft, haunting caress in my ear.

I had lived for that.

Even if it was fucked up. Even if it was twisted.

It was all I'd ever needed.

Having her by my side was all I'd ever craved.

Her mask was gone. Mine wasn't needed anymore, so I threw it on the desk.

"Playing hide and seek, Miss Whitenhouse?"

She tilted her head, a look of confusion crossing her face.

"I've been searching for you for an hour, everywhere. Guess time's up. You win."

She chuckled ever so slightly before a sigh left her lips.

Her eyes met mine.

"We need to talk, Angelo."

"Yeah, we do," I murmured, stepping closer, inch by inch, until there was barely a breath of air between us.

Her head tilted up, her lips parting, quivering like she was bracing herself for what was coming.

"But first, you need to tell me what's bothering you, so I can fix it."

She let out a dry, biting laugh. "Fix it? What if the problem is me, Angelo? What's your fix then? Shoot me too, like Pauline Dupont?"

My jaw tightened at the mention of that name.

"Pauline Dupont made her choices. She earned her bullet. You're not her. Don't ever compare yourself to someone like that."

Her chin tilted up defiantly. "And if I did deserve it? What then?"

"If you think I'd ever kill you, you're out of your fucking mind. But anyone else causing you problems? They're dead the second I know their name."

I didn't know what the hell was tearing her apart, but I'd never seen her this wrecked—like she hated herself more than anything I could ever kill for her.

Her silence stretched, her lips parting like she wanted to say something, but the words never came.

I leaned in. "Let me make this clear. If you've made a mess, I'll clean it up. If someone's hurt you, they're already dead. But if you think for one second I'd ever hurt you, you don't know me at all."

She shook her head, her voice barely a whisper. "You don't get it—"

"Then make me understand, sweetheart."

A tear fell, but she quickly wiped it away, biting her lip. "I can't."

"Then listen to me, Jade. I need to say this. Something I've been keeping for too damn long."

"No, Angelo. Please—"

"I love you," I forced out, the words breaking past all the walls I'd put up around my heart. "I've loved you since the moment you burst into my life—riding your high horse, throwing your big ego around, pouting like you owned the damn world. And maybe you did, because you've owned *me* from the start. I've never been able to look away from you ever since."

She went still, like my words had paralyzed her.

"I've loved you every day, more and more," I continued. "Working with you, arguing with you, just *having* you in my life ... It became my routine. My anchor. You changed everything—how I saw the world, how I saw myself. And I know—" my voice cracked, barely audible now. "I know I've hurt you with my words over the years. God, I hurt you, and I hate myself for it. But, Jade ... I never meant a single one of them. Not one."

Her lips parted, but no sound came.

"I said those things because I didn't know how to say the truth. Because the truth—*this* truth—terrified me. I was scared that the second I let it slip, the second my hands let go of this, you'd fly away. And I couldn't bear the thought of losing you."

Her eyes shimmered with unshed tears.

"So, please. Let me be yours, Jade. Let me be the one for you."

Everything I'd kept buried for years came rushing out, raw and untamed. My mask cracked, but it didn't feel like relief—it felt like everything was slipping through my fingers.

"I can't—We can't—" A sob broke from her.

I took a step forward, but she stopped me.

"You can't love me, Angelo. Not after what I've done."

She turned, walking to the window, the lights of New York glowing brighter, everyone gearing up for the countdown to New Year's Eve.

I glanced at the time.

11:58 p.m.

I moved towards her, wrapping my arms around her waist and pulling her back into me. She cried silently, her hands resting on my arms, my head pressing into her neck.

For a moment, I just held her—letting her break.

I pressed a kiss to the crook of her neck.

"There's nothing you could do that would ever make me stop loving you, Jade."

Another sob left her lips. "Don't say that ..."

"I mean it."

She sniffled, her head dropping back onto my shoulder, her eyes fluttering shut.

"I love you too, Angelo," she whispered. "So much. Too much, and I shouldn't. But for some reason, my heart betrayed me and chose you."

Relief washed over me, settling deep in my chest.

I had seen it in her eyes, felt it in the way she'd kissed me, but hearing her say it … that made it real. It erased all the fucking doubts away.

I nuzzled her neck, inhaling the scent of her—*so* intoxicating, *so* fucking addictive, that I couldn't stop myself. I kissed her neck again, feeling her shiver under my lips.

"What do you mean?"

She stayed silent, her body trembling in my arms, eyes closed as if she couldn't find the strength to speak.

But just as I thought she might, the sound of fireworks exploded outside, bursting in the sky in a dazzling array of shimmering colors. The flashes lit up the windows, casting fleeting shadows over her face.

I felt her heart race beneath my fingers. It matched the chaos outside—wild, uncontrollable.

My arms tightened around her waist, pulling her closer.

We stood there in silence, the fireworks outside lighting up the sky in bursts of color, but the space between us felt thick, like time had come to a standstill.

Slowly, she turned to face me, and my hands dropped to her hips instinctively, pulling her closer.

She didn't wait—her hands cupped my face, drawing me in until our lips met.

It wasn't a kiss of love.

No.

It was hunger, fierce and unrestrained, like she needed something from me—something she couldn't even explain. Her lips were urgent, almost desperate, as if she feared that if she didn't let herself feel this now, it would disappear before she could grasp it.

I leaned back, my forehead dropping to rest against hers.

Her hands slowly slid from my face, fingers trailing down my neck, before they settled over my chest.

"I've put my resignation on your desk. Please let me go, Angelo. Don't try to stop me."

The moment the words hit me, it felt like acid had been poured over my skin.

My eyes landed on the envelope on my desk.

"Resignation? Why? What the fuck is going on?"

Her eyes met mine, calm, like she'd already made peace with this, and that just made my blood boil even more.

"I don't want to do this anymore, Angelo."

"And you think I'll just let you walk away?"

Her gaze never wavered. "If you love me, respect my choice."

My jaw clenched.

The words hit like a fucking slap, and for a moment, I didn't know if I was going to rage or fucking collapse.

But I didn't move as she turned and left, the door shutting behind her like it was slamming a part of me into the dark.

CHAPTER
FORTY-ONE

"After all, it's one thing to run away when someone's chasing you.
It's entirely another to be running all alone."
—**Jennifer E. Smith**

Jade

I crammed the last of my clothes into my suitcase—the ones that didn't feel like they weighed a thousand pounds from guilt alone. My vision blurred with tears, and my throat tightened again, like it was punishing me for even trying to breathe.

The bathroom was next. I swiped my hygiene products into a bag.

The second I had gotten home, I'd ripped off my dress, the fabric burning against my skin, the sting of betrayal—mine, his, ours—digging deeper than I could handle.

Yoga pants and a hoodie had seemed appropriate for someone who was running away once again.

My job in New York? Over. Done. Finished.

By the time the city woke up from its champagne-soaked haze, they'd be feasting on the juiciest scandal of the year. Angelo Lazzio, the untouchable Don Juan, completely exposed.

And all thanks to me.

The one he trusted. The one he *loved*.

A bitter, pathetic sob broke free as I sat down on my bed, pressing my palms against my face like it could hold me together.

Years of planning, plotting, promising myself this moment would feel good, and yet here I was.

Empty. Guilty. Hating him, hating myself, hating everything.

But I'd done it. I'd done what I said I would.

So why did it feel like I was the one who'd been destroyed?

I forced myself to get up, shut off the lights, and head to my secret room.

Six years of my life stared back at me: a mess of files, photos, and every shred of evidence I'd spent so long collecting.

All I wanted to do was set it on fire and watch the flames erase me, him, and every terrible decision in between.

My eyes landed on a picture on the ground, and the second I saw it, my heart twisted like someone had taken a knife and just ... twisted it.

I dropped to my knees, my hands shaking—probably from the sudden rush of guilt, probably from the realization that this was the last thing I'd needed to see.

It was a photo of Stella and me.

God, we must've been so young—maybe ten and five—

laughing like idiots, wearing swimsuits that were too bright for anyone's eyes. That was before the world had turned ugly, back when I'd thought we'd always be okay, that I could always protect her.

I pressed the photo to my chest, my breath stuttering in my throat.

Then I carefully set the picture down.

My fingers moved to my necklace, the gold chain catching, trembling under my touch. Two little butterflies dangled there —one for my father, the man who had once seemed untouchable. The other for Stella, the little girl who had thought I could do no wrong.

My life—my whole existence—had been reduced to a couple of charms and a picture I couldn't even look at without falling apart.

"I did it, Stella," I whispered, my voice barely a breath. "And I'm sorry. I ... I'm sorry I fell in love with the man who took you from me."

My eyes closed, and the tears came—hot and choking.

"I hope you can forgive me."

I got up and dusted off my pants, just as three rough knocks echoed through my apartment.

It must be Mr. Jones, my concierge, coming up to help with the suitcases.

Running away had been part of the plan, a one-way ticket to Edinburgh in my bag, and zero clue what came next.

Scotland—of all places.

I didn't know a soul there, hadn't even thought about the country before. But it was far enough away, and no one would think to look for me there. Not Angelo. Not his family. Not the journalists, nor his partners who'd want my head on a platter by sunrise.

I sighed, turning off the lights, the darkness swallowing up the life I was leaving behind.

Hurrying to my room, I grabbed my bags, slipped on my sneakers, and tried not to think too hard about what I was doing.

Just go, Jade.

The knocks came again, louder this time, and I rushed to the door, pulling it open.

But it wasn't Mr. Jones.

With a gasp, I tried to shut the door, but his hand stopped it cold.

I pushed harder, leaning my whole weight into it, but it didn't budge.

"Jesus," I breathed as the door swung open effortlessly. "Are you the Hulk's long-lost son or something?"

He stepped inside, closing the door behind him.

His gaze swept over me slowly, before it dropped to the suitcases on the floor.

A flicker of anger passed through his eyes, subtle but unmistakable, as his thumb brushed over his lips.

"You weren't planning to leave without saying goodbye, were you, Miss Whitenhouse?"

The ice in his voice was enough to send a chill straight down my spine, and I instinctively stepped back.

If I'd thought Angelo was terrifying when he was angry, this was something else entirely.

He looked *deadly*, yet so beautiful my heart hurt.

He stepped closer, his hands loose at his sides.

"Goodbye, Lazzio."

"Off to hell, or something?"

"Hell can't be worse than staying here with you."

Another step.

"What are you running from?"

"You," I admitted, the word slipping out in a shaky breath before I could stop it.

His head tilted slightly. "Why?"

I shook my head and spun on my heel, aiming for the safety of my bedroom, a closet, *anything*. But before I could make it two steps, his arms wrapped around my waist, yanking me back against his chest.

"Let me go!"

My nails dug into his skin, my elbows jabbed into his ribs, and I even tried to stomp on his foot.

He didn't flinch. He didn't loosen his grip. And he sure as hell didn't let me go.

"Keep going," he whispered in my ear, his breath hot against my neck. "I told you I'd enjoy the fight."

Stronzo!

I twisted in his arms, glaring up at him. "What do you want, Angelo?"

"You," he breathed out. "You, and only you."

My chest tightened, and I could feel that all-too-familiar panic rising like a tide. My vision blurred, my heart thundered in my ears, and my throat felt like it was closing up.

He saw it.

I could tell by the way he let go of me, turned me around, and pulled me close. My face pressed into his chest, tears spilling down my face, soaking his shirt.

He didn't say a word. He just held me, letting me cry in his arms once again.

Angelo Lazzio, my savior and my reaper.

The one who had carved scars into my soul, whispered promises through blood-stained lips, then dragged me back into the darkness.

Suddenly, he carried me, and my legs and arms circled his body as he walked to my sofa and sank into it, his arms strong around my back.

I cried into his neck, his hands caressing my hair, whispering words I didn't deserve, and then madness took over.

I grabbed his face and lost myself in him.

He kissed me back, though his hands fell back at his sides, like he was surrendering to me but also scared that if he touched me, I'd stop.

I was so hot I felt like I was burning with fever.

I don't know what took over me, but I couldn't stop.

Overwhelming lust erupted through me, tightening in my chest before making its way between my legs.

He leaned back, eyes half lidded, lazily dropping to my lips again.

A flicker of confusion passed, like he truly was lost and didn't know what I was playing at, but it didn't stop me. Even though it should've.

But I didn't care; I was too far gone.

I drew my tongue across his neck, sucked the skin, then bit it hard.

Then my hands grabbed his hair and yanked it back, giving me more access, and I licked my way up his neck as a low groan vibrated through his chest. The fire between my legs burned hotter.

I continued to lick and suck his neck, grinding against him, the fabric between us slowly driving me mad.

Angelo cursed under his breath before grabbing my ponytail and twisting it around his wrist—once, twice, three times.

I ignored him and let my hands drop to the zipper of his pants, lowering it. His boxers followed, and I grabbed his cock in my hands, pumping it, precum already making its way down his length.

"Fuck—"

I lowered my yoga pants until they dropped to my ankles, brought him to my entrance, and shoved him inside. Stars exploded between my legs, making me moan.

I didn't wait—I couldn't, as I rode him fast and rough, my hands grabbing his shoulders, nails digging into his skin as his hand yanked my head back harder.

"That's what you needed, *amore*? My cock inside you?" His accent was rougher than usual.

I moaned his name, unable to speak as my vision blurred, tears streaking down my cheeks. His cock was so deep I could feel it in my stomach.

He let go of my hair, slapped my ass hard before grabbing my hips and slamming me down hard, fast, and rough. The naughty noise filled my apartment.

His lips dropped to mine again, his tongue forcing its way into my mouth, swallowing my breath. I felt it pulse between my legs when he sucked on my tongue.

I had always enjoyed kissing, making out, but with him, these were my favorite things.

I'd never admitted it before, but I was obsessed with the way he kissed me. It always felt as if his mouth was making love to mine.

I leaned back, breathless, feeling my orgasm make its way up my legs, bursting through me as my pussy tightened around his cock, my head thrown back.

Millions of little butterflies fluttered between my legs, my juices pooling down his shaft as he let go of my hips and I rode him slowly now, my eyes locked on his like I couldn't look away.

"I love you," I breathed, going down slowly, watching his length disappear inside of me before I came back up again.

"I love you too, *amore*," he said as his hands grabbed my

face and his lips found mine again, this time softer, as I felt him pulse inside me.

His fingers dug into my skin before he groaned in my mouth and came inside me for the first time.

He leaned back, realizing what he'd done, and we both stared down as his cock softened and slid out of me. His cum leaked down my pussy, drop by drop. His finger reached down, smearing it on my folds, circling my clit as I hummed, pressing my forehead against his.

Then he forced his cum back inside me, his finger entering me slowly.

"Feel better?"

I shook my head, closing my eyes as a sigh escaped my lips.

I felt him reach for my thong and pants, pulling them up before he adjusted me onto his lap, settling me properly.

"Tell me what's wrong."

"I did something bad, Angelo. *Really*, really bad."

His lips dropped on mine again. "What did you do?"

I lied to you.

I betrayed you.

I tore apart everything we had, Angelo, even though you're the only man I've ever loved.

I took a deep breath, letting it settle in my chest, before pulling away.

"I'll be back," I muttered.

I stood up and made my way to the bedroom, desperate to find what I needed so we could put an end to all of this.

As I rifled through my nightstand, his phone rang.

I heard him answer, his voice rough.

And then ... complete silence.

My fingers found what I needed—the weight of it familiar in my hand.

When I walked back into the living room, he was standing in front of the window, facing away from me, his phone still gripped tightly in his hand. I stepped closer, and the moment he turned around, his eyes found mine.

It took no more than a second for him to understand what was happening.

The look in his eyes wasn't surprise.

No, it was something darker—something much worse.

He knew.

He knew *everything.*

His gaze slid down to the gun in my hand, and for a brief, sickening moment, I thought he might actually laugh.

"Why?"

The word was simple.

Why?

Why did I betray him?

Why did I spend six years pretending we were something we never were?

Why did I let myself fall so deeply in love with him?

I didn't have an answer. Not a real one. Not anymore.

I swallowed the bitter lump in my throat. "You should hurry. The feds are already looking for you. They'll be here soon enough."

His jaw clenched, and if looks could kill, I'd be dead ten times over.

"I don't give a damn about the feds." His voice dropped, the coldness sharper. "Why are you running? Why would you fuck me and then sell me out to them?"

A sick laugh bubbled up, but I swallowed it back. "Pick your poison. Murderer, cheater, liar, home-wrecker ... Take your pick."

His gaze sharpened, and there it was again. *That* look—the

one that told me I was pushing him too far, and he hated it, but couldn't seem to stop coming closer.

He didn't get it. He couldn't.

Not unless I told him everything. And I couldn't do that. Not now.

"Answer me," he ordered.

I almost choked on the air I was breathing, heart racing.

He took another step toward me.

Without thinking, I raised the gun, pointing it directly at his chest. "Don't. Move."

But of course, he didn't listen.

He ignored me, his eyes blazing with so much anger, but there was that crack—tiny, barely visible—betrayal. Hurt.

I saw it, and it made everything worse.

Another step.

"Angelo, stop!"

He stepped closer.

And for a brief moment, everything inside me froze.

I hesitated—just for a split second—and he took another step.

"This time, I'll aim lower, Lazzio."

He stopped, a dark amusement flickering across his face before he wiped the ghost of a smile off his lips with the back of his hand.

"You said you were from Philadelphia."

"I lied."

"You swore you'd never tell a soul about my past."

"I lied."

His eyes darkened as he stepped closer. "You told me you *loved* me."

"I do," I breathed out.

He laughed, but it wasn't real—it was empty, bitter, like he couldn't even believe the words coming out of my mouth.

"You really are a better liar than I gave you credit for, Miss Whitenhouse."

He stepped closer, his chest pressing into the barrel of the gun now, and I swear to God, I could feel his heartbeat against it.

He didn't care. He wasn't scared.

But I was.

"You're going to tell me, Jade. *Now.* Why are you doing this?"

The question shattered me, cracked the last mask I'd been holding on to.

And I screamed, a raw, jagged sound that felt like it tore me apart. "Because you killed my sister!"

Then confusion flashed in his eyes. "What?"

"Nine years ago. Lake Kendrick, Boston."

He took a step back, his hand running through his hair.

"What the hell are you talking about?"

I lowered the gun, my hand trembling, and tucked it into the waistband of my pants at the small of my back.

My breath hitched as the memories clawed their way to the surface.

"The Cyrus Project."

"The Cyrus Project? That's—" He stopped mid-sentence, his words cutting off as realization flickered in his eyes.

The Cyrus Project, the key to the ache in my chest.

"You sent men to plant mines," I said, my voice breaking. "Because Lucius Cyrus stole that project from you. You wanted to ruin him, ruin everything... but you ruined me instead."

His silence stretched, suffocating and heavy.

"My sister ..." My throat tightened, the pain clawing up my chest, making it impossible to breathe. "She and her boyfriend had a fight that day. She called me crying, told me to come find her at the lake, and I—" My voice cracked as tears blurred my vision. "I went to her. I tried to bring her home, but they stepped on *your* mines."

"Jade—"

I shook my head, stumbling back. "The sirens from the police spooked us. She stepped back, and the ground—" A sob ripped through me, jagged and uncontrollable. "It exploded. She was right in front of me, Angelo. One second she was there, and then ... she wasn't. She was gone, and I—"

My knees buckled, and I hit the floor, gasping for air, my hands clawing at my chest. "She b-burned alive. She d-died because of *you*."

His footsteps thundered toward me, and then his arms were around me, pulling me against him no matter how hard I pushed.

"Don't touch me! Don't—" My voice cracked as the fight left me, replaced by the unbearable weight of grief. "You k-killed her, Angelo. You killed my sister. And when y-you did, you killed me too."

The room felt too small, his arms too strong, the air too thick to breathe.

"Shhh," he murmured, his voice softer than I'd ever heard it.

His hand moved in slow, soothing circles on my back.

But I didn't want comfort.

Not from him.

I tried to pull away, but his grip only tightened, his fingers steady as they found my chin. He tilted my face up, forcing my eyes to meet his.

"Jade, I'm not the one who put those mines there."

"Stop lying, Angelo!" My voice was raw, shaking as I shoved against his chest. "I've spent six years digging through your dirt, six years tearing my life apart to find proof. And I did.

Emails, texts, contracts—everything." My breath hitched. "So don't stand there and tell me you didn't do it."

His thumb dragged across my cheek, wiping away a tear.

"Jade," he murmured. "I'm not claiming to be innocent. God knows I'm not. I've done things you can't even begin to imagine. But I'll tell you this—I didn't put those fucking mines there. You can hate me, you can shoot me, you can burn my entire goddamned world to ash, but don't accuse me of something I didn't do."

His hand cupped my face, his fingers warm against my skin, his grip unrelenting as he forced me to meet his eyes.

They were dark, heavy, not with anger, but something far deeper, something raw, something that seemed to tear at him just as much as it was tearing at me.

"You want revenge?" he murmured. "I can help you get it, *amore*."

My heart hammered against my chest, my head spinning.

I didn't want to hear it. I didn't want to hope, not like this—not after everything, but the possibility that he might be innocent ... it gnawed at me.

"How?"

"I know who did it, Jade. And I'll give you everything you need to make him bleed. But only if you trust me."

I shook my head, confusion clouding every thought, but there wasn't time to process it.

Just as I opened my mouth, the front door burst open, slamming against the wall. Four FBI agents stormed in, guns raised, red lasers slicing through my apartment as shouts filled the air.

"Angelo Lazzio, you're under arrest for the murder of Pauline Dupont."

Angelo barely reacted.

Instead, he turned to me, his hands threading into my hair, his lips finding mine in a kiss that stole the air from my lungs.

Before I could even register it, he pulled away, his fingers brushing down my neck.

One last glance—cold, unreadable—and then he walked out, calm as ever, following them.

The door slammed shut, and my hands flew to my neck.

Gone.

He had taken my necklace.

CHAPTER
FORTY-TWO

"Sometimes, we have to say goodbye to the love we wish could stay forever."
— **Manisha Manjari**

Jade
23 years old
Seven years ago

"Why the drugs, Jade?"

I scoffed, my legs on the couch, my arms crossed tight. "Why the twenty questions?"

Dr. Morano sipped her coffee, her face calm, steady—unshakable. "It's my job to ask questions, to get past whatever wall you've built around yourself. The more I know—"

"The better the diagnosis?" I cut in, my voice biting. "Pretty sure we already agreed I'm crazy."

Her smile was soft, infuriatingly patient. "We agreed you weren't crazy, Jade. You're just—"

"Weak? Selfish? Stupid? A mess of bad decisions, wrapped in guilt?"

"Hurt."

That single word hung in the air, too heavy, too simple, and yet impossible to argue with.

"Ah, pain," I muttered, letting out a bitter laugh as my eyes drifted to that awful painting on her wall. A picture-perfect family walking through a field of sunflowers. It was insulting, really. "My one and only constant companion."

It had been two years now.

Two years since Stella and Thomas had died.

A year and a half since I'd crawled out of the psych ward and started wandering through life like a ghost, hollow and aimless.

Three months ago, I'd tried to fill the void—or drown it—with ink on my skin.

That tattoo had set off the spiral. Cocaine. Alcohol. Nights I could barely piece together.

For the first time in two years, I thought I'd cracked the code, and had found the answer to the pain.

I'd overdosed.

But instead of rotting away in the bathroom of my favorite bar, I'd woken up in a hospital bed. They couldn't even let me die right. The ER doctor had handed me two choices, like I'd had any say in my own fate: rehab or therapy.

I'd chosen therapy. Not because I'd wanted to. Rehab had just sounded worse.

And that's how I'd ended up here again, in Dr. Morano's office, after over a year of avoiding it.

When she'd opened the door and seen me, her eyes had

flickered—sadness, pity, maybe even a flash of disappointment. She hadn't said a word, just motioned me inside.

I hadn't hesitated to throw myself onto the couch, shutting my eyes.

In a way, facing her was harder than facing myself.

Dr. Morano didn't push—not yet.

She let me stew, probably waiting for me to crack first.

I stared at the ceiling, letting out a dry laugh. "What's the plan here? Sit there all day until I finally break down and bare my soul?"

"Only if that's what you need, Jade."

I rolled onto my side, my eyes landing on that sunflower painting again.

God, I hated that thing. It was too bright, too happy, too ... wrong.

"I don't even know why I'm here."

"You're here because you don't want to be dead."

The words hit like a gut punch, knocking the air out of me.

I turned my head just enough to glare at her. "I never said that."

"You didn't have to." Her voice softened, but it didn't lose that edge of truth I loathed so much. "You could've chosen rehab. Or you could've vanished entirely. But you didn't. You came here. That means something, Jade."

My throat felt tight. "Or maybe I just suck at making decisions. Wouldn't be the first time."

"Or maybe," she countered, her eyes locking on mine, "there's a part of you that still wants to fight. Even if you don't see it right now."

I sat up, crossing my arms over my chest, like it could shield me from her words. "Fight for what? There's nothing left, Doc. Nothing worth saving."

Joy had long since abandoned my life, leaving nothing but an empty shell.

And maybe that was a mercy.

Happiness—so bright, so intoxicating—was nothing more than a cruel mirage.

It lifted you high only to send you crashing down. And the fall? The fall tore through you, leaving scars so deep they never truly healed.

The wreckage it left behind was never worth the fleeting light.

"That's not true, Jade."

I scoffed, shaking my head as I looked away. "You don't know what the hell you're talking about. You don't know what it's like to lose everything, to watch the people you love—" My voice cracked, and I bit down on the words, swallowing the lump in my throat.

Dr. Morano stayed quiet for a moment, letting the weight of my outburst settle. "You're right. I don't know exactly what you've been through. But I know pain, Jade. And I know it doesn't have to define you."

"Feels like it already has, Doc."

I'd tried everything—every trick, every lie, every distraction. Drowning in work, chasing highs, numbing myself to the point of oblivion. I clawed at normalcy like it was some lifeline I could hold on to, tried to keep the monsters in my head chained up tight. But no matter what I did, I always ended up back here. Back at square fucking one.

Because that's all I was—a goddamn failure.

I hadn't been able to save my mom from falling apart after she'd lost the love of her life.

I hadn't been able to stop my sister from stepping onto that mine.

I hadn't even been able to pretend that I was fine. Not for anyone. Not even for myself.

Failure is all I'd known.

And maybe it was time I stopped fighting it. Maybe it was time to let it win.

Dr. Morano studied me with that maddening calm, the kind that made me feel exposed.

She leaned forward. "Maybe the missing piece isn't about forgetting or pretending, Jade. Maybe it's about finding a real purpose again. Something that matters. Something worth living for."

"Purpose?" I shot back, the word tasting bitter on my tongue. "What's the purpose of dragging around a body that feels like a corpse?"

"That's the thing about ashes, Jade," she whispered. "They're not the end of the story. They're the roots of it. Ashes feed the soil. They're where things grow. Where life starts over."

The air felt heavy, thick with something I couldn't name.

Hope? No, that wasn't it. Hope was dangerous, like a flame you couldn't control.

This was different.

This was something raw, something I wasn't sure I was ready to touch.

But her words lingered, their weight settling in the cracks I thought were too far gone to hold anything.

Ashes weren't the end. They were a beginning.

They were now the dawn of my revenge, and the dusk of my pain.

A twisted rebirth, where every burn, every scar, fed the fire that would burn down everything in its path.

CHAPTER
FORTY-THREE

"Thoughts and prayers won't stop a speeding bullet."
— **DaShanne Stokes**

Angelo

The cold of the interrogation room did nothing to still the brutal pounding in my veins, each pulse threatening to tear me apart. My breaths ripped shallow and uneven, my vision clouded with raw betrayal.

Oh, Lazzio. I've got too much dirt on you. I could ruin you.

Jade Whitenhouse.

The woman I'd been obsessed with. Crazy in love with. Head over fucking heels for. The one who had haunted my every waking thought.

She hadn't just *ruined* me—she'd ripped me apart from the inside out.

She'd forged her own black blade and drove it straight into my chest. Buried it so deep that the last ember of life in my heart, the one I'd fought to keep alive for thirty-six fucking years, had snuffed out.

Six years.

Six goddamn years.

The devil herself had been plotting my destruction for over half a decade, carving out my downfall piece by meticulous piece. Every fragment of my life—good, bad, dangerous—turned into a weapon. She had collected it all, crafted it into documents sharp enough to cut me down.

She'd unearthed everything: how my mother had nearly lost me before I was even born, the fevers that almost killed me as a child, the kidnapping when I was nine. Every triumph and humiliation. My master's degrees—international business at Columbia, data security engineering at Cornell. Every deal I'd struck, every contract I'd signed for Lazzio Entertainment Group and Lazzio Exhibits Inc. Every woman who'd ever warmed my bed, single or married. Every soul I'd sent to the grave without remorse. Hell, even my fucking allergies were in that folder.

She'd handed them *everything*. Every. Last. Detail. About me, my family, my empire.

She had made it her life's mission to tear me apart, to burn everything I was to the ground, and watch it all turn to ashes.

And she'd succeeded.

Just not in the way she'd thought.

Jade Whitenhouse had made me fall for her, so fucking deep, I was already lost—just to watch me crawl to her, and destroy me.

The words I'd said to her a few weeks ago keep playing in my head, taunting me.

I'm starting to think you might kill me, Jade. And you know what? I'd let you.

But if I had only known back then how fucking wrong I'd been—how the very flames of her love, which I had thought would heal me, would end up burning down the last shreds of my soul.

I scoffed to myself.

Her love.

Was she even fucking capable of it?

Was it all fake? Just some goddamn act?

I swear to fucking God, I'd seen it in her eyes—the love, the admiration, the fucking longing.

Had I mistaken it because I had wanted it so damn badly to be true? Because I'd been desperate for her to love me just as much as I'd fucking loved her for the last six years?

You can't love me, Angelo. Not after what I've done.

If I wasn't sitting in this fucking interrogation room with these bastards watching my every move, waiting for me to snap, I'd destroy every goddamn piece of furniture in here, furious at myself.

I'd told her there was nothing she could ever do that would make me stop loving her.

But this?

Betraying me, lying to me, stealing from me ...

"I love you too, Angelo," she had said. *"So much. Too much, and I shouldn't. But for some reason, my heart betrayed me and chose you."*

When Vittori had called me tonight, telling me that Alia Jasper, head of the New York City FBI field office—the woman he'd befriended and occasionally had in his bed—had informed him that her own sister, Alexandra Jasper, Fox News' top journalist, had compiled a sixty-two-page folder detailing my life, and accusing me of murder, embezzlement, kidnapping, threats, and more.

I had been not only fucking shaken, but utterly destroyed.

Then I'd turned around to see her—*mia diavoletta*—gun pointed high at me, ready to shoot.

She'd claimed I had killed her sister.

Stella. The same name she had cried in her sleep many times.

But the Cyrus Project had been the reason her sister had died, not fucking *me.*

If she had just fucking come to me and been honest, I would have helped her get the revenge she so desperately needed—because I knew exactly who was behind it all.

La freccia della tua vendetta ha colpito il cuore sbagliato, amore.

A heavy breath clogged my lungs as I checked the time again.

2:35 a.m.

When I'd entered the feds' car, Vittori had texted me that his Alia would get me out at 2:45 a.m. That I had to stay at least twenty minutes to pretend, for the employees there, that I was a nobody—without money to buy this fucking country and every bastard that came my way.

The doors opened, and a pretty agent—Detective Naomi McLauren—sat down, her cheeks pink, eyes wide as she scanned my face and lips. She explained why I had been arrested, but in the process, was unable to hide how attracted she was to me.

I barely listened to her, my mind still on Jade, waiting for her to explain the fucking sinful lies that had slipped from those pretty lips.

When my Rolex hit 2:45 a.m., I put my blazer back on and left.

Despite every fucking betrayal, my soul was still fucking empty, craving its soulmate—even though she was the reason I was in this mess in the first place.

Jade Whitenhouse.

My employee. Mia Diavoletta. My light.

How could this woman be my redemption and my ruin in the same breath?

"Well, shit. All this just to save your ass from the feds on the day of your goddamn New Year's party."

I slammed the passenger door, rubbing my eyes as if I could scrub away the exhaustion, the nerves, and the simmering anger.

Vittori's hand gripped the wheel as he steered the car out of the parking lot.

"Yeah, *grazie*. Who knew you fucking their head agent would actually pay off one day, huh?"

A smirk tugged at the corner of his lips as he slowed for a red light, pulling out a pack of cigarettes and offering me one. I took it, and he lit both mine and his, drawing in the smoke with a satisfied inhale.

The chill air bit at my skin as he rolled the window down.

"Beautiful Alia Jasper." A lazy grin spread on his face. "I've always known how to pick my women, Lazzio. You, on the other hand ..." He gave a low scoff, shaking his head like I was the dumbest bastard he'd ever met. "Still haven't figured it out, apparently."

My glare could've burned through stone.

"Can't believe your little *diavoletta* almost ruined *you* entirely—just to bring your empire down. And for what?"

"She thinks I killed her sister."

A beat of silence.

His brow barely lifted. "Well ... did you?"

I exhaled sharply. "No. I didn't even know she *had* a fucking sister—let alone that she died in a damn explosion!"

Doubt and fucking shock now swam faster in my mind.

I still couldn't fucking believe it.

Six years.

Six fucking years I'd been obsessed with a woman who'd turned out to have a hidden agenda sharp enough to gut me. Six years of wanting her, needing her like an addiction I didn't want to kick—only to find out she was plotting my downfall from the start.

All because of something that wasn't even fucking true.

But now, I couldn't even separate the truth from her lies anymore.

Every touch, every batting eyelash, every moan, every goddamn caress—how much of it had been real?

What had been part of her little performance?

She'd told me she fucking loved me.

The words I'd dreamed of hearing for years, spilling out of her mouth like salvation. And now? I didn't even know if that was a lie too.

Fuck.

I'd told her about my past—the things I'd buried so deep.

I'd handed her my scars, my truths, my fucking trust.

And what had she done? She'd wrapped it up in a pretty little bow, just to hand it over and ruin me.

"What are you gonna do now?"

He pulled the car into the parking lot of my condo, throwing it into park.

I sat back, closed my eyes for a moment, and let out a slow breath.

"Now?" My voice was cold, clipped. I turned to him, a shadow of a grin curling at the edge of my lips. "Now, I need your help with something."

Because one way or another, this wasn't fucking over.

CHAPTER

FORTY-FOUR

“Revenge, the sweetest morsel to the mouth that ever was cooked in hell.”

— **Walter Scott**

Angelo

“Long time no see, Greg.”

The bastard spun around, eyes wide like a cornered rat, his hand twitching toward the railing of his jet stairs.

I leaned against the doorframe of the jet, arms crossed, a slow, deliberate smirk playing on my lips.

“What the *fuck* are you doing in my jet, Lazzio?”

It had taken me ten minutes to track Greg down.

Ten. Fucking. Minutes.

That’s all I had needed to learn that the second he’d

slipped out of the masquerade ball, he'd swung by his house to pack a bag before making a break for Thailand.

The bastard thought he was clever, timing his little getaway for when the feds would be breathing down my neck, thinking I'd be too preoccupied to stop him. And here he was, at four a.m., standing on his shiny private jet, smugly assuming I was someone else's problem now.

Judging by the look on his ugly mug, though, he wasn't just surprised to see me.

He was scared.

I let the silence hang for a moment, just to watch the panic tighten his shoulders, before I pushed off the doorframe and shrugged lazily.

"You're not paying your pilot enough, *stronzo.* Told him I had something *very important* to discuss with you. Slipped him fifty grand in cash, and—well—who the fuck says no to fifty grand?" I grinned, slow and sharp. "Certainly not your guy."

Greg froze, panic flashing across his face, before his instincts kicked in. Like the rat he was, he spun on his heel, lunging down the stairs in a desperate sprint.

I stayed where I was, leaning casually against the jet's door frame, and pulled my gun out in one smooth motion.

"Run, and you're dead," I called lazily.

The bastard didn't stop. Of course he didn't. Greg was always the kind of idiot who thought he could outrun consequences.

Bang.

The shot cracked through the night, clean and sharp. The bullet hit the ground at his feet, sending up a spray of dust and concrete. He stumbled, nearly eating shit on the bottom step before skidding to a stop.

I took my time descending the stairs, the barrel of my gun aimed directly at him.

"I don't miss twice, Greg," I said, my voice calm, almost bored. "You know that."

He turned slowly, hands already raised, his face a cocktail of fear and disbelief.

"You're insane," he breathed.

"No," I said, stepping closer, each movement deliberate. "I'm fucking *pissed*."

I stopped just a few feet away, cocking my head as I looked him over, my gun still trained on his chest.

"Did you really think you could run? That you'd be halfway to Thailand, sipping your shitty cocktails, while I was sitting in a fucking federal holding cell?"

His lips parted, but no sound came out.

The bastard was too terrified to even lie properly.

I clicked my tongue, shaking my head. "You disappoint me, Greg. I thought you'd at least try to grovel before you went full coward."

Anger flashed behind his eyes. "Fuck you, Lazzio."

A low laugh rumbled out of me, the kind that made him flinch even though I hadn't moved an inch.

I leaned closer. "*Fuck me*?" I repeated. "You're cute, Greg. Truly. It's almost enough to make me forget how badly I want to put a bullet in your head."

He was trying to play tough, but his twitching fingers and the way his eyes darted to the stairs gave him away. Fear was an ugly look on anyone, but on Greg? It was practically pathetic.

"You're lucky I need you alive tonight," I continued, straightening and adjusting the cuffs of my sleeves. "Come on. My girl's waiting for us, and I'm not a fan of making her wait."

I shoved Greg toward the car, his feet fumbling to catch up as he glared over his shoulder at me.

His lip was split from the punch, and I caught the flash of anger in his eyes, but he didn't dare say another word.

Until he did.

"Your girl?" he sneered, like he thought it was funny. "You mean the bitch who sold you out to the feds? I figured you'd have put a bullet in her by now."

Would you kill me too, if I betrayed you?

No, amore. I could never kill you.

And I was fucking right—no matter how much the world screamed for it, no matter how much she deserved it, it was the one thing I could never do.

He stiffened as I approached, but I didn't stop until I was close enough for him to feel the cold press of the gun barrel against his cheek.

"Run that mouth again, Greg," I said, my voice cold as ice. "See where it gets you."

I yanked him forward by the collar, slamming him into the side of the car.

The door swung open, and his chauffeur gave me a polite nod.

Guess money really does buy everyone, huh?

I leaned in, close enough that he could feel my breath on his skin, my eyes never leaving his. "Got it?"

He didn't answer, just nodded, his eyes wide.

I shoved him into the car and slammed the door behind him.

The bucket tipped, and the cold water hit Greg square in the face, a satisfying gasp ripping out of him as he sputtered and coughed. The water pooled on the floor beneath him, soaking into the grime and leaving him shivering.

I leaned back in the chair, arms draped over my knees, watching as he thrashed and groaned. His wide, unfocused eyes darted around, desperate for clarity, until they landed on himself—on the ropes biting into his wrists and ankles, in the bloodied state I'd left him in before he so rudely decided to pass out.

His face went as pale as a corpse.

Good.

When we'd pulled up to the location earlier, his mouth wouldn't stop. Snide remarks, desperate insults—shit meant to get under my skin. I'd let him talk until the pounding in my head hit its limit, and then I'd dropped him with one punch. Lights out. The silence after had been a goddamn blessing.

But now, after an hour of peace, Greg was finally coming back to life, blinking against the dim light, his breath ragged and uneven.

"You didn't," he croaked, his voice a whisper of disbelief.

I barked out a laugh. "Oh, I fucking did."

He groaned, thrashing against the ropes like that'd do anything. His chair creaked under the effort, the pathetic sound of his struggle grating on my ears.

"Now what, Lazzio, huh?" he spat. "An eye for an eye?"

"Something like that."

The warehouse door groaned open, its metallic echo rolling through the cavernous space. Cold light spilled in, illuminating Greg, who flinched like a cockroach caught under a lamp. His thrashing against the ropes stilled, but his breaths came quicker, sharp and panicked.

I didn't move. I just leaned back in my chair, tilting it onto two legs, my eyes fixed on the black SUV gliding inside. Its engine purred like a predator, unhurried as the tires crunched to a stop on the concrete.

The driver's door opened first, and out stepped Vittori.

"Satan's pissed," he said, nodding toward the back seat. "She's not getting out of that car. Good luck."

I wiped the smile off my face with the back of my hand.

Of course, she wouldn't.

I made my way to the car, ignoring Vittori as he leaned against the hood, that smirk on his face like he was enjoying the whole damn thing a little too much.

I ignored him, pulling the back door open and ducking inside.

The scent of leather and something distinctively *hers* hit me immediately.

I shut the door behind me with a soft click, my gaze finding her instantly. She was still, like stone—eyes locked out the window, face unreadable. I knew better than to think she was just ignoring me. She was probably plotting, calculating her next move, just like always.

For a moment, I just watched her.

Pretty face, full lips, sleek hair—so fucking beautiful. Too beautiful.

The woman I had given my heart to, only to watch her crush it in her hands.

She crossed her arms, irritation flaring.

"How the hell did you even get out of jail?" she shot at me. "Guess blood money really is the ultimate pass to freedom, huh?"

"No proof, *amore*."

"No proof? Really? Because those *big* folders I handed over sure seemed like enough proof that you're a psychopath, a murderer, a liar, manipulative—"

I leaned back, a smirk playing at the corner of my mouth. "Fuck, you've never looked sexier, Jade."

Her glare could've burned me alive.

"Who would've thought, huh? You fucking snitching on me just makes me want you even more."

She exhaled sharply, rolling her eyes. "Oh, perfect. You've lost it too. Listen, your stupid buddy kidnapped me on my way to the airport—unwillingly, I might add—and now I'm stuck in the back of a car in some deserted warehouse. I was supposed to be sipping champagne in first class, flying to Scotland to celebrate my sweet revenge, not here. So do me a favor —Let. Me. Go."

"I didn't kill your sister, Jade."

Her eyes squeezed shut. "You're lying."

"Get out of the car. You need to hear the truth."

She pressed her hands to her ears, shaking her head as if to block me out.

"I don't believe you, Angelo."

I grabbed her wrist and lowered her hand.

"You have to trust me, Jade."

Her eyes met mine, and in that moment, I saw it all—hope, anger, confusion, and something deeper.

She wanted to believe me, but she was too fucking scared to admit it.

"Trust me, *amore*," I breathed out.

Just like I fucking did, before you tore it all apart.

Her eyes searched my face, and after a long pause, she swallowed and gave a slow nod. She unbuckled her seatbelt, the faint scent of her perfume lingering in the air as she pushed open the door and stepped out of the car.

I stepped out of the car and made my way toward her.

Her eyes locked onto Greg, and I saw her flinch, her pupils dilating like she couldn't quite believe what she was seeing.

"Lazzio, I don't want to be a witness to the blood on your hands!" she snapped, her voice shaky with a mixture of fear and disgust. She tried to turn back to the car, but I was already in her way, blocking her.

"James Greg is the one who destroyed the Cyrus Project. He's the one who killed your sister. Not me."

Her breath hitched in her throat, and for a moment, her eyes went wide, that fragile mask of control slipping for just a second.

But she quickly regained herself, her fists tightening at her sides.

"Lazzio, I swear, if you're lying, I'll grate your dick in a grinder and feed it to you."

I couldn't help but smirk at the threat, my hand reaching out to grip her chin, tilting her head just enough to catch her lips in a quick, possessive kiss.

Her eyes fluttered shut for a second, a brief moment of surrender before she pulled back, her breath shaky.

"Noted," I whispered, the taste of betrayal lingering on her lips.

"Not that I'm not enjoying the show," Vittori's voice sliced through us. "But you two lovebirds better hurry the fuck up. I've got shit to do."

I snapped my gaze over to him.

He was leaning casually against the car, cigarette dangling from his lips, his eyes glinting with amusement.

"Greg," I said, turning slowly. "Let's talk about the Cyrus Project."

His gaze seethed with hatred, his body straining against the ropes as if he could break free. "Fuck you, Lazzio."

Vittori laughed. "Wrong answer, buddy."

My gun was out in an instant, and I shot him straight in the calf.

An eye for an eye.

The blast echoed, his scream following immediately after.

Jade flinched, her hands pressed to her ears, her face twisting in disgust. She spun away, her body colliding with mine as she buried her face in my chest, desperate to shut it all out.

"It's alright, *amore*," I murmured low, my hand sliding down her back. "Now, Greg, where were we? Ah, that's right. The Cyrus Project."

His face twisted, sweat dripping down his forehead. "W-What about it?"

I smirked. "Don't try to play the innocent card now, Greg. Tell us how you thought you'd fuck over my old man because he didn't hand you the project."

His eyes burned with rage. "Your father's a piece of shit! Just like you, Lazzio! This project was supposed to be mine! Only fucking mine!"

Vittori sighed, shaking his head as he casually drew his gun, but I stopped him with a hand.

"What did you do, Greg?" I asked.

He spat blood onto the concrete, a twisted grin curling his lips. "Wasn't gonna let your old man get a fucking cent of my cash, Lazzio. So I rigged the whole damn place with explosives." He let out a low chuckle, dark and cruel. "Yeah, Jade. Your sweet little sister and her boyfriend? They were just the unlucky ones who happened to be there. Small world, huh? They were the perfect setup—collateral damage, nothing more."

Jade's hands dropped to her sides, as she turned slowly.

He grinned darkly, continuing, "You think people were pissed about the Lazzios taking the land? That was the cover-up. The bodies, though? That's what really got people's blood boiling. Innocent lives gone, and the Lazzios became the fucking villains."

Jade's fingers brushed down my hand, slowly wrapping around the gun.

I didn't stop her.

"At least that was the plan," he sneered, shaking his head. "Of course, the Lazzios always get away with everything. They pinned it on Jonathan Cyrus, said he was the one behind the investment. Then they killed the poor bastard years later." He tilted his head, a cruel smile creeping onto his face. "Took you six fucking years to figure it all out, Jade. A bit late, don't you think?"

A sob tore from Jade's throat, her shoulders shaking as she gripped the gun tighter.

I stayed back, watching, letting her take the reins.

This was her moment.

"You killed them," she spat, her voice low but trembling. "They were innocent. Just—just living their lives. They didn't deserve this."

Greg sneered. "Deserve? Nobody 'deserves' anything in this game, darling. Wrong place, wrong time. That's all it was."

"Wrong place?" Her voice cracked, climbing to a painful pitch. "I was there! I saw them—blown into pieces. Do you have any idea what that's like? Watching someone you love ripped apart, and there's nothing—fucking *nothing*—you can do?"

Her sobs came harder.

I'd seen pain before—hell, I'd caused it—but nothing like *her* pain. It filled the room, suffocating, bleeding into every corner, and for once, I didn't have the words.

"Nine years. I've carried that for *nine fucking years,* trying to forget, to move on. And now I find out it was *you.*" She raised the gun, her hand steady despite the tears streaking her face. "The only thing you deserve is the same fate."

Greg flinched, his mask of arrogance cracking as real fear seeped into his eyes. "Wait—wait, hold on! You think this'll fix anything? You pull that trigger, and you're no better than me."

"Maybe I am just like you," she whispered, as she racked the gun.

I stepped forward, not to stop her but to make sure she knew I was there.

He sneered through the panic, his mouth running to the bitter end. "Look at you two. You should *thank* me. You wouldn't even know each other if it weren't for me. The kidnapped kid and the lonely addict. Tragedy, huh? Almost makes me wanna—"

The shot rang out before he could finish.

One clean bullet to the head. His body slumped back, dead before he hit the ground.

She stood there, frozen, the gun slipping from her fingers like it weighed a thousand pounds.

Before she could spiral, I grabbed her, spinning her around and pulling her into me, even though every fucking part of me screamed to push her away after what she'd done.

Her grip on my shirt was tight, almost desperate.

I nodded at Vittori, who moved without a word, tossing a cover over Greg's lifeless corpse.

"Let's get you home," I murmured.

She followed without a sound, her eyes fixed somewhere far ahead, avoiding the blood pooling behind us. I opened the car door, and waited as she climbed in.

The drive was quiet, the low growl of the engine filling the silence between us.

Her head rested against the window, eyes shut, but I could see it—the tight set of her jaw, the faint tremor in her hands.

She wasn't okay. And I sure as hell wasn't either.

So I did the only thing that might offer us some kind of relief.

I reached over, my hand closing around hers in the space between us, despite the fucking chaos inside me.

Her fingers were cold, unsteady, but she didn't pull away.

Instead, she let me hold on, her grip tightening just enough to remind me she was still here, still fighting not to fall apart.

I didn't say anything—there was nothing to say.

The world outside could keep fucking burning; right now, all that mattered was her hand in mine.

CHAPTER
FORTY-FIVE

"One day you will kiss a man you can't breathe without, and find that breath is of little consequence."
— **Karen Marie Moning**

Jade

I sank deeper into the bath, the foam teasing my eyes, the warmth of the water easing the tension in my muscles. My head tipped back against the tub, but no amount of heat could relax the chaos in my chest.

I had just *killed* someone.

I had just killed the man who had not only taken my sister from me, but had also hurt the only man I had ever truly loved.

The emotions swirling in me were so tangled, so high, it felt like I might drown in them.

What was I supposed to feel? What was I even supposed to do with all this?

It wasn't regret.

I sure as hell didn't feel bad.

The bastard was dead, and the world would be a little lighter without him in it.

It wasn't guilt, either. That wasn't the problem.

But it wasn't pride. Not even close.

I closed my eyes and let my head dip beneath the water, staying there just long enough to let the silence swallow me, letting it drown out the noise in my head.

One, two, three.

I rubbed the water off my face and slumped back down, wrapping my arms around my legs and pulling them tight.

Well, I'd done it.

My revenge was checked off the list.

I just hoped the man I'd wrongly accused could somehow find it in him to forgive me.

I cleaned myself up, stepping out of the bath, drying off with Angelo's luxurious towels—soft, fluffy things that felt like they were made for a king. I slipped into the clothes he'd left for me: one of his T-shirts that fell to mid-thigh, and a pair of boxers that were way too big, but I managed to fold them over my hips anyway.

I tried to dry my hair, but then I realized I was about five seconds away from collapsing, so I just let it air-dry and walked out of the bathroom.

When Angelo said we were going home, I'd figured he'd meant my place. But, of course, he had brought me to his. When he'd parked in his lot, I hadn't bothered arguing. Honestly? I had been terrified of being alone with my own damn thoughts. After everything, he was probably the best distraction I was ever going to get.

I padded into the living room, but he wasn't there.

I wandered around, eyes scanning, until I noticed the door to his office slightly open.

I swallowed the lump of guilt rising in my throat.

Last time I was there, I'd stolen his burner phone and gone off to ...

Yeah. Whatever.

I was an idiot.

I pushed the door open just enough to see him sitting there, back to me, staring out the window. The reflection of his face flickered against the glass.

He was holding something in his hand. My necklace.

I circled his desk slowly, unsure. When I finally reached him, I slid between his legs and settled on his lap. He'd just showered—his hair damp, wearing a simple t-shirt and low gray pants.

He didn't push me away. He stayed still, his hands on the chair's arms, eyes locked on my necklace, his fingers twisting the butterflies between them.

"Angelo, I—"

He cut me off. "Tell me everything, Jade. Don't leave anything out."

I nodded, my arms wrapping around his neck, my hand brushing against his cheek.

So I did.

I told him about my parents—the love they'd had for each other, so pure, so deep. I told him how my father had passed away when I was too young, leaving us three behind, how Stella had still been too little to remember him.

I told him about Stella and me—how we had been more than sisters, we had been best friends. How I'd loved her fiercely, even when she'd take my clothes, my makeup, or the posters on my walls. Sundays had been ours, a time to bake cookies and watch movies, just the two of us. The world had felt simple then, like nothing could touch us.

I talked about Lake Kendrick, how it had become our sanctuary. We'd spent countless hours there, the quiet beauty of it giving us a space to breathe.

Then the words got harder to say, but I forced them out.

I told him about the day they'd died, how I'd watched it all happen, how I hadn't been able to save them. How I'd survived, but a part of me had died that day too. It felt like I'd been living in the shadow of their deaths ever since, even when I hadn't wanted to admit it.

I spoke about the year I'd spent in the psych ward, the way my mind hadn't been able to accept the reality of losing Stella. It was like I had been stuck in a dream, hoping to wake up and find everything back to the way it had been.

And then, I confessed the part of me that still haunted me —the addiction. The time I'd overdosed, the darkness that had pulled me in, and how I hadn't touched anything since.

But the cravings, they still came.

A hollow ache in my chest that I couldn't outrun, no matter how hard I tried.

"When was the last time you really wanted it?"

I swallowed. "A few months ago, when my mama passed."

He cursed under his breath, his hand running through his hair.

I told him how revenge had become my purpose, my only reason to keep going.

"Why did you start working for me?"

A faint smile tugged at my lips. "I did some digging into New York's elites, and your name came up. Angelo Lazzio— most eligible bachelor, part of the big three. I was curious, so I dug deeper and found out about the families. I knew working for you would give me access to the world I needed to tear down."

He nodded, his gaze never leaving me.

I told him how, over the years, I'd built a web of information about the New York elite, how I had dirt on every single one of them.

And then I told him the truth—the part I hadn't expected.

Somewhere along the way, I'd fallen for him.

"When I first met you, I thought you were cold, controlling ... attractive," I said softly, my hand falling to his chest. "Then, the more time I spent with you, the more I became ... drawn to you. I remember the night you got me out of jail, carried me home, and thought, *I wish this man would take me to his bed*. But I quickly shook that thought away."

My throat tightened, words clogging up as my eyes burned.

Come on, Jade. You can do this.

"I fought so, *so* hard not to let you in, Angelo. To keep you out of my heart, to force you out of my head," I whispered, my voice breaking as I clenched my fists in my lap. "But then, last year on Christmas night, I looked through your computer. I found an email—about explosives. And for me, the puzzle finally clicked. It was you ..."

The air in the room grew thick, suffocating me.

Before I could spill any more of my tangled thoughts, he cut me off.

"This was my hacking email address, Jade," he said. "The email you found wasn't mine. It was from the contractors to James Greg—the night before he gave the signal to turn them on."

My breath faltered, my chest tightening as if the truth itself was strangling me.

"All it would've taken was one word. One *fucking* word, Jade. I would've helped you. I would've torn the world apart for you if you'd just—" His words died, and he leaned back in the chair, dragging a hand over his face.

The weight of his disappointment crushed me more than any shout ever could.

Tears burned my cheeks, but I didn't bother wiping them away.

"Life has taught me that trust is a weapon, Angelo," I whispered. "One that can always be used against you. I couldn't ... I couldn't take the chance. I couldn't have known you were innocent."

His eyes locked on mine, heavy with betrayal so sharp it felt like a dagger twisting in my chest.

Then, out of nowhere, his hands reached behind my neck, and I sucked in a shaky breath as he clasped my necklace back in place.

My fingers found it instantly.

"My therapist gave me this necklace," I sniffled, a weak chuckle slipping past my lips. "Stella had one just like it—Mama bought it for her birthday. I always loved it. When Dr. Morano saw a picture of Stella wearing hers, she gave me this one. Said it was meant to represent hope," I murmured, the edges of a bittersweet smile tugging at my lips. "I added a charm for my papa too."

A shiver ran down my arm.

Pain had been my constant for the last decade—pain, sadness, and too much self-loathing. A part of me feared that now, after reaching the goal I'd been chasing, I'd fall back into my demons and drown in it all over again.

"I don't expect you to ever forgive me, or forget." My eyes met his, steady but weighed down with regret. "But I need you to know ... I'm sorry. I'm sorry for using everything you gave me against you. For making you trust me. For letting you fall in love with me. I'm so, *so* sorry, Angelo."

He ran his tongue across his teeth, eyes never leaving mine, his silence deafening.

His fingers grazed my cheek before sliding down to grip my neck, pressing against my pulse. I pressed my hands flat against his chest to steady myself, but it was pointless—every inch of me was pulled into him, unable to escape the heat that radiated off his skin.

"When I pulled you out of jail on your birthday, and heard about that yoga instructor, I lost it. Found him at his place after the ER. Shot him cold. Same with Nathan Simons, and every other asshole you entertained over the years." His grip tightened ever so slightly around my neck. "You wanna know why?"

He had killed Nathan Simons?

Well, that explained why I'd never gotten a follow-up text after our little sexcapade.

Unusual, really—most men couldn't help but come crawling back for more.

I shook my head.

He yanked me closer, his fingers digging deeper into my neck.

"Because the mere thought of anyone else touching you, making you smile, taking any part of you—it drove me fucking insane. I needed *all* of you. Your eyes, your mouth, your thoughts, your dreams ... hell, even your insults. All of it. For myself. And the fact that you gave them to other men? Under my fucking nose ..." He let out a low, humorless laugh. "I couldn't hurt you for playing me, torturing me. So I made them suffer instead."

I knew a part of me should be terrified, but even with the blood of all my ex-flings slipping down his hands, tainting me,

I couldn't shake the feeling that I was safer with him than I'd ever been with anyone else.

I hummed softly, my nails digging into his chest. "That's a really unhealthy coping mechanism, Lazzio."

His lips were now inches from mine, his breath warm against my skin.

"You have no fucking idea what I'd do to keep you," he murmured, his lips grazing mine with a teasing restraint that only stoked the fire. "I've spent years drowning myself in work, running halfway across the world just to put some distance between us—to starve this obsession for you, to pretend I could cut you out of my mind. But now? Now, I'll go to whatever lengths it takes to make sure no one else touches you, tastes you, claims you."

I felt a shiver crawl up my spine.

His voice dropped, low and deadly. "Go ahead—drag my name through the mud, shoot me, steal from me, lie to me, try to destroy me. But you'll never get rid of me, Jade."

My lips parted slightly, my eyes growing half lidded as his other hand gripped my hips.

"What if I run away?"

He tilted his head. "You could try. Change your name, erase every piece of yourself, disappear into the shadows. But I'd still find you. I'd tear the world apart to do it." His voice dropped, sharp and possessive. "And when I do, I'll just remind you who you belong to—body, mind, and soul."

I nodded slowly, letting his words sink in, every syllable wrapping around my throat like a chain I didn't want to break.

"Do you forgive me, Angelo?"

His eyes dropped to my lips, dark and cold. "No."

My chest tightened.

My arms circled his neck, pulling him closer until my forehead pressed against his.

"What do I need to do to be forgiven, then?" I murmured, my breath brushing his lips.

I would do *anything* for him to forgive me and silence the guilt that gnawed at me.

His gaze darkened. "Take me to Lake Kendrick."

CHAPTER
FORTY-SIX

"I'm oxygen and he's dying to breathe."
— **Tahereh Mafi**

Jade

Angelo parked the car with a soft stop, and I exhaled the breath I'd been holding since we'd left New York that morning—first the helicopter ride to Boston, then the car ride to Bay Village.

Not a single word had left my lips since last night. Not one.

Every time he'd asked me something or spoken to me, I'd simply nodded, lost in my own thoughts, trying to brace myself for this uninvited, unwelcome journey ahead.

Part of me wanted to scream when he'd said he needed to see the place that had made me—the place that had broken me, shattered me. The place where my pain had been born, the place where I'd lost everything that had mattered.

I had wanted to slap him. Tell him to go to hell for making such a demand.

But that was when I'd known I couldn't keep running anymore.

Nine years. I'd spent *nine years* hiding from the truth, from my own reflection. Avoiding everything that might break me further. But there was no running anymore. Not now.

So, I'd told him I'd do it, then had stood, left the room, and gone to sleep in the guest bedroom, thinking maybe he'd wanted some space too.

But in the dead of night, his body had pressed against mine, his arm around my waist, his head buried in the curve of my neck.

Relief washed over me, unexpected and bittersweet. I'd closed my eyes, letting sleep take over. Even the haunting image of Greg's dead eyes glaring at me had faded, pushed aside by the heat of his skin against mine.

He turned off the engine.

That was it. I had to get out and—

A wave of heat hit me, making the world tilt.

Black dots swarmed my vision, and my throat tightened.

Not now, not here, please.

"Breathe, Jade."

I squeezed my eyes shut, trying to steady myself. My hands curled into fists, and I forced a slow breath, fighting the panic that had a grip on my chest.

"Good girl," he murmured. His fingers wrapped around mine, pressing my hand to his lips. "I'm here, *amore*."

I nodded, feeling the warmth of his touch seep through the fog in my mind.

I exhaled, the pressure in my chest finally loosening.

It took a moment, but eventually, I could breathe without

feeling like I was drowning. My heart steadied, the panic fading into something heavier.

Angelo got out and circled the car to open my door. He unfastened my seatbelt, zipped my coat, and carefully eased my hair free from the collar.

Then he cupped my face, his thumb lazily caressing my cheek.

"You okay?" he asked, his gaze steady on mine.

I nodded.

Stepping out of the car, I led him toward the forest path. Mud and snow clung to my boots as we trudged forward. The trees thinned out, revealing a barren stretch of land littered with signs screaming "Do Not Trespass" and "Private Property." Cheap red ribbons fluttered in the wind, barely hanging onto the posts meant to warn people away.

We climbed over them anyway.

The ground turned slick with snow and sludge as we moved closer.

Finally, we stopped in front of a faded red sign, its peeling letters spelling out one word: *Mines.*

I froze. My hands trembled.

The place was quiet, lifeless, but the memories weren't. They clawed their way to the surface—images, sounds, everything I'd spent years trying to forget. My breath caught, sharp and shallow, as if the air itself had turned against me.

"This is it?"

I blinked, his voice cutting through the fog in my head. "What?"

He shrugged, his expression unreadable. "You said it was the nicest place around here. Doesn't seem worth it to me."

For a second, I wanted to slap him, the heat rising to my face.

Was he seriously making light of this?

But then it hit me—he wasn't mocking me.

He was pulling me back.

As if sensing my realization, the corner of his mouth lifted in the faintest hint of a smile. His gaze drifted ahead.

"You're an ass."

"Maybe. But you're not passing out on me here, Jade. Not today."

I rolled my eyes, but the edges of my mouth betrayed me. "You're lucky I didn't bring a shovel."

His laugh was quiet, the kind that snuck under your skin and settled there.

My gaze wandered ahead, scanning the expanse of nothingness that was *everything*.

I inhaled deeply, my chest tight as if it was trying to keep me together while my mind unraveled.

"What do you want to say to Stella?"

I crossed my arms against myself, not for warmth, but to stop the tremble that threatened to give me away.

What would I say?

I'd been talking to her in my head for years. Whispering to her in the dark when the world felt too loud. Telling her about my failures, my victories, the milestones she hadn't been there for. Hoping—God, *always* hoping—that somehow, somewhere, she had been listening.

I swallowed, my throat dry, my voice barely audible. "I'd tell her I miss her more than anything I've ever lost. More than flowers miss the sun when it disappears, leaving them to wilt in the dark. And when she crosses my mind—which is every day—it's the only time I feel whole, like she's still here. I'd tell her that I'm *so* scared of losing her again. Not just her, but the memory of her. The way she looked, the way she laughed ... the way her voice sounded when she teased me, or how she'd cross her arms and pout when she was mad. Every little detail. Every stupid, perfect thing."

The words choked me, but I couldn't stop them.

"I'd tell her that each day I feel her slipping further away from my mind. And it kills me. But not my heart. Never my heart. She's there, always, locked inside, and I hope to God she knows that. I hope wherever she is, she feels how much I love her. Because it's the only thing I've got left to give her."

By the time I finished, my chest was heaving, and the tears were running freely.

For once, I didn't wipe them away. I let them fall, heavy and hot, as if they could reach her.

Angelo's fingers brushed against mine.

I turned to look at him, but his eyes were already on me, warmer than I'd ever seen. "What would you say to your mother?"

I let out a bitter, humorless laugh. "Too much. I wouldn't even know where to start."

"Try," he said, his voice rough around the edges. "For me."

For him.

I swallowed the lump in my throat. "I'd tell her I'm sorry."

"For what?" he asked softly, his voice barely above a whisper.

"For not being with her when she needed me the most," I choked out. "When my sister died, I—I didn't stay. I should've held her. I should've cried with her. But instead, I ran. I left her alone with all that pain, because I couldn't handle it myself."

The words hit the air like stones, heavy and jagged, and I pursed my lips, trying to keep the sobs from breaking loose.

But they did anyway.

"And I didn't stop running," I continued, my voice shaking. "I spiraled—into drugs, alcohol, sex, anything to numb it. I got arrested. I became this person she wouldn't even recognize.

This person she wouldn't *want* to recognize. I made myself unworthy of her love because I thought ... I thought if I didn't deserve it, maybe it wouldn't hurt as much when I lost it."

I blinked hard, the tears blurring everything in front of me.

"She begged me not to go down that path, Angelo. Begged me not to destroy myself for revenge. She told me she didn't want that for me, that it wouldn't bring my sister back." My voice cracked again. "And what did I do? I *ignored* her. I spent years consumed by it—by hate, by this gnawing, endless need to get even. I wasn't there for her the way I should've been. I was too busy plotting, too busy running from everything she asked me to face."

I looked away, fixing my gaze on the snow-covered ground as though it could somehow ground me.

"And then when she got sick ..." I could barely push the words out now. "I tried. God, I *tried.* I visited. I held her hand. I told myself I was there for her. But I wasn't. Not really. I was so scared of losing her too, so scared of what it would do to me, that I couldn't—I couldn't let myself get close. Not the way I should have."

I clenched my fists until my nails dug into my palms.

"I thought if I just kept my distance, if I braced myself, maybe it wouldn't destroy me when it happened. But it did anyway. And I can't—" My knees buckled, and before I could hit the ground, Angelo was there. His arms steadied me, his hold strong, like he'd been waiting for me to fall all along.

"I didn't get to tell her," I sobbed, my voice muffled against his chest. "I didn't get to tell her how much I loved her. How much I *still* love her. I didn't get to tell her I was sorry for every single way I failed her. That I'd carry her with me for the rest of my life, even if it killed me."

Angelo's hand cradled the back of my head, the other

wrapping around me like he thought he could hold all the broken pieces of me together.

"You think she didn't know?"

"I don't know," I whispered. My fists clenched weakly at his dress shirt, the fight gone out of me. "I don't know if she did, Angelo."

"She knew," he said, his voice rough, but certain. "You think love like that just disappears? She knew, Jade. And she *still* does."

I let the words settle, let the weight of them press against the ache in my chest.

And for the first time in months, I let myself cry for her—not just for the loss, but for the love too. The kind that never really fades, no matter how far you run.

Angelo swept me up, cradling me against him as my nails dug into his skin, desperate for something to hold on to. I buried my face in his neck, tears soaking his shirt, shaking with everything I couldn't say.

His grip was unbreakable, his body strong as he carried me back to the car.

I tossed the damp towel into the basket, steam curling in lazy tendrils from the bathroom. I was wearing one of Angelo's T-shirts—something I'd found in the bag he'd packed for me. It was soft, loose, brushing just above my knees.

The door creaked open, and fog spilled into the room as I made my way to the bed, my legs heavy, my mind even heavier.

After my breakdown, Angelo had held me in the car, letting me fall apart in his arms until exhaustion had taken over. I didn't remember much—just the warmth of him and the steady rhythm of his breathing. I must've passed out, because the next thing I'd known, he had been carrying me into the hotel lobby.

He hadn't said much—just that I should shower and relax. Then he'd left, promising he'd be back.

Too numb, and too drained to question him, I'd done as he'd said.

I slipped under the covers, pulling them tight around me, like they could shield me from the world. The room was heavy with quiet, the kind that crept into your chest and refused to leave. Shadows bled across the walls, stretching and twisting with the dim light outside.

It wasn't late, barely past five, but I didn't care. I just wanted to stop feeling.

And yet, I couldn't deny it—I felt lighter. Raw, wrecked, but lighter.

Angelo had done it.

He'd broken me apart, dragged out all the things I'd buried so deep they'd started to rot, and had forced me to say them out loud. It had hurt like hell, but the pain wasn't as unbearable now. It was something else, something almost ... freeing.

I stared at the ceiling.

The ache was still there, but it wasn't crushing me the way it had used to. For years, I'd carried it alone, letting it fester and eat away at me. But today, Angelo had taken some of that weight. He hadn't fixed me—he couldn't—but he'd made it bearable.

The silence wasn't so sharp anymore. It didn't cut as deep.

I'd let it out, all of it, and the world hadn't ended.

Angelo hadn't looked at me like I was broken beyond repair.

If anything, he'd looked at me like I was worth holding on to, even when I couldn't hold on to myself.

My fingers traced the edge of the blanket.

He had stripped me bare—not just physically, but in ways I hadn't thought anyone ever could. And somehow, instead of feeling exposed, I felt ... safer.

Speak of the devil.

The door clicked open, and Angelo walked in, two bags in hand, his eyes finding me instantly. Always.

He moved toward the living room area, setting the bags down on the counter before shrugging off his coat and heading straight for the bed. He sat down at the edge, close enough that I could see his cheeks were slightly red due to the cold.

"I brought food—chicken noodle soup and tea," he said, his voice low, his eyes tracing my face.

I shifted against the headboard, my fingers picking at the blanket. "Thank you."

"Feeling better?" he asked, leaning forward slightly.

I nodded, even as my hands fidgeted. "A little."

"I bought you something else."

My head tilted slightly, curiosity edging out exhaustion. "What is it?"

He stood, moving to where his coat hung on the chair. His hand dipped into the pocket, and when he turned back, a small box rested in his palm.

Without a word, he came back to the bed and placed it in my hands, his fingers brushing mine.

"Open it."

I glanced down at it, my fingers brushing over the edges, but instead of lifting the lid, I set it aside on the bed. My hand reached for his without thinking, my fingers curling around his.

"Have you forgiven me, Angelo?" I asked, my voice quieter than I intended.

His brows pulled together, the faintest shadow of something crossing his face—hurt, maybe. Or anger. It was hard to tell with him, the way he hid his emotions behind a mask so effortlessly.

"For what?"

"For lying. For stealing. For trying to destroy everything you've ever worked for. For ruining everything. For not—" I shook my head, unable to finish.

He shifted closer, his free hand reaching up to tilt my chin so I couldn't look away.

His gaze pierced through me, darker than the night.

"Wasn't this trip supposed to be the price for my forgiveness?"

My lips parted, but no sound came out.

"You brought me *here*. This—" He waved his hand, a subtle motion, but it said more than any words could. "This was all I needed, Jade. It's enough."

"So, is that it?" I whispered, almost too afraid to ask. "Am I *really* forgiven?"

His gaze softened. "*Sì, amore mio.*"

A lump rose in my throat.

"I don't deserve it," I whispered.

"Maybe not. But you don't get to decide what I forgive." His hand dropped from my chin. "Open it," he said again, softer this time.

I let out a shaky breath, my fingers trembling as I reached for the velvet box.

I opened it slowly, and the sight inside stole the air from

my lungs. A tiny, delicate gold butterfly, identical to the ones that hung around my neck, gleamed softly in the light.

"You said the two around your neck symbolized your papa and sister," Angelo's voice was low, like he was threading his words carefully. "One was missing for your mama. Now the three of them will be together, watching over you."

I looked at the butterfly in my hand, feeling something break open inside me.

"How did you ...?"

"It wasn't hard to find," he murmured, his gaze warm, watching me like he always did—always seeing more than I wanted to show.

I closed my eyes, swallowing hard, trying to keep myself together, but it was impossible. The butterfly wasn't just a gift. It was everything. A piece of the puzzle I didn't know I was still trying to solve.

A way to keep them close. A way to remember them all.

"Thank you," I whispered, barely able to get the words out.

Angelo didn't say anything. He didn't need to.

His hands gently slid behind my neck, unclasping my necklace. The delicate motion felt impossibly intimate, his fingers warm against my skin. He added the gold butterfly charm before securing the necklace back around my neck.

His hand grazed my skin, sending a little shiver straight through me before he cupped my face and yanked me closer, his mouth slamming against mine. It was hot, fierce—like he was marking me. Telling me, in no uncertain terms, that I was his and he was mine.

"I love you, Jade," he muttered, his voice rough. "But from now on? No more fucking lies."

I pulled away just enough to meet his gaze. "I promise."

He leaned in, his lips brushing mine. "You better mean it."

"I do," I said, a little too breathlessly for my liking, but damn, he had that effect on me.

His lips crashed back to mine, deeper this time.

I cupped his head, my fingers threading through his hair, pulling him even closer. The pressure of his mouth against mine was almost punishing, but in the best way—like he was erasing all the mess, all the bullshit, with every swipe of his tongue.

He groaned into me, his hand sliding down my back, pulling me flush against him.

When he finally pulled back slightly, his breath ragged, his hands still gripping me like he was afraid I'd slip away, I could see it in his eyes—the raw hunger, the need.

And it made me feel alive.

Angelo Lazzio needed me—just as much as I needed him.

"Make love to me, Angelo," I whispered against his lips.

He didn't waste a second.

His lips crashed back into mine, pulling me to him like I was the air he needed to breathe. Every inch of his touch was a claim, a demand, and I let him take what he wanted—again and again—until there was nothing left but the two of us tangled in each other, our skin on fire.

I forgot everything else.

All that existed was him.

All that mattered now was him.

CHAPTER
FORTY-SEVEN

"The phoenix must burn to emerge."
—**Janet Fitch**

Jade

"I never thought I'd say this, but ... I'm going to miss you, Miss Whitenhouse. Who am I going to gossip about now that you're leaving us?"

I let out a scoff as I packed my things into cardboard boxes for the movers. The office was almost empty now—just a few picture frames, mirrors, and personal knick-knacks left behind.

Six years in this office, and I'd be lying if I said leaving wasn't tugging at my heart. But the adventure ahead was far more exciting.

"Grace," I sighed, sitting back behind my desk, my heels tapping against the floor. "We may have hated each other over the years, but I need to be honest with you."

Her brow arched, curiosity piqued.

"You make the best chocolate muffins ever."

Her eyes widened in realization. "*You* were the one stealing them from Mr. Lazzio's fridge?"

Oops. I'd definitely just screwed up.

I cleared my throat, suddenly fascinated by the contents of my bag. I rummaged through it, searching for ... nothing, really. Anything to dodge the flames of her wrath.

"You little devil!" she practically shrieked. "Were you also the one stealing the chocolates my husband got him every year for his birthday? The ones filled with—"

I snapped my bag shut with a decisive *click* and bolted to my feet. "Oh, would you look at the time! Totally forgot—I have an appointment with the accountant. Bye, oldie!"

I made a beeline for the door, her indignant curses trailing behind me like a bad perfume. By the time I reached the elevator, I was frantically tapping the button like my life depended on it.

When the doors slid open, I ducked inside, safe for now.

Today was my last day here, and if I was leaving, I was doing it on my terms—with a bang.

Or, more accurately, by annoying my boss—*or soon-to-be ex-boss*—one last time.

It had been a month since our trip to Bay Village. Three days of strolling through my childhood memories—my old school, the house I'd grown up in (now home to a sweet couple with twin daughters), the spot where I'd gotten my one and only tattoo, and even the place where I'd had my first kiss.

Naturally, Angelo had asked for a name.

Naturally, I hadn't told him.

I wasn't about to hand him a reason to hunt down some guy who didn't even remember me.

I asked him about Luciana, his uncle's wife, and why he had helped her vanish into the shadows. He had said it was to free her from the weight of her demons, to give her a chance to breathe in a new life.

I'd told him he had done the same for me, and he'd kissed me—deep and wet—whispering against my lips that I was the one who had saved him from his own.

I'd also introduced him to my Aunt Krissy and Uncle Jack, and the reunion was ... heavy. Emotional, guilt-ridden, bittersweet.

The way they'd looked at me—shocked, hopeful, hurt—was something I'd carry with me forever.

But it had brought a strange kind of closure, too.

I hadn't realized how much I'd needed it until I had stood there, watching my past collide with my present.

When we'd gotten back to New York, Angelo had returned to work, and I'd asked for some space to think things through. Of course, "space" hadn't meant what you'd think. Before I'd left, he had me pinned beneath him in bed, arms trapped above my head, fucking me into a promise I'd stay in the city—and most importantly, not run off to Scotland.

Honestly, I had been so close to coming, I would've promised him my kidneys if he'd asked.

Since then, I'd emptied my apartment. I'd cleared out the room where years of resentment and bitterness had festered, burning paperwork, files, and pictures until there was nothing left but ashes.

Angelo had lasted three days without me. On day four, he'd showed up at my apartment, unapologetic as always, and declared he couldn't sleep without me. He'd told me if I needed space to think, I could do it during the day—but at night, he was staying. I hadn't argued. Amazing sex, nightly massages, *and* breakfast in bed? That hadn't been space—it had been a bribe.

And I wasn't complaining.

But today was different. Today marked the end of this chapter.

I was packing up my life and preparing to step into the unknown, but not before making sure I'd left my mark here—on him, on this office, and on the memories we'd built.

The elevator dinged at his office level, and I stepped out, my heels clicking against the floor.

I strode down the corridor, pushing the door open without a second thought.

But what—or more accurately, who—I saw froze me in place.

"Hello, Miss Whitenhouse."

My throat tightened, but I swallowed it down. "Hello, Mrs. Greg."

Laurie Greg.

James Greg's wife.

The wife of the man I'd killed—coldly, without hesitation, and without an ounce of remorse.

Angelo's voice broke the charged silence. "Please, sit, Miss Whitenhouse."

I moved on autopilot, walking to the couch and sinking down beside him. He didn't look at me, but the way his hand brushed against mine as I settled was enough to steady my nerves.

Laurie Greg sat in the armchair across from us.

Her presence filled the room, cold and immaculate. She was the kind of woman who didn't just wear vintage Chanel, but made it feel like it had been designed just for her—a pale pink two-piece that should have softened her, but didn't.

Her hair was twisted into a tight bun, her features sharp and striking, every line of her face etched with a beauty that hadn't faded with age, but had only grown more lethal. She had to be in her early sixties, but the years had done nothing to dull her.

If anything, they'd made her more dangerous.

Her eyes—icy, pale blue—cut to me first, then Angelo, her lips curving into a smile that wasn't really a smile.

"My husband," she began, her voice smooth as silk stretched taut, "has been missing for over a month."

The words hung heavy in the air, each syllable like a stone sinking deeper into my gut.

Angelo leaned back, his arms folding across his chest. "We're sorry to hear that."

Laurie let out a laugh—a quiet, hollow sound that managed to be both elegant and vicious. "Sorry?" she repeated, tilting her head. "Funny choice of words, considering you two are the ones who got *rid* of him."

Her gaze flicked back to me, cold and assessing, like she was peeling back my skin to see what was underneath.

Angelo didn't blink. "That's a serious accusation, Laurie."

Laurie leaned back in her chair, her smile growing wider and somehow crueler. "Oh, it's not an accusation," she said softly, almost sweetly. "It's the truth and ... I wanted to thank you both."

What?

"James," she continued, her tone smooth, almost bored, "was a bastard. Cheated on me with anything that had a pulse. Beat me, insulted me—stripped me of every shred of dignity, until I didn't recognize myself anymore."

The way she spoke made it sound like she was commenting on the weather, but there was venom under it, seeping into every word.

"I used to lie awake at night, fantasizing about killing him. How I'd do it, where I'd leave him. But ..." Her gaze darkened. "I never had the guts to follow through. Not until you two stepped in and tied up my loose end."

My stomach tightened, but I kept my face as blank as I could.

"So, you're *thanking* us," he said, his voice low, even, dangerous.

Laurie tilted her head, the smile on her lips sharpening. "Oh, Angelo, not just thanking you. I'm here to ... express my gratitude."

"Gratitude?"

"Yes, Miss Whitenhouse. Gratitude. For doing what I never could. You've given me something no one else ever has."

Angelo shifted slightly. "And what exactly is that, Laurie?"

Laurie's smile didn't falter. "Freedom."

Freedom.

If I had felt even a sliver of it when I had ended her husband—the man responsible for so much of my own pain—then I couldn't begin to imagine the weight that must have lifted off her shoulders, knowing he was gone.

She rose gracefully, her manicured hand reaching for the Chanel bag resting on the seat beside her, and she adjusted it over her arm.

Her kitten heels clicked softly on the floor as she turned to leave.

But just as she reached the door, she paused, glancing back at us over her shoulder.

"Don't worry," she said, her tone as smooth as polished glass. "Your secret is safe with me. I told the feds that James ran off to Thailand with his mistress after I 'found out.' They won't come looking for him. But then again ..." Her gaze flicked to Angelo, her eyes gleaming with something dangerous. "I know the dirty feds are already in your pocket, Lazzio. Impressive work, I must say."

And with that, she strolled out without a second glance.

I exhaled, a nervous laugh escaping my lips as I glanced at Angelo.

"Damn," I muttered, leaning back as he closed the distance between us. "That woman ... she's something else."

Angelo chuckled low and deep.

Then, without warning, his hands found my waist, and before I could even think to protest, he lifted me effortlessly, as if I weighed nothing at all, and plopped me onto his lap. I gasped, instinctively wrapping my arms around his neck to steady myself.

His face dropped in the crook of my neck, his lips grazing my skin as he growled softly, "I missed you."

I let out a hum, shifting slightly. "We saw each other this morning though."

His hands slid to my waist, pulling me closer, pressing me against him as he grinned, lips teasing my skin.

"Too long ago," he muttered, then kissed my neck.

I let my fingers slide through his hair, tugging him closer as I tilted my head back, giving him full access to my neck.

"I finished getting all my things," I breathed out. "I'm officially boss-Lazzio-free."

He chuckled softly, the sound low and teasing, before he leaned in and sucked hard on my neck. My nails dug into his scalp as I fought to hold back the moan threatening to escape.

"Would you like one last promotion before you leave, Miss Whitenhouse?" he murmured.

"Actually, there is something I'd like, boss."

I smiled slightly, pushing him back playfully and getting off his lap. I reached for his hand, not missing the way his eyes darkened with interest.

He arched a brow, but didn't hesitate, his long fingers wrapping around mine as he stood and followed me.

. . .

My fingers traced the edge of the table, tapping lightly against it.

"I've always liked this room, even if meetings dragged on forever. The way the sun breaks through the window, the oval shape of the room, the plush chairs ..." I tilted my head, letting the words hang in the air. "It's the perfect place for my little promotion."

Angelo settled back in his chair, facing away from the window, looking like a king waiting for his subject to either beg for forgiveness, or beg for freedom.

He leaned back, legs spread wide. "Tell me more, Miss Whitenhouse."

My nails clicked against the table, the sound deliberate and sharp.

I reached behind me, fingers brushing the zipper of my dress.

I pulled it down slowly, letting the movement drag, watching the way his eyes followed every inch. His tongue flicked over his lips, barely a whisper of a reaction.

The dress slid down, pooling at my feet. I stepped out of it, just as a low curse slipped from his mouth.

I'd been planning this, had it all figured out this morning. A little fantasy come to life—being fucked in this meeting room. The windows were all glass. Anyone who came up here would see us.

I was in a black thong, garters pulling my stockings tight against my skin, bows at the back of my legs. Nothing on my tits but two heart-shaped stickers on my nipples, barely covering anything.

I crawled onto the table, slowly, making sure he saw every inch of me.

The cold surface under my knees only made the heat between my legs tickle.

I stopped in the middle, sinking into my knees. My hands slid up my body, grabbing my tits, squeezing them together, fingers gently brushing over the heart-shaped stickers.

I tilted my head, meeting his gaze head-on, a flicker of challenge in my eyes.

He exhaled sharply. "Come closer."

I chuckled, shaking my head. "Not yet, boss. I haven't finished my presentation."

I pushed up onto the table, hands dragging along the surface—legs, hips, tits, my fingers combing through my hair as I moved. Every shift was slow, making sure he caught every detail, the way my body curved and swayed.

His jaw tightened, eyes following me.

I tilted my hips, swaying from side to side. "I've been working hard to get your attention," I said. "Guess it's finally paying off, huh?"

He leaned back in his chair, eyes darker than ever. "You've always had it, Miss Whitenhouse. But now? Now it's *all* yours."

I turned away, letting my black hair fall like a veil, fingers brushing through it before I swept it to the side, showing my tattoo.

My naked back was exposed, the curve of it teasing him as I glanced back, catching the way his eyes ran down my spine.

He shifted in his seat, clearing his throat.

Angelo Lazzio was turned on.

Very turned on.

The bulge in his pants was practically giving me a standing ovation.

"You know," I whispered, "sometimes I'd spend extra time in your office—pretending to go over your files—just to feel your eyes on me. I'd drop something, on purpose, just so you could watch me bend over. Just so you'd get a peek at my ass."

I gave him a slow, wicked smile, my fingers brushing over the soft curve of my waist. Then I slowly slid my thong down my hips, letting it pool around my heels before stepping out of it.

"Would you like a demonstration, boss?"

His gaze was locked on me, a slow nod of agreement.

I parted my legs and bent forward, my wetness slipping down my thighs, my pussy warm under his watchful eyes.

I knew he could see *everything*.

I straightened up, a smirk playing on my lips as I turned toward him, dropping to my knees.

Then, I gripped the edge of my thong between my teeth and, with a devilish smile, slowly crawled toward him.

His gaze never left me as I stopped at the edge of the table, settling on my knees. I took the thong in my fingers.

"Open your mouth."

He obeyed without hesitation, and I slipped it between his lips.

With a smirk, I positioned myself at the edge of the table, letting my legs hang loosely, parting them slightly as I leaned back on my hands, so he could see how excited I was.

His hands immediately roamed up my legs.

I whispered, "You can fuck me now, but there's one thing you need to do first."

His brow furrowed, curiosity and need written on his face. I straightened up, pulling the thong from his lips and tossing it behind me.

"I want your lips on mine."

He leaned in, but I stopped him with a single finger.

"Not those, Angelo."

He growled, his gaze locked on mine as I leaned back on my hands again, parting my legs further, inviting him closer.

And he did, so fast I gasped. He buried his face in my pussy, his tongue so warm against my folds I couldn't help but moan loudly.

My hand brushed his hair away, my fingers lingering in the strands.

"Look at you," I giggled softly, watching him. His hands gripped my thigh as he sucked on my clit. "Such a good boy, listening to me."

He chuckled darkly, but didn't have time to say anything because I grabbed a handful of his hair and yanked his head back a bit, his face glistening with my wetness, which he licked from his lips.

"Say it, Lazzio."

His eyes narrowed. "Say what?"

"That you're a good boy."

A flicker of something dark crossed his face. "Jade—"

"Say it. *Please.* It's my last day, remember?"

He ran his tongue over his teeth. "I've been ... such a good boy, Miss Whitenhouse," he said roughly, the sound sending heat to my pussy. "So *please*, let me fuck you, now."

I released his hair with a soft chuckle, a hint of a blush creeping up my cheek.

Damn.

He really had been a good boy, and I knew forcing him to say it out loud was going to get me punished for it.

Hard.

And I couldn't wait.

"Go ahead."

He stood up quickly, and pulled me to my feet.

Without warning, he turned me around, pushing me down onto the table, my chest pressed against the cool surface, my cheek resting to the side.

In one swift motion, he shoved my thong into my mouth.

Before I could even process it, I heard a zipper drop, and he slammed into me, making me gasp.

His grip on my hip was bruising, his fingers digging into my skin as he pounded into me with unrelenting force. Each thrust was a punishment, each one harder than the last. The sharp crack of his hand slapping my ass echoed in the room, the sting spreading heat across my skin.

"There," he said breathlessly. His hand gripped my hair for some support. "That's my fucking reward."

I tried to push back against him, to meet his rhythm, but he was relentless.

He slapped my ass again, harder this time, making me cry out against the fabric stuffed in my mouth.

His hand snaked around my throat, pulling me up, his lips brushing against my ear.

"Want me to stop, *amore*?"

I shook my head furiously, desperate.

"Good," he rasped, his teeth grazing my neck before biting down just hard enough to make me shiver. "Cause I want you to ride me now."

He let go of me and sat back in his chair, the smug bastard, as if he hadn't just fucked me senseless. I turned around, taking my thong out of my mouth. I ran my fingers through my hair, like I wasn't shaking inside, and stepped over him. His cock, still hard and glistening, twitched as I straddled his lap.

"Ready?" I asked, grabbing him firmly, my grip making him hiss.

His jaw tightened, but he remained silent.

I sank down onto him slowly, my lips parting as he stretched me wide. Inch by inch, I took him, my thighs trembling as he filled me to the hilt.

I gasped, my head falling back. "God, you'd think by now I wouldn't feel like I'm splitting in half."

His hands clamped down on my hips, his breathing harsh. "You talk too much."

I rocked my hips once, a slow, deliberate grind that had him biting back a low groan. "And you love it. Admit it, Angelo—what's better, fucking me or shutting me up?"

"Both. But if I had to choose ..."

He thrust up hard, filling me so deep I swore I saw stars.

I gasped, clawing at his shoulders for balance, and his eyes darkened, that sharp, dirty edge slicing through his voice.

"... shutting you up while I fuck you. Best of both worlds, don't you think?"

I tried to fire back, but he bucked his hips again, stealing the words right out of my mouth. His hands slid up my back, pulling me flush against him until my chest pressed against his lips.

I rode him hard, my lips trembling, my legs burning, every nerve alive and screaming. My heart raced, my stomach coiling tight, and then I shattered, crying out as the release ripped through me. My body collapsed against his, trembling, legs instinctively locking around his waist, like I needed him to anchor me.

But Angelo wasn't done.

With a low growl, his hands gripped my ass, holding me down as he drove up into me, relentless, rough. Two, three more thrusts, and his head fell back, a filthy groan tearing from his throat as he spilled into me.

For a moment, the only sound was our ragged breathing, my body still trembling as I rested against his chest.

"You truly are the best employee I've ever had."

I brushed damp hair off my face. "Glad to know I've exceeded expectations."

He smirked, his fingers trailing down my back. "Shame it's your last day. Though ... I might have another position in mind for you. But fair warning—it's a 24/7 kind of gig."

I cocked a brow, unable to hide my grin. "Oh? What's the role?"

"My wife."

I blinked, caught between a laugh and a gasp, my heart stumbling over itself.

His wife?

Mrs. Jade Lazzio.

"Angelo, your cock is still inside me. If that's your proposal, I'm gonna have to decline. Because, quite frankly, it's lame."

"Ah, lame, huh?"

I tilted my head, letting my fingers trail lazily over his chest. "Mmm, yeah. I mean, no ring, no speech, and you're still balls-deep. What happened to romance? Or are you just hoping to screw me into saying yes?"

His lips curled into a dangerous smirk. "Careful, *diavoletta*. Keep talking, and I might just screw you so good you'll beg me to ask again."

I leaned in close, my mouth brushing his ear. "That's cute, Lazzio. But if you want me to say yes, you're gonna have to try harder than a dick-meets-wedding pitch."

He chuckled low, the sound vibrating through his chest as he caught my mouth again—deeper this time, hungrier.

Best last day I'd ever have.

CHAPTER
FORTY-EIGHT

"Sometimes the dreams that come true are the dreams you never even knew you had."
— **Alice Sebold**

Jade

"Just two steps, and we're there, *amore*. Careful, though—there's a little step."

My hand clung tightly to his as Angelo guided me through the room.

My view was pitch black, courtesy of the scarf he had tied over my eyes to keep his "little surprise" under wraps. Romantic, right? Except I was already tripping over my own feet, one stiletto threatening rebellion, while he strolled ahead.

Not working for Lazzio Exhibits anymore had given me plenty of free time—too much, honestly. Time to overthink, time to adjust to my shiny new routine as Angelo Lazzio's girlfriend.

If you'd imagined diamonds, lavish trips, and champagne at breakfast, well... you'd have been right. But it was more than that.

You'd think the CEO of one of the largest, richest groups in the West would be chained to his desk. But no. When it came to me, Angelo's calendar might as well have been titled *24/7: How to Worship Her*. And yeah, I had used to joke about him being obsessed with me—until I'd realized it hadn't been a joke.

The way his hand would find mine the second I walked into a room, like it was instinct.

The way his body would plaster itself against mine at night—leg slung over me, hand cupping my chest, head buried in my neck like I was the only pillow worth having.

The way his eyes would always, *always* track me, dark and heavy, as if I'd disappear if he blinked too long. And let's not forget how his voice, usually sharp enough to cut, would soften to a dangerous murmur whenever he spoke to me.

Warmth bloomed in my chest—along with the faint, smug satisfaction of knowing Angelo Lazzio was mine. Completely, obsessively, *irrevocably* mine.

And honestly? I loved every second of it.

He had made me feel cared for in ways I hadn't known I needed. He'd sit and listen to me rant about my failed nail appointment, the six-inch heels that had turned my feet into torture devices, or the hour-long saga of blow-drying my hair. And then, instead of rolling his eyes, he'd grab the blow dryer himself. Angelo Lazzio—the man who could crush empires—blow-drying my hair, without a single complaint.

When he had to leave for work, I'd poke and prod at him the whole day just to hear his exasperated laugh. But he never snapped, not anymore. Now, he'd just look at me with that dark amusement in his eyes, lips curving into a wicked smirk, before pulling me in for a kiss that stole my breath—and left me wondering how I had survived his absence at all.

By the end of March, he'd suggested we move in together.

I'd frozen at first, my fear of the unknown gripping me. But Angelo, ever the persuasive devil, had whispered in my ear all the *ways* he'd make the experience worthwhile. His tongue on my skin had been surprisingly convincing.

So I'd caved.

Three weeks in, and I was even more in love—with him, with this, with everything. I loved how his scent filled every corner of the space, how my things now mingled with his, and how he was never more than a room away.

I was hopelessly, recklessly, *irredeemably* in love with him.

And, as terrifying as it was, it was also the most freeing thing I'd ever felt.

We'd gotten even closer as I'd started opening up about everything—my past, my family, my dreams, and even the messy parts I usually kept locked away. I'd told him about my days of chasing highs that always ended in lows, about every mistake I'd ever made, every regret that kept me up at night.

And Angelo? He had never judged me. Not once.

On the contrary, he'd leaned in, fascinated, like I was a puzzle he couldn't wait to piece together. Every detail had seemed to make him want to know more, like peeling back another layer of me was his favorite pastime.

He had opened up too, sharing bits of his childhood—Italian summers spent devouring gelato, strolling through the cobblestone streets of Positano and Florence, and baking cakes with his *nonna*.

His voice would soften when he talked about her, and I

couldn't help but picture a tiny Angelo, cheeks dusted with flour, proudly holding up a cake.

A few days into living together, he'd told me his mama wanted to keep Georgino, his little fluffball of a dog, with her because she needed the company.

Now, I'd never been a dog person—had never had one, never planned to—but Georgino was different.

The so-called "monster" was actually a saint wrapped in fur. Sweet, quiet, well-behaved ... and yet, I'll admit it: I was *jealous.*

Yes, jealous. Of a *dog.*

Because Angelo gave him *so much attention.*

He'd pet him, talk to him, look at him like he was the center of the universe. Meanwhile, I would stand there like, "Hello? The love of your life is standing right here. Pet *me.*"

So when his mama asked to take Georgino, I had thought it was a genius idea.

Angelo, of course, was annoyed at first, muttering something about "family obligations" and how his mama had *plenty* of company already. But it didn't take him long to realize the setup was perfect.

Turns out, his mama had started bringing Georgino to work every day, so Angelo could still see his precious angel without the dog hogging all his attention at home.

And me? I had my man *all* to myself.

Win-win.

I had also started seeing Dr. Morano again. Angelo had insisted it would help me handle the grief better, and, well, after a heartfelt little reunion, the doc and I had decided on weekly two-hour calls.

I hated to admit it, but he had been right. It was helping. More than I'd like to admit.

He stopped me abruptly, his hands gripping my hips, as his hot breath skimmed the back of my neck.

"You ready?"

I hummed. "*Sì.*"

"That's my girl," he murmured, and then his lips brushed the side of my neck—a kiss, soft at first, then bolder, like he couldn't help himself.

The scarf loosened, and with one slow pull, he slid it off.

The space was massive—too massive—just an expanse of gleaming marble tiles, white walls that seemed to stretch forever, and ceilings so high they made my neck ache just to look up.

I frowned, confused. "I don't get it," I muttered.

His arms circled my waist, pulling me close until his chin rested comfortably on my shoulder. "You said you've always loved fashion," he said, his voice warm against my ear, "so I bought you this place."

My heart stuttered in my chest. "What?"

I turned around, my hands pressing flat against his blazer.

He kissed my forehead, utterly unfazed by my shock. "You can open your own store, create your own brand. Whatever you want, *amore*."

His hands squeezed my hips, grounding me as my brain short-circuited.

"Consider me your first-ever investor," he added with a grin so smug, I wanted to kiss him and smack him all at once.

I blinked, trying to process. "Angelo … this is a lot more than buying me flowers."

"I'm not a 'just flowers' kind of man," he said, leaning back to look at me. "You deserve more. Bigger. Better. The world, if I can give it to you."

I opened my mouth, but no words came out.

I was torn between swooning and screaming.

My own store. My own brand.

God, how did this man know what I wanted and needed even before I did?

"You're insane," I finally managed, but it came out soft, barely a whisper.

"For you?" He tilted his head, that devilish smile spreading again. "Always."

I let out a shaky laugh, overwhelmed. "So, you just ... bought me a *whole* building? Probably worth tens of millions of dollars?"

He shrugged, utterly unbothered, as though this grand gesture was as casual as holding the door open for me. "Why not? It's an investment—for both of us. Besides," his voice dropped, a dangerous edge slipping in, "I like spoiling you. Watching you get flustered is my new favorite hobby."

My cheeks burned. "You're impossible."

I turned back toward the space, my gaze sweeping over the vast, marble-floored expanse, the high ceilings that seemed to stretch into infinity, and the stark white walls practically begging for color and creativity.

"You're serious about this?" I asked, my voice quieter now, the weight of his offer finally sinking in.

He came up behind me, his presence grounding, yet electrifying. His hands slid up my arms, his touch both soothing and possessive. "I've never been more serious. This is yours, *amore*. Do whatever you want with it. Make it your empire."

My empire.

The words settled in my chest, foreign but thrilling.

"What if I fail?" The question escaped before I could stop it, a flicker of doubt slipping through my defenses.

Angelo's grip on me tightened, his lips brushing against my ear. "You won't."

I turned my head, catching his gaze.

It was unwavering, as steady as his heartbeat against my back.

"How can you be so sure?" I whispered.

"Because I know you, Jade. And because I won't let you."

I didn't bother with words—I couldn't. My chest was tight, emotions too big, too overwhelming to cram into a neat little "thank you."

So, I did the only thing that made sense at the moment.

I grabbed his face, my hands tangling in his hair, and kissed him.

Hard. Deep. And forever.

CHAPTER

FORTY-NINE

"Come sleep with me: We won't make Love, Love will make us."

—Julio Cortázar

Jade

I readjusted my mask, making sure it was perfectly in place, then checked my dress.

Everything was flawless.

I was wearing a buttery, white Elie Saab gown, sleek and seductive, with sheer white gloves that barely grazed my wrists, and a mask covering my eyes, decorated in feathers—white and gold. The gold butterfly necklace dangled at my neck, and the tiny "A" choker from Angelo sat snugly.

I stepped out of the condo and took the elevator downstairs, my driver waiting as always, silent and patient.

Tonight was exhibition night—*The Fallen Masks*. Angelo's brainchild, a masquerade ball of sorts, but with a twist. It was mandatory to wear Venetian masks and gowns, celebrating the shift into spring.

I couldn't help but feel a thrill buzz through me—not just because of the exhibition itself, but because this time, I planned to *enjoy* the night.

My throat tightened as memories of the last masquerade crept in—how I'd shattered Angelo's trust, how I'd broken him, all while trying to tear us apart.

Sometimes, at night, when everything else was quiet, I'd lay awake, watching him sleep beside me, my fingers brushing over his face. The guilt still clawed at me, and I wondered how he had ever forgiven me. How he could look past all the shit I'd done, and had still found a way to love me.

I'd been running from myself for so long that I still couldn't believe he wanted me—wanted *this*.

But maybe that was the thing about love, right? It didn't care about your mistakes. It just dug into the darkest parts of you and wrapped around your heart like mercy you didn't deserve.

I made my way to the driver, who opened the door for me with a quiet nod. I slid into the back seat, the door clicking shut behind me. The car began to move smoothly through the city, but as I settled in, my gaze fell on a small, carefully wrapped gift resting on the seat beside me.

I frowned, curious, before I grabbed it and noticed a card attached.

I tore it open, reading the words written in Angelo's familiar script:

Your first surprise of the night.
It's time to use your pain as art, amore mio.
x Angelo

. . .

A flutter of excitement ran through me.

I wasted no time unwrapping it, my fingers trembling slightly in anticipation as the sleek paper came apart. Inside, I found a file—simple, but mysterious.

I opened it, the contents catching the faint light from the street-lamps as the car sped through the city. My pulse quickened as I flipped through the papers.

Until I found a contract.

Contractual Agreement

*This agreement acknowledges that **Mayor Nicolas McKingston** of **Bay Village**, through this contract, hereby affirms that the property known as **Lake Kendrick**, encompassing **ten acres of land**, is now the sole property of **Miss Jade Whitenhouse**.*
*Following extensive negotiations and the inactivity of the land due to the tragic explosion of Mines nearly a decade ago, the property has remained in a state of standby awaiting a new owner. **Mr. Angelo Lazzio** has purchased the land for seventeen million dollars and, in turn, **has granted Miss Jade Whitenhouse full ownership and custodianship of the property.***

I was frozen, staring at the contract, my heart pounding in my chest.

He bought me Lake Kendrick?

How?

Why?

Tears were already welling in my eyes, but I refused to let them fall.

I quickly grabbed the note again and reread it.

It's time to use your pain as art, amore mio.

Oh my god, Angelo.

I felt my stomach drop. That land ... It wasn't just any land. It was where my sister had died. The place where everything had changed for me. I had avoided it for so long, buried the memories as deep as I could, and now Angelo was giving it to me.

Not just a plot of land. *My* land.

The car came to a halt, and the driver opened the door, offering me a smile. "I'll keep your present safe in the car, Miss Whitenhouse, until you're ready to head back."

I nodded, giving him a brief smile in return, then stepped out onto the red carpet.

As I made my way through the crowd, I spotted some old clients and acquaintances, but I barely slowed my pace.

Tonight, I wasn't here for small talk or forced pleasantries. I only had eyes for one person.

I reached the top of the grand staircase and looked around the ballroom, my gaze scanning the crowd. But no sign of Angelo.

With a frustrated sigh, I pushed my way down the stairs.

The crowd parted just enough for me to slip through, but still, no sign of Angelo.

It was like he was purposefully hiding.

"Jade?"

I spun around so fast I nearly gave myself whiplash, my heart in my throat—but no. Of course, it wasn't him.

"Oh," I said, recovering quickly with a smile. "Monica."

Monica Lazzio. Angelo's mama.

I almost didn't recognize her under the dazzling red-and-gold mask, her fiery gown sweeping dramatically across the floor, like she'd just walked out of a Renaissance painting. She looked fabulous.

"How are you, *dolcezza*?" she asked, her voice warm. "I'm so sad you resigned from Lazzio Exhibits Inc. Angelo will never find another like you."

My smile stretched wider. "*Grazie*, Monica. I just needed a change of pace."

She tilted her head. "Hmm, I understand. Angelo told me you moved in together." Her lips curved into a knowing smile, her eyes sparkling with something dangerously close to maternal mischief. "I'm so happy, Jade. In thirty-six years, I've never seen my son in love."

Her words hit me square in the chest, but I managed to stay upright. Barely.

She stepped closer, taking my hands in hers. "*Grazie*, Jade. Thank you for helping him understand he deserves love, too."

I tried to hold it together, but a little laugh bubbled out—half sob, half disbelief.

"He's the one who taught me I deserved it, Monica," I said, my voice breaking despite my best efforts to play it cool.

She squeezed my hands, her smile so radiant it was almost blinding.

Then, she leaned in, kissing my cheek.

"Next week," she said decisively. "Lunch and shopping. My treat. And no arguing."

I nodded.

As she turned to leave, she glanced over her shoulder.

"I can't wait for you to be part of our family one day." She winked and left.

La famiglia.

I stood there, rooted to the spot, my cheeks flushed.

The word settled over me, heavy and sweet, like honey warmed by the sun.

I let out a sigh as the music softened into a tender ballad, couples melting into each other as they glided across the floor in perfect harmony.

I tried to make my way through them, carefully dodging sweeping gowns and clasped hands, but before I could take another step, a hand caught mine—strong, steady, and oh *so* familiar.

Before I could process it, I was spun effortlessly, my breath catching as I collided with the unyielding warmth of a chest I knew better than my own heartbeat.

I looked up, and there he was.

Angelo.

Mio Angelo.

The world faded, the glittering ballroom, the music, the whispers—they all disappeared. It was just him, with his dark eyes smoldering beneath his mask.

"Looking for me, *amore mio*?" he murmured, his voice a low, velvet caress.

I whispered, "Always."

His smile, achingly tender and devastatingly beautiful, made my knees weak.

"I haven't been much of a gentleman with you, have I?" Angelo murmured, his voice low and rich as he extended a hand. "I've never even taken you to dance. Shall we?"

I hesitated. "I've never been much of a dancer, Angelo."

Clubbing? Sure.

That was survival mode—dim lights, sweaty crowds, and music loud enough to drown out my two left feet. I could flail like a caffeinated hyena and still blend in.

But *real* dancing? Like, actual ballroom? With rules and grace?

Yeah, that was uncharted territory.

"Lucky for you, I've got enough practice for the both of us."

I couldn't help but laugh, the sound shaky, caught somewhere between nervous and utterly charmed.

My heart swelled, ridiculous and euphoric, as his hand settled on my waist, warm and steady. I looped my arms around his neck, trying to ignore the way my pulse seemed to echo in my ears.

"How did you recognize me?" I asked.

I'd tied my hair in a bun, and the mask hid half my face—surely enough to make me unrecognizable in this sea of glamour.

"I'd recognize you anywhere, Jade," he said softly, the words like a vow. "Even in a sea of souls, mine would find yours. Always. Unfailingly. As if drawn by fate itself."

Always.

"Even in hell?"

The corner of his lips curled, a whisper of a smile. "Especially in hell, *amore*. Because finding you there would make it feel like heaven."

I pressed my face against his chest, letting the steady thump of his heart remind me I wasn't dreaming. His hand trailed lightly down my back, sending little sparks through me. The song *Love in Portofino* by Andrea Bocelli wrapped around us.

And then, in that perfect, quiet moment, I felt his breath on my ear.

"*Ti amo, Jade.*"

God. His Italian? It should be illegal to sound that good. It went straight through me, hitting me like an electric jolt. I swear, if I hadn't been so damn close to him, my knees would've given out.

There was something about the way he'd said it that just ... wrecked me.

He could probably tell too. He always could.

I almost cried right then. Something in me was just so overwhelmed by him, by the night, by everything—like this whole thing was too beautiful, too perfect, too damn real to believe.

"I think you're making me fall harder than I already have," I muttered against his chest.

He let out a soft chuckle, leaning back just enough to look at me. "Good. Because I've got another surprise for you."

I didn't even need to ask. I followed him willingly, heart thumping in my chest.

Funny how love could make you feel both silly and speechless.

But honestly, if this was what being in love felt like, I was all in.

We reached the elevator, and as he hit the button for the rooftop, I realized we had about five minutes. Perfect timing.

Without thinking, I spun to face him, grabbed his face, and kissed him hard. My hands buried themselves in his hair, his grip pulling me in closer, fingertips digging into my ass.

"Have I told you how fucking stunning you look?" he whispered, lips still brushing mine.

I pulled away slightly. "Nope, you didn't. Not very gentlemanly of you, Lazzio."

His eyes glinted with mischief as he leaned in again, lips pressing to mine with a hunger that made my pulse race. His tongue swept across mine, teasing, making it impossible to think of anything else.

I pulled back, breathless.

"Thank you, for Lake Kendrick."

He smiled softly. "You're welcome. Now you have the

chance to create something beautiful in a place where so much of your pain once lived."

I nodded, tears starting to blur my vision. "I think Stella would have liked this."

"I'm sure she would have," he said gently.

The elevator door opened with a soft click, and a light breeze from the city brushed against my skin.

He stepped in front of the door, blocking the view.

"I hope she would have supported what I'm about to do," he said, his voice tender as he moved aside.

My brows furrowed in confusion before my gaze shifted to the rooftop.

Oh. My. God.

The entire rooftop was transformed into a sea of red dahlias, their velvety petals spilling over every inch, hiding the pavement beneath. A delicate glass pathway glowed softly, leading to the center where the air shimmered with rainbow-colored lights.

In the distance, a wall of diamonds sparkled, catching the light like a thousand stars scattered across the night sky.

Angelo stepped closer, his hands gently removing his own mask before taking mine off with equal care. He placed both masks down, his touch lingering for a moment before he took my hand.

We walked together, my heels clicking against the glass.

I was utterly speechless, butterflies in my stomach, knowing what was coming.

We stopped in the center, and Angelo's hand gently cupped my cheek, his thumb brushing over my skin in a soft caress.

"Are you ready for my speech?" he asked, a playful glint in his eyes.

I couldn't help the giggle that slipped out, my hands trembling as I nodded.

His smile softened.

"For six years, Jade, I've loved you," he said, his voice low, almost reverent. "I've spent every moment in your shadow, watching from afar. And in all that time, I've never met anyone like you. You've made me feel things I buried long ago—things I didn't want to face, but couldn't escape. But there's no running from it anymore. Not from you, not from what you do to me."

He took a deep breath, his gaze never wavering from mine.

"Despite everything we've been through—the betrayals, the lies, the way we tore each other apart—it was *always* you. Always. And even when I tried to force you away, when I made it seem like I didn't want you, it was only because the thought of never being able to have you was a weight I couldn't bear, suffocating me more than your absence ever could."

His thumb moved across my cheek.

"I hope you'll stay with me, because you are both my deepest torment and the most beautiful gift I could ever receive. And I need you, Jade. More than you'll ever understand."

Tears welled up as I tried to steady my breath, overwhelmed by everything he'd just said.

Angelo dropped to one knee, and for a second, I thought I might faint. He pulled out a red velvet box, so elegant it looked like it belonged in his museum, or a high-security vault.

The ring he held was a masterpiece.

The emerald-cut diamond at its center was striking. Flanked by two smaller, round diamonds that added just the right amount of brilliance. The gold band was simple, but elegant—quiet, like it knew its worth without saying a word.

That was the kind of jewel that could only be worth millions.

I couldn't help but stare at it, my fingers trembling as I brought my hand up to my mouth.

Angelo reached for my hand.

"I'd choose you every time, in every lifetime, *amore*. But for now, let's start with forever." He paused as he held the ring before me. "Would you marry me?"

"You want forever with me?" I whispered, my voice barely a breath.

"I've always wanted forever with you, Jade."

My chest squeezed.

I've always wanted forever with you.

God, how did I get so lucky?

"Yes, Angelo," I said, overly excited. "Yes, I'll marry you!"

He slid the ring onto my finger, his movements quick and sure. I giggled, feeling like the happiest woman alive, and in one smooth motion, he swept me into his arms, spinning us in joyful circles. Our laughter danced through the air.

When he set me down, his lips found mine in a kiss that made the world fall away. As our lips parted, the sky erupted in a blaze of fireworks—each burst of color painting the night. Reds, blues, golds—flowers of light blossomed in the sky above us, lighting up the towering skyscrapers of New York, the city humming with love around us.

"Not too lame, huh?"

"No," I breathed out, my heart soaring, "Not even a bit."

We stood there, the fireworks exploding above us, colors bursting in the sky as his arms wrapped around my waist, pulling me closer. My arms rested over his, and I felt him, solid and warm, tucked behind me with his face buried in the crook of my neck.

There was something calming, something right about this moment, and I couldn't help but smile.

As we watched the sky light up, my heart settled into this peaceful rhythm.

And that's when it hit me.

The greatest blessing in life was often hiding in plain sight.

We spend so much time running from our pain, from loss, from the pieces of ourselves we think we can't face. We wear masks to survive, trying to protect ourselves from the world, but also from the truth.

We lie—to get what we want, to shield ourselves, to fit into something we think we're supposed to be.

But sometimes, if we're lucky, we meet someone who sees past all that.

Someone who sees the scars, not as flaws, but as part of who we are.

Someone who doesn't just see our lies, but understands them, even loves them.

And there, in Angelo's arms, under the fireworks and stars, I made myself a promise.

I would never lie to myself again.

I would hold on to the people who saw me for who I truly was—who saw the good and the bad, the messy and the beautiful—and never let me go.

And, in my heart, I would always hope that the people I loved could feel just how much they meant to me, how deeply I cared for them, just as they had always done for me.

In a way, I was grateful.

My sinful lies had become the twisted path to my redemption, guiding me back to a part of myself I'd thought I would never see again—to the happiness I'd thought I had lost forever.

EPILOGUE

"Tell me every terrible thing you ever did, and let me love you anyway."
— **Sade Andria Zabala**

Angelo

Detective McLauren sank into the chair at the far end of the table, her eyes narrowing as she brought her cup of coffee to her lips, still suspicious, but there was a flicker there—something more than just professionalism.

She hadn't changed since the last time I'd seen her, back when I had gotten arrested. Same tight bun, same subtle makeup, but the dark circles under her eyes suggested she wasn't getting much sleep. Guess the job was wearing on her. Pity.

"I have to admit, Mr. Lazzio," Detective McLauren began,

her voice carrying that same sharp, calculating edge I remembered from the night she'd slapped cuffs on me. "I didn't expect to see your name on my schedule. Especially since your wife nearly handed you over on a silver platter last time. Seems like the kind of thing that would make a man swear off the FBI for life."

Her words were sharp, but her gaze softened just enough to betray her curiosity—or maybe something else. She leaned forward, her eyes dragging over me, lingering longer than they should have.

"Jade has always had a flair for theatrics. Keeps life ... interesting."

Her lips curved, just slightly. "Oh, I bet it is. You know, I believe the last time we spoke, you said she was the devil who took possession of your soul?"

I leaned back. "I wasn't lying."

Today was our anniversary. Our two-year mark, and while the world had seen our wedding in Portofino as the event of the decade—complete with *The Times* calling it the wedding of the century—Jade and I had known the truth. The grandeur, the guest list with royals, business moguls, and celebrities—it had all been just the icing on the cake. What had really mattered was the quiet, private ceremony in Aspen weeks before, where it had just been us.

And it had felt like that moment had set the tone for our life together.

Our honeymoon had been a masterpiece. We'd torn through Europe like a storm—Paris at night, Rome drenched in history, Vienna with its quiet elegance.

When we had come back, I had bought us a house in New York. Not some penthouse in the sky, but a two-story place with a garden she could fill with flowers. She loved it. Loved that it was close enough to Alexsei and Caia's house that we could walk over for those chaotic family dinners. Their twin girls ran wild through our backyard, and Jade looked at them like they were a glimpse of our future.

Sometimes Volk and Sofiya visited from Moscow, their kids bickering in Russian while we'd sit back, amused.

Work was thriving—Lazzio Exhibits had tripled its visitors, and was now one of the top three tourist destinations in New York. But the real spectacle was Jade, and her empire.

She had launched her luxury brand, *S & C*, in honor of her sister and mother, and her first runway in Milan hadn't just been a success; it had been a coronation.

Scarlet had showcased her pieces on tour, propelling the brand into the spotlight, but Jade hadn't needed the boost. She was a force all on her own.

Seeing her like this—thriving, conquering, fucking glowing—it did something to me I couldn't even explain.

I'd never been the kind of man to believe in fairytales, or bliss, or whatever bullshit they sold you in the movies. But now? Now I understood it. Leaving her in the morning felt like I was ripping myself apart, and the second I was gone, all I could think about was her.

She was my obsession, my salvation, and the one thing I'd never fucking deserve, but would fight like hell to keep.

Jade had made me believe in forever.

And somehow, someway, I'd gotten her.

How the hell did I get this fucking lucky?

She let out a low scoff. "What's this, Mr. Lazzio? You here to rub it in—how you found love and the rest of us didn't?"

"Something like that."

I put the file on the table.

Her brow lifted. She grabbed it, flicking it open.

Inside was the sum of James Greg's pathetic life: every penny he'd stolen, every woman he'd shattered, every blackmail scheme, everybody in the ground with his name written all over it. The man had been rot personified, and I'd wrapped it up with a bow just for her.

She didn't look up as I stood, buttoning my blazer and flicking a glance at my cufflinks.

"I don't get it." Her voice was laced with confusion.

"Greg was a fucking bastard," I said, my voice calm, even. "He made his wife's life hell. Mine and my wife's too. So, I dealt with him. Found everything you need to close the file on him and start giving his victims what they're owed. His widow, Laurie? She's keeping half his money. The other half's going to the people he destroyed. Consider it my good deed for the year."

Her head tilted, eyes narrowing. "You *dealt* with him? Who made you God, deciding a man's fate?"

I lifted a shoulder. "He tried to rewrite mine. I just returned the favor. And in the process, I found the only thing that matters. *My wife*."

I took a step toward the door, my shoes echoing against the cold tile floor. But just as I reached the threshold, I stopped. Turning slightly, I glanced over my shoulder, catching her eyes still fixated on the file.

"Good luck, Naomi. Hope you find the love you're searching for."

Her head shot up, her expression flickering between surprise and something else she didn't quite manage to mask.

I smirked. "I know I did."

And with that, I walked out, leaving the past where it belonged—behind us.

THE END.

AUTHOR'S NOTE

To the women who've ever been told to stay quiet or follow a path carved by someone else—this is for you. Be bold, be defiant, and live fiercely. Your voice matters, your choices matter, and the life you create for yourself is your greatest rebellion. The world may try to silence or shape you into something smaller, but never forget your strength.

Live unapologetically, on your own terms, and never settle for anything less than the freedom to be yourself!

Writing *Sinful Lies* has been an intense and transformative experience, and I couldn't have done it without the incredible people in my corner.

To Mae: your sharp eye and dedication as my editor have elevated this book in ways I can't thank you enough for. Your guidance and insight have been invaluable.

To my sisters—bound by blood or by the threads of fate that tie our lives together—thank you for believing in me and urging me to chase my dreams. You have had a front-row seat to my doubts and failures, yet you always stay, cheering me on. I love you all deeply.

To my beloved sinners who first fell for *Sinful Promises*, walked beside me through *Sinful Games*, and now stand here with *Sinful Lies*—you have my endless gratitude. Your unwavering support, your words of encouragement, and your love for my stories breathe life into my work. Even in moments of fear, exhaustion, and uncertainty, you remind me why I write.

And finally, to anyone who's ever felt trapped or unheard: **your story is yours to write.** Take the pen and carve out the life that feels right for you—not the one expected of you. You owe it to yourself to live fiercely and authentically.

With endless gratitude,

Marie.

After swooning over Mikhaïl Volkov in *Sinful Promises*, Alexsei Romaniev in *Sinful Games*, and Angelo Lazzio in *Sinful Lies*, it's time to meet the ultimate French temptation: **Théo LeRoy.**

He's not just a dream—he's your dangerously irresistible bodyguard, armed with a sharp tongue, deadly skills, and a gaze that could melt steel.

Ladies, brace yourselves.

Théo doesn't just protect—he owns every room he steps into, and he'll soon own a piece of your heart. The Sinful series is about to get hotter, darker, and naughtier than ever.

Are you ready to surrender?

Sinful Desires coming soon! ;)

About the Author

Marie Annilla's novels are packed with complex, electric, and tantalizingly spicy characters. Her stories have strong, audacious female leads and men who will ignite your wildest fantasies and linger in your dreams.

She writes with one purpose: to ensure every girl finds the man she never knew she craved.

Marie has always dreamed of being a writer, weaving tales that bring her wildest imaginations to life. Living in a quaint village in England, she spends her time reading, writing, or enjoying her garden. When she's not lost in her stories, you'll find her teaching tricks to her mischievous cat, Tiger.

You can email her at: marie.b.annilla@gmail.com

Printed in Great Britain
by Amazon

62029330R00313